KAMAL

"The emotional anatomy of a terrorist . . .
The writing is vivid, the insight deep . . . the
story exciting."
American Examiner

"Stunning . . . Explosive . . . Tautly told."
Richmond Times-Dispatch

"Filled with moments of great passion and
sensuality."
Los Angeles Herald-Examiner

"Plots and counterplots rush past before the
reader's eye."
Chattanooga Daily Times

"The suspense never lags . . . I was hooked
from the first page."
Springfield News-Leader

"KAMAL is a first-class novel."
Kansas City Star

KAMAL

D.W. ARATHORN

AVON
PUBLISHERS OF BARD, CAMELOT, DISCUS AND FLARE BOOKS

Grateful acknowledgment is made for permission to reprint:

A quotation from Rimbaud's *A Season in Hell*, translated by Ovid Demaris, in his *Brothers in Blood*. Copyright © 1977 by Ovid Demaris. Reprinted by permission of the author.

Quotations from *The Koran Interpreted*, translated by A. J. Arberry, Copyright © George Allen & Unwin Ltd., 1955. Reprinted by permission of Macmillan Publishing Co., Inc. and George Allen & Unwin (Publishers) Ltd.

AVON BOOKS
A division of
The Hearst Corporation
1790 Broadway
New York, New York 10019

The Harper & Row, Publishers, Inc. edition contains the following
Library of Congress Cataloging in Publication Data:

Arathorn, D.W.
  Kamal.
  I. Title
PS3551.R323K3 1982   813'.54   81-47682
                                          AACR2

First Avon Printing, December, 1983

To Dad

part one

Kamal

ALLEZ, mon vieux. Run your stubby ink-grayed fingers over the pages again. A fourth time. Check the printer's marks, the cut of the paper, the registration of the punch holes. And now look up the number in your stolen-passport list. Not counterfeit, not stolen. Hmm. What are we to make of this, mon gars? Let's try the photo now. Stamp embossing looks good, evenly raised all over, crisp. No plaster job. Ah, maybe it's not really me! Check again, flesh against photo. Eyes, yes, nose, yes, shape of mouth . . . My features are hardly so ambiguous that they call for this laborious comparison. But you are a clerk, you under your blue kepi, and you have your procedures. Yes, I know. Some synapse is warning you that this is not just another tourist before you, so your duty to France obliges you to exercise your tedious procedures. Carry on. I'm in no hurry.

"Vous êtes Américain?" You watch for signs of nervousness in the throat, where they cannot be disguised by a nonchalant expression.

"That's what it says on the passport: U.S.A." And the accent is genuine Yankee too, isn't it? You haven't run into a problem like this before.

"Kamal . . . Jibral, your name?"

"That's what it says." All true. Though I can see

3

you are asking yourself, How does a Kamal Jibral with a scimitar nose like this one, and these lethal cheekbones which make the eyes seem like beasts peering out of caves . . . how does he come to be carrying an American passport? Let me tell you. A sad, some even say bitter, vicissitude of History. A betrayal. Of which your fine Republic is not entirely innocent, monsieur.

"Mr. Jibral. What is the purpose of your visit to France?"

Vengeance. "Tourism. Le tourisme, m'sieur."

"You are arriving from Switzerland."

"Yes."

"And before that I find only the recent stamp of India."

"Yes." Though what you are really looking for you won't find.

"You have been traveling long. The latest exit stamp from the U.S. is dated July 1970. You have been living in India since then?"

"Hare Rama."

"Yet I find no entry stamp from India."

"You know how the colonials are, old boy. Very loose." So loose, in fact, that they will never discover the odd coincidence of one Bernard Guzman having landed in Delhi and never departed while one Kamal Jibral flew off from Delhi having never arrived. Bernard Guzman, represented by a forged passport, I left oxidizing in a tiny brazier. He warmed a few chapatti for an old beggar near the airport. His last good deed for humanity. I imagine it is this Bernard Guzman you would like to apprehend, monsieur le passe contrôle. Yes, Bernard was decidedly a fellow worthy of your interest. You might not even have let him enter your fine Republic. But, alas, he has flown off to join Shiva, leaving you with this rather uninteresting character Kamal Jibral. Whose passport is entirely legitimate, by the way.

4

"How much money are you bringing into France, Mr. Jibral?"

"About twelve hundred dollars, mostly in traveler's checks." Quite a bit for a lad who looks like a student in his patched-elbow jacket and running sneakers. Quite a bit indeed, you think as you sharpen the end of your already keen nose between thumb and forefinger.

"You are aware that you may not work in France without applying for a work visa. May I ask your profession?"

Revolutionary, monsieur. Assassin, kidnapper and bankrobber. Smuggler and counterfeiter, too. "I am an artist, monsieur."

"Oh, yes, I am sure you are." Sneer, sneer away. The hollow thump of your rubber stamp will now dismiss me from your mind. How many borders I've crossed in these last two and a half years. At every passport control desk in the world official permission to pass sounds like a rap on an empty coffin. Thud to ink, thump to stamp.

"Passez." Sûreté Nationale, Orly, 18 décembre 1972, France 24. And with that you have forgotten Kamal Jibral already. What a mistake!

Behind a knee-high platform a dour stalk of a customs inspector paces, frowning on a tiny woman struggling to reclose her giant suitcase. She does not expect him to lift a finger. She knows France. Suddenly, out of the passport gate something interesting saunters into his numbing boredom. He straightens up with the briefest glance at my light Adidas bag.

"Quelque chose à déclarer?"

"Two pounds of cocaine."

I used to watch Latin American customs men wave travelers by for this kind of joke. But I was never in a position to risk it. Now that I finally can risk it I find myself in a country where the officials don't have a sense of humor.

5

"Ouvrez. Open it." He grimaces at the crumpled wad of sweaty underwear. He doesn't want to put his hand in. "Take it all out."

"If you're so interested, you take it out."

Another douanier is closing on us. This son of a whore is going to make a scene. A third is suddenly behind me, with his hand resting on the butt flap of his holster.

"Come with us please. Take your baggage." His kepi is pulled so low his eyes are invisible.

Idiot Kamal! You didn't need this.

"Espèce d'arabe," I hear one of them mutter.

I flip all my junk out of the bag onto the inspection table, hoping to forestall the body search. But I can see in their faces that they are set on the humiliation.

"Come with us, please. You may leave your baggage where it is."

Idiot Kamal.

Fortunately the pat-down is perfunctory, and carried out in privacy. But it is still pure intimidation. You're helpless, Arab. We can do anything we want with you. When they lead me back to my bag I'm already thinking about leaving them with a souvenir.

Idiot Kamal! You didn't need this, you don't need more. Remember what you're here for. Pack your bag and act contrite. Let them have their intimidated wise-ass. What does it cost you?

Of course it is this intoxicating smell of freedom in my nostrils which tempted me to this nonsense in the first place. I will forgive myself. After two and a half years of granitic sobriety how could I resist the first opportunity to taunt a man in uniform, the first time in two and a half years free of the gnawing fear of unforeseen consequences to myself, to comrades, to Movement, to History. For urban guerrillas in

6

Montevideo there is no act or word, public or private, that is purely personal. Even in hiding, every time I took a shit I found myself wondering if there wasn't some police agent counting turds in the sewage to see if there were more than the registered number of people in the household. But now I am in France. Now I can loosen the sphincters at both ends.

A puzzling sensation overcomes me on the bus ride into Paris: a mescalinelike intensification of sight renders colors so palpable they might come off on my hand if I touched them. It has been raining. The highway pavement is a palette of swirled zincs, purples and silvers dappled by the spray of cars which slick past us in their rush homeward. The sky above the city, showing through holes in the piles of soft leaden cloud, is absolutely lavender. I've never seen anything like it before.

My twenty-thousand-mile escape route from Uruguay ends with the dying shudder of the bus engine beneath the Invalides terminal. In the silence I continue to sit for a minute to absorb the sensation of motionlessness. Of not being chased. Immediately the other passengers have crowded toward the exit, leaving me the last to debark. The young woman just ahead has high tight calves. Like my mother's. It must be a characteristic of French women. Her calves lead the way to the street. I've been told I must find my way to the district near Boulevard Saint Michel: the district of students and emigrés. Among certain South American circles everyone knows where to go in Paris. Sooner or later they all expect to end up exiled here, so the stories and the city maps get passed around. In Monte I heard talk of a Bar Américain and a Mr. Magoo's as if they were just off the Rambla rather than an ocean away. All the revolutions of the Third World are plotted over coffee on the sidewalks of Paris, it was said. The cafés of Paris are more private than the bedrooms of Montevideo.

So I am already no stranger to Paris as I tread the long blocks of Boulevard Raspail. I've been carrying a picture of it, built up conversation by conversation, embroidered by maps and postcards. And I carry another image, vaguer and more romantic, inherited from my mother. Paris was her dream, too. Though not for its political, but for its moral and emotional freedom. To the eyes of a girl from sullen Normandy this city must have shimmered like some exotic paradise. Perhaps because she never lived here her dream kept the freshness of longing. The vision she passed on to me makes me expect to find Paris a city of women as well as of political refugees.

Where Saint-Germain forks off Raspail the sidewalks begin to spring to life. Even the December chill, rain and overcast haven't chased everyone inside. Here is some sort of sculpture gallery holding an opening. The party spills out onto the sidewalk. Photographers are everywhere with their strobes. Cross the street, Guzman! a warning blares inside my skull. Cameras are the enemy's friends. And though a calmer voice urges a course straight through the throng, residual clandestine paranoia still has the stronger grip on the reins. Don't forget, it chides, that Jibral-Guzman is no common apparition.

And that is true. Though my mother's fair French genes passed me this anomalous wavy blond hair and diluted my complexion to a medium olive, they did nothing to soften the hawkish bedouin physiognomy I inherited from my father. But from the shadowy side of the boulevard my caution feels absurd. Those photographers are celebrity hunters, not police spies. There may come a day when they will claw each other out of the way for a chance to record my face, but at present they wouldn't waste even a

8

single frame. Rather, they would wish all such scruffy passers-by had the good taste to keep to the dark side of the street.

Later I check into a hotel: under my own name for the first time in two and a half years. The signature feels awkward. But there is no suspicion in the eyes of the concierge, only sympathy for a traveler so tired he can barely hold a pen.

"You want with bath?" Seeing my passport, she tries English.

"Sure. With bath."

She hands me the keys. Her voice also jingles. "Third stage. I hope you like."

Welcome back to the world, Kamal.

"I'm sure I will. Merci, madame."

Wide awake after little more than an hour of sleep: already my mind is whirling far ahead on the trajectory of my plans. Tomorrow I must begin to make contact with the Palestinian underground. Too much History has hurtled by since I first submerged into the moldy cellar of Pollo Rojo. History quickly loses its meaning under the floors of someone else's life. Once a week the upstairs people would bring down their newspapers. Today's, or the previous month's, who knew the difference? Or cared? Censorship smothered the local stories like a fog. If you strained you could sometimes discern vague outlines of events in Chile or Argentina. Allende running into difficulties? The Movement would shudder. As I might have, once upon a time. But after you have had a friend machine-gunned in front of you, you are no longer inclined to believe in bloodless revolutions. Particularly from a cellar. Down there only the news from abroad could stir the blood. Two hijackings in the spring, a mad kamikaze attack by Japanese in the airport of Tel Aviv, a glorious demolition at a refinery in Trieste late in the summer. And then, in

9

Munich, the commandos of Black September turned the television cameras from the Olympic athletes onto themselves: it burned in my mind with the glow of revelation.

After twenty-five years my discarded, humiliated nationality suddenly shined as a badge of courage. But on other chests, not mine. For in Uruguay I was not even Kamal Jibral but the counterfeit Bernard Guzman, cowering in a Tupamaro safehouse cellar waiting for the dynamite of the Death Squad to cave in the walls. I knew if there was to be a place in History for me it would be as Kamal Jibral, not Bernard Guzman. Even if it were no more than to die in a crossfire under a burning helicopter on the tarmac of another Fürstenfeldbruck, at least there would be the sweetness of the mourning of kin. . . .

But tonight, months later and thousands of miles distant in the heart of Paris, I am just as far from even a first step toward Kamal Jibral's place in History. Suddenly the city sounds vast and alien outside my hotel window, and Kamal Jibral seems no more than an incidental passer-through. Here I have no Esteban to conduct me to the heart of the struggle as in Uruguay. Here I will have to chip my way in from the outside, and the walls sound very thick. Experience tells me it takes time, that I must have patience. But patience is one of the resources I exhausted in the cellar of Pollo Rojo. Which leaves me entirely at the nasty whim of Good Luck.

At the foot of Saint-Jacques, tourists stand with their heads cocked back to take in the towers of the cathedral. But a few steps away, under the awning of this cafe, no one could care less about architecture. I hear my mother's voice prodding me to at least take a stroll across the Petit Pont and have a look inside the great monument. Later. There is more important business to attend to. I have discovered a round of bars and cafes where young Arabs hang out. They are mostly North Africans. Whenever they have to speak in English or in French they become formal and defensive. None of them recognize me as kin of any sort. "Ah, Américain," they chuckle in their guttural French as I shoulder up to the afternoon crush at the stand-up. Mostly they want me to put my money into the jukebox or the fusbol game. There is scarcely a Frenchman to be seen. There is almost everything else: Latin Americans, Africans, Vietnamese, Arabs of every sort. Except Palestinians.

"Used to be a pack of Pallies who collected around here," a drunk English girl assures me, "but they've all quite disappeared in the last month or two. I used to sort of date one— Not go to bed with him, mind you. Never know what you might pick up from an Arab. But he was so delightfully angry. All the time and about everything. He used to live out in the bidonvilles like the rest of them. Two dozen to a room. That made him angry. And he had to leave the bars by half past eleven in order to be on the platform for the last train back at twelve-ten. That made him angry. He once even coaxed me that far. To show me that no one on the platform was white. He said that made him angry. No whites except me, I pointed out. Which made him angry too, because he really preferred his own women but they wouldn't let him touch them and he couldn't afford to get married as a result of the class oppression by the Jews and the English so he was going to take me home and fuck me till I begged him for mercy. I told him he could fuck himself till he begged himself for mercy. And left him on his sooty platform with the rest of his sooty, angry Arabs. You wouldn't be an Arab, would you?"

"Not if I could help it."

In fact it seems I can't be an Arab even when I do try to be one. I lack the one attribute by which all

11

Arabs decide who is one and who isn't: Arabic. I am deaf and dumb in the language of half my ancestors. My father reserved his native tongue for trysts with old friends from the "countries" who brought tales of woe and intrigue which I and my brothers were not to hear, understand or remember. To us Arabic became the language of plots and secrets. Most of the family business was transacted in English, though when my mother was feeling romantic she spoke to my father in French. Usually he squirmed and grumbled and replied in English. So she taught us her French, instead, and slipped into it to coax, endear and comfort us. Discipline and disappointment descended on us in English. The two languages were sufficient for all family purposes. When we periodically pressed to be taught the language that would initiate us into the world of dark secrets, my father would make his standard refusal, loaded with bitter irony:

"For what? Your future lies in this country. You are Americans. If you want to go back and live with the flies of the camps, go ahead, learn Arabic. But if you want to become a beggar you can just as well hold out your palm in Greenwich Village as in Borj al-Barajina."

His tone convinced us, even if his words were melodramatic. There was nothing he craved more profoundly than to leave the past behind. Powerless to cut himself loose from it, he became all the more determined to prevent it from snagging his sons. It was the grasp of the language he feared most.

You wouldn't be an Arab would you? the English girl asked. Not if I could help it.

But I can't help it. For even without recourse to the language, the past like some desperate uprooted vine has found other cracks through which to slip its tendrils into my soul. Its path must have been as twisted as the mazes of our traditional art. My father, however, can be glad that only one of the five of us has fallen back into its grip. If there is any contentment in the grave he must find it in knowing that he sired four perfectly American sons. If I have gone bad, well . . . he always said that History demands individuals, even entire peoples, to be sacrificed to its progress. Four steps forward, one step backward: as a family we are way ahead of the percentages my father's revered Lenin declared acceptable. He can't complain.

"But if you are looking for Pallies," the English girl persists, "and you can't find any in the bars or on the train platforms, you might try the Sorbonne or Nanterre. They all belong to the General Union of Palestinian Students, or whatever their club is called. They keep a desk up there somewhere."

Is that so? Are we Pallies a particular interest of yours, sister? Wouldn't you love to know that a student organization is the last place I'd go to make contact with the underground movement; those student groups are the first place the oppressor directs his agents. Or maybe you wouldn't love to know that. Maybe you don't give a damn about student organizations and clandestine movements and are just sitting here chatting up another angry Arab because it gives you a thrill to send us home horny.

Sometimes I envy my father the peace of his grave and my brothers their militant complacence. And I have to wonder what is so different about me that I am driven to stalk this vocation even when it is desperately trying to elude me, as it is now. Or even more strange, that I have so little urge to elude the vocation when it is stalking me. Those are the worst times: when the threat behind your back becomes so oppressive that soon you are ready to walk into the open hoping to draw some fire. Just to prove that it isn't entirely your own imagination doing the stalking. For your own imagination is the most lethal assassin of all. It gets you with your own weapons. You sit day after day, or night after night—it doesn't matter, because night and day are the same down there—chewing over the same dry scraps of experience until they become so twisted and shredded that you are no longer sure that the hardliners on the Committee who are so dedicated to seeing you shot are not justified. You are doing the hardliners' work for them. Then it dawns on you, in the last moment of partial sanity, that you have become the victim of someone inside your own skull, and this infiltrator has to be hunted down, exposed and killed before the effects of his treachery destroy you.

But how do you smoke him out? By razing the doubts he feeds on. By rebuilding your certainties in iron. What are the facts? Fact: Esteban was betrayed. Nobody outside the cell knew we would be in Punta del Este that weekend. Only three of us knew beforehand where in Punta we would be hiding: Esteban, me and Alain Castellan. Fact: Esteban is dead, and the rest of us would be too if I hadn't been the one to start shooting back. So there is only one possible conclusion: the one that required me to put a bullet in the head of Alain Castellan. The rest of our cell had no difficulty recognizing that conclusion was the only logical one—they just could not bring themselves to act on it. They left it to me. And that is what the Committee could not tolerate: that I was the one to act.

But why am I still worrying over it? The Committee held their inquest. I was not found guilty. Even the hardliners on the Committee knew I was right. When their chance came they kept their voting hands in their laps, pinned by the logic of my defense:

"Esteban was my friend a decade before the Tupa-

14

maros were a gleam in his or your eye. It was he who came to the States to beg me to buy guns for you. I did not seek him. If I had been meant to conduct him to his death, would I have waited two years before getting around to it? And if I were responsible, would I have waited around for this inquest to exonerate me? Hell no! I would have made a running leap into the U.S. embassy and you would never have seen me again. So by what Byzantine reasoning are you supporting these suspicions?"

They are hooded but I think I recognize the woman's marble-hard diction:

"We also note that Alain Castellan was acquainted with Esteban for nearly as long a period. So the logic, comrade Guzman, by which you convinced yourself that Castellan was the betrayer and that you had the right to judge and execute him must have been even more Byzantine. Unless, of course, you were simply silencing a possible accusation against yourself. That would be straightforward logic indeed."

"I am intelligent enough to realize that executing Alain Castellan would hardly silence any accusation against me. Quite the opposite. Yet it still had to be done, to protect the others from further betrayal."

"You must forgive us, comrade Guzman, if we find your interpretation somewhat ironic."

Shit! All interpretations are ironic. The curse of underground existence is that any action, any word can be construed by some elaborate chain of reasoning to be the action or word of a provocateur or spy. Though proving it is another matter. That is why I am still alive.

"The Committee reaches no conclusion in the matter of Guzman. But the ambiguities and uncertainties raised by the extraordinary, brutal and unauthorized action of Guzman require us to sever from the Movement. . . ." The list of criticisms droned on for an hour.

The Committee concluded that Guzman would be required to re-educate himself while they further evaluated the implications of the Castellan execution. Guzman would remain in isolation and be obliged to study basic revolutionary texts under the guidance of the political education section. In short, I was exiled, like my father, to a paper revolution. It was the worst humiliation they could have devised.

Some might be grateful to escape with their skins from such a nightmare. Some might convince themselves that it is possible to sever themselves from their own past. But try. Whether you sit in your cellar "re-educating" yourself or merely sit there fuming, or try to disappear into fantasies of the glory waiting across the ocean, your past never gets farther from you than the inside surface of your skull. It talks to you. It wheedles you. It accuses you. It parades before you the evasive glances of those you were sure once trusted you, and the murderous irises of the judges' brown burlap faces. It echoes the conversations you never hear: "Do you think Guzman really is a traitor?" Until finally you have to clear yourself before these doubters inside your skull, unambiguously, regardless of the risk. "What kind of traitor would walk out into the bright sunlight and execute a Death Squad commander in front of his own house?" No traitor. So you pry out the Colt Python which you have stashed inside the doorjamb and study the list of Death Squad goons exposed by the informer Bardesio and you forsake the dark security of your cellar to squint into the dazzling morning sun, reading the street signs until you have found the one and your eyes have remembered how to focus more than eight feet away. And when the man emerges from the solid peaceful house with his briefcase swinging in anticipation of another profitable day at the Ministerio del Interior, belching his breakfast into the cool breeze off the Plata, and smirking at the memory of his mistress's tongue, you raise your Colt until his shiny white forehead gleams over its black sights, and you remind yourself to squeeze. You even see the back of his head splash the beige stucco of his garden wall. And, as if waking out of a dream, suddenly become aware of all the other people on the sidewalk wakened out of their sleepwalk by the piercing crack of the .357 and now gaping in half-comprehension at the sprawled figure, the blood- and brain-spattered stucco, your shining black revolver, and you explain in a very calm but authoritative manner, "This man was a murderer of the people."

But as you walk away, suppressing a gathering urge to scamper for the nearest dark place, you see in those stupefied faces the question: "Murderer of the people? You mean us?" And that is when you know you don't belong here in Uruguay and never did, that these are not your people and don't want the revolution you are making for them. That is when you comprehend, without a single hesitation, There is nothing to redeem here: it is time to go.

Yet what idiot superstition persuaded me I would leave Uruguay further behind by flying the long way around the world?

The Atlantic does not put me very far out of reach. There are Uruguayans all over Paris. One just checked into my hotel. I saw his name in the guest register: Ramon Valdivia. But he could be anybody. And I am unarmed for the first time in years. I must find a pistol. But even more important, I must get myself out of the flow of transients and into some quiet out-of-the-way apartment. Or else I will come back to this hotel room one night to find a man sitting on my bed with a silenced revolver greeting me.

"The concierge was kind enough to let me wait, señor Guzman."

During the first weeks of January I learned that Paris was not the open city I had heard described in Montevideo. It had no place for a foreigner without credentials. Day after day I watched the faces of landlords close up like shop shutters when I presented myself in response to their listings. Narrowed eyes studied my features, cocked ears dissected my accent, and my American passport and traveler's checks were to no avail. Where were my recommendations? If one carries no recommendations one must live in a hotel, they said. So I remained in my hotel and listened carefully at my door before entering the room each night.

The matter of a weapon would not solve itself either. I quickly discovered that a foreigner cannot obtain firearms. That is even difficult for a citizen. One afternoon I lingered near a fancy gunshop behind the Palais Royale until I convinced myself there was no way to burglarize it. Through the glass I watched a portly businessman being fitted with a shoulder holster and a small automatic. A man with credentials. He emerged after half an hour and glanced around with that guilty furtiveness of a man not used to carrying a gun. A perfect mark. Yet as I began to tail him up Saint-Honoré I realized it was just an exercise. Even if I managed to knock him down and steal the pistol, where would I run? I could not disappear in Paris as I could in Montevideo. To disappear one has to have connections, and if one has connections one doesn't have to risk mugging armed gentlemen to obtain a pistol. I broke off pursuit somewhere in the Sixteenth Arrondissement and rode the Métro back to my own side of the river.

Nothing up till now had demoralized me as much as this futile chase. In the midst of the greatest concentration of revolutionary organizations in the world I was as isolated as a traveling brush salesman. By now I knew every cafe, restaurant, bar and bookstore in every alley in the Latin Quarter. I knew the faces of their regular customers, and the scripts of their conversations. In South America this would have already led me to the so-called political element. And among these would be the liaison to the clandestine world. But here in Paris everyone belonged to a political element. In South America, under repression, people guarded their words. Here everyone with any kind of opinion made certain everyone else within shouting distance was informed of it, in detail, whether interested or not. There were few places to escape if one wanted to eat without being provoked by some dogmatic idiocy. That evening I needed peace more than usual and so I slipped into a tiny Vietnamese-run restaurant on Rue Sommerard where the restrained demeanor of the owners imposed itself on the diners and made it the quietest eating place in the Quarter.

But not that evening. For just as I began pecking at my rice a machine-gun rattle of Latin American Spanish filled the narrow room. The argument came from behind me. I did not want to give it the encouragement of turning around, but I could not help listening.

"You and your precious Allende"—a young woman's voice thick with the bitter sarcasm which Spanish is peculiarly capable of carrying—"will be the end of every revolutionary movement in the world. You ask us to wait for the masses to elect socialism in countries where there are no elections."

"In Uruguay there are elections." An older man's voice, tired and pedagogic.

Immediately interrupted by the young woman's blurting, "In which the Frente Amplio collected scarcely twenty percent of the vote. If the electoral

19

process is so holy, you should hark its voice and kneel at the altar of the reactionaries who get the votes."

"The failure of the Frente Amplio," the man persisted, "was entirely the doing of the Trotskyite provocateurs."

"If you are referring to the Tupamaros, please remember that you Communists supported the front as well. But you Communists are very bad at taking your share of blame for a failure. You should be glad we exist. What would you do if there were not an unending supply of Trotskyists to crucify?"

"This is too much!" A female voice, older than the first, hoarse with outrage.

"Calm, calm." The pedagogue again. "By this time, my dear, you should recognize the argumentative technique of the Fourth International: When you do not have a theory, yell your confusion louder. Even Trotsky himself thought he could intimidate the dynamics of history with torrents of sarcasm. They have only learned from their master. How else can one explain why they pour all their energies into vituperation instead of organization."

"You are a good Communist, Antonio: a master of understatement. Regrettably, what you understate is the truth. Yes, we do not spend all our energies in organization. As a result we are not stultified in bureaucracy. And yes, we put some of our energies into vituperation. But how else can we respond to the backpedaling and backbiting of those who should be our comrades-in-arms but refuse to pick up arms because loud noises upset them."

"No. It is simply that we do not confuse loud noises with revolutions. Nor, it should be pointed out, does the class enemy. How many more millions of dollars are the Yankees spending to undermine quiet Allende than to suppress your noisy Tupamaros, ERP and whatnot. Eh, Justina? Perhaps the CIA is consulting your Fourth International comrades in New York to determine who poses a threat to American interests and who doesn't. As I understand it, even the Yankee Trotskyites can see the historical futility of these popgun antics in Montevideo and Caracas and São Paolo and Buenos—"

"It is pointless to argue—"

"You mean that it is hopeless to argue."

"I mean that it is pointless to argue with someone who has all the answers and each one tells him to keep sitting on his ass until a messiah comes, whether named Lenin or Allende. That is a luxury one can indulge only thousands of kilometers from the battle."

"Unfair, Justina, unfair. I ask you which of us emigrés is not guilty of indulging in pontificating from a safe distance. That is what keeps us together, us emigrés. It is our unifying principle. No one else will listen. And why should they?"

I could no longer resist the urge to turn around and have a look at the contestants. They sat two tables away, a slight dark girl braced against the wall and an older couple facing her. They were all now glaring into their soup. I wanted to lean over and tell them how many times I'd sat through the same debate in the very heart of Montevideo. But I was only momentarily provoked. You get used to overhearing the pronouncements of these vicarious theorists. And you learn to shrug when you'd really like to walk over and plop a dud hand grenade in their soup and watch them faint dead away.

I buried my nose in the rice for the rest of dinner and left afterward without a glance in their direction. But a week or so later, when I slogged into the restaurant after another futile search for a weapon, the dark girl was there again. Alone this time. We nodded at each other. She seemed prettier than she had that noisy evening. Political wrangling doesn't flatter anybody's features.

I commented in Spanish as I passed her table, "Are you continuing the struggle this evening?"

"No, gracias a dios." She had peculiarly strong regular teeth for such a delicate, even frail jaw. "You are North American?"

"Yup." I sat down at her table. She did not object.

"I recognize your accent. States or Canada it had to be."

"States. But you are the genuine article."

"Genuine? Oh, yes. I was born in Havana."

"But no longer a citizen? An exile of '59?"

"That's right. But I will be a French citizen soon."

"Your family is here?"

"Not any longer. They went back to Miami."

"Poor folks."

"In every way, they are."

"Where did your Stalinist friends of the other evening start out?"

"Oh them! Venezuela. But does it matter? They are all exactly alike. Though I suppose they would say the same about us."

"Us?"

"Well, you did label them as Stalinists, so I just assumed . . ."

"Actually I don't keep a political theory. For the same reason I wouldn't keep a poodle: finicky, demanding and always snapping at other breeds."

"That's very clever. What is your name, George Bernard Shaw?"

"Kam." I used my nickname to spare a round of explanation.

"Kam? I've never heard that name before. I am Justina."

"Like De Sade's—"

"Not at all like De Sade's, I assure you."

Our banter through the rest of the meal scrupulously skirted politics. She insisted upon paying for her own, but accepted to be invited to a movie. She insisted on seeing Zeffirelli's *Romeo and Juliet,* promising it would put her in a tender mood. Afterward she led me to her apartment: barely more than a room, but tucked away near the dead end of the Passage des Patriarches. A perfect hideout.

The night did not quite satisfy the longings aroused by the movie. Justina was not a beauty, and was the type who never let herself forget it, even lying there in our sweat.

I heard her murmur, "She is so lovely."

"Who is?"

"Juliet."

"Naturally."

Justina must have known it was futile to fish for compliments this way. We lay in silence, each filling in the unspoken conversation. I thought about trying to be gallant, but knew I couldn't pull it off. I never could. Instead, I reached across and began playing with her nipple.

"I have a rule not to make love with a man until I know his full name. I have broken that rule once tonight. But not twice, all right?"

"What's in a name?"

"A little trust."

"I could tell you any name."

"Tell me any name then."

"Moishe Washington Wong."

"What? No, at least a name I can believe."

"Let me think."

"Think all you like, but take your hand away until you come up with something."

"How about Kamal Jibral."

"You are an Arab?"

"No. My father was an Arab. But that was before I was born."

"It sounds complicated. I won't pry anymore. You can put your hand back."

"That's better."

But the next morning she began prying again.

"How can you afford to live in a hotel? You aren't on somebody's payroll, are you?"

She was dressing as she asked this, lingering by the window to let the morning sun fall on her skin. The window looked onto a narrow courtyard and the facing building blocked all but a narrow band of sunlight which fell near the window, leaving the rest of the room in obscurity. She could not see my expression, but sensing a reaction she peered intently into the shadow.

"I can't afford to live in a hotel. But I can't find an apartment. What do you pay for this, Justina?"

"About eight hundred francs. That's a bargain for Paris."

"You ought to paint the walls white instead of this . . . whatever this was once. White would make it much more cheerful."

"If the landlord wants to improve it he can do it at his own expense." This was said with the vehemence that politicos reserve for landlords and the few other oppressors with whom they have direct contact. Even political women usually do something to make their nests attractive, but this had no adornment. Not even a poster.

"Do you live here alone, Justina?"

"Yes. I prefer my privacy. And you, you have no friends here in Paris?"

"Only the kind you have to buy a beer to get them to talk about the weather."

"That's too bad. But if you know no one, then why did you come here?"

"They said it was an exciting town."

"Who said that?"

"They . . . Everyone. Everyone who's been here. Or maybe everyone who hasn't. My mother grew up in Normandy, but she's always loved this city."

"Ah, your mother is French. I wondered how you knew French so well. That is very unusual for an American. But you are hardly the typical Yankee."

"What do you want? A cowboy hat?"

"A kaffiyeh would look more appropriate. It would cover up the blond hair which spoils your image. Let's see." She started to drape a pillowcase over my head.

I grabbed her wrist. "I am not an Arab."

"Oooh! I'm sorry." She finished dressing and leaned out the open window. She was hiding her face by this gesture. "I guess I'd better be going, Kamal."

"Where?"

"Why, to work."

"At this hour? What do you do?"

"I have a job at a bookstore. Odd hours."

"What do you do with the rest of your time?"

"Sometimes I am a student. And I work on a small newspaper."

"You write?"

"Write, edit, type, copy addresses. We all do everything that comes up. It is our principle to avoid hierarchy."

"Political sheet?"

"It's called *La Flamme*. You see it everywhere around the Quarter."

"I'll pick one up."

"Well, I should be going."

"I'm not stopping you."

"Do you . . . I mean, should we meet somewhere later?"

"Why not?"

"Rue Sommerard again?"

"That's all right. But how do you afford to eat there every night on a bookstore salary?"

25

"I can't, Kamal. But once in a while we all need a special occasion. At nine?"

"At nine."

Poor Justina. She was obviously the type who refuses to take a hint. I did not want to poison her own apartment with the bitterness of a rejection. It would be much cleaner to cool her off in a public setting, and I had the rest of the day to think up the least painful excuse. To have to do this after one night made me a little sad and a little angry. Why, with all the beautiful, proud women in Paris, did I have to take home this one?

Resentment and frustration continued to peck and to nag at me all day as I milled aimlessly up and down the sidewalks of the Latin Quarter, staring at shopwindows while the hollow under my ribs sucked harder at every step. Why did I take home this one?

A camera store near the Odeon had artistic nudes on display in the window. Coppery limbs, glistening breasts. Why didn't I take home one like that? But wishing was only making the hollow worse, so I wandered on toward Invalides.

Two hours later I found myself stopping in front of the same display. Kamal Jibral leching at pinups: he had fallen pretty low. A salesman in a white lab coat was watching me through the window, wearing a sneer. I turned from the window, about to hurry away, when a rage suddenly closed around my chest like a huge fist. You dare to sneer, you pathetic counter clerk? You think Kamal Jibral is just another rootless, horny emigré whose claim on this city extends no further than the seat that comes with price of a cup of coffee?

I strode into the shop, straight to the sneering salesman. "I'll have the Nikon. The same model as the one under those photos."

He blinked as I yanked out my traveler's checks

and ran off to fetch the camera. He returned unctuous and eager for conversation. I let him talk and said nothing. He asked where I was from. I stared. He flustered and concentrated on filling out the forms for the guarantee and the tax refund.

"Votre nom, ici, s'il vous plaît."

My name? Here's my name. I crumpled the forms.

"Mais alors, this is worth fifteen percent . . ."

I left him with his precious forms. But as soon as I was out on the sidewalk the frustration and anxiety swept over me again. And with the camera in its silly little box under my arm I felt like a fool. Double the fool for having been provoked by a clerk's sneer. And suddenly I was very anxious to see Justina again.

Justina

"ALLÔ, RAYMOND? C'est Justina."

"Why are you telephoning? The regular time is not far off?"

"Something special has happened."

"Can you talk freely?"

"Yes. I'm alone in my castle."

"Castle?"

"Yes." The walls are meters thick and soar to the sky; the masonry is out-of-print books. "I am at work. There is no other extension on this line, Raymond."

"Well?"

"Do you remember the photographs you showed me that you got from Uruguay?"

"I remember that I showed you photographs."

"Do you remember the strange-looking guy: blond, with the nose?"

"Most of them have noses, Justina."

"Only one of them had eyes as mean as this."

"I don't recall. But what about him?"

"I've met him, Raymond. Here, in the Quarter."

"You are certain it's the same one?"

"Absolutely. He hasn't even changed his clothes. Turtleneck shirt, blue jeans, tan corduroy jacket, white Adidas with green stripes. He's absolutely the same one, Raymond."

"If it's true, well done, my girl. Do you know where to find him?"

"Oh yes. I am seeing him tonight."

"Be careful, eh? Did he say what he's doing in France?"

"No."

"What name is he giving?"

"Kamal . . . Jibral. The name on the photo was something else. Something odd, like two different nationalities."

"What did he claim his nationality to be?"

"American."

"American! How's his English?"

"Perfect, Raymond. And his Spanish is excellent, if a little accented. So is his French. By the way, he said his mother grew up in France, Normandy, and his father *was* an Arab before he, Kamal was born. Whatever that means."

"How old is he?"

"Twenty-four, twenty-five. My age."

"Did he say anything about Palestinian origins?"

"No. But I'll bet you're right."

"Try to find out. I can't locate the dossier or the photo right now. Can you call me back in an hour? From a different phone."

"Yes. I'll take a break."

"Good girl, Justina."

Now that is a good sign. Twice on the telephone in one day. It is no trivial matter when Raymond drops his sarcasm. If this turns into something big there will be no more questions about my "seriousness."

28

He'll stop treating me like a cockroach. But on the other hand it could turn out to be nothing. Maybe I'm mistaken about the photo. What happens when Raymond discovers I've made an error? Mon dieu! Telephoto pictures are so misleading: all the coarse shadows on the face and the way the head seems to bunch up on top. But no, this time I don't think I'm wrong. My instinct tells me it's the same man. I recognized him the instant he walked into the restaurant. And when I made him turn around to see what all my hysterics were about, I knew for certain. Same face, and he barely contains himself from jumping up at the mention of the Tupamaros. And even then I waited a week to make doubly sure. He looks dangerous. I wonder what he could be doing here? A hired assassin, like the Jackal. My God, Kissinger is here in Paris for the peace talks! Why didn't I think of it? Justina, you are dumb. No wonder Raymond was so excited.

"Allô, Raymond? Justina ici."

"That was a short hour. But I found the photograph. Was the name, do you recall, Bernard Guzman?"

"That's it! What does it say?"

"When are you seeing him again?"

"Tonight, at nine. What does it say?"

"Justina, remember your training, please."

"I'm sorry."

"Are you going to spend the night with him?"

"Raymond, if you please!"

"Spare me the false modesty, if *you* please."

"Do you want me to spend the night with him?"

"You already have, if I surmise correctly. So why not again? But don't throw yourself at him. Sois un peu la coquette, hein?"

"Yes, Raymond."

"Urge him to talk, but don't pump him. Talk about

yourself freely. That might loosen him up. Remember that it will be the subjects he avoids, leads away from, that will be the ones most of interest to us. Remember the subjects he avoids."

"I will."

"Bring up the Palestinians at some point. He has an Arab name. It is natural to ask how he feels about Israel."

"He insists he is American."

"Ah ha! So we already know the first subject he is anxious to avoid. Treat it gently but don't let go of it if you can help it."

"I will try, Raymond."

"Good. Call me tomorrow if you can, but don't lose contact with your new friend."

"Then he is important."

"I did not say that. He is an interesting case, that is all. At this moment. A bientôt, Justina."

"A bientôt, Raymond."

Suddenly this adventure is going sour. Why are you doing this, Justina? Here is the first interesting boy you've met in ages and you've already made a criminal out of him. And for what crime? If the Uruguayan butchers identify this man as their enemy, isn't he then your comrade, Justina? You had nothing to fear from him until you told Raymond about him. So why did you do it?

I don't know.

Yes you do know, little liar. It was for that quick flush of pride, for the thrill of hearing Raymond's compliments, for the taste of a little dollop of power over the pathetic creatures who share your demimonde. And naturally, it was to prove your loyalty to the country which will soon take you to its bosom. Don't forget that, Justina. You will go crazy with guilt if you forget why you are doing it. Remember, you are doing it because until you receive that slip of paper that makes you a citizen the Direction de Surveillance du Territoire owns your little soul. Remember, Justina, the DST owns your soul.

Kamal

WE WERE BOTH half an hour early to that rendezvous, and both a bit embarrassed by our urgency. So I showed her my new camera while we waited for dinner to be served. She was curious about what I planned to take pictures of: a curiosity that had a nervous quiver in it. Perhaps prurience.

"Dogs copulating under the Eiffel Tower. Actually I have no idea. I don't even have any film. I saw the camera and wanted it. Just like you might see a puppy and have to take it home."

"Did you ever just take home a puppy, Kamal?"

"No."

"I didn't think so. You don't seem the type."

"Well, I never brought home a camera on the spur of the moment either. So there's hope."

"A camera isn't a puppy."

"And a puppy isn't a woman? Is that what you're saying, Justina?"

"Oh, I'm not as demanding as a puppy. I promise."

"But can you compete with a Nikon? This one has a built-in meter."

"If you want me to keep a meter, that can be arranged."

"Oh, I didn't mean that, Justina."

"I know you didn't. But you gave me the line; I couldn't resist. You'd better get used to that. I can't help myself."

Used to it? As if we had already taken vows. But I did not protest, because I also had a sense that we were beginning something long enough to do a little getting used to each other. It was no courtship of

31

love. Both of us knew that. But courtships of need are equally compelling, and far more common than the romantic sort in the circles Justina and I inhabited.

Somebody once observed that at both ends of the social spectrum there is a leisure class; in both, romance is subordinated to alliance. What Justina offered me more than compensated for her pinched expression and bony chest. She had a safe apartment and, from all appearances, she had connections in the Movement. My connections had all gone up in Bernard Guzman's smoke. Through her I could accomplish in a month what it might take me a year to do on my own.

But what she thought I could give her in return was not at all clear to me. Often it is worth a great deal to a woman who thinks of herself as a dog to be seen on the arm of a man she assumes specializes only in foxes. But Justina seemed a little too shrewd to comfort herself with such a hollow vanity. Like me she was a creature of the Struggle. She had hung on through too many fallow years to be just another spring semester radical. She had plans for me, and I guessed it would not be long before they revealed themselves.

We continued to see each other almost every evening. After a week I moved my bag to her apartment and had another key made. At least I could stop putting my ear to the door before unlocking it. Life improved rapidly. Before long she invited me to *La Flamme*'s offices, a three-room apartment over a grocery store not far from Patriarches. The door, which stood open, carried three hefty locks: one engaged a steel bar that ran the width of the door. Justina leaned over the desk which guarded the entrance, greeted the pale, heavy woman who sat behind it with a perfunctory peck on each jowl, then presented me.

"Françoise, Kamal."

The large woman had a very firm grip and a suspicious air. Her dourness made Justina chirpy.

"Is Pierre here? I'd like to introduce—"

"Justina, since when does one expect Pierre to be here when one wants to see him. There was even a man from *L'Express* looking for him earlier."

"*L'Express.* Really?"

"Why not? They pay. Does your friend write?"

"I don't know. Do you write, friend?"

"Not particularly."

"Too bad, Justina. Then you will have to do the piece on Kissinger or push it off onto Hervé. Pierre will never get to it."

"I don't know a thing about Kissinger, Françoise."

"Pierre can give you all the information. We have to get it out in this issue, what with this phony cease-fire they are talking about. I don't know why they don't make the Americans surrender just like any other defeated army."

I had noticed as we entered two photo posters on the wall behind Françoise: one the tight, tough visage of Madame Binh and the other, next to it, Henry Kissinger's smear of puffy features with cross hairs sketched crudely over them. Typical student stuff: posturing. Whoever had cartooned the cross hairs had probably never squinted through a telescopic sight at a deer, let alone a man. No one who has can make a joke of it. It jolts you to the core the first time you realize just how easy it is to kill. Or how easy for someone to kill you. It takes so little imagination to see yourself under the cross hairs, going about your normal business, oblivious of the barrel lined up on your temple, about to be denied even a fraction of a second to absorb the most important event in your life. Those cartoon cross hairs made me furious.

Justina worked in a small side room crammed with three desks and innumerable cartons of papers stacked between them. She had to turn sideways to slide to her own chair.

"No quiere a los hombres," she muttered under her breath, jutting her chin toward the comrade I had just been introduced to.

"She makes no secret of that."

"I'm sorry. I was hoping Pierre would be here."

"No matter. Some other time."

Even this was a good start. In a few weeks I knew I would meet everyone in the office. Over the desk facing Justina's hung a PFLP poster: a thick fist thrusting a silhouette AK-47 into an orange and red sky. The text was in Arabic. Presumably whoever normally sat at that desk could read it. That person might even be a member. This was the closest I'd come yet. This inconsequential visit left me so encouraged that I insisted on taking Justina out to dinner on the Right Bank. The secret bourgeoise in her soul kept the revolutionary from protesting this little decadence. The effects of the burgundy and the sauces and the art nouveau self-indulgence of the decor liquidated the rest of her resistance. The waiter treated us like a married couple: m'dame, m'sieur. If I had proposed, perhaps just after the tarte, that we move into a quiet house in Orsay and raise three children Justina would not have objected. But coffee and the breeze on the river as we walked back to Patriarches restored her social conscience.

"If you ever tell anyone at *La Flamme* that we ate like this, Kamal, I'll never see you again. Never. What you spent on that meal would have fed everybody at *La Flamme* for half a month. I won't have it known that I'm stepping out with a Rothschild."

"Come on, it wasn't all that fancy. We can try Maxim's next."

"Don't you dare. How can you afford this, anyway? And your fancy camera? How long have you been traveling without working?"

"I'd rather keep myself a little mysterious."

"It makes me nervous."

"Don't you trust me, Justina?"

"I don't trust what the others may make of you. I hate having to say 'I don't know' to all the questions they ask about you."

"Tell them I'm a Saudi prince. Radicals are always impressed by royalty, even if they hide it."

"A Saudi prince who doesn't speak Arabic? What are you really? French and what? Palestinian?"

"Something like that."

"That's what I figured from the start. What's the big secret?"

"I'm the head of Black September."

"And I'm Anastasia."

Several days later I met the man who had tacked up the PFLP poster: a sinewy, suspicious Algerian a few years older than me who, even sitting, kept his chin tucked down like a boxer on guard. This was the Hervé mentioned by Françoise; and he had, in fact, been stuck with the unwanted Kissinger piece. He already knew that I was an American and launched into his subject as soon as I walked in the door.

"Did you know that your man Kissinger is a flunky of Rockefeller?" His tone accused me of being Rockefeller's flunky as well.

"Did you know that your man Boumédienne is a flunky of Baron Biche?"

"I don't joke."

"Then we're going to have a hard time communicating, Hervé." I sat down on Justina's desk, but Hervé wasn't ready to drop the subject.

"We have an entire analysis of the function of Henry Kissinger as ruling class intellectual. Did you know that he advocated that the U.S. take over the colonial war in Southeast Asia as early as 1958? Isn't it a pretty irony that he who lit the conflagration should be the one to win the accolades for putting it out?"

"Are those your cross hairs on the picture of Henry in the other room?"

"No, not mine. Françoise drew them, probably."

"Good. I would not like to think you had any prejudice before you sat down to write this article on poor Henry."

"Prejudice! I am of Jewish descent myself. I can have no prejudice against Henry Kissinger. His betrayal of his own class condemns him. I need no prejudice to condemn him. But it sounds to me as if you approve of him. That surprises me. You must be aware of Kissinger's rabid Zionism. With him it is not only a religious instinct. As the leading theoretician of U.S. hegemony through alliance, the American-Israeli incest is particularly precious to him."

"Of course."

"Of course? I would have thought, with your origins, that this Kissinger would be particularly odious to you."

"My origins? My father always said, It's a waste of emotion to begrudge a wolf the fact that he acts like a wolf. Considering origins I could just as well wonder how you can sit comfortably under Habash's AK-47."

"I have Jewish ancestors. I am not a Zionist. I support the secularization of Palestine. Have you not read Maxime Rodinson? Or your own I. F. Stone?"

"Is this something you read about, Hervé, or something you act on? What I mean is, are you a member of the PFLP, for example?"

Hervé did not answer. He glowered for a moment, then with a twitch of a sneer turned his attention to the stack of typed paper in front of him.

I waited a few minutes while he read, or pretended to read, then in the smoothest tones I had, commented, "I didn't hear your answer."

No reply. I saw myself drag him across the desk by his wiry hair and stuff his fucking Kissinger notes into his mouth, so if he wasn't going to answer at least he'd have an excuse. At that same moment I felt Justina's hand reach under my jacket and hook my belt. As if her tiny fingers could hold me back if I'd really been ready to blow.

"Suelta, Justina."

She let go. Reluctantly. I slid off her desk and leaned over Hervé's with my hands on either side of his papers. He still did not look up.

"Mon cher Hervé, I'll be back tomorrow to see if you find your tongue." His hair smelled of sweat. Aren't you going to stand up and tell me to go to hell? He continued to pretend to read instead. This Hervé was no different from the "movement intellectuals" I'd run into at Columbia in the old days; the kind who attacked you with words and then acted offended if you threatened to defend yourself with your hands. Of course you were also threatening to expose their dark secret, that they didn't really take words as seriously as hands. Afterward they hated you twice over because you had exposed their hidden shame of their own medium.

Justina caught up with me outside the grocery. "I'm sorry for grabbing you. I thought you were going to beat him up."

"I may yet."

"Hervé is a difficult person. Maybe from growing up Jewish in an Arab city."

"I grew up Arab in a Jewish city."

"New York is not Algiers, Kamal."

"Paris isn't Algiers either. Or hasn't he noticed?"

"Listen, Kamal. When you've spent a little more time here this city will stop looking to you like a Renoir. There is nothing more despised in Paris than an Algerian Jew. The contempt may be silent but it is absolutely poisonous. Hervé has a tough existence.

37

There is a reason he looks as he does. Have a little compassion. You're not exactly a marquis yourself."

"I hope you're not asking me to go up and apologize to him."

"No. Just be friendly the next time you see him. Pretend nothing has happened."

"Not if he pulls that act again."

"He won't."

"How do you know?"

"I know Hervé. Believe me, I know him."

"I see. That's the problem."

"It's a good part of the problem."

"How touching."

"I'm sorry."

But Justina was right. The next time I came to the *La Flamme* office Hervé ventured a careful smile and offered, "This must be a gratifying day for you."

It was January 27. Every headline on the newsstands trumpeted that the Vietnam cease-fire was to be formally signed today by Rogers and Madame Binh and the others here in Paris and simultaneously go into effect on the other side of the world.

"Gratifying? For Madame Binh and General Giap. Why for me? America needs a war like Vietnam. It can't feel anything without a war. Now it will settle like sludge. Look at France. It hasn't felt alive since the Algerian war, right? Except for tiny twitches like May '68. But you know what I'm talking about."

"Perhaps that is merely a symptom of the imperial vampire becoming anemic without colonial blood to suck."

"Or perhaps it is human nature."

"Under imperialist nurturing, yes."

"Why, hasn't it been a little slow for you, Hervé, since '68?"

"I am a product of this same society. My instincts are formed by it too. But things change, no? Ho Chi

Minh once said that America would be transformed by the war in Vietnam."

"Did he? Perhaps it was wishful thinking. I've heard abandoned spouses reassure themselves with very similar predictions. Haven't you?"

Justina spiked me from behind with her finger, but Hervé did not seem to take offense.

"It's true. Algerians wanted to believe France would collapse economically without its main colony to suck dry. The last decade has been rather disappointing in that respect, but that's neo-colonialism for you. A mere change of costume."

He was offering me the peace pipe of shared rhetoric. He couldn't know how the very sound of it raised my hackles. I felt Justina's glance urging me to accept the pipe and take a puff.

"Kamal, I would like you to glance at this piece on Kissinger before we have it set. I am interested in your opinion as an American." The final pass of the pipe.

"Why not? I'll probably learn a good deal about the man myself." I winced inside for my unconvincing act. But again it seemed to meet Hervé halfway. He was probably wincing for his own part. And Justina for both of us. But we forged ahead, set a time to meet and discuss the papers which he handed to me warily, as if handing over a weapon.

"What did I tell you?" Justina exulted when we were alone.

"Is it all over between you two?"

"Are you jealous?"

"No, just curious."

"I spend every night with you, don't I?"

"I'll take that evasion as meaning it isn't over between you."

"Is anything like that ever completely over?"

"Oh yes, sooner or later. But it's all right, Justina. I don't mind."

Justina

I CAN'T MAKE this man feel anything: not tenderness, not jealousy, not even anger. And the longer I fail to make him respond, the more of myself I plunge in to fill the void. Though against my will, against my better judgment and against Raymond's advice.

"What does he want, Justina?"

"Want? He doesn't ask for anything. He's very generous in fact. He takes me out to fancy restaurants in the Sixteenth."

"Then clearly he's after something."

"Maybe he likes me."

"Resist the temptation to flatter yourself, Justina. Always favor the most bitter interpretation of the facts. That way reality doesn't come as a double blow."

"You're such a gentleman, Raymond."

But of course he is right. Kamal doesn't like my body. His desire seems to spring from his brain, which is never still, not even when he makes love. He is a very competent lover. I shouldn't complain. Not after Hervé's wild excursions between ice and satyriasis. But Kamal's self-control chills me. I am getting used to it enough to take care of myself. And Kamal is not selfish. Not at all. If I only knew what he wants from me. I scarcely know what I want from him. If Raymond instructed me to break off with Kamal . . . Well, I wouldn't. It's beyond that now. I sense a driving passion beneath his control. Hints nip at the surface: that first encounter with Hervé. Kamal reminds me of a hand grenade. Hard, smooth shell. Inside, all coiled springs and explosive. Any woman wants to tap a little of that each time she makes love with a man. Why can't I with him?

His body could not be more right for me. Long, narrow and stringy like a distance runner's. And sheathed in skin as thin and smooth as an onion's. A similar color, too. He is an artist's ideal. At even the slightest shrug the action of a hundred muscles animates the surface. The effect is almost a translucence. It is a body that should be more sensitive. Unless his imperviousness is a perfectly executed act.

He claims to be indifferent to food. Yet spends money willingly in fine restaurants. He can eat almost any amount and not gain a gram of fat. Or not eat at all and not notice the lack. He also claims to be indifferent to music, yet is constantly pointing out subtle currents of emotion in our acquaintances' tones of voice. His eyes seem to me unusually keen, and always restless. When we are walking he is always observing goings-on behind distant windows. At night he will watch from our darkened room pantomimes of ordinary life in the apartments facing us, as though dining and shaving were forbidden rituals. In vain do I try to drag him from this embarrassing spying. It is deeply embedded in his nature; so many of his habits have the quality of a search for something just missed. He sleeps so lightly that the softest footfalls in the corridor wake him to full alert. But he can drop back to sleep just as quickly. Patriarches is fortunately a very quiet corner of the city.

How long will it be before this sentry state of his drives me crazy? Sometimes I think he's paranoid. Certainly when I'm panting in his arms he has nothing to fear from me. What I would give for the tenderness he lavishes on that grotesque rhinoceros at the Vincennes zoo. Maybe I'm not ugly enough for him. Kamal is the only person who can touch that leathery old dinosaur without gagging. From the second time we went there, the beast has lumbered over to the concrete barrier of his pit as soon as Kamal appears. And the gratitude that shines through the lonesome eye, almost lost in a continent of gray, wrinkled parchment, for some reason touches Kamal more deeply than anything else can. Certainly more deeply that I can. For me his eyes remain as dry and hard as camera lenses. Click. Yet he himself can't stand to be watched. He hates his own stone features. Ozymandias, he calls his face. He likes me to keep my eyes closed when we make love: that is fine with me. It is hard to come staring into a pair of gun barrels.

Kamal

HERVÉ CHOSE the place. It isn't the kind of cafe I would choose to hold a quiet, considered conversation on the structure of the American ruling class. I've known this alley for a while; it was on my circuit for a few weeks when I was looking for Palestinians in the street. Here there are three cafes within fifty meters. Hervé's choice is the most raucous of the three, the only one with a pinball machine. Its rattling and clattering set the rhythm for everything else that goes on inside. Neither the pinball nor the jukebox is ever allowed to rest. Almost every customer is a stand-up, not simply to save the forty percent on the price of a drink, but because sitting down violates the spirit of the place. Along the foot of the bar is a handsome brass toe rail on solid lathe-turned stanchions. This is the line of scrimmage. You have to tough your way to it before you can get one of the surly whitejackets to take your order. The whitejackets are very nearly the only Frenchmen in here. The average skin hue of the patrons is two f-stops darker than mine. But business is good enough that the bartenders don't feel they have to pretend to like us. They spill half an inch of every drink dropping the glass onto the counter. Contempt is considered style. To protest it is considered total lack of style.

Hervé is not at the bar when I saunter in. He's cornered the pinball machine, and has his beer set down on the sloping glass to free both hands for englishing the box. The tallest of the three whitejackets has noticed this and is yelling over the dark heads that he doesn't want his machine full of sticky beer. But Hervé is oblivious. He is attacking the machine with an intensity which would topple the State. Standing up, he is bigger than he looked behind his desk.

"Salut, Hervé." I wait until the ball has finally dodged his flailing bats.

"Merde!" He already has another coin on the way from his pocket. "Ah, bon soir, Kamal. So what did you think of my piece." He rams home the coin; the line of balls click into place.

"Not bad. Not at all bad. But you have to decide if Henry is a flunky or a Machiavelli. How can he be both?"

"Very simply. He started as a flunky, Kamal. But he absorbed the taste for power." Clack. Hervé is suddenly lost to the trajectory of the stainless steel ball, but continues once it is safely rebounding from target to target at the upper end of the box. "Yes, he acquired a taste for the power to which he offered himself as apologist. You've heard the story before: the resentful servant who discovers that the master's shoes fit him better than they fit the master himself. It's almost classical drama, the story of Kissinger. There are only two ways to make one's presence in history— Merde, I took my eye off it." Clack. "To climb on the backs of those who already have power. Or to step on their necks. Kissinger epitomizes the first option. You and I the second."

"You and I? What makes you think I have any desire to step on anyone's neck, Hervé?"

"Hah!" Clack. "Perhaps not to step. To chop? Yes, you could play Robespierre without acting. . . . Eh! that was a good one. Eight hundred points! Did you see?"

Hervé is twice as big down here as up there in *La*

43

Flamme. The reducing potion must have been Justina's presence. He sends the plunger hammering into the next ball. And then speaks in a low voice between the dinging of the target bells. "Speaking of losing heads . . . you wanted to know . . . if I belonged . . . to the PFLP, hein? One can't just ask questions like that . . . these days. After what happened . . . to Hamchari . . . yes, speaking of losing heads. Ah merde! Do you have another franc?"

"Here's a franc. Now what about losing heads?"

Clack. "You know Hamchari, the PLO man? Had his head blown off by a bomb in his telephone. . . . Clean off. Picture in one of the tabloids of his girlfriend drenched in blood . . . out of her mind . . . holding the body with no head. Powerful propaganda."

"When did—"

"Just last month. Right here in Paris." Clack.

"Who did it?"

"Who? Surely you're not that innocent. Who blows up Palestinians, *you* ask that? Mossad. Wrath of God. . . . And before Hamchari they blew up the Palestinian library. That is why . . . you don't ask . . . your friends . . . if they are in the PFLP." Clack. "Your curiosity might be . . . misinterpreted."

A pulse of fear abruptly flushed by fury. Is that a threat you just made, Hervé? Possibly an insinuation that I'm an Israeli assassin? Strange indeed to be coming from you. As a Jew in the PFLP you yourself would be a prime candidate for Mossad's vengeance. You would be keeping that association a closely guarded secret. But if you are not a member, why are you going to such lengths to give the impression that you are? Who can know what goes on in a mind like yours anyway? When a Jew takes the side of the Arabs there is something deeper than humanitarian sympathy behind it. Something as unpredictable as a scorpion and as fatal to overlook.

Hervé slams the machine with his fist as the last steel ball drops past the bats.

"Merde! Well, enough francs lost to this. Henry Kissinger still waits."

Through the rest of the encounter the currents of threat and suspicion are kept carefully below the surface, or diverted onto poor Henry. We finally part with forced smiles and a still handshake. But walking back to Patriarches in the dark I am warmed by a certain satisfaction: the meeting has not been without a purpose. Now, at least, I know for sure why my efforts to contact the Palestinian underground have been meeting a wall. Everyone with any connection at all must have done a duck dive to keep out of the way of the Israeli assassins, while Kamal the innocent has been bounding around Paris like a lonely puppy begging for someone to throw him a stick.

Justina

I SHOULD BE thankful, at least, that it is still a long way to spring. Raymond used to have me meet him for our once-a-month meetings at the Deligny swimming pool so he could stare at the bare-breasted women sunning themselves on the deck while we discussed which comrade was leaning toward which faction and who had come in from Frankfurt or Milan to talk with whom. But now it's my turn to ogle. Although, being a typical male-chauvinist middle-aged Frenchman, Raymond is not even aware that his soccer players' muscular thighs could do the same thing for me that women's suntanned boobs do for him. For the last few months we have met on the sideline of the field in the Bois de Boulogne and watched the men hurtle back and forth as

45

we trade our lethal gossip. And today again. It is cold and clear.

Raymond is early and already very involved in the game, bouncing up and down on his toes either out of excitement or trying to keep warm. His dense gray and black hair almost looks like a tweed hat. From behind he looks immense, though he is not particularly tall. I suppose I'm used to Kamal's lean build. Or perhaps it's Raymond's raincoat.

I slip into the line of spectators next to him. This is an excellent meeting place. Like the pool on the Seine, it is very unlikely to be frequented by the political demi-monde: sports are the opium of the masses. Raymond turns when he feels my shoulder against his arm.

"This is the best match yet. Some of these boys could be professional. Look at the tall African there. Formidable. Un vrai Pelé."

The one he is talking about is almost blue-black and built as straight as a lamppost. His side has just kicked the ball past the goal and he is loping back toward the middle of the field, so easily and gracefully he seems hardly to touch the ground. He is close-cropped, almost to the skull. Everything about him is elegant, even his accented French as he shouts instructions to his team. He makes French sound almost a masculine language.

"Raymond, I have important news."

"Good! We can talk on that hummock and still watch."

We leave the line of spectators and stroll toward a rise overlooking the field and backed against a stand of trees.

"Well, what is our friend up to?"

"Kamal? Mostly nothing. He is bored stiff. He might leave Paris."

"To go where?"

"He doesn't know. He is just another confused

46

American hippie looking for the meaning of life. I wouldn't be surprised to receive a postcard from an ashram in Nepal six months from now: 'Have found God. He's far out. Love, Kamal.' "

"You are certain he is as directionless as you say?"

"Oh yes. One day he thinks he is Jean-Paul Belmondo, the next he wants to pet rhinoceroses. My important news is not about Kamal but about myself."

"And what is your news, Justina." Sarcasm already creeping into his voice.

"I am quitting, Raymond. I can't do this any longer. I've got to start living a normal life or I will go crazy. I'm so tired of seeing everybody as a suspect criminal I want to scream. I've finally got something I want to keep. Sooner or later this will poison it."

"That's too bad, Justina. Of course, I will not try to coerce you."

"You will not stop my citizenship papers?"

"Ah, Justina. You know that is not up to me. I can only give you the opportunity to prove your loyalty. If you do not want to use that opportunity, what can I do? It is up to others to decide whether or not your past associations and activities disqualify you from citizenship. If you want to quit, I can certainly understand that urge. What you are doing is difficult and alienating. The rewards are few. It more often than not seems futile, even destructive. Who hasn't wanted to quit? I often do myself. It is just a pity now when you are on the verge of accomplishing something significant that you should run out of courage and will. But that is not uncommon, so I am not surprised. Only disappointed."

"Don't try to make me feel guilty."

"I'm not."

"Yes you are. You're accusing me of dropping something very significant; isn't that the word you used? What is it that makes me so important?"

"I oughtn't tell you if you are going to quit."

47

"A lousy bluff, Raymond. You insult my intelligence."

"Not at all. It is simply better that you quit not knowing information that could harm you."

"Give up, Raymond. Kamal is as insignificant as I am."

"If you insist. But to be realistic, where will you go now?"

"Maybe to Switzerland. I can use my languages there."

"You know that they have had troubles in Switzerland. They will not look benevolently on your political associations. Particularly with the German anarchists. The Swiss are afraid of the Baader-Meinhof madness creeping across their borders."

"I will tell them I was working for you, Raymond. For the DST."

"I assume you are joking. You know perfectly well we would deny it. Or worse. If pressed we might even hint you are working for the Cuban DGI. You know that most Western governments consider the Cuban service just an office of the KGB. That would be a particularly sticky association to try to shed."

"Maybe I'll go to Sweden. They do not have as many political paranoias as the rest of Europe."

"Brr. I can't see a Latin like you adjusting to that climate. Nor will they ever grant you citizenship. But it is a life, I suppose. Whatever you do, Justina, be sure to get far away from your boyfriend Kamal. That is, if you want to avoid some real complications."

"Oh, don't try to pull that shit, Raymond."

"Well"—throwing up his hands—"I've given you the best advice I can. But when your Kamal hijacks a jet, or assassinates some government official, remember what I said."

"This is ridiculous."

"You will be the first person the Police Judiciaire will interrogate. The very first. Of course, don't try to tell them that you were working for us when you got involved with him. We will deny that, too. Anyway, enough of these somber cautions. I wish you best of luck, Justina, in your new—"

"Raymond, wait."

"I've said too much already. Best forget everything. Remember what I said about not knowing information which could harm you."

"Raymond, please. Who is Kamal? What did he do in Uruguay?"

"Uruguay is Uruguay. We leave that to the Uruguayans to worry about. I can only tell you, Justina, not to mistake his apparent inactivity for lack of seriousness. He is merely being patient when he has to be patient; that is the sign of a professional. He did survive several years underground in Uruguay. For a foreigner that is remarkable. Get him to tell you what it is like to be an urban guerrilla in Uruguay. Of course if you ask him that he will know immediately that you're a spy. But if he grows to trust you enough, maybe he will confide a few of his experiences. That is if you don't run out on him as you're running out on us. But enough. Au revoir, Justina. And good luck."

"You smirky pig, Raymond. You've got me into it up to my neck, haven't you? Proud of yourself? Don't be. If it takes the joint efforts of the SDECE and Police Judiciaire and God knows who else to keep me working for you, you've got nothing to be proud of."

"Calme, du calme, Justina. Not all of us together can make you continue if you don't want to. You can still quit, and hope for the best. Perhaps you are right about your Kamal. Perhaps he will end up in an ashram in Katmandu, and you will have nothing to worry about. Think it over. And call me if you change your mind."

I've always wondered how they hang on to their agents against the pull of conscience. Now I see how

49

easy it is. You're standing in a cocked bear trap. You dare not move in either direction. The status quo is the only situation that isn't fatal, and when you realize it you're suddenly ready to do anything to preserve what you've got.

I leave Raymond absorbed in the last few minutes of struggle on the field. He has won his match. In a store window I catch a glimpse of what defeat does to me. The way I look now I would dispirit a Mongol horde. Kamal will take one look at me and throw me out into the street. It seems I need Raymond regardless of what happens now. He is the only one who can protect me from the consequences of what I've been doing for the last couple of years. And I need Kamal, because to lose him would plunge me to a depth of despair I might not be able to recover from. And if what Raymond hints at is in fact true, losing Kamal's affection could even be lethal. It is really a simple situation. You're a bug on a twig in a flood, Justina. Steady as she goes.

Kamal

DAYS DRIFT by. I have grown so used to inactivity I don't know how to end it. Life is comfortable at Patriarches. A regular little family scene. Justina cooks now. And is taking better care of herself. She's done something to her hair that keeps it back from her face, and unburdened her feet of those thick-soled clodhoppers that looked like veterans of the Long March. Now she wears something that reminds me of Cinderella's slipper. The comrades at *La Flamme* are apparently blaming me for this bourgeoisification of their little Pasionaria. It wasn't my idea, but I like the improvements and especially enjoy the discomfort it creates in the Circle. I don't have much to do with the *La Flamme* collective now. There is another circle from Justina's bookshop who are not political. Their enthusiasms focus on music and poetry and "film" and have led us to a few chamber concerts and the Cinémathèque. More simulations of normal city life; these activities may not be vital but neither are they entirely déjà vu like the debates at *La Flamme*. And since I've been almost three years without "culture" these diversions don't do me any harm. They would make my mother happy.

The only addition to our political circle has been a German named Dieter who, passing through Paris on business, recognized Justina in the street. Justina knew Dieter from the "old days," meaning '68. At that time he had some connection with Red Rudy or Danny Cohn-Bendit. Now he is working as a salesman for Siemens. He hints that he is still active with some German and Italian groups. His job gives him perfect cover to travel about. He stayed with us three days, camped on our floor between the table and the stove. The company pays him a per diem for hotels and food, which he pockets, minus the cost of a couple of bottles of wine with which he expresses his gratitude for our floor and then ends up drinking the best part of by himself. But he has a certain boyish charm. One would feel niggardly denying him hospitality. When he's a little high he can tell a good story, mostly made up but entertaining. He's useless for real information.

Meanwhile my search for the Palestinian underground has all but ceased. Those who will say anything all give the same advice: Go to Beirut; there they recruit openly. So I am again considering the journey east. But peculiarly, whenever I let my mind wander to Beirut, it automatically makes the jump south to Jerusalem. "I left on my feet. I will return on my feet." All through childhood I heard my father chant that same vow. I, who left in the womb, will not even make it back in a shroud, at the rate I am going. So far the farthest I've gotten is to a fancy travel agency on Avenue de l'Opéra. Even that was on an impulse. The Valkyrie behind the desk caught my eye. I waited for her to finish with her client and then asked in French the price of a one-way flight to Jerusalem. Immediately her expression hardened.

"Vous n'êtes pas français?" It was phrased as a question but was a statement, and had no bearing on the price of a ticket.

"Non, pas français." What's it to you?

"Vous parlez très bien le français. Vous êtes Syrien?"

"Américain."

"Oh, excusez-moi." She flustered and hurried to supply me with more information than I wanted. Then she confided in English, "I advise to go by El Al. *They* know how to make it safe from Arabs."

"Do they, madame?" We'll see about that.

It took me an hour to cool off afterward. It was lucky I still hadn't located a pistol. The world would have been treated to the first hijacking of a travel agency.

Justina returns this afternoon with a large cardboard tube. She pops me gently on the head with it, and then on the butt. She is strutting around to show me a new pair of jeans. They are almost skin-tight. She is beginning to look like a regular Parisienne.

"What's in the tube?"

"Color, my love. Color for a colorless wall. Look." She slips out three prints and holds up the first for my approval.

"Jesus!"

"What's the matter, Kamal?"

"My father had the same poster over his desk." It was one of the 1917 Bolshevik issues, in reproduction, of course. A fierce black and white Lenin raising his fist against a red sky filled with Cyrillic letters. "What are the other? Stalin and Trotsky?"

"Sorry." She unfurls the next. Windmills in a meadow of flowers against a cool sky tufted with cumulus. "A better view than our window, anyway . . . Monet."

"It's fantastic, Justina. Where's the original?"

"In the Louvre."

"Let's go steal it. I can't live without it."

"Kamal! I didn't know you cared for art."

"There's plenty you don't know about me. Let's see the next. Ah, Renoir." A slightly sad buxom blond barmaid staring at me over the carousing melee of a turn-of-the-century nightclub. Her figure seems to move, perhaps sighing.

"Not Renoir, my love. Manet."

"Oh well. I wonder how he does that?"

"Does what, Kamal?"

"Makes her appear to be breathing."

"She does, doesn't she? I never noticed that. Are you a painter?"

"I might have been."

"But?"

"Things got in the way."

"What things?"

"History."

"You're being vague."

"Am I?"

"I know you have secrets. I've never pressed you for them, have I?"

"No."

"But I am a little bit curious. Isn't there anything you can tell me?"

"What can I tell you?" She sits on the bed with the Renoir in her new denim lap watching me with tender eyes. Why shouldn't I tell her? A little bit, at least. Though every reflex tries to suppress it, I mumble, "I was in Uruguay for a while."

"I always thought you spent time in Latin America. Your Spanish is so good. You must have spent more than a year."

What harm to go a little further? "Two and a half years as a matter of fact."

"What were you doing there?"

"This and that."

"I won't ask. Just tell me when you're ready."

"Some revolutionary work."

"Serious?"

"Everything there is serious. Unlike here."

"There's serious work going on here, too."

"None that I've been able to find. I don't mean to hurt your feelings, but by the standards I'm used to . . ."

"You mean that what we are doing is not serious because it does not advance the armed struggle."

"More or less."

"Then why don't you join the armed struggle here?"

"Where is it, Justina? I can't find it. It must be so far underground that they don't know what year it is."

"It does exist though. I don't know where it is either. But all the bombings, the hijackings, the . . . assassinations. Something happens every week in Europe. Those people must live somewhere. They must have some organizational base, mustn't they? I don't know how terrorists work, but they can't be on their own, can they?"

"Not unless they can manufacture their own weapons, their own explosives, forge their own papers, rent their own safehouses, and so on."

"Did you ever have any contact with the Tupamaros, Kamal?"

"Hold on. This conversation is going further than I wanted it to. Let's change the subject."

"I wasn't trying to pry. But it's a little hard not to be curious about one's lover's experiences. You do know so much more about me that I do about you."

"And so it shall remain."

"I don't mind, Kamal."

"Good."

"Do you want some dinner? I bought a chicken."

"Sure, anything."

Now you're really slipping. No self-control at all. In a few minutes you would have been blabbing about Esteban. That's why they warned us about comfort and companionship. You lose your psychological muscle tone. You get soft. For a tender glance you will sing like a canary. For a pair of warm breasts to rest your cheek on you will throw aside your historic purpose. There was a reason why Lenin forswore the intoxications of music and mortified himself on the cold rigors of the chessboard. If the Man of the Iron Will was afraid of being softened, why is Kamal so confident? Not long ago he thought he was mortifying himself on the bony chest of Justina. But apparently Justina's chest is not bony enough anymore. Go ahead, Kamal. Why not give in the rest of the way? Tell her all your secrets, marry her and get a job. You're no longer the revolutionary. And everybody knows it but you.

Justina

So KAMAL NEEDS to confide, just as Raymond predicted. But I am not flattered by the confidences; I am horrified. I don't want to hear any more of them. Not because they themselves are so terrifying, not at all. It is my own curiosity which horrifies me. Raymond has made my natural inquisitiveness into a disease.

Suppose Kamal is picked up for nothing more than a few questions about an acquaintance. And then a few questions about himself. The information I have passed Raymond will come back at him, full circle.

And Kamal's no dummy. He'll know in a second where it came from.

If I can't quit working for the DST the very least I can do for Kamal and myself is to choke off the flow of information. Bore Raymond. Put the DST to sleep with regard to Kamal. Yes, this I can do. This I must do. It is a month already; quiet days pass quickly. A few more quiet months and Raymond will start barking up another tree. All it takes is endurance, Justina.

"Good morning, Raymond. No soccer today?"

"Maybe they're late. Damn. No point in standing around with nothing to watch."

"No point in standing around with nothing to say, either."

"Eh, Justina? You have nothing to tell me?"

"I'm afraid not."

"Nothing new, eh?"

"Nothing."

"I see one thing that's new. You're fixing yourself up. You look almost pretty; even pretty, I mean. It must be true love. Who's paying for it?"

"I am."

"It must be very important to you then. Has he noticed?"

"Of course."

"He likes his women to look good, eh?"

"What man doesn't?"

"All men do. But some are afraid to show it. He's not like your Trotskyist comrades, is he?"

"No, not at all like them."

"What does he think of them?"

"He doesn't much care for them. He probably thinks we're a bunch of poseurs. Big talkers."

"Of course he does. You know very well how the Arabs sneer at you European—"

"He doesn't think of himself as an Arab."

"No? He's never talked about going to the Middle East?"

"Not seriously."

"Ah, but he has talked about it. Which city, Justina? Damascus? Beirut? Aden?"

"He's mentioned Beirut. Mostly Jerusalem though. To see his father's home."

"So he still considers it home. That's very significant, don't you think?"

"It seems a natural enough curiosity."

"Really? When are you leaving for Havana, Justina?"

"He's just talking about it. He's not going."

"How do you know that? You'll only know when he gets on a plane and goes. In the meantime, we can only guess at his intentions. Didn't you tell me at some point that he was going around to bars where Arabs collected?"

"He doesn't do that much anymore."

"He does it a little bit?"

"How do I know where he goes during the day?"

"My thought exactly, Justina. I think we had better find out where he goes during the day, since you cannot give us that information."

"How are you going to find that out?"

"He must get lonely when you are away at work, or at your newspaper. Maybe we could find him another companion."

"Raymond, if you do . . ."

"You don't leave me much choice, being so uncooperative."

"I'm not being uncooperative. There's simply been nothing significant."

"Let me be the judge of significance, Justina. Your job is to report facts, details, impressions. So let's begin again, and see if we can't come up with a clearer picture of what our friend is about."

57

Kamal

WHAT TRIVIAL INCIDENTS can turn life to shit. Justina
staggers home from work with a bloody bandage
around her right palm, having put a packing staple
clean through it with the power stapler she uses to
seal boxes of books. Has she had it looked at? Oh,
yes. They carried her to the Faculté de Médecine a
few blocks away, where a medical student yanked
out the staple, inspected the wound with a shrug,
poured alcohol on it and wrapped it in gauze. It was
nothing, he said. It would heal in a few weeks.

But Justina hasn't recovered her color now for two
weeks. To me the wound looks infected, but she refuses to ask for any more medical attention. She
doesn't want to be shrugged at again, she says. I
think she wants to suffer. She must have gone out of
her way to get her right hand under the stapler in
the first place. But you'd think she stapled closed her
cunt for what it's done to our sex life.

The effect of her injury on my mood has been like
blood to a shark. I can't get violence off my mind.
And the news hasn't helped: first the Israelis shooting down a Libyan passenger jet, then on the same
day sending raids halfway across Lebanon to tear up
a couple of refugee camps. Their excuses get more
audaciously incredible as their raids go deeper. This
time they've captured secret PLO documents which
turn out to be nothing less than plans for "a terrorist
raid which will put Munich in the shade."

Nobody can say the Israelis lack imagination. Nor
could they say that about Black September. It's
taken them only a week to respond. And who would
think of Khartoum? Nobody, obviously. So they were
able to waltz into the Saudi embassy during a party
and nab the U.S. ambassador, the Saudi ambassador, a Belgian chargé d'affaires and a small herd of

other officials. It seems everybody is in action. Except me.

I went to see *Day of the Jackal* two afternoons in succession. It started me thinking about alternatives to the course I set myself when I left South America. Why not go mercenary? I've got the skills. I can kill with a pistol at distances a regular soldier would miss half the time with a rifle. There must be people who would pay me to use that talent. I can make a list as long as my arm of heads of state who more than deserve a .357 slug in the temple. It could lead to a profoundly satisfying retirement: sipping rum on the deck of my yacht in the Caribbean sunset, cherishing the memory of the faces that exploded in my sights: Franco's fat one, Park's smooth one, Somoza's puffy one, Lon Nol's round one, Pahlevi's smug one, Hussein's pretty one. I'd have some unusual stories to tell my grandchildren.

But on the way back to Patriarches after the second watching I have to admit I'm no Jackal. I can't work alone. I'd go crazy without anyone to trust. Perhaps I'm not another Esteban who drew people like a warm fire on a dark winter night, but I'm no solitary. Not by choice. I need a following. I am a natural leader. People gather behind me like ducklings in an emergency. When Esteban fell, it was me they turned to by instinct. There was no planned succession. Nothing anyone took seriously, because it was inconceivable that Esteban was mortal. He was too big, too needed. Another Fidel.

And even when he did fall, his corpse continued to protect us. His dead body still had charisma. No pasaran! It was so massive that it blocked the door against however many were out there trying to push it open. He gave me the seconds to grab my AR and begin shooting back. While the others just stood there in shock. That's why they turned to me afterward. We alone had driven off the murderers: his warm bleeding body and my cold will. Who else was there to turn to? Who else was there cool-headed enough to organize an escape, to single out the betrayer, to take the necessary steps? Yes, the cell was more than grateful for me to take command. It was the Committee, far away from the realities of action and survival, that took it upon itself to undermine me. I didn't fit into their theory. I was a foreigner, a North American devil. I had no doctrine, no line. I was an individualist. I was bad stuff.

Perhaps that was all true, in their context. They needed leaders who could be loved, who could become legends to their people someday. I was too strange, too chilly a figure to take Esteban's place for more than the moment of survival. I have to admit I sensed that even then. I knew I needed to find the place and the people who would accept me and warm away the chill. I convinced myself that place would be Paris.

Yet here I am, measuring myself against the chilliest and most solitary character of all time: Jackal. I must have been wrong about the place.

As Justina once predicted, I no longer see Paris through impressionist's eyes. Though once in a long while a new angle on the city will catch me by surprise. Today from the colonnaded Métro trestle crossing the Pont de Bir-Hakeim, a rain-stippled jade-green Seine fretted by the bright stone of its bridges seduces my glance upstream, where, from a Michelangelo sky, a divine rod of sunlight bursts through the dark piling clouds onto the spires and slate roofs of the Ile. But the crossing lasts only forty seconds and the vision vanishes behind the grimy facade of apartment buildings. The duration seems appropriate. Anything longer would create an illusion that a more sensual life exists here than in other metropolises. It ain't so. The city makes us pay dear for our forty seconds of grace.

Every person I meet is a victim of the city. But then I meet only the refugees, rejects and radicals, who are already victims of something else before they come here: Africans, Arabs, Russians of once noble families, Vietnamese whose wounds are so deep that they refuse to react to anything alive, bitter South Americans. All of them clawing for a place, for an income, for a bit of respect, for reassurance that they will be allowed to stay. It is not impossible. Justina is almost a citizen, she says. And for me it would be a mere formality. After all, my mother is French.

But France doesn't touch me. Arabia touches me. The Levant touches me. Places I've never seen, but have such a grip on my heart that I wince at posters of the desert as if the sunlight and desolation are really in front of me. Just like my father, who was once brought up so short by a photo of Jerusalem in Doubleday's window that he lurched as if a fish hook had caught in his cheek. He was melodramatic by nature and never hid the least twinge of emotional pain. But that book cover photo drew tears, cascades of tears, rolling down his dark, fierce face while behind him five kids and a pretty blond woman watched his and their own reflections in the clean glass. That was my first taste of humiliation. I felt the blood gorging my face, and silently hurled a curse damning him to die on the spot. Later, in the shame of that wounded afternoon, the episode formed into an indelible warning. I was only eight at the time—it must have been right after Suez—but its message was implacably clear. Words could never have been so unambiguous. The terror of sinking into such a humiliation has never left me since.

He did try to explain himself that evening at the dinner table. "If it weren't for you children," he confided in that embarrassing, vulnerable tone, "if it weren't for you children I would have joined the

61

fedayeen. Of course I am doing what I can now, but I'm afraid someday I will die of a broken heart. For not having done enough."

It was impossible for us to understand his loss then. We affected somber faces. We listened. But it had no reality to us. We lived very well. He was a banker. We had a large apartment overlooking the East River and the UN building. We ate sumptuously. My mother loved to cook. Like all of his friends, the businessmen and UN bureaucrats who kept us awake with their impassioned debates, he had grown round and soft. Like a Lebanese. His face no longer fit his body. Did he want to be like those bony and haunted fedayeen in the pictures in the magazines he received from abroad? Why? I was ashamed to ask. Instead I searched through his magazines to find the answer. But not able to read the strange script, I never found an answer. The photographs showed lines of ragged tents, corrugated tin hovels, dirty haggard people with empty eyes. Was this what he missed? My father's world was a mystery to me.

And my detachment, born of that incident, became a mystery to him. He was provoked when I sat unmoved through his laments. Finally he would turn on me. "But, of course, what should I expect? You are just an American 'kid.' Sports mean more to you than history." Then he would turn rueful. "But in the last analysis, isn't this all my own fault? I brought you here. I have given you an American standard of living. I have exiled us from our own history. So what right have I to expect you to be other than an American 'kid'? What right have I? It is I, by my cowardice who have made you such."

By this point the tears were already choking his voice and blurring his eyes. I kept my eyes fixed on my plate until, overcome by self-accusation, he would stagger off to the bedroom, quickly followed by my mother. My brothers and I would finish dinner in silent disgust.

I'm so regular at these damn bars I've become invisible. Step in from the dark street, survey through blue fumes of Gauloises the faces at the tables and the backs of heads at the bar: all familiar but none friendly. So step out again into the damp obscurity, pad along the sidewalk to the next. At the head of the meat-red stairway leading down to the subterranean Bar Américain four wire-haired Tunisians sniff around a pair of German girls in tight Levi's and elastic bodices that show off their nipples. I'm getting sick of the predictability of every tableau in the Quarter. But the Bar Américain has a good stereo, at least, and clear strains of Country Joe and the Fish waft up like hash smoke tendrils from the sous-sol into the street.

> I'm stuck on L.A. freeway
> Got rainwater in my boots.

I want to go home. If the U.S. is still home to me. It's been too long to make any assumptions.

There is one stool vacant. That is a luxury down here. I can stay as long as I care to continue buying drinks.

This Vietnam rock makes me nostalgic the way nothing else can. No other place in the Quarter has a sound system which can bring Hendrix back to life. Nor Janis. On the cafe jukes they sound like they're playing from their coffins. Froggies don't know the difference, never having heard them live. Not only do I want to go home, I want to go back. About five years. Though there probably isn't a soul down here regardless of nationality who wouldn't want to jump back five years and land two months before May 1968.

"Hi." The voice is as flat and broad as Nebraska, female, but low, in the register of, say, Mary Travers. She turns out to look not unlike Mary Travers: round-faced and blond, bleached, I am guessing, because her eyes are dark, dark brown. When I get a chance to look down I see full hips and thighs stretching a tight skirt. "Hi. Can I squeeze in here next to you?"

"Anybody's guess. How did you know I was American?"

"Oh, I've noticed you around."

"I haven't noticed you."

"You're not very polite, are you?"

"Strike one."

"That's all right. You're very unusual-looking. Anyone would have to be blind not to notice you. Your name is Kamal, isn't it?"

"Is it?"

"Yes, it is. And mine's Elaine."

"Is it?"

"Yes, it is. And you're a Leo."

"Am I?"

"Yes, you are."

"And what are you, Elaine?"

"Aquarius."

"I meant, what do you do for a living, Elaine?"

"Now, now. Let's not get hostile."

"What do you want?"

"Beer will do."

"Have mine."

"You're not thirsty?"

"I'm feeling a little crowded here."

"Why, so am I! Let's go someplace quieter, where we can hear ourselves think."

"You can hear what I think right here. I think you're wasting your time, Elaine. Or whatever your name is."

"Not nearly as much time as you've been wasting,

my dear Kamal. Not even as many minutes as you've been wasting months."

Suddenly this obnoxious blonde deserves a closer look. She appears calm, but her eyes, which have a decidedly Slavic tilt to them, are defying me. Defying me to do what? Punch her in the mouth?

"You never answered my question, Louise. What do you do and what do you want?"

"Elaine. I teach English."

"I already know English."

"I want to talk to you. In English. But not here." This she says in an almost inaudible voice.

"Will the sidewalk do?"

"The Quai will do better."

It takes only minutes to reach the stairs down to the bank of the river. Notre Dame blocks out half the sky. A few silent bodies lie as much hidden as possible along the foot of the masonry wall; the law in its majesty still prohibits rich and poor alike from sleeping under bridges. But the English teacher doesn't seem too concerned about the sleepers overhearing her.

"I have friends—"

"One wonders how you keep them."

"—I have friends who are interested in you, Kamal."

"They must be life insurance salesmen."

"They are revolutionaries. Palestinian revolutionaries." She's smart. She takes me to a place so dark I can't see her expression. By day I suppose she wears shades for these approaches.

"Why are these Palestinian revolutionaries interested in me?"

"It is said that you have been looking for the Palestinian underground."

"Said by whom?"

"That I do not know. My friends asked me if I would make contact with you. That's all I know."

"Why didn't they make contact themselves?"

"They did not want to compromise you, in case the rumors were wrong."

"*You* don't compromise me?"

"I am just a lonely American looking for companionship." She takes my arm to illustrate.

"What organization do your 'friends' belong to?"

"The Popular Front for the Liberation of Palestine. You have heard of it, I assume."

"Once or twice." If this is what she claims it to be, it is the first and only break to come my way. If it is not, it can only be a police trap. But why now? Why after all these months of futility does this suddenly drop into my lap? Suppose it is a police trap. It can't be against the law, even in France, to express some interest in fellow Palestinians. So if this is a setup, the punishment will be extracurricular: a little roughing up, a few threats. Nothing worse. Unless she is fronting for Uruguayans. But if *they* knew where to find me, they would have already bumped me off. The only other possibility is Mossad.

"Well, are you interested?"

"I'm interested in knowing why someone like you would be in the middle of something like this."

"Cautious, aren't you? Do you want to meet my friends, or not?"

Even the Israelis would have nothing more than a little pre-emptive discouragement in mind for me. There's no excuse but gutlessness for being this finicky. Once upon a time Kamal would have leaped at this without a blink. But he doesn't trust his instincts any longer. He's gone timid. The wages of domesticity. If he balks a second longer, blondie, just inform your 'friends' they'd have no use for such a pansy anyway.

"Like my old pappy used to say: Don't never look a

gift horse in the mouth, but don't never stand behind 'im neither."

"I suppose I'm to take that as meaning Yes, you do want to meet my friends. All right. I just have to make a phone call and they'll meet us."

"Where?"

"They'll tell me that on the phone."

"Tell them I suggest the rhinoceros pit at the Vincennes zoo."

"Why there?"

"The rhinoceros is a friend of mine."

She phones from a cafe directly across from the Palais de Justice. I like the irony. The phone is, as usual, next to the potties on the sous-sol. I loathe the smell which emanates from the hole-in-the-floor type, but I'm willing to put up with the odor not to let Elaine out of earshot.

She is inside the phone cabinet arguing. She sticks her head out from the pebbled glass door. "They won't go for the zoo."

"Tell them I'll keep my rhinoceros on a leash."

"They want to meet in Bois du Boulogne. I told them it's too far and too cold."

"Tell them to meet us right here where it's warm and light. Stuff this Peter Lorre crap. I'm going upstairs and having a drink."

A minute later she finds me at a table near the front.

"Well?"

"We're meeting her. I told them you were fed up with their paranoid antics."

"Thanks for starting me out on the right foot."

An extraordinary nervousness has welled up from nowhere. My palms are sweating. A cold trickle runs down my ribs. My knees have a bad case of sewing machines; every time I stop thinking about them they start jouncing violently under the table. If anybody is watching me they must think it's my first date. In a way it is.

Elaine is up from her seat suddenly. "Ah, quelle coincidence!"

A short prim Egyptian-looking fellow waves, hurries over, kisses her on both cheeks. Elaine introduces me as her "friend from America." I have no name. The newcomer is introduced as Ghassan. He initiates the conversation. "Are you finding Paris to your liking?"

"It's an entertaining city."

"Ah, but don't you find that tourism as a constant diet is a bit like living on baclava? One needs also the meat of work and the wine of accomplishment."

"And the cabbage of idleness and the grapes of wrath."

"Excuse me? I did not understand."

"It was a bad joke. Not worth explaining."

"But I have the impression you like to travel. The ideal is to combine work and travel. To give one's travel a larger purpose."

"That would be ideal."

"Where would you like to travel next, for example?"

"Where would you suggest? I have already seen South America."

"That must have been interesting. You will have to tell me about it some time. Have you ever been to Southeast Asia?"

"No."

"You could try Spain. Of course one risks getting blown up by the Basques."

"Or mistaken for an Israeli agent and being shot dead."

"Ah, you read about that. It was not a mistake. The Israelis confirmed that the man was in fact an agent."

"That's reassuring."

"Have you ever been to Israel, by the way."

"You mean Palestine? No. In fact I have often thought that would be my next excursion. I have always wanted to see Jerusalem."

"Do you have relatives there?"

"No. Not that I know of."

"Have you considered traveling to Israel by way of North Africa? That is a very unusual way to go, and one can learn some extraordinary things in North Africa. Things which will be very useful to know when you travel further east."

"Is that so? Which country did you have particularly in mind?"

"For scenery Morocco. For archeology Egypt. But Libya, you know, there's a country often overlooked. Some friends of mine were very affected by having spent time in Libya. I myself have not been there, however."

"Perhaps I should speak to these friends of yours who have."

"That is exactly what I was thinking. Yes, you must meet them as soon as possible. Are you free tomorrow evening?"

"I believe so."

"Very good. I will arrange a little party for tomorrow. Elaine knows where I live. She can conduct you there. Is that agreeable, my dear?"

Elaine's attention has been wandering off during this hokey banter. "My dear" brings her back abruptly.

"What? Is what agreeable?"

"You will bring your friend for a pleasant evening of conversation at my flat. At eight, tomorrow evening."

"Why naturally!" There is a heavy sneer in her voice.

Ghassan stands, with a hint of a bow.

"Please excuse me for interrupting your tête-à-tête, my dear. I was just passing and recognized your lovely blond hair. It has been so good to talk to you and your friend. Good evening, and à bientôt."

Excusing myself shortly afterward, I stroll toward Patriarches trying to form a concrete image of what has happened in the last hour. It still seems impossible, after all these months, that it should transpire so simply: Hello, we're from the PFLP; we're interested in sending you to Libya for commando training and then on a mission into Palestine. But why not? There must be a dozen or more people around the Quarter who have a good idea of what I've been after, and simply did not want to make their connection with the organization known to me. At least one of them must have reported my desire to make contact. These things take time. I know that from Montevideo. Still, it is so difficult to accept success when you've resigned yourself to failure.

But Justina senses the lift in my spirits as soon as I'm through the door. "You're certainly cheery."

"You make it sound like a crime."

"No. I'm just surprised. After the way you've been for the last month."

"Things have suddenly changed."

"Changed? How?" She is choking with breathless worry, probably thinking I've taken another woman.

"They've finally found me."

"They? Oh. Congratulations."

"It fell right out of the blue. Just the first approach, so far. We'll see what happens. It better not be somebody's idea of a practical joke."

"Oh, I'm sure it's not, Kamal." But she says this so weakly that it comes across as, I hope it is. She knows that we haven't much time left together.

Justina

SUPPOSE KAMAL BEGINS to suspect? Then what? He'll twist my skinny neck until I squawk. Fini. A revelation like that could even reconcile Kamal and Hervé: brothers betrayed. Now there's a revolting thought. Even in normal circumstances a woman must never let her ex-lovers become friends. None of us could survive that kind of stereoscopic examination. But in my situation the outcome could be lethal. And even if neither of them could go through with it, they could turn my life so gruesome that I might wish one of them would. There's still enough of the Church left in me to keep me from ever doing it to myself. A real handicap.

Nor do I have any hope of getting out of this on my own. Kamal will have to make the move. Maybe they'll send him somewhere far away, like Iraq. Whoever "they" turn out to be. I wonder what goes on in his mind when he lies staring at the ceiling like this. He watches with the fixity of someone in front of a movie screen. I find myself involuntarily glancing up at the flaking paint which hangs there by nothing more than tradition, hoping to catch out of the corner of my eye a glimpse of whatever it is that grips him so. Maybe this is his silent way of telling me he suspects the trap that is being laid for him. God, I hope not. What will I do? Call Raymond again. It's Raymond's scheme; he had an answer for everything when he announced it to me.

"But, Raymond. He will get suspicious if, after all these months of nothing, a man walks up to him and says, Good day, I'm from the Palestinian terrorist underground and we would like you to join us for a little bombing and hijacking this afternoon."

"Justina, in the state your friend is in, if Jacques Tati walked up to him and said, I'm George Habash, your friend would probably believe him. At least he

would try his best to believe him. There is a phenom-
enon we observe very frequently in people like Kamal who are drawn to terrorism: they progressively
blind themselves to all parts of the world which do
not conform to their delusional systems. But you
know this, Justina. The longer your comrades' efforts yield no results the more fervently they expect
a reversal delivered by a genie from a lamp. Why
else do they run out to every little street demonstration hoping that somehow it will rub itself up into
another May '68? Your friend Kamal, I'm certain, is
quite ready to take to his bosom any old genie we
care to spring on him. Alas, it is when the trout is
hungriest that he should be the most wary of fat insects landing on the water. But it is not in his nature
to be so, or we fishermen would never catch a trout.
We already know that Kamal will snap at—Never
mind."

"I'm very glad you did not say whatever vicious
thing you had in mind then, Raymond."

"Realistic. Not vicious, Justina."

"You still haven't told me how your genie is going
to present itself."

"Nor will I. In fact, the only reason I'm mentioning this at all is so that if Kamal should muse
out loud over the extraordinary bit of good luck that
is about to come his way, you can encourage and not
discourage him from believing in it. Kamal will be
told that he has been recommended by an acquaintance who needs to keep his association a secret. If he
should bring up the subject, you will reinforce this by
saying you think that a number of your common acquaintances must have clandestine connections,
though you have no ideas which ones. Is that clear?"

"I understand. Will I be meeting this genie?"

"I doubt that the genie will let that happen."

"But what will you get out of it? That is what I
don't understand. Suppose that Kamal believes the

genie is from Fatah or PFLP or whatever. Then what?"

"I see you really do not understand. This genie will truly be a member of Fatah or whatever."

"But if you have this agent already, why do you need Kamal?"

"Because Kamal will undoubtedly reach heights, see sights, that this one could never dream of. This one is only trying to save his own compromised skin. He is merely a low functionary who can recruit Kamal into the organization. We would never ask more of him than that. But Kamal will be given a chance to do whatever his ferocity drives him to. He will not be restrained by the knowledge that he is compromised, because he doesn't know that he is compromised. He will be an unwitting agent. Just as you were, Justina, when you conspired to help those two German anarchists enter France. Do you remember how easy it was for us to persuade you to cooperate? There is no one easier to recruit as an agent than a person who is compromised from the outset and whose comrades are more dangerous to him than the police. But I am lecturing an expert, unnecessarily."

"You are implying that Kamal is compromised by his association with me and I by my association with you."

"Exactly. That's the old agent's daisy chain. It doesn't even require that the associations be presently alive. That's what makes the chain durable despite the poor material it's forged from."

"Suppose one of us miserable creatures decides to give our violent comrades *your* name, Raymond. What then?"

"That would be your own death warrant, not mine. No organization whose existence in France is tolerated by the DST—and that includes all the ones you are likely to have heard of—none of those organizations will use up its bonne volonté with us by assassinating one of our officers. They may knock off one of our agents from time to time, but never an officer. Not since the OAS was in its prime has the DST lost an officer by assassination. And you may recall what happened to the OAS."

Kamal

THE NEXT TWENTY-FOUR HOURS stretch to ten times that, drawn to a fine brittle thread by the waiting. I've been ready to explode all afternoon. When I find Elaine again she is staring at the dark facade of the Palais de Justice, two empty beer glasses in front of her.

"You're late, lover."

"You mean you've got a head start."

"Can you afford a taxi?"

"To where?"

"Benghazi."

"Sure. Anything for you, kid."

The taxi driver senses we're not his typical fare. He keeps glancing back at us in his rearview mirror.

"We're still here, mon vieux."

Elaine tells him to stop. We are outside the Périphérique. In Villejuif. A nice irony. After the taxi takes off we begin to walk. She leads us down a cobbled street to a small apartment building across from a construction site. Lights from cars passing south on the autoroute sweep the dark walls of the building every few seconds. We pause to let a 2CV van pass by, rattling like a broken snare drum, then step into the building. She knocks at a door on the third floor. I realize I am expecting spotlights and a steel chair but am going to be disappointed.

The door is finally unlocked and opened by Ghassan. Inside two men are sitting on a threadbare sofa smoking. The thick sweet fumes are vaguely reassuring. My father's friends used to smoke a similar tobacco. Ghassan nods me in, but Elaine remains behind and when he closes the door she is outside. I hear her slow footsteps descending. It's tough being a courier. I know.

The two men on the couch do not stand but extend their hands as Ghassan introduces them.

"Tony." Burly and almost as dark as an Indian, with big soft hands and humorous eyes. A thin mustache widens his smile. He wears his hair long and hanging almost to his eyebrows.

"Saleh." Almost my double from the neck down, but darker. His hand is hard. We have a momentary contest of grips. But nobody wins that one against me. This man immediately senses that he won't and offers a cigarette, forcing me to free his hand.

I wave it aside. "Devout Mormon."

He doesn't understand but he looks offended anyway.

Ghassan directs me to a stuffed chair facing the sofa, and he straddles a dining chair to my right. All very informal, they are telling me.

GHASSAN: "I should ask, would you like something to drink."

KAMAL: "Let's get on with the interrogation."

GHASSAN: "Interview, my friend. Not interrogation."

KAMAL: "Whatever you want to call it."

GHASSAN: "I understand you do not speak Arabic."

KAMAL: "It is true, but how did you find out?"

GHASSAN: "The same way we accumulated the rest of your biographical data. From patient research. Here is the compilation. You may tell us of any errors."

He hands me a single typewritten sheet with a single paragraph sketch of my life. There is a space

75

left after BORN IN. Also no mention of South America. It is gratifying to know that Guzman left no obvious traces to Jibral. Or vice versa. There is almost as much about my father as about me. They must have talked to one of his old friends from UNRWA or IntraBank days. It's a cozy little world sometimes.

KAMAL: "I was born just outside of Amman. I was still a fetus when we left Jerusalem in May '48. The rest of it is correct. How long did it take you to get the stuff on my father?"

GHASSAN: "I believe we have been working on your case for about six or seven weeks, if that is what you are asking. I am sorry that we could not have talked to you sooner, but these things take time. We were aware of your impatience."

KAMAL: "Who told you about me?"

GHASSAN: "Of course we cannot tell you that. But I can tell you that we have been aware of you since you first began asking around the students' quarter to make contact with us. As I recall, that was at the start of January."

KAMAL: "Close, close enough. Actually I started nosing around the last week or two of December."

GHASSAN: "That was an unfortunate time to choose because of the murder of Hamchari. Because of that we had to assume the worst of anybody asking questions about us. But that is past history. Now that we meet you in the flesh we can come to know you better. Let me ask you, When did you start to think of yourself as a Palestinian?"

KAMAL: "I never thought otherwise. I suppose I had to deal with it seriously after June '67. Before that I was still a kid."

SALEH: "But your mother, she is French. Did you never consider yourself French?"

KAMAL: "No."

SALEH: "And you carry an American passport, you

are a citizen, you are in all respects a native of the United States. Then why with the choice of three nationalities do you choose Palestinian?"

KAMAL: "Why with a choice of thirty-two teeth does the tongue always go to the one with the cavity?"

SALEH: "You answer me in riddles?"

KAMAL: "No riddle. It is where one is wounded that one automatically identifies. It would be a peaceful world otherwise."

GHASSAN: "There is profundity in that, my friend. Let me ask you then what you would be willing to do to avenge these wounds? Would you kill?"

KAMAL: "If necessary."

SALEH: "But you might not be able to judge the necessity. Would you kill if ordered to kill? That is the real question."

KAMAL: "That would depend on who was giving the order."

SALEH: "You are already expressing reservations. That is not a wholesome sign."

KAMAL: "Let me explain my reservation. I have no idea who you fellows really are. That dossier could have come straight off the Interpol wire. You could be French agents, Israeli agents, CIA agents. It would be rather indiscreet of me to be making commitments to violence here, wouldn't it?"

GHASSAN: "A very reasonable reservation. Let me put it to rest."

He reaches for a thin newspaper lying on the dining table behind him and holds it up. The writing is Arabic, but the letters PFLP appear below the banner. Below that is a photograph.

GHASSAN: "Do you recognize the photograph?"

KAMAL: "It is Saleh or reasonably close."

GHASSAN: "You cannot read this, I know, but it is an article about a man who was recently released

from an Israeli prison where he was kept two
years. The man is Saleh."

KAMAL: "What was your crime?"

SALEH: "I was organizing our people on the West
Bank. But they accused me of transporting explosives. There was no trial. They had no evidence,
because it was a lie."

GHASSAN: "Take this paper. Let someone translate
the article for you. Does that reassure you, my
friend?"

KAMAL: "It helps."

GHASSAN: "Ah, you are a cautious one."

KAMAL: "I'm still alive."

GHASSAN: "Does this mean that you have been in
danger of your life before?"

KAMAL: "It could mean that."

GHASSAN: "Please elaborate."

KAMAL: "Not until I know who you are and what
your functions are in the organization."

What-are-we-to-do-with-him glances are flying between them. I don't even know why I'm pressing the
issue, except that instinct tells me these are low-
level types. I want to be handed to the top man, and
not get shipped off to Libya or stuck in some periph-
eral cell as a courier, like Elaine. These fellows know
nothing about me. They think I'm just another green
recruit.

GHASSAN: "I can say that as a group we act as the
screening committee. What our individual functions may be is of no real concern here. We can, as
a committee, recommend you for training at one of
our bases if we find you suitable."

KAMAL: "I am already trained. I already have experience in clandestine action. I have held command.
And furthermore my cover is intact. I have no in-

tention of blowing it for the privilege of running around in the dirt with an AK-47."

GHASSAN: "Then what is your intention, if we may be so bold as to inquire?"

KAMAL: "My intention is to be put in touch with your top man in Paris."

GHASSAN: "That is not our ordinary practice."

KAMAL: "I am not your ordinary volunteer. I have skills only your top man will be able to put to use."

SALEH: "What skills are those?"

KAMAL: "To quote your colleague, that is of no real concern here."

Saleh starts to mutter in Arabic. Immediately Tony, who has made no sign before this, raises his hand to cut him off. Is he thinking that perhaps I do understand Arabic? What a curse that I don't.

GHASSAN: "I think we should adjourn this meeting until we have instructions on how to handle your case. I do not know if what you want is even possible. You will have to wait, you realize."

KAMAL: "I know how to wait. But I also know that you can reach your commander of clandestine forces in hours if you need to."

GHASSAN: "I will see what can be done. But I make no promises."

KAMAL: "Send Elaine to the Bar Américain a week from tonight. I'll be there."

GHASSAN: "And so will she. Though it may be with a somber message."

KAMAL: "If so, there will be no point in wasting any more of your time or mine. Now it is still before midnight, I believe. I would prefer not to have to walk all the way back to the city, so I will bid you gentlemen a good evening and à bientôt."

Ghassan leads me cordially to the door. Quite to

79

my surprise the other two stand up as I am shaking Ghassan's hand. They are not quite certain whether to offer their own, as if I might ignore the offer and thus leave them with a small humiliation. My tactic has worked better than I had a right to expect; they are deferring, bent by nothing more than the force of my will. If their elusive top man can be reached, the message I have left here tonight will reach him. None of these three would dare to thwart me now.

The Direction Paris platform is empty, but the station master promises, "One more train; you are lucky." I feel lucky. Things have rolled my way. I am in motion at last. They've cleared an entire train car for me, even. Just like for Lenin. Twenty minutes later at Gare Luxembourg, my own Finland Station, all the dark heads on the adjacent platform swivel. I am the only one returning to the city at this hour. The rest, on the outbound quai, are waiting to occupy my special carriage. Something about me is drawing their attention. What do they want? A slogan? All right, I'll give them one: "Comrades! We shall now proceed to build the terrorist disorder."

Justina

IT HAS to be Kamal coming up the stairs four at a bound. He does the three flights in a few seconds when he is in a good mood. One morning when he did the same thing at Trocadero everyone stopped to watch him flying up the marble steps, his legs stretched nearly horizontal like a lanky Nureyev. He told me he was once an athlete: he used to race at his university. I've never been attracted to a man who wasn't an athlete. Even Hervé wrestled once upon a time.

Dieter, who has been sitting with me and chatting

over a bottle of Côtes du Rhône, all very relaxed, suddenly tightens at the clatter in the stairwell. Dieter is the very antithesis of an athlete. He is big and soft and slow. He should be blond to complete the image, but his hair is a sort of woody brown. For all his softness, though, he can turn very hard. The warning is in his eyes, which are the most toneless gray I have ever seen: exactly the gray of the concrete pillboxes the Germans planted throughout the French countryside and which still remain, impervious to every method of demolition. I have always thought that in another time Dieter would have made a top Nazi. Now he has no outlet for his ruthlessness, so he expresses the other side—the affable drunk.

Kamal springs through the door, but spotting Dieter, immediately raises his guard. "When did you arrive, Dieter?"

"Ach, Kamal, how are you?" Dieter's voice can be very warm and jolly. His soft Bavarian accent sometimes gives him the air of a ski instructor. "I am on business again, on my way to Italy in a day. It is tedious, but I have, this way, the opportunity to visit friends I never would see otherwise."

This does not put Kamal off his guard. It is a classic situation: Man comes home to find his woman slightly drunk with a male friend.

"Don't let me interrupt you. What were you talking about, Dieter?"

"I was talking of events in Germany."

This is not quite true. We were gossiping about the sex lives of old friends, some of whom were Germans who came to Paris for the Events of '68.

"Well, go on. What's happening in Germany? Besides Meinhof and Baader?"

"Nothing happens besides Meinhof and Baader. Things happen around them and because of them. We are laying the foundation of the Fourth Reich in response to the Rote Armee Faktion."

81

"We?"

"By we, Justina, I refer to the stratum of neo-Nazis which lies just under the visible surface of German society. Even my own parents, who sympathize with all the new repressions, you should hear them . . ."

"You are referring to the new prison at Stammheim? I saw a photograph of it."

"Not just the prison, Kamal, but the new laws and ordinances which could fill the prisons in a day if they put them into use. And the augmentation of the Stapos and the Popos. Suddenly these so-called policemen are showing up on the street in tanks and with automatic weapons. I swear, you see the specters of 1930 rising right before your eyes."

"What is going to happen?"

"It is very simple, Justina. The middle, like my parents, will pull to the right. And with that the possibility of reform vanishes. Leaving only armed rebellion. In Italy it has already begun. Another militant wing splits off from the Communist Party every day and disappears underground. Today they are collecting guns. A year from now it will explode. In Germany it may take a little longer, but it will happen."

Dieter's eyes are not the kind which glow, but the tremor in his throat makes me wonder about the purpose of this speech.

Kamal, too, is wondering, for he asks, "Are you planning to get involved?"

"In Germany I am already involved. But we must forge alliances across the borders. What about you two? There is nothing happening in France. It is just a giant safehouse. You should come to Germany."

"Are you recruiting, Dieter?"

"You know, whenever I come to France I see only long cynical faces and shrugs of ennui. I prefer to see my friends with their blood hot, not tepid. That's what we were talking about, eh Justina, when you came in."

"He's right, you know, Kamal. There's nothing happening here in France anymore. We are rotting while we wait for '68 to continue."

"What the situation calls for in Germany, Kamal, is a dramatic act to complete the polarization. You cannot imagine the reaction in the last weeks to the demand by Black September from Khartoum to free the Rote Armee prisoners in Germany. Palestinians demanding the freedom of Germans, Kamal! Imagine if they had succeeded, if they had held just a few more important people after killing the U.S. ambassador. That would have been the opening shot of the revolution."

"Why don't you just go spring them, Dieter? The hell with hostages and demands. In Uruguay they popped one hundred and fifty of the most important political prisoners in one jailbreak. It didn't start the revolution, but what the hell."

"Believe me, if I could form a commando of the right men—and women—I would try to break right into Stammheim. But to find the right people, that is the problem. No Germans really want to start the shooting, the guilts of the past lie too heavily on German consciences. Once the shooting starts, the guilts will come flying off like veils. But the people to set the spark will have to come from outside Germany."

"Sorry, Dieter."

"Oh I didn't mean that. I was just giving vent to a thought. As I said, I am just on tedious company business." He points wearily at the heavy black case he has brought with him. He has pushed it almost under the table, as if to stay as far away as possible from it. "That is the thing I spend my days trying to sell to skeptical engineers."

"What is it?" Kamal asks, but clearly not caring what the answer is.

"A new kind of oscilloscope for finding elusive little troubles in big computers. Look at this machine." He pulls the case to his feet, unlocks the top and tips out a metal box whose face looks like a small television with a hundred knobs. "Do you know, if I could sell this and keep the entire sum I could take a very nice vacation."

"Why don't you?"

"The Kripo are very good at tracking down larcenists. And once they started tracking, who knows where they might follow me. Didn't Bob Dylan say, 'To live outside the law you must be honest.'"

"I don't think that's what he meant, Dieter."

"Ah well, English isn't my first language. And now, I have kept you both long enough. As I have told Justina, there is another person I have plans to see tonight. I will not have to sleep on your floor if I leave now. But we can have lunch tomorrow and continue our conversation. Yes?"

"Of course. Who's your late-night friend?"

"I'm sorry, Justina, but she is married and so I must be discreet. Even Paris is a small town when it comes to infidelities." He shrugs and throws up his hands. Dieter can also be very cute when he wants to. "That's life among the petit bourgeoisie. Be thankful you don't have to split your life in two as I do. By the way, Kamal, do you mind if I leave this fragile electronic albatross here and pick it up tomorrow? I'd rather not have to appear at this assignation weighed down like a station porter."

"I understand."

"Thank you and adios until tomorrow, friends."

Kamal already has his shirt and shoes off by the time Dieter lugs himself out the door. He sits picking at the worn rubber soles, listening to the heavy steps descend, then, after they have ceased for a minute, lies back on the bed staring at the ceiling again.

"How did it go tonight, Kamal?"

"Fine. How did what go?"

"I don't know. You didn't tell me where you were going."

"It went fine. Better than fine."

"I'm glad."

"What's Dieter doing here in Paris if he's on his way to Italy? It's hardly the direct route."

"Dieter is not very direct himself."

"Exactly what I was thinking, Jus. I wonder what that lecture was all about?"

"It was not vintage Dieter. All that business about forming a commando group and storming Stammheim. He never talked like that before. Maybe he was rehearsing a line for his new girlfriend."

"An odd come-on to throw at a petite bourgeoise."

"Maybe she isn't really a petite bourgeoise, Kamal. Maybe she is someone we know."

"Who cares about Dieter's sex life."

But when Dieter fails to show up for lunch the next day as he so volubly promised, his sex life becomes suddenly more interesting. We begin to speculate on who could be detaining him. And when we fail to hear anything from him by midnight, our speculations turn sinister. Could he have been picked up for questioning? Had he suddenly suspected surveillance and left Paris in order not to lead back to us? I can talk about these things without my heart pounding now. Sometimes I am surprised by just how enthusiastically I can participate in spy talk. At *La Flamme* it is a favorite of conversation to speculate on comrades behind their backs. It means nothing. When Kamal showed up, how the tongues wagged. He, of course, was a CIA agent, no question.

When I first suffered the anxieties about being discovered, Raymond pointed out that there were only two ways I could be exposed. If I were followed twenty-four hours a day for a month by a small army of specialists, they might be able to stick with me through my evasive maneuvers and observe my meeting him. Or if somebody very clever planted a story through me which would provoke a response from the DST. But Raymond reassured me the DST had other sources of information with which any startling news of that sort would immediately be cross-checked.

And when I worried that I might accidentally blow myself, he provided me with the agent's first commandment: You are your cover. "There is no act you have to sustain, Justina. You are a genuine Trotskyist. We would never choose a Gaullist for this purpose. You are your cover. Keep doing exactly what you've been doing. Once a month you have an appointment to keep with me. Simply think of it as coming to see a psychiatrist. Once a month you come to talk to me for an hour or less about the people you know, what they say to you and what you say to them. Your hour at the psychiatrist's is no one else's business, is it?"

That mental trick worked enough for the habit to take root. Now I can stand back detached and listen to Kamal fret and worry over Dieter's disappearance. The one thing I know with certainty is that uninformed speculations are always wrong. Therefore Dieter has not been detained. Nor is he leading a tail away from us. And certainly he hasn't been bumped off. Sooner or later we will hear from him and what we hear will be ridiculously innocuous: like a case of food poisoning or appendicitis.

Kamal

A WEEK as slow as death, put behind me by sheer will power. I still know how to wait. Of course there is no guarantee that Elaine will be waiting with a message. But my luck feels good; something will happen. Justina senses it too and has slid into a funk. She chooses to wait until I have my hand on the door to remind me that it has been a whole week since we have heard from Dieter. I've nearly forgotten about him, and at this point don't give a damn.

Justina has also managed to recruit the sky into a conspiracy to dampen my enthusiasm for this rendezvous. The first cloudburst in a month catches me at the head of Saint Jacques and chases me all the way to the river before I recall that we are to meet not across from Justice but down in Bar Américain. I haven't run this far for over a year. All the memories wound into my muscles are being set loose. I used to run in a rain like this down to another river, the Hudson, daydreaming of the Olympics. I needed the daydream to keep me going at the pace. And here's an irony I never thought of before: It would have been the '72 Olympics, the Black September games, I was dreaming of during those early-morning training runs down to Riverside Park. It was no idle fantasy either, with Coach goading me daily to make a grab at world class in the 440 hurdles. All I had to do was keep leaping for those next five years, he said. That was spring of 1967. A year later events had swung my ambitions so far from Olympic hurdles that I barely noticed being dropped from the squad.

I walk the half block back to Bar Américain panting. Winded by a short half mile downhill at a warm-up pace—that is a little depressing. My Olympics were over only six months ago.

Elaine is leaning on her elbows at the bar with three empties in front of her and a fourth on its way. She smells of damp wool and demoralization.

"Mind if I squeeze in?"

She swivels her head, still propping her chin so the words buzz through clenched teeth. "That must be a proposition. You're panting already."

"You must have something I want pretty bad."

"Do I? You Arabs are so rude."

"Only to you Yankee women who all come on like whores."

Pulling the collar of her greenish jacket up to just below her eyes: "Does that calm your incontinence, beni couscous?"

"Let's go, Louise. I'm running out of patience."

"Go where?"

"To visit your three stooges."

"Three stooges! My God, you really are an American. And all this time I thought you was an A-rab, Ahab."

"Let's go, Louise."

"Elaine. I'm Elaine. And I'm from Ohio. I'll bet you're from Missouri. Being so suspicious and all. I think I'd rather be from Ohio. That way you get to go to Kent State without payin' tuition. I'll bet you don't believe I went to Kent State. You're wrong. I got a bullet hole to prove it. Right here, look."

She yanks open her shirt and lets a fat breast flop out. There is a small elliptical scar on the side near her ribs. "See?"

This brings a few whistles of appreciation. Somebody elbows me in the ribs and spits, "Formidable!" in my ear.

"Pin a medal on it and let's go, Louise."

"Your place or mine, A-rab?" She tucks herself away.

"Their place."

"Whose?"

"Theirs."

"I don't know *them*. Don't *them* have names."

"Come on outside, Louise, and let's sober up."

"Oh, *them*! Of course, effendi, anything you say."

I have to steer her up the narrow crimson stairway. I'm afraid she's going to vomit all over the carpet. Fortunately the rain has stopped, and she isn't as drunk as she's pretending. Though not sober yet either.

"How long have you been working for these guys, Louise?"

"This isn't work. This is fun and games."

"How long?"

"A year, a little more. I don't remember."

"How did you get hooked up with them?"

"That's a dumb question. How does a blonde with big tits get hooked up with anything? Did you meet the one who calls himself Tony?"

"Barely. He didn't say anything."

"He hasn't got a good grip on the language. He couldn't keep his eyes on the blackboard. But he has the best stash of hash in Paris. And some other things."

"How much do you know about these guys? I mean in terms of their importance."

"Oh, they're important. They're important, all right. Every one of them, each one more than the other. Listen, have you ever met an Arab who will admit he doesn't count for shit, except beside Allah? But I know who really counts. Yes I do. What has two eyes in front and two eyes in back and still can't see?"

"I give up."

"A dollar bill. It's got George's eyes in front and the eagle's eye and that crazy eye over the pyramid in back. Now, could you imagine what stories a dollar bill could tell you if any of its four eyes could see where it's been. Sometimes I feel like a dollar bill, the way I get passed around by you A-rabs. I've even been left as a tip."

"Who's stopping you from walking out?"

"I am. It keeps me from getting bored. I know that someday I'll go home to Akron, get married and raise three kids in a station wagon. I figure I'd like to have something to remember. A secret to drop on the hubby and squash him like a bug if I ever have to. 'My dear,' I will say one morning over the Kelloggs, 'did you know that I've fucked and sucked every Arab terrorist in Europe?' Actually I'd like to tell my pa, but it would kill him. Then I'd be the terrorist, wouldn't I? But what was I talking about?"

"Dollar bills with eyes."

"That's right. Well I've got eyes which can see what goes on in front of me. So I know that Ghassan and Tony and that other one are pipsqueaks. There was this A-rab party Tony dragged me to, in a fancy mansion near Versailles, full of minor consulate types and businessmen who must have something going for them, because Ghassan and Tony and the other one were clucking around them kissing ass. But suddenly, about one in the morning, this bearded guy comes in and suddenly everybody's whispering and pushing into a circle to shake his hand. Later the Beard comes over to Tony. Tony introduces me. The Beard is very gallant. We keep brushing tit to elbow for the next hour, and finally we get to talking. Tony stands by beaming. At about three in the morning the Beard and Tony have a little huddle. Then Tony says to me, I have some important business which takes me away now, but Mohammed has offered to conduct you home.

"That turned out to be his home, naturally. But who was I to quibble? Anyway this Mohammed was a lot smarter than Tony. He said he was an actor and a playwright. I never could find the plays. His name was Boudia, Mohammed Boudia. Ever hear of him?"

"No."

"But he really was an actor. With some little theater in the city, I've forgotten the name. But that wasn't why they were all whispering and wanting to touch his hand. That was no theater crowd. My gallant Momo Boudia is a big-shot terrorist. And he sure played the part. I never stayed with him twice

90

in the same apartment. And he always carried a gun, which he kept under his pillow at night. And I was one of about forty women he was seeing at the time."

"You don't see this Boudia anymore?"

"De temps en temps. Why? Do you want to meet him?"

"I wouldn't mind."

"I'll bet you wouldn't mind, O master of understatement. But what have you ever done for me? Huh?"

"I bought you a couple of drinks."

"I'm sorry. You're just not in my league, fella. Let's get going. Weren't we supposed to be meeting somebody?"

Elaine, completely sobered by her tale, steps into the street to hail a taxi. When we've piled inside she orders it to the Bois du Boulogne.

"What's this change of venue mean?"

She shrugs. "I just take orders."

Again she has us dropped off short of the destination. The paths of Boulogne, as always after dark, are haunted by sexual predators and prey of every permutation. We are immediately tracked by a pair who finally decide to approach us under a lamp. They are in the costumes of elegant middle-aged bourgeoisie; they appear to be a couple, man and wife even. But out here you can never judge by appearances, they say. The couple ask us our price, tous les deux, for both of us together. Elaine tells them ten thousand francs. They snort and stalk off into the shadows. We continue another few hundred yards, only to be approached by another pair: two males this time, one quite burly. The nearest lamp is some distance behind them. Their faces are in complete shadow, but there is something about the certainty of their walk which warns me that the approach is not sexual. Automatically my hands go to my pockets for some kind of weapon. Nothing but a house key. Elaine is slowing up and stiffening. This isn't part of the expected scene. The two men seem to have no hesitation.

"Ça va, Elena?" One can't tell which one spoke.

"C'est toi, Tony?" Elaine's voice trembling slightly.

"Oui."

"Ah, bon. Et qui avec? Oh, mon Dieu!"

The shorter one comes striding up to us with both hands extended. It takes me a moment to see there is nothing in them. It is a greeting. "Comrade Kamal Jibral, I am Mohammed Boudia. You have been wishing to meet with me."

Statement or question? The delivery of the phrase almost made it a command. His hand, softer and more sensual than I expected, feels like an antenna tuning in on my nervous system. I can see almost nothing of his features, as he has carefully choreographed this meeting to keep the light directly behind him. The backlit ends of the hairs of his beard form a glowing corona around the darkness of his face. I can imagine him smiling and scrutinizing me with shrewd restless eyes.

Tony, whose position to the side allows the lamp to light his face obliquely, is watching my hands. He has the nervous air of a secretly armed man who isn't used to being armed, and expects everyone else around him to be armed as well. Sensing Tony's jitters, Elaine has instinctively moved for cover behind my shoulder. For a moment I think I'm feeling Justina's breath warm on my neck. Boudia has completely ignored her presence.

"Yes, comrade Boudia. If you are who I have heard you claimed to be, I have been waiting months to meet you."

"And who have you heard me claimed to be?"

"A commander of clandestine forces of the PFLP."

"That is a rather grandiose way of describing my

92

function. I would call myself a freedom fighter. It happens that one must now conceal oneself if one fights for freedom."

"You imply that you have no greater authority than the men I have met so far."

"It happens that Fate has placed in my hands certain responsibility."

"Then you are the one I have been waiting to meet."

His arms gesture up from his sides in mock supplication, the lamplight catching white starched cuffs protruding from the dark jacket sleeves. "Meet me on what matter, my friend?"

"To offer my services."

"Are you a domestic?"

"Excuse me?"

"A revolutionary does not offer his services. He volunteers to join the struggle.

"I apologize for the overcautious phrasing. I've been sitting on my ass for months. I'm ready to leap into the battle."

"We generally train our fighters before letting them leap into battle."

"I am trained."

"So I have been informed. But whether your training and experience are of any use to us remains to be determined. Come, my friend, let us go for a walk together. Tony and Elena will follow far enough behind to allow us to pursue this discussion in privacy. But first, as a matter of routine, I must ask you to submit to a brief body search. It implies no distrust. We simply require it to subdue anxieties which interfere with open conversation. . . . Tony, if you would do it quickly, please."

The search touches the armpits, waist and ankles. If I were armed he would not discover it, since he has skipped the only place I ever carry a pistol: in the small of my back. But, as Boudia said, the search is a formality. Perhaps a warning that the possibility is not being overlooked. Immediately afterward Boudia gestures toward an unlit dirt path forking from the paved one. Still without letting a ray of light hit his face, he guides us onto it, while Tony and Elaine wait until we have put twenty yards between us and them, then begin to follow. Boudia keeps the pace slower than an amble. He does not want to use up the darkness of the path before our conversation is done.

"So, what is the nature of this training and experience you would not reveal to our comrade Ghassan?"

"I was two and a half years with the Tupamaros."

"You implied to Ghassan that you had seen action."

"Yes. I was very close to the leadership. Because of my unusual identity I was entrusted with special tasks."

"Of what nature?"

"Negotiations in kidnappings, certain intelligence work, smuggling of weapons, for example."

"You do not mention armed action."

"I have killed, if that's what you are asking."

"I was not asking. But it is interesting to know. You did well in asking to speak to me directly. Ghassan is used to dealing with the ordinary class of volunteers. We have so many these days we have to sort them in some expedient manner. The rigor of military training in one of our bases in Syria or Libya or Lebanon strains out the dilettantes, leaving us with the dedicated and the spies. The spies do not wish to call attention to themselves, so they stick to the herd. The fact that you insisted so vehemently on setting yourself apart was extremely interesting to me. It meant that you were either an uncommon volunteer, or a very uncommon spy."

"But now you are convinced I am not a spy."

"Certainly not. What, my friend, would have convinced me of that?"

"Some leaders claim they have an instinct."

"Those quickly become dead leaders. Successful spies depend on their victims' instincts. Logic and experiment are the enemies of the spy. Not instinct. You do know about the great Sorge."

"I have heard of him."

"If you are a spy, my friend, I highly recommend researching his career diligently. He, too, was a man of ambiguous nationality. As are many successful spies."

"My ambiguous nationality is not my fault."

"Nothing that happens in childhood is ever the child's fault. Nevertheless, as are the roots, so grows the tree."

"One does make choices."

"Why did you choose revolution instead of something like medicine? Some don't have that choice. You did."

"I don't know. Perhaps my conscience."

"And where did your conscience learn to make such harsh demands?"

"I don't know. It was always that way."

"Ah, so you see, whatever you are now, hero or spy, was forged into you at a very tender age. Now I must perform the assay to discover what, in fact, was forged. You have an American passport. A legal American passport?"

"Yes."

"So you are free to travel to Israel."

"Yes."

"You enjoy a liberty that few refugee Palestinians enjoy. You have not taken advantage of it yet?"

"No. But I have intended to."

"By any chance do you know how to use a camera?"

"Of course."

"Ah yes. I forgot. You Americans know how to use

every sort of gadget. Do you happen to own a camera?"

"No. . . . Yes, as a matter of fact I bought one recently, but haven't used it. A Nikon."

"A Nikon. Very nice. I assume you would naturally take it with you on any journey."

"I am a fighter, not an espionage specialist, Mr. Boudia."

"As always, the American crashes straight to the point, without the pleasure of foreplay. It is true. We would like you to take some pictures for us. You said you were involved in 'certain' intelligence work in Montevideo. That did not make you an espionage specialist, did it? This will not make you a spy either. It is a reconnaissance which is needed and which will test your loyalty at the same time. For an American the risk is negligible, whereas for less fortunate compatriots . . . Do you want me to continue?"

"You are very persuasive, comrade Boudia."

"As you no doubt know, since infamous September our advance bases have had to be relocated from Jordan to Syria and Lebanon. This has been a tremendous disadvantage, because the border crossings, particularly from Syria, have to be made into difficult terrain and hostile populations like the Druzes of the Golan area. Since '67 the Golan area under Mount Hermon is being developed into a combination fortress and resort under the assumption that Israeli tenancy there will be indefinite. The settlements are a particularly important part of the occupation. That is the Zionist principle. So it is an equally important part of our resistance to let these settlements know that their foothold is extremely tenuous.

"That's the dirty work of our struggle. It's not like living it up here in Paris. It barely makes news in the Israeli papers when a raid reaches its destination, and most of the time they don't even get that far. The Hermon is the most difficult kind of terrain. It changes character at every elevation. In one spot there is cover, fifty meters to the side the slopes are bare. You can fall into a crack, step off a cliff, get lost if you blink your eyes. It is a military nightmare for both sides. But since most of our fighters have never been there, they are at a severe disadvantage against patrols who have been trained there, and fought there in '67. Our boys must make do with photographs."

"The Israelis must control access to the area very strictly."

"No. Because it is also their playground. In the summer it is crowded with hikers and sightseers. In the winter they ski there."

"I will take your pictures."

"I am very pleased to hear that. Very pleased, my friend. Tony will show you the maps of exactly the area that interests us, and will explain how to go about it. How do you feel about doing this?"

"A little scared. Proud. I need some time to absorb it."

"Of course. By the way, we would also prefer if you would fly by El Al. We like our 'special people' to gain as much familiarity with their airline security as possible. It could be valuable later on. We would also prefer if you would fly from an airport outside of France. We try to keep our activities away from the countries which tolerate our presence relatively gracefully. I would suggest Milan."

"I suppose you would also prefer it if the Israelis could not trace me too easily back to Paris."

"Yes. In Europe one travels by train if one does not want the transit recorded in one's passport. I assume you have already been stamped for Paris when you arrived."

"Yes."

"That is too bad. But it is still better than having

the ticket written from Paris. The ticket stays in their files. While your passport stays with you."

"We encountered the same kind of problem in South America."

"When you return we will talk at greater length about your experiences in South America."

"How will I get in touch with you? I don't like to depend entirely on Elaine."

"Rightly so. You will find in the Paris phone book a Dr. U. M. al-Ghazw. Telephone early in the morning or late at night. It may take several days before you get an answer. Identify yourself as . . . let me see . . . Huckleberry Finn. A meeting place will be arranged. Of course I needn't tell you, if you are being followed . . ."

"Don't worry. By the way, have you spent time in Russia?"

"Why do you ask that, my friend?"

"Just a question."

"No question is just a question."

"Let's save it until I get back. Both question and answer."

"As you wish."

Boudia turns around. Tony's and Elena's footsteps scuff in the dirt somewhere. They are hidden in shadow. This darkness is unnatural for a park inside a city. They must have gone to some trouble to find a path under a canopy dense enough to block out the skyglow. Boudia's voice is so familiar already that it seems inconceivable I haven't seen his face yet.

"My friend Kamal, we have said all that has to be said now. I wish you best of luck and hope we may meet under, let us say, more illuminating circumstances. Please wait here. I will send Elena up the path to you. She knows the way out of the jungle." Without a handshake he slips from my side. His footsteps crunch quickly away.

A minute or two later Elaine's uncertain steps come into earshot. "Kamal?"

"Here."

"Whistle or sing so I can find you."

"I'm sing-ing in the rain . . ."

"God, you're a real cornball." She collides with me.

"Don't overdo it, Louise."

"I was just bein' friendly, fer Chrissakes."

"Did you and Tony have a nice chat?"

"Smell." She exhales in my face.

"Do that three more times, and neither of us will be able to find our way out of here."

"What's the hurry. You're always in such a god-damn hurry. Let's find ourselves a nice little patch of grass and make some splendor."

"Hey Louise, you shouldn't let on that you're edu-cated. It spoils your charm."

Justina

EACH OF KAMAL'S sudden comings and goings affects me like stepping out of a fog to the edge of a preci-pice. Now an entire night away from Patriarches. He is seeing another woman, of course. But what right have I to protest. His betrayal is so paltry beside mine that I should whip myself for feeling offend-ed. And yet he's the one who acts guilty. When he slipped home at four in the morning he expected me to be fast asleep. He jumped when I switched on the light. There was a flicker of fury, perhaps at think-ing he'd been caught, which was quickly quenched in explanation.

"Well, Jus. The search is over. I'm in."

"Oh, well that's very good. You must be happy."

"Happy? Not that exactly. It's like reaching shore after being shipwrecked."

"I didn't know you'd been shipwrecked too."

"I didn't know you were so literal."

He stalked into the bathroom. A few seconds later both taps were roaring into the tub. Washing away the other woman's juices. He's "in." What a choice of words! Couldn't even get out a real lie. It turned out to be the longest bath he ever took. The great revolutionary hiding from his girl in a locked bathroom. Finally he emerged wrapped in a towel.

"Now that you're 'in,' what happens, Kamal? More all-night meetings?"

"No. I'll be going away for a little while."

"Going away? Permanently?"

"Didn't I just say 'for a little while'?"

"How little?"

"A couple of weeks, maybe less."

"But you will be coming back?"

"I damn well hope so."

"You mean . . . it's a mission."

He didn't answer for a moment. Then, with his back to me, he muttered, "That's your interpretation." He rolled into bed with his back to me still. I didn't dare ask another question.

But now, after a few more hours of tossing, I find myself perfectly willing to believe in this mission. If it still doesn't make my fears of another woman vanish—I don't know how women know, but when there is another woman, we always do know, even when we convince ourselves otherwise—the cold fact that he is going on a mission somehow mitigates it. Perhaps this is why men offer themselves up as soldiers: It's a collective excuse for their faithlessness. And doesn't it work, too. When he awakes I am cooking him breakfast, American style, to help him recover from his night out.

"By the way, Justina, what did you do with Dieter's black case? It's not under the table."

"Somebody finally came by for it last night. A

friend of Dieter's. Or a colleague. He said Dieter wasn't working for Siemens anymore, and had asked him to pick it up."

"A German?"

"No. As French as they come. A real engineer type. Not much bigger than me. He could barely carry it."

"Did he know what happened to Dieter? Why Dieter didn't show up?"

"No. I asked. He just shook his head and mumbled something about Dieter being unreliable. Good old Dieter. He probably got chased out of town by the woman's husband. And then got fired."

"Did the guy leave his name? A card or something?"

"He said his name. Jean-Jacques . . . let me recall. Jean-Jacques . . . Froyat. That was it. Why?"

"He didn't show you a letter from Dieter, or a note."

"No. He said Dieter phoned him. He must have spoken to Dieter. How else would he have known it was here?"

"That's true."

I thought that would be the last we'd hear of Dieter's black case, but it wasn't. A day or two later I came home to find Kamal glowering over some sheets of paper.

He didn't greet me. His first words after I closed the door were "Justina, did you pick up that thing of Dieter's? I mean did you actually carry it?"

"Yes. For a moment, when I handed it to the guy."

"What would you say it weighed?"

"Oh, it was heavy. I could barely lift it. Twenty-five kilos, perhaps."

"At least twenty-five. Possibly over thirty. Look at this."

It was a glossy brochure with a picture of Dieter's machine on the cover. The writing was in German.

"Where did you get that, Kamal?"

"From the Siemens office in Paris. It's in German, but you can read this. At the very bottom of the specifications: 'Gewicht—13.8 kg.' Suppose the carrying case weighed another five or six kilos. Under twenty total. What do you make of that, Justina?"

"It's very odd."

"And even odder is the fact that the Siemens office had never heard of Jean-Jacques Froyat. Nor of Dieter."

"What does it mean?"

"What it means is that we've been used as a drop. For who the hell knows what. Guns, explosives, ammunition. There could have been twenty kilos of anything inside that metal box: five kilos for the box and its screen, five kilos for the black carrying case, and five RPG rounds, or two dozen grenades, or five Skorpion subs, or a dozen Tokarevs, or enough plastique to take down a 747 three times over."

"Or twenty kilos of heroin. Knowing Dieter, that's more likely."

"Look, it's amazing that anyone would trust Dieter to carry as much as a few thousand dollars' worth of contraband."

"Kamal, maybe we were just wrong about the weight. Maybe the machine just seemed heavier than it really was."

"Then who was Jean-Jacques, eh?"

"Well, it's gone. There's nothing to worry about now."

"Now. But suppose our little Jean-Jacques had been followed here. We'd be up to the elbows in shit. For what? I don't like being used. Particularly without my knowing it. He damn near fucked everything I've been working for with his little black case."

"But it didn't work out that way. They were careful."

"Not careful enough."

Kamal was too upset about this for me to think clearly until after he had taken his aggravation out for the evening. He had another "meeting." Once alone, all sorts of explanations for the discrepancies poured into my mind. There might have been books or batteries in the case, or it may have been a different model machine from the one on the paper brochure. And as for the little fellow, he never said he worked for Siemens. He only said he was picking the case up for Dieter. He didn't seem to be the clandestine type, either. I've known enough of them now to have some faith in my judgment. But as Raymond warns, it is just as dangerous to acquit as to condemn on appearances.

Kamal has been gone another entire night. This time he comes back agitated instead of guilty. This is worse. It gives me vertigo. It calms me a little to feed him. Routine is reassuring. But he is totally preoccupied.

"Is it still on, Kamal?"

He looks up surprised. Then nods sharply.

"When?"

"Soon."

He bolts down his breakfast and rushes out. I feel a little more peaceful when he isn't here. If this keeps up I'll be looking forward to him leaving.

I suggest a movie for the evening when he gets back. He has bought a pair of desert boots at Vieux Camper, a rucksack and some other little camping items. He stomps around the apartment in his boots, wondering aloud if they're going to be comfortable. And later wears them to the movie theater.

It doesn't help. The night passes in little fits of nervous sleep. I can feel his mind whirling like a whetstone, throwing off sparks. I try to calm him with my hands. He pushes me away. His skin feels like rubber. Finally I can do nothing but turn my back and let my exhaustion carry me away from him. When daylight wakes me he is also finally asleep, but lying twisted and snoring in a way I have never seen him before. I am wondering how soon is "Soon." And how much worse it will get before then.

I have coffee and fresh croissants waiting for him when he wakes. The croissants are a real luxury. He pulls on his pants and staggers to the table and gives me a little pat on the thigh when he sees what's on his plate. He is worn but calm, like a drunk or a sick man convalescing. I want to ask how soon is "Soon" now, but am afraid it will put him right back to yesterday. And just as I am thinking this there is a knock, a rather brash knock, on the door. I jump up to answer it, hoping to let Kamal stay in his lull. But that is futile, because it is Dieter at the door. He sort of marches right past me with a sunny smile across his round face. I was afraid we hadn't seen the last of him. But at least he's not here to cause trouble.

"Hullo, Kamal and Justina, it's been a little longer than I planned, but—"

"Late for lunch, my friend. You make it hard to be a good host." Kamal rarely shows the Arab in him. When he does it comes out in threatening ambiguities of tongue.

Dieter, like anyone who senses a half-hidden blade, immediately goes on the defensive. Which in Dieter takes the form of ingratiation: "Lunch I can find in any restaurant. But with whom else can I talk about the things we talk about?"

"With anyone, Dieter. I can take you to half a dozen cafes where you will hear more grandiose schemes than yours being discussed in very loud voices. Loud enough so that everyone will be sure to know what a stud the speaker is."

"The difference"—Dieter wondering if and why he is being attacked— ". . . the difference is that I do

104

not want to be overheard. Nor does anyone whose intention is carrying his words into action. That is why I came here. I think of you as a man with that intention, Kamal."

"How flattering. But I'm afraid you overestimated me, my friend. I'm not as courageous as I look. You see, I don't think my consciousness is developed enough to guide me into battle for a couple of suburban jerk-offs like Meinhof and Baader. Nor is my analysis refined enough to permit me to perceive the mortal oppressions cast down on the people of Western Europe by their department stores and state universities. And my working class orientation is so weak that I feel no solidarity with drug addicts and insane asylum patient collectives. No, Dieter, I'm not the man you think I am. I'm just blinded by brutish and narrow Third World prejudices. There's just no place for me in your high-technology vanguard. But maybe you could make just a little donation to my poor backwater struggle."

Dieter has entirely changed during this. His round face has grown edges and corners. You can almost read the calculation on his slate irises. He's getting close, but he can't quite see what Kamal is leading up to. He knows ingratiation hasn't worked. Now he'll try a counteroffensive.

"I should have known better than trying to talk to a Palestinian. Ever since Munich you think you are gods. For shooting up eleven Jews. I suppose that puts your vanguard out so far in front that no one has the right to a struggle of their own. You're just like the Jews: you sell your suffering. Well, take your superior Palestinian suffering and stick it up your ass. Keep it warm there, because pretty soon everyone else will forget about it. You are just a momentary drama. A flicker in the flame of oil. The Russians will drop you when they have a bad winter and need American wheat. And the petroleum countries, why should they want you to have a homeland? They'd lose their cheap labor."

"Dieter, can it and get out of here."

"Not until I'm finished replying to—"

Kamal starts to rise from his chair; so liquid, so deliberately sinuous is the motion that we are not seeing a human but a reptile uncoiling. It stops my breath and Dieter's word in midflight.

He is swallowing the stuck word, now stammers, "What . . . Kamal, what have I done?"

This is genuine. Despite Dieter's advantage in height and weight, he seems a child. Cloud before steel. The muscles in Kamal's bare chest are so coiled Dieter is afraid to take his eyes off them.

"You . . . and Jean-Jacques . . . have abused . . . my hospitality."

At this, whether out of nervousness or disbelief, there's no way to know, Dieter coughs up a little smirky giggle. But the smirk is wrenched away in an instant by horror as he sees the springs in Kamal's chest unwinding, and the arm and hand they drive flying upward and straightening with a half twist just under his chin. The blow whips him back like a reed. He falls against the door gagging and clutching his throat; his writhing drives whatever little breath is in him out, but he can't open his tube to get more in. His eyes are so bugged out, I have a wave of nausea just looking at him. I'm sure he's going to die.

But Kamal just continues to stand and watch. Dieter finally manages to wheeze in a breath. Kamal steps over him and drags him to his knees. Dieter still tugs at the flesh of his Adam's apple as if trying to hold open the tube. Kamal leans and whispers something in his ear. I can only make out the hiss. Whatever he said brings Dieter wobbling to his feet. His eyes are blinded with tears of choking or fear. He's gone completely white. Kamal opens the door, Dieter staggers out still doubled over. He starts down the stairs and nearly topples. Then he stops, steadying himself with a hand on the wall and twists his head up to say something. But he can't get it out. He gags on it, his eyes flood and he half falls down the rest of the flight. Kamal closes our door on the nasty scene. He looks very relaxed. His chest is smooth again.

"He's either an agent or an idiot, and we don't need either one. Is there any more coffee?"

I'm as gagged up as Dieter. And my eyes feel equally bugged out. I pour the coffee and marvel at Kamal's calm. I have an urge to run and lock the door. I'm terrified we haven't heard the last of Dieter.

I am awakened in the middle of the night, no it is early, early morning, by a shuffling. Kamal is not in bed next to me. He is dressed. He is pushing things into his Adidas bag which sits on the table.

"Now?"

"I told you, soon. Isn't this soon?"

"Too soon." But actually it isn't. I'm glad he's going. So I can recover from the Dieter episode. Whenever I look at him I see his hand whipping Dieter backwards across the room. Nobody should be able to do that with one hand. Not to a heavy man like Dieter. Not to anybody.

"I'll be back soon, too. Don't worry about me."

"I don't. I worry for the people who may cross your path."

"Don't waste your worry on these people, Justina."

"You are going to Israel!" The obvious dawns so slowly.

He clamps his jaw and keeps his back to me as he finishes packing. Why couldn't I keep my mouth shut?

No more sleep this morning. I lie awake after he

leaves trying to decide if I am hoping he makes it back. My guts are roiling and bubbling. Even a liter of milk barely quiets them. I have to call Raymond first thing. That will calm me down.

Raymond is in a bad mood. I am only supposed to contact him in the most serious emergencies.

"Well, Justina, I hope whatever you have dragged me out of bed to tell me is worth the taxi fare."

"Oh, I'm sorry. I thought you'd come by Métro. It isn't worth more than two francs."

"Don't waste my time with weak humor, please."

"All right, Raymond. I just thought you'd like to know that Kamal has left Paris."

"When?"

"This morning. Very early."

"Permanently?"

"No. He said he'd be back, but I don't know . . . given the place he's going."

"Where?"

"Israel."

"By your mother's balls, Justina, don't joke. He told you he was going to Israel?"

"I guess. He didn't deny it."

"How long ago did he leave?"

"I told you, just a few hours."

"Did he say anything more?"

"He said he'd be back soon. A few days or a week."

"How long have you known this, Justina?"

"Just a few days. They've been crazy days. I couldn't get away before. I couldn't take the chance. You see, he said he'd just made contact with the Palestinian underground. I didn't believe him. I thought he was making it up to cover the fact that he was seeing another woman. You didn't send him another woman as that genie to conduct him to the—"

"Another woman?"

"A blonde. I found a hair under his jacket lapel.

You once threatened to find him another 'companion.' Don't you remember?"

"Poor Justina. Don't take everything I say so seriously. Do you imagine I would jeopardize the relationship after all the effort we've put into establishing it? That would be rather self-defeating."

"I haven't produced much information."

"What? Were you expecting to stumble on an unpublished Magna Carta? Intelligence is collated gossip. . . . But you know that."

"One can know something and not believe it."

"Do you think this blonde is threatening the relationship?"

"I did. That was why I didn't call. But now that he's gone off on this . . . I don't know anything anymore. I'll just have to wait and see."

I should tell him about Dieter. But suddenly it seems too complicated to even narrate episode by episode. Certainly too complicated to explain. Or maybe I'm just too tired to think. Or too dispirited.

Raymond senses the withholding, as he always does. "Anything else, Justina?"

"No, Raymond. That's all. I should think it was plenty, but you're so damn greedy."

"I do appreciate it, Justina. I really do. And I imagine it will be appreciated by those who are handling your papers."

"Don't start that, Raymond."

part two

Kamal

THE WINDING EASTWARD DESCENT from the verdant
crest of the Jura suddenly brings into view the cod-
dled plain of Switzerland. Months ago, when I
landed down there coming from India, it was full
winter: gray, misted and snowing. A dour land, I
thought. Now, just into April, it is transformed.
Through several leagues of the purest air I have
tasted for months the Alps glisten, too crystalline to
be mistaken for cloud. Geneva and its lake lie
painted on the plain below. Cruel vicissitudes of history, that one child's ancestors should have planted
themselves here on this most favored patch of terrain with the prospect of twenty thousand years of
peace and plenty, while another child's ancestors
clung to a desert offering no more than shrubs and
boulders and dust storms.

The key to it, of course, is water; there is more
water before my eyes at this very moment than has
fallen on my desperate land in those twenty thousand years. Geology dealt to us off the bottom of the
deck. And the irony is that here I am on my way back
to fight for that crookedly dealt card. Don't ask too
many questions, Kamal.

"Schön," comments the driver as he wheels his
BMW down the switchbacks. He has hardly said

much more than this the entire trip from Macon, where he picked me up. He was a lucky choice. I haven't had to pay for my ride by entertaining him with conversation. He prefers to concentrate on his driving technique, he says. That is why he drives this road instead of flying to Lyons and back.

At the boundary of Geneva he slows for the first time since the border. "Look." He is pointing to a sign by the road and reads PRUDENCE. He shakes his head. He has the kind of straight blond hair that always falls back into place exactly. "That is Geneva. You are not staying here?" he asks with quiet disgust.

"No."

"You may continue with me, if you wish."

"Thanks, but I'm heading south."

"To Chamonix?" There is a glimmer of excitement.

"To the tunnel, and then south into Italy."

"Ah well. If you come back to Switzerland and need a place to stay, here's my card. We can go mountain climbing. You look fit enough."

"It's good to know there are people whose doors are open."

"You won't find many in Switzerland. Too many of us take that sign seriously: PRUDENCE. What is your name, by the way?"

"Kamal."

Not even a blink of surprise.

"Well, good luck, eh? On whatever your journey takes you to." Almost as if he guesses.

But when the scarlet BMW hums out of sight I slip his card into the nearest trash basket. He meant well, but he has no idea what kind of trouble that little card could drag him into if discovered on my person during the next few weeks. It must be wonderfully relaxing to be so innocent. I, in contrast, cannot afford to stop calculating for a minute. Now I

114

must hitch back out the last few miles of the way we came to get to the airport. No, I am not going on to Milan, as Boudia recommended. There is no reason he should be able to anticipate any more of my movements than necessary. Just in case. This is also why I jumped train at Macon instead of continuing as my ticket was written. By this shortcut I will be landing in Israel about the time I should have been pulling into Milan. Now remains one last question: whether to fly El Al as Boudia more or less ordered.

At the airport concourse the El Al personnel wait with the air of gunfighters: chins up and feet spread. Even the short-legged dump who checks the bags. She must think her bulgy belly deserves the attention of every passer-by. They can certainly afford to put her in a uniform that fits less critically. You could excuse that kind of thing in South America. The airlines had bigger troubles to occupy their minds. But in Monte we all considered hijacking a coward's game. There was nothing much to gain from it, unless you were escaping to Cuba. It was not felt as an act against a system so much as an act against God, whose substantial grace was manifest in the fact that the metal machines stayed in the air at all.

But here it is a different matter. There is no God in Switzerland. There is only System. And its strutting pilots eyeing the queues, its agents herding stray passengers like maverick cows, its clerks poking away at their computer terminals and occasionally raising their eyes with disgust to be certain that there is a lump of flesh to go with the name on the screen. But even this doesn't make me want to hijack so much as to wait at the end of the runway with a cage full of starlings. Still, there is no harm in seeing what this famous El Al security is all about.

"Passport," demands the potbellied clerk when my turn comes to ask for a one-way to Tel Aviv.

115

There is no visible reaction when she sees the name. "One-way Geneva-Lod, tourist or first, please?"

"Tourist."

"Smoking or non-smoking, please?"

"Window in either one."

"No windows left on this flight." She is a machine with a potbelly as a disguise. Who would give a robot a potbelly?

"Ma'am, are you Israeli?"

"No. I am Swiss, of course."

"Of course."

A special check-in area has been constructed for the flights to Lod. Men and women are separated into two queues outside two temporary plywood cubicles. JRA boxes, I have heard them called. Our luggage has been tagged but not checked in. We push it ahead of us in the queues. Passengers on other lines pass by staring. We must look like refugees, burdened and frightened, guarded on both sides by Swiss police with submachine guns. The flight is scheduled to leave in less than an hour. Yet the lines advance less than one person a minute. They will have to delay take-off. Amazing that three Japanese crazies could inject so much fear even a year after the fact.

Passengers in both lines keep glancing at my Adidas duffel. Odd baggage for a traveler, they are thinking. Maybe he's an athlete. Or . . . Munich made the sports duffel a trademark of the terrorist; but this is pure coincidence, since I have had this bag for over two years; the legacy of a minor-league soccer player in Buenos Aires. This bag once carried the equivalent of forty thousand dollars out of a poorly protected bank. It has nostalgic value to me, like a great racehorse put out to pasture. But this one may yet see adventure to remind it of the old days, even if it can't tell from the collection of innocuous junk it's carrying now. Innocuous, but too new. That's my

116

only worry. I'd have liked to have a little more time to knock the boots around and scuff up the camera. Boudia might have told me in advance, knowing that Tony would have a difficult time communicating alone. Elaine would have been worth her weight for once, but security demanded we do without her linguistic talents; she was asked to take a walk, poor kid, while Tony unfolded the details of my mission on her kitchen table. Even unfolded they remained nearly indecipherable.

"You must to maintain the apparel equilibrate."

"What?"

"Equilibrate!" Tony must have thought louder meant truer. Fortunately I began to recognize the linguistic short circuits. He was translating through French from the Arabic. But he refused to speak in French, insisting his English was better.

"You mean I must keep the camera level."

"Yes. Perfectment equilibrate. Then to put in the middle horizontalment before prizing. Then you must to escribe his pointing. From the com-pah, yes?"

After some work we decided he meant that in each picture a key feature was to be centered in the field of view and the compass bearing of the feature was to be written down with the number of the frame.

"Yes, yes. But still to equilibrate. Nivel the camera."

"Keep the camera level regardless of the elevation to the key feature. I get it, Tony."

"Yes. We from this make the calculus of angels."

"You and Saint Thomas, Tony."

"Saint Thomas? No, other one. You no know him."

The procedure was pretty obvious. I don't know how Boudia expected me to commit the map to memory. It was drawn on a scale of five hundred meters per centimeter: every ripple of terrain showed up. And all the features, except elevations, were in Arabic script. The key points had been circled in red ink and lay along the southeast slope of the mountain ridge which defined the border with Lebanon. The demilitarized zone separating the Syrians and the occupation forces appeared to run down a buttress perpendicular to this ridge. Somewhere, not marked, and Tony wasn't sure where, was an Israeli fortified observation post. That was something I had to record, and if possible discover depressions in the terrain which were out of its line of sight. This was the most dangerous part of the assignment. If the Israelis caught me with a notebook full of bearings and a couple of rolls of pictures of their fortification my troubles would be over. I would be guaranteed to spend the rest of my life in my homeland.

Tony reassured me before our briefing was over, "Israelien not shoot spions. Only enprisonate them for the during of life."

The whole operation was a big joke to him. Safely back in Paris screwing Elaine. While I am being subject to a search unlike anything I've been through before in an airport. My bag is spread open on the rough plywood counter by a grim middle-aged woman. This one is Israeli. They trust only their own when it comes to security. Behind her a compact but very fit-looking man is watching the proceedings. I have no doubt he is armed. He scrutinizes the passengers while the woman rips apart our luggage. The compass, a cheap camper's model, oddly does not interest her. The camera she treats methodically, removing the lens, peering inside, replacing it, until she notices the bubble level clipped into the accessory shoe. She points it out to the compact man. He mutters something in Hebrew. She turns back to me.

"What is this?"

"A level."

"For what is it?"

"For keeping the camera level when I'm taking pictures of buildings. So the sides don't converge." I indicate the perspective with my hands.

"I see." She pushes the camera back into my bag and zips it closed.

As I reach to reclaim it the man behind her steps forward. "Je voudrais voir votre passeport, monsieur, s'il vous plaît." His accent is very heavy. I can't help but smile in appreciation of the richness of his little gambit. In one moment he is able to observe half a dozen factors: how anxious I am to have my luggage back, how I react to an unexpected challenge, how reluctant I am to have my passport examined a second time, how firm is my command of French—which would help distinguish a North African from a Palestinian—and whether or not I am used to going armed. An armed man reaches into his jacket without letting it swing open.

Reading his intention, I have to suppress a whimsical urge to set off every one of his alarms. I recall Orly. I can't afford the luxury now. Instead I respond with my best tourist bumbles.

He flips through the passport quickly, then asks, "You are an American citizen by birth?" The inevitable question.

"Yup." Not strictly true, but close enough. My parents had the foresight to claim New York as my birthplace on all my records. So it is right there on my passport.

"Please come with me. Take your bag."

He guides me to a small office down a hall from the concourse, where he hands the man behind the desk my passport. This one has a tanned shaved skull and enormous hands. He, too, flips through the passport, more casually than the first. Then he picks up his phone, dials, waits, then rattles off something in Hebrew, followed by my name. Now he has to wait. We try to outstare each other. He has very cold blue eyes

119

and flared, cavernous nostrils. Finally he thanks whoever is on the other end of the phone and hangs up.

"I am sorry for this inconvenience. You understand . . ." He flicks the passport to the edge of his desk. There is a little smile on the bottom half of his face. You understand.

"I understand. If my name were Cameron Gabriel it wouldn't be necessary."

He shrugs. I was almost expecting a retort. It is an odd sensation to be confronting a Jew who is this hard.

"How long do you expect to be in Israel, Mr. Jibral?"

"A few weeks."

"Where will you be staying? Relatives?"

"I have no relatives there. Hotels, I expect."

"Which cities?"

"Jerusalem. That's all I know, so far."

"Enjoy your visit. I have to ask you to submit to a body search before you board. It is required of all passengers."

I raise my hands.

"You are not being arrested." He waves my hands down and gestures for the man who escorted me here to make the search. He is fast and thorough, and does not miss the small of my back. While he is doing this, the phone rings. The call is very brief.

"Mr. Jibral, we mustn't keep you any longer. Your plane is boarding. They have called to say there has been a problem of overbooking. You would not object to traveling first class as a compensation for the trouble we have put you to? At no additional charge, of course."

"Who would object to that?" Only a terrorist who had a logistical reason for being in tourist class.

"Good. Have a pleasant vacation." He nods to the man who brought me in. I am led out to the boarding gate. Here too there are armed Swiss police. The passengers are placing their baggage on the platform of a loader just at the foot of the boarding ladder. This precludes anyone putting luggage into the hold without himself boarding the plane: at least partial insurance against bombs which might have escaped the baggage inspection.

There are four other passengers in first class. The stewardess directs me to the front row of seats: three free and a man in the window seat on the left. She lets me choose, so I slide to the window seat on the right. No one else comes into first class. When the engines start and the blast of cold air from the ventilation nozzle over my seat hits me, I feel a chill. I've been sweating profusely without realizing it. Immediately the fear goes to my gut and limbs.

As we taxi out under the Jura from which I've descended just a few hours ago I am rooting around for any one of the heroic fantasies I keep tricking myself with. The face of that man in the office frightened them all away. Suddenly there is no fervor, no cause. Just a blank in my imagination, and fear in my veins. Like some burnt-out grunt on one more useless patrol. And nothing's happened yet. It's a bad start, Kamal.

Twenty minutes into the flight the stewardess comes forward with the drink cart.

"Are you not feeling well?" Not much feminine sympathy in the question.

"I'm just hot."

"It is not hot in here."

"That so? Why don't you just pour me a straight scotch on ice."

She complies in the manner of a nurse loading a hypodermic syringe.

When she has wheeled out of the compartment the man sitting by the opposite window slides to the aisle seat, leans toward me and confides, "I used to be terrified of flying here, too." He is chubby and jolly; his florid face looks incongruous lapping over his natty business grays. "All this terrorism, aie! It's enough to make anybody sweat. I assure you, don't worry about it. Not in the air, anyway. Once you are in Tel Aviv, that is another matter."

He picks himself up and slides, uninvited, into the seat beside me. "You are an American. I was too. You get used to anything. I will tell you what I saw flying back to Lod one time. I was up in first class as usual. We were about halfway home, when suddenly a commotion motion breaks out in the main cabin. Oh no, I thought, this is the end. It's that Khaled girl or one of her friends. Then suddenly again, after some talk, there are thuds and cries of pain, cursing, screaming. And one instant later they come crashing in here. Into first class, I mean. Four Arabs, young men, with their hands behind their backs, pushed ahead by the crew and other security men. Perhaps just passengers. Some of them had guns though. Small guns, I suppose so that there is no danger of puncturing the plane. I hope so, anyway.

"They tied the four Arabs right into these front four seats, right across here. I saw one of them spit teeth out. And blood. Some of the crew went back to calm down the passengers. Even one of the security men went back with them, but he returned a minute later with a stack of towels over his arm. What are they going to do, I wondered, give the Arabs a bath? But no, they began gagging them, one towel around the mouth, one around the neck. Very strange, I thought. But what do I know about tying people up? Not much. Certainly not what I saw next. The biggest security man, a regular ape of a commando, took out a long knife and slowly moved the blade right in front of the noses of the Arabs, one by one. Nodding at each one and saying something in Arabic. Somebody later said he had lived in Iraq as a child, so you can hardly blame him.

"Where was I? Oh yes. Then he went back to the first, over where I was just sitting, and slipped the knife in under the towel around the kid's neck. And then drew it straight across. The other three watched it all. His hand came out covered with blood. Then he took the knife to the next one. And then to the one where I am sitting now. I saw this one the most clearly. The knife went in the whole way and then he made a sawing motion. He held the Arab by the hair as he did it. Like something out of the Old Testament. And then he went on to the one in the seat you are now sitting in. Can you imagine? He had seen all three of his companions die like that. He struggled a little, but there wasn't much hope. When we landed at Lod, even before the plane stopped rolling, they opened the door up here and threw the bodies out onto the runway."

"How come they let you sit and watch the entire spectacle?"

"Perhaps they didn't notice me. Or perhaps tourist class was filled up. Like today."

Or perhaps you are a security man with a prepared tale.

"I never heard about the incident."

"Perhaps it was not material for the newspapers. One can understand why. As it is, they don't have many people traveling first class."

He nods solemnly and returns to his seat. A word to the wise, he is thinking.

Landing at Lod only continues the threats made by my loquacious seatmate. The airport is armed for battle. Three tanks squat by the side of the taxiway, hatches open. Our plane halts a quarter mile from the terminal and does not open its doors until two jeeploads of soldiers have deployed from the ladder

123

to the terminal. Finally we are allowed to deplane in a nervous, sober procession past the muzzles of their Uzis. The inside of the arrival room is also cleared for a field of fire. Every passenger is searching the walls and floor for stains of the carnage of eleven months ago. We do not step clear of an Uzi muzzle until customs has cleared our bags.

But the firing range atmosphere abruptly ends at the doors to the main airport concourse. Suddenly we burst back into a civilian world reverberating with emotion and exaggerated gestures of greeting and parting, frustration and joy. It's a little like home, like New York . . . A little like home. Great line, Kamal.

I hurry out of the terminal to feel the sun of home pouring out of the blue talcum sky, to feel its grass struggling underfoot, to smell its yellow dust blown from just beyond the airport fence. But this isn't quite home. This is still something transposed, makeshift: heavy construction equipment parked next to cars, a dusty half-track parked just outside the chainlink fence with its pintle-mounted machine gun pointing casually at the sky. Like a fist in the face.

No. This isn't my Middle East yet. There is one more step to take. A short step, but first I must go back inside to the car rental desk and weather one more inspection of my passport. Home is always a little further away than one thinks.

Katamon! Repetition planted that story in so many private corners it used to ambush me, like the worm of an unwanted song in my ear. Once again my father's words are spilling from the overfilled bucket as the rented VW rattles over the rough road climbing toward Jerusalem.

"They attacked us, Katamon in particular, because they could not bear the thought of barbarian

Arabs living more graciously than civilized Jews. What was their excuse this time? Defense of a Jewish neighborhood? We were all Arabs—Christian, Moslem or neither—but all Arabs, living in peace. There was no possible excuse. So they said it was 'strategic.' Hah! I'll tell you the 'strategy.' They looked. They saw we were wealthy. They asked themselves, Is it worth the effort to drive poor Arabs from their hovels when with the same bullets we can expropriate solid homes filled with food, clothing and furniture?

"We had been hearing rumors for months. Since the vicious bombing of the Semiramis Hotel in January. You go to sleep when you hear rumors too many times. But even when the attack did begin, that was the last week in April, we were not totally unprepared. The Mufti sent men in to defend us, commanded by a young man named Abu Dayieh. They were reinforced by Iraqi volunteers soon afterward. The Jews, of course, chose to attack the very symbol of our area: the Saint Simeon monastery, which stood on the highest ground. As if the invasion of a Greek Orthodox monastery were not itself sufficient sacrilege, the Jews then completed the desecration by the most brutal kind of attack. Some of the wounded defenders were brought down to our house. What horror you were spared, inside your mother's womb. The Jews had advanced from room to room behind hand grenades. Kamal, hope you never have to witness the effect of a hand grenade on a human body."

I must have been eight or nine when I first heard this account. It left me with a permanent curiosity about grenades.

"So the Jews captured the monastery. But only briefly, before our men counterattacked with mortar and sniper fire. The Jews were soon trying to escape from the stronghold, which was becoming an inferno. They did not succeed. I saw with my own eyes a group of twenty or thirty try to run from the rear of the building. Our Iraqi volunteers cut them down like grass. I saw but one or two reach cover out of the range of our rifles. We were on the verge of a decisive victory.

"But then suddenly our men stopped firing. For no apparent reason. Through binoculars I saw a detachment of Jews approach the monastery by the same grove of trees in which their compatriots had been mowed down just a few hours before. Now they simply ran up to the monastery without a single casualty. That was the end of the fighting. And there was only one explanation. Betrayal. It wasn't the first time, and it wouldn't be the last that we had victory snatched away from us by treachery. They never uncovered the traitor. Our men just slipped away in the night, leaving Katamon undefended.

"Of course, we couldn't see them leave. But we felt it. Despair descended like a gas upon us. Our neighbors were talking of waking in a Jewish Katamon. I tried to silence the defeatist talk. Who rightfully could be asked to risk his life to defend homes abandoned by their own inhabitants? A few fled right away, in the dark, to more securely held districts in the eastern part of the city. Through the night, more people quietly disappeared. We and a few others stayed through the night. But by the first light we could see that the pessimists had been proved right. From our windows we could see the Haganah advancing up the street. And before their advance, Arab families, our friends, were pouring from their houses carrying their children and little else.

"It was a terrible, tragic morning. I don't know if you will ever be able to appreciate the horror, Kamal. It was beyond imagining. We had fifteen minutes, fifteen minutes to decide between the humiliation of a lifetime, of generations, or death. But

126

if you yourself have children, Kamal, you will understand that you cannot sacrifice them to concepts of honor they are too young to comprehend. And so we, Kamal, with you already in your mother's womb, accepted the humiliation with the rest of Katamon. And, although we did not fully realize it at that time, with the rest of Palestine."

Now, twenty-five years later, only one month short, I am about to re-enter this very Katamon which remained the barb in my father's heart until that heart finally failed him. My own veins are pounding. Just ahead, a bus from the airport jammed with sweating tourists lumbers up the long rise, belching black diesel fumes onto my windshield. You'd think they'd put in a four-lane road to connect their two main cities. But no. I have to risk my life overtaking the bus while the oncoming traffic swerves to a stop, seeing that I'm not going to retreat. Honk up your own asses, motherfucks. These Israelis are not invincible, after all.

A few minutes later I whisk past the crenellated wall that must contain the Old City. At the far end there are a dozen more buses idling their black fumes into the air. And checkered tourists gaping like idiots at yellow stones. The map is clear in my mind. It is here I turn right and speed south, not far, a dozen blocks perhaps, then to the top of the hill. . . . Suddenly I realize the real risk of this. What if the place cannot explain the persistence of my father's agony?

Even through tears I can see it is not the place my father described. A sour odor of poverty and conflict hangs over the streets, stirred by restless dark teenagers who coagulate wherever there is place. These kids could be my cousins, by manner, by mood, even by appearance—except for ubiquitous six-pointed stars which flash from unbuttoned chests, emblazon berets and sleeves. Instead they are my enemies.

And though the monastery still caps the hill, this is not my Katamon. Where are the low villas of Jerusalem lime set back behind stone fences and rows of cedars? Somewhere jammed between cubes of concrete apartments with wrinkled laundry hanging from every balcony like limp banners of contempt: Hey you, eat my fucking underwear!

Still, I can't tear myself away. I prowl the district, methodically crisscrossing, all the time carrying in my mind's eye an image like an antique hand-tinted photograph of a particular stone house set back behind five cedars, two to the right and three to the left of a flagstone path leading to a heavy door under an arch of bright tangle-patterned tiles. But either the image is faulty or the original has been erased, for I notice that I am doubling back on my earlier path.

So now, Kamal, you must accept that this Katamon holds nothing for you. As you knew from the first. Why else did you so avoid coming here? History has erased your father from these streets with the same obliviousness it erased his life in America. The only traces of him survive in the minds of the few of his family who care to keep his troubled presence alive. Is there any agony worse than this? Than these sobs which you can barely keep caged within your ribs. How many other sobs has this terrible city finally ripped from supposedly impregnable vaults of toughness or stolidity? Know that at least you are not alone.

Somehow I have wandered down near the Old City. Escaped from Katamon. Below are excavations, miles of them. They say this is the national sport, this disinterment. What are they turning the buried past inside out for? Do they expect to find some key dropped by an antique ancestor which will finally prove their right to tenancy? If this heap of 200-generation-old relics leaves you Israelis still hungry, imagine the hollow in my gut. I can find no mark of my own father from less than twenty-five years ago. In this city of inheritances, whether of walls or ideas, too solid to be erased by millennia, why is there none for me? Would it have cost my father that much more effort or courage to have left a little proof of his existence? So that it would not now be left on my shoulders to prove it.

A deep depression overwhelms me on the long walk back to where I parked the VW in Katamon. The evening has finally fallen. How is it possible that I saw the sun rise in France this morning, somewhere between Paris and Macon? A time warp. It took the Crusaders over a year to make the same journey.

"Are you an Arab?" The voice comes from about waist level, a careful mixture of British and Hebrew accents. An incongruous little girl, dark and tousled in a faded dress, stares daringly into my eyes. An even littler boy—her brother?—circles behind her. "Are you an Arab?" she repeats.

I am at a loss to reply: too guilty to lie, too embarrassed to answer the truth: "I don't know." Instead I challenge her rather dryly: "How did you know to speak to me in English?"

She points at my running shoes. "Only Americans wear those. But you're not Jewish."

"How do you know that, little sister?"

"The way you look." She has already trapped me in her precocious interview.

"How do I look?"

"Like a skinny bird with a straw nest on its head." She breaks into laughter, and translates her cleverness for her little brother, who also breaks into laughter and begins stamping in circles around both of us.

"In that case I'm going to fly away."

But before I manage to escape into the car she is

grabbing the tail of my jacket. "We will show you the city for two dollars."

"Your parents wouldn't like that, would they?"

"Why not?" She is truly perplexed.

"It's late. Aren't you afraid strangers might hurt you?"

"Only Arabs."

"I might be an Arab."

"You said you were American."

"I might have lied."

"You speak English too well."

"You speak English well, too. Are you an American?"

"Of course not."

"Then maybe I'm not either."

She points to my shoes again.

"You're too smart for your own good, little sister." I tug her fine dark hand from my jacket and escape into the VW.

"You're too dumb for your own good" are her parting words, followed by more laughter and another translation. The boy throws a stone at the car as I pull away. Katamon . . .

The weight of the dark hauls down this curtain of fatigue I've been barely holding back for the last hour. I manage to follow some tourists to their hotel and check in for the night. But sleep will not come, kept at bay by too foreign cadences of the sounds slipping through windows which must be kept open because the room is so small. From below, hollow steel clangs which defy identification, rasping coughs of an old diesel going nowhere, gutturals of insistent Hebraic argument echoing off the opposing apartments, and warbling sirens from the distance heralding over the roofs a message of violence—man's or God's, it doesn't matter. They reach the fear just the same.

I have made a profound mistake in coming here. Suddenly I have nothing to fight for. Except the past. Katamon? They can keep it. Shall I now wander about this little country looking for something pretty enough that it will boil my blood thinking about how they've taken it away? Absurd. I am an American. I have Yosemite, the Grand Canyon and the Chesapeake Bay without a fight. These Jews have taken nothing from me. What they took they took from my father and the other Palestinian fathers, leaving most of them soft and bent and sorrowful like my uncles. But the sap survives. We have sap, my brothers and I. We've got the only inheritance which counts in America: quickness of mind or hands or tongue or legs. I inherited all four. I am damned well equipped to make it in America. So was my father. So what's all this fuss about a grubby little slum? Fuck it. If my father wants it back, let him come down and fight for it. I'm going home.

Machine-gun fire through the door, Kamal rolls for cover behind this white soft barrier, behind his brother's massive corpse, which is making a line of small red blooms amidst the white where the bullets hit pft, pft, pft, wait, your brother isn't that big, it's your father, my father?, yes your father, you'd better crawl to him and save him, I will, but Kamal's legs have been paralyzed, have I been hit, oh no!, and drag useless as he pulls himself forward on his arms toward your father, but that can't be my father he isn't big either, Kamal, answer the door will you please. I thought you were dead, dad. Stop daydreaming and answer the door.

Oh, knocks, not shots. And what am I doing on the floor all tangled up in my sheets and pouring sweat? The room is as hot as a steam bath. I must have gotten up in my sleep and closed the window. And it's bright daylight. Nobody's at the door either. Only an old man with arthritic knees sticking out of his checkered shorts.

"Did you knock?"

He turns with a sneer. "And why should I knock at *your* door?"

"And why shouldn't I knock your false teeth down your throat?" Maybe nobody knocked. He gives me the finger as I slam the door. Why am I always—not always, but usually—a kid in my dreams? Anyway when my brothers or father are in the dream too.

Now I catch sight of the Nikon sitting on the dresser, a little black demon demanding homage. Did I dream Boudia, too? To trick myself into coming here? There's no Boudia, just like there's no Katamon. Inventions to suit an obsession. But he said the photos are important. Your brothers are getting mowed down crossing into the Golan for lack of those photographs. That is no invention. Revolutionisme oblige, Kamal. So pull yourself together, take the damn pictures, and fly out of this godforsaken hole. You can worry about your existential dilemma back in Paris, where that is the specialité du maison anyway.

"You are lucky," says the man at the desk. "Two minutes later we would have had to charge you for another day."

"So what?"

"So what?"

"That's right. So what? Look, I'll pay you for two days if it will make you happy. Or three or four or a week. Whatever you want."

He glowers. He thinks I'm playing some kind of trick on him.

"Well?"

"Well nothing. You pay me for one day and never come back here again and that will make me happy."

"Mazel tov."

Outside the sun is blinding, falling straight from overhead and bouncing off the bright yellow stone on all sides. The door handle of the VW is painful to the touch. A blast of overheated stale air escapes into my face as I swing open the door. At the same moment I am clamped around both arms just above the elbow, my bag is yanked from my right hand and I am slammed against the edge of the roof. I have a move for this. But the response is viscous, it lags far behind the intent. I am supposed to shove right off my left foot and clear a space between me and the attacker to my left so I can twist and bring my knee into play against his balls. But I find that both my feet are kicked out from under me and that I am hanging with my chin on the scalding metal and the rain gutter digging into my Adam's apple. They are running hands over me. I am being robbed. My papers first. Now in my crotch and down my legs. I should have stayed in bed and paid the extra day. I am not being robbed. I am being arrested.

When they let me regain my feet again my hands are already cuffed behind my back. The whole operation has taken the time of one breath. They've got me turned around before my shins start to give and push me stumbling across the street toward a Land Rover next to the entrance of the hotel. I didn't even notice walking right by it. I have to jump up into the rear door to keep them from smashing my kneecaps into the bumper. Two men in uniform climb in after me. A third is already at the wheel. The goon nearest the door, facing me, is bull-shouldered and coarse-featured. He is spitting at me in Arabic. I feel a laugh coming on. I've been arrested before. In '68, like everyone else. Arrest is no big deal in a democracy. And this is a democracy, isn't it fellas?

The big one backhands his knuckles into my cheek and across my mouth. He mocks me with a heavy laugh, "Hu, hu, hu," to show me what I've gotten hit for. I yuck back at him, bow my head, and lunging forward drive my forehead into his nose. He responds with his fists into my undefended ribs, but I manage to twist to the floor of the Land Rover coiling up my legs, ready to kick him through the roof. But the smaller cop is now restraining him. He spits on me instead.

I wriggle back up to my seat and stay there the rest of the ride. The goon perches with his fists clenched, mopping a trickle of bloody snot off his mustache with his khaki cuff. The smaller one looks exasperated. They avoid each other's eyes. I don't feel too bad. I got in a good shot, considering the handicap.

We pass by the wall of the Old City heading north, then turn left. In Paris I heard that all of the really hard prisons are out in the desert or on the West Bank. We don't seem to be leaving the city. That is when I'd start worrying. But the Rover abruptly lurches from the street into what appears to be a compound of temporary barracks erected within a courtyard formed by a square of aging institutional buildings three and four stories high. The effect is of a spy movie stage set: somewhere in Eastern Europe, 1946. But for all the barbed wire, this isn't very menacing. The gate stands open and unguarded. There are people coming and going from the street. Our driver is snaking us through a jam of parked police vehicles toward the rear of the compound. He halts in front of the furthest barrack. Here they push me out of the Rover and march me up an alley between two of the barracks. I am in good company. There are dozens of Arabs around, many in kaffiyeh. They watch silently but closely as I am pushed by them. This reminds me a little of the Harlem precinct stations, except no one is laughing.

As we enter through a side door into the barrack it is a relief to be out of the sun. I still can't muster any anxiety over this little adventure. My father would have said that I have been brainwashed by propaganda to believe the Israeli democracy is just an extension of the U.S. democracy. Well, I've gotten rapped across the face by an American cop too, but for turning over his car in Morningside Heights. Perhaps this is pre-emptive arrest in anticipation of my turning over their Land Rover.

They push me, quite gently now, through the fourth door off the corridor into a tight room with steel mesh over the door and a dozen folding chairs lined up along the walls. A waiting lounge: there are four teenagers inside already. They have been talking, but cut their conversation off cold as I stumble in. Now they look me up and down, nod cautiously, but do not resume their talking. I can't tell if they are Jews or Arabs. Whoever they are, they must think I am a spy thrown in to overhear their conversation, because they don't say another word. I don't mind. I have finally identified the lightly hovering ghost of déjà vu that has been accompanying me since I first felt the grip on my arms and has kept me from taking the arrest seriously. I used to daydream a very similar episode long, long ago, an adventure I made up from overheard conversations which echoed up the parquet hallway to our bedroom along with the clinking of glasses and ice. My father had been keeping count of the arrests in Gaza. Every time there was a new wave of them he announced this to the guests, who muttered their reverence and commiseration for the heroic victims. Yes, they were heroes. While we—ignored, dismissed and forgotten in our beds—didn't count for anything. Just frivolous, useless American kids.

But I knew how to make myself count. I had myself arrested too. Almost every night, by Israeli troopers who looked like Irish cops in dark blue uniforms and carried nightsticks and Smith and Wesson

.38s. They would frog-march me down to the precinct station and chuck me into the cooler, where I sneered at them and dared them to do their worst while I plotted escapes with smuggled explosives to blow out the back wall. Then I would lead my schoolmates to freedom in the forests of New Hampshire. And far away, back at home, my father would recount my exploits to his awed and adulating guests. . . .

Heavy metalic scrapes of a bolt being drawn interrupt this nostalgic musing. A spidery silver-haired gentleman slips in through the partially opened door, surveys us a moment, then cocks his head back toward the corridor as if listening to instructions from off stage. He has the sharply cut features and erect posture of an Austrian count. A definite step up from the two chimps who grabbed me. He gestures to me to stand up and turn so he can remove the handcuffs. He could do that in the hall, but the fact that he chooses to do it here suggests a show of benignity for the four teenagers. Whatever the motive, I am glad to have my hands back.

He conducts me down the length of the building.

"Please." Crooning like some high-class jeweler inviting a customer to inspect his best diamonds, he opens the door to a little office. But all the cubicle contains is a black metal table and three armless metal chairs. There is a smell of chlorine, and no window to let it escape. The room is lit by three photographer's lamps on long stalks. On the table there is a single manila folder and a hairbrush. The two chimps have followed us down the hallway and now join the Count and me inside the cubicle.

"First, if you please, a photograph." He holds out the hairbrush.

"Not without a contract. My agent says never without a contract."

The Count waves the manila envelope threateningly. "This is your contract."

The smaller chimp is already adjusting the lights. He has brought in a camera on a tripod. I hold out my hand for the manila folder.

"Please do not underestimate, Mr. Jibral, how serious is your position."

"Isn't that pretty relative?"

"Relative?"

"Relative to the possibilities. Is my position more or less serious than rounding Cape Horn in a canoe, for example?"

He spins a heavy gold ring on his left forefinger. "It could easily become more serious, Mr. Jibral."

"Heavy."

"You have assaulted an officer. And that is only the beginning. Before we go any further, comb your hair and let us have our photograph." He signals the big chimp to rise in a threatening manner. He is armed with a cosh. They are going to get their photo one way or another, so I might as well give it to them gracefully. I accept the plastic brush, smooth out my hair and assume as innocent a smirk as I can staring into three spotlights. If this photo is going to be circulated it should look as benign as possible. Unfortunately, my features never look benign.

"Thank you for cooperating, Mr. Jibral. Please have a seat."

The metal chair in front of the table is bolted to the floor. The Count takes up an interrogating stance behind the table. "Mr. Jibral. Who did you contact in Katamon yesterday?"

They had me followed!

"What's Katamon?"

"It is where you spent the late afternoon yesterday."

"Ah ha. I was looking up Yehudi Menuhin."

"Mr. Jibral, enough jokes."

"I was just wandering around. Sight-seeing."

"There are no sights in Katamon, Mr. Jibral. We

are not fools. You land at Lod. One hour later you are in Katamon. If you had gone directly to the Wailing Wall, or in your case, to the Dome of the Rock, this I would find quite normal. But Katamon, no. You parked your car. You began to walk. Where did you walk to?"

"If you know so much, how come you don't know where I walked to?"

"Mr. Jibral, I am the one paid to ask the questions."

"Aren't you also paid to listen to the answers? I told you I was walking around sight-seeing. If you have other information please tell me. I'm really curious to know what I was doing in this Katamon. You see, I was under the impression I was wandering around."

"You went deliberately there."

"That's right."

"Why?"

"My parents used to live there."

"And why did you not tell me this when I first asked?"

"You didn't ask what I was doing. You asked who did I contact. I contacted nobody. Except a smart-ass little girl who wanted to sell me the city for two dollars."

"A good bargain."

"I was thinking of going back and asking her for a date."

"Where are your parents now, Mr. Jibral?"

"My mother is in New York."

"And your father?"

"You'll have to ask him. He crossed the great river five years ago."

"So why have you come back?"

"To see what they left behind."

"Why have you come back, Mr. Jibral?"

"To see what they left behind."

"Why have you come back, Mr. Jibral?"

"Your needle's stuck."

"Are you aware that it is illegal here to be a member of a terrorist organization? You can be imprisoned."

"For what crime?"

"For the intention of committing violence against the State of Israel."

"Intention is a state of mind."

"Intentions precede acts."

"Which acts?"

"That is exactly what we intend to find out."

"Find out, or invent?"

"Mr. Jibral, where were you before you came to Israel?"

"Geneva."

"And before Geneva?"

"Here and there."

"And before Geneva, Mr. Jibral?"

"You're stuck again."

"Paris, Mr. Jibral. Now where were you before Geneva?"

"Paris? Isn't that what you said?"

"And how long were you in Paris?"

"You have my passport. It's stamped in there."

"And what have you been doing in Paris since September?"

"December."

"I'm sorry, December."

"Screwing girls and drinking wine. What else does a tourist do in Paris? Go to museums, if he is the serious type."

"He makes contact with the terrorist organizations which the French tolerate on their soil because expedience costs less than principle."

"You're rather a bore, you know. If you can't come up with something more specific than that I think I'll be on my way." My butt is barely inches off the seat when a sidehand blow crashes into my neck just above the shoulder, setting off flashbulbs inside my head. When I try to turn my head it is held firmly by the hair on both sides.

"Mr. Jibral, we are not playing. You have been sent here on a mission. We are going to find out what it is."

He is looking for an excuse to torture me, to send me out to one of those desert prisons where the Oriental Jews take their revenge for *their* parents' misery.

"I demand to speak to the U.S. embassy."

Another blow to my neck sets off more flashbulbs. Now I can't focus. Two Counts loom above my head, fuzzy and shadowed. As they start to converge into one image I see that he is turning one of the lamps down toward me.

"Who did you see in Katamon, Mr. Jibral?"

"Gestapo."

"What did you say?"

"GE-STA-PO," I shouted at the top of my lungs. Another blow.

"GE-STA-PO, GE-STA-PO, GE-STA-PO . . ." A big hand clamps over my mouth. But I hear the chant echoing from another room: "Ge-sta-po, Ge-sta-po."

"GE-STA-PO." Now the big chimp is pulling my hair. But the adrenaline has completely anesthetized my body.

"Ge-sta-po, Ge-sta-po," echoes back.

I've started a demonstration!

"GE-STA-puh—" They've finally got a gag around my mouth, and now they're wrestling the handcuffs back on. For some reason I'm still not trying to resist.

"Ge-sta-po, Ge-sta-po," continues to chime from somewhere in the building. The Count leaves the room, slamming the door behind him while the chimps finish strapping my arms to the back of the chair and my ankles to the legs. This is why the chair is bolted down. I start to laugh into the gag. I don't know why. If this were happening in Monte I'd be drowning in my own fear sweat.

"Ge-sta-po, Ge-sta-po . . ." Finally it dies out.

My neck is starting to throb. And then to cramp. Worst pain in the world, neck cramps. Who was the informer? My mind is not clear enough to reason it out, but clear enough to wonder why they didn't wait to catch me red-handed with a camera full of espionage. Then they'd have a real excuse to break my balls. This is a lucky break. Apprehensio praecox.

At least an hour passes before the Count returns. He immediately signals the two chimps to unbind and ungag me. They even help me to my feet. The Count is hovering and pacing. "Stretch out the muscles, Mr. Jibral. It will keep them from cramping. We are having coffee brought. I am embarrassed to admit there has been a terrible, terrible mistake. You have been confused for someone else."

"Is that so?"

"I realize that what we have subjected you to is absolutely inexcusable." He is reciting. He's gotten orders to let me go. They've discovered their screw-up. They've grabbed me too early. They've looked at their records and discovered that a family called Jibral really did live in Katamon, so I was telling the truth. They're telling me I've been confused with someone else to persuade me to go on with my mission. How dumb do they think I am? On the other hand, what choice do they have? If they hang on to me, sooner or later I'll get a message to the U.S. embassy and then they'll have to let me go anyway, since they've no evidence to back their charge. So they're letting me go and hoping for the best. The worst I can do is protest to the embassy. Show them a couple of black and blue marks. Big deal. On the other hand, if I'm dumb enough to believe this ridiculous excuse and continue with my mission they'll end up with a real prize.

"Mr. Jibral, if there is anything we can do . . ."

"There is. You can book me a seat on the next flight out of this fucking country. And have one of your goons drive me to the airport."

"Please, Mr. Jibral, I understand your indignation. Allow yourself some time to cool off. You must certainly not permit this, our mistake, to spoil your vacation."

"It's a bit late. Where are my things?"

"They are being brought. Do you care to wash up?"

"Mustn't look like I've been beaten up when I walk out of here, huh? Maybe you'd like me to put on a little makeup."

"You should rest overnight before flying."

"I am flying this afternoon whether you make the reservation or not."

"To where would you like me to reserve?"

"Anywhere in Europe."

"I believe there is a flight to Athens."

"Athens is lovely. There is also the matter of the car I rented. Would you please return it."

"You can drive it yourself to the airport."

"I would rather have one of your goons along, just to make sure I don't do anything suspicious."

"That is quite unnecessary. But as you wish."

This is the last I see of the Count. Adnan, the smaller chimp, speaks some English. As we are pulling out of the compound I ask him what this place is.

"It used to be a hospital. But it was a police station for the British when we took it over."

"Is that Shin Beth I was just visiting?"

"Oh no. Miutim. Minorities."

142

"That's nice."

"Not for you, eh?"

I like this guy. He's the only one with a sense of humor.

We don't talk much on the highway to the airport. I feel a rage slowly gathering which I don't want to provoke along any faster. I have to get out of here before I do something stupid. It's not their rough stuff that's getting to me; it's being thwarted. They've made me fail. Or someone made me fail. Lucky for me the people on this end muffed it. I don't count on the Israelis making too many mistakes like this one.

The airport is a welcome sight this time. Even with its herd of tourist buffoons. They're more restrained at this hour. It's getting close to dark. Adnan stays with me all the way to the boarding lounge. At the search cubicles he flashes a card or badge from his wallet to spare me what he senses would be more than an irritant to me now. While we are waiting a flock of Japanese tourists pass through the search lines. Everybody stares at them; memories are still fresh. They know why they are being stared at and keep their eyes to the floor. When the boarding to Athens is called they file onto the plane like prisoners of war, moving nothing but their feet, barely speaking.

Adnan shrugs. "It wasn't their fault." Silently meaning, Yet every one of us is held responsible for what his own race does.

We shake hands. Watching the Japanese has made me calmer.

Adnan is almost moved by the spectacle. "I am sorry, eh?" Meaning, It's a tough world and I did what I had to do.

"It could have been worse, Adnan." You're a gentleman even if you're my enemy.

"You know, one is lucky, very lucky to be able to

143

be living in America." Meaning, Go home while you still can.

"I guess I'm just a lucky guy, Adnan." But America isn't home.

His parting nod is creased by a wry grin. Meaning, I guess I may be seeing you again.

My parting nod, enigmatic. Unfortunately for one of us, you will certainly be seeing me again.

Justina

So THIS IS HOW women send their husbands and sons off to war. You stay numb until he is beyond your clutch, then let the gales of contradictory emotion hit you. The ordinary stew of terror and pride must be bad enough. But stir into those my special guilt, and the result is very difficult to keep down. If only Raymond had not been so interested in this venture of Kamal's . . .

That is what scares me. The French don't cooperate with the Israelis the way the Americans do. If anything, they cooperate with the other side. Or so they say. But you never know. In France, government policy can be one thing and the policy of an agency like DST quite the opposite. The DST has old traditions and loyalties; they don't change every week like the government's. But what are those loyalties? Nobody issues statements to make them clear. In this business all you can be sure of is that nothing is as it appears to be. The rumors start to gnaw away at what you have taken to be bedrock under your feet. Like the Algerian passports. Now why would the Algerians want to issue blank passports to Fatah or whomever it was, then promptly report the serial numbers to SDECE and the CIA? They might as well have handed the men directly to Mossad. Did Boumédienne know about this, or does he have his own little DST working against him? It all makes me feel like a child drifting through the adult's world in a fog, the grownups' conversations always out of earshot or incomprehensible to my childish mind.

And now my playmate has suddenly grown up and gone off to seek his fortune. I wandered through the first day of his absence disoriented and despairing. I fretted half a dozen hours away under the stacks of books and cartons, warily avoiding the stapler until the very last hour, by which time the urge to put another staple through my hand had subsided enough to let me get safely through the packing.

Why do I always find myself in jobs where there is no one to talk to? Because that way you'll have a few hours of the day when you're not a spy. Oh, it's not that bad, Justina. Yes, it is. It's absolutely poison. Slow, painless, but lethal.

Yet by evening the sense of loss was beginning to acquire a certain sweetness mixed with the bitter. After all, it was an accomplishment for me to have had someone to lose. Yes, that was progress. I decided to look at it that way. I slept well. Feeling sorry for myself had exhausted me so thoroughly I slept through the alarm in the morning. Finally it was the hot sun pouring through the window that sweated me out. Throwing back the covers, I continued to lie spread-eagled, nude under the heavy rays, slipping in and out of drowses whose dreams grew increasingly erotic, and half waking with the memory-feeling of Kamal's tongue on my nipples. Then suddenly I was jolted by a vision of him sidling through an East Jerusalem alley, aching to glance behind him but suppressing the fear, gliding like a cat through a low arched hole in the ancient masonry where two tough men in mufti grab him in the darkness, muttering in Arabic, while here I am basking like a starlet in Saint-Tropez with my fingers inching down toward . . .

I bolted out of bed, spindled up by a cataract of cold shame, threw my clothes on over my sweat, and hurried over to the *La Flamme* office. There was no answer to my knock. I fished out my key, let myself in and went straight to my typewriter. I knew there was something I should be working on, but couldn't search my mind for it, because now Kamal and the two men in mufti were pushing blocks of explosive into his new rucksack, carefully, so carefully. But this was interrupted by the back-and-forth rattle of a key in the already unlocked door. Then heavy steps, which could belong only to Hervé, advanced and halted halfway through the outer office.

"Eh? Qui est là?" Nervously, as if he feared burglars or other intruders. Normally I would have played a joke on him: banged a drawer or rustled papers. Instead I remained quiet, hoping he would scare himself off. But after a moment he stepped hesitantly to our door and peered in.

"Oh, c'est toi, Justina." Disappointed and relieved all at once. "You're the last person I expect to find here these days. And alone particularly. Where's your Palestinian?"

I wanted to wipe the sneer clean off his face. My Palestinian is on a mission inside Israel, you pompous prick. But Kamal said not to tell anybody where he was going.

"Out of town for a bit."

"It must be some 'bit' for you to be looking so wilted, Justina. A permanent bit, perhaps? You were looking quite the gamine for a while in all your new presents from Galeries Lafayette. We were beginning to despair. Françoise said, 'I preferred the old Smudge to this new Candy Wrapper.' But I assured her that it was the same old you underneath, and that as soon as the Palestinian left it would be just like old times again."

"He'll be back, Hervé."

146

"Oh? You say that with certainty. You must know where he went."

"No, I don't."

"Aha! A secret mission. How romantic. And here you are pining away with worry for your bedouin James Bond. How bloody touching. It must be a dangerous mission. To the homeland perhaps? To do in the insidious Golda Kleb. No wonder you're wilting, Justina. Is that it?"

"What I want to know is why you're so damned interested, Hervé. It's unnatural." Back him off with suspicion.

"I am not interested one small hard shit."

"Good. Because this conversation is at an end."

Hervé had settled himself behind his desk as if he meant to stay. I yanked the blank paper from my typewriter, folded it into an envelope, scribbled a nonsense address on it and marched out. Kamal was at that very moment making his way toward a particular cafe with his rucksack slung casually from his shoulder, a particular cafe where Israeli soldiers met their girlfriends for coffee and cake.

Later I called up my old Venezuelan Stalinist friends. I hadn't talked to them since the night I first saw Kamal. They insisted on taking me to dinner at Sommerard. It would be a long time, I realized, before Paris would be something other than a grid of reminders of Kamal's absence.

Kamal

NO FLIGHTS OUT of Athens tonight. And to taxi into the city for a bed seems a little decadent. I've slept sitting up in airports before. An airport sheds its camouflage of bustle after midnight and becomes as fragile as an empty crabshell. I feel like a virus in a sleeping body. The airport has let down its defenses.

Not that the defenses of this one are particularly strong even during the day. It would be a perfect staging ground for a hijack. The guards don't really believe there is a danger. They go resentfully through the routines prescribed by some far-off agency, but their expressions apologize and dismiss what their hands are performing. Earlier I watched a blond California hippie lug his backpack past the baggage inspection grumbling, "This is bullshit, man. This is fucking bullshit." He was late for the last flight out to Madrid. The inspector shrugged, shook the pack and waved him on. The guy must have made the flight. Or maybe he's down at the boarding gate sleeping, trying to sleep, without toppling off his chair, like me. No, not him. He'd just find himself some floor and stretch out: Fuck dignity, man.

I will have to tell Boudia about this airport. He might be able to make use of it. That is, if I ever see Boudia again. Or if he will believe anything I say if I do see him. Putting myself in his position, what would I make of Kamal's failure to complete his mission? Of his premature arrest? Of the cursory interrogation? Of the patty-cake beating? Of the hasty release and the phony excuse for it? If the Count had wanted to concoct a more damning scenario, what last fillip could he have added? It would take a genius to improve on what he did. If I were Boudia I wouldn't touch me now. I'm blown. I've been waltzed right into Fool's Mate.

But by whom?

God help his tender testicles when I find out.

But by whom? The list can't be all that long. Boudia himself? To what end? If he'd wanted to nail me for some nefarious reason he would have told them exactly where to pick me up red-handed with a camera full of espionage. Same for Tony. Elaine didn't even know I was going to Israel. And besides which, if she were an Israeli agent she would have led them to cut down the big shot Boudia himself and not wasted time on a small fry like me. The same applies to Ghassan and Saleh, who also did not know I was being sent to Israel. So, in short, it could be none of you or any of you, or someone who doesn't come so obviously to mind. But these things have a way of coming to light in ways and at times you would never expect. Betrayal is something I know like the flex of my fingers. I was born under it. It was my nursery rhyme. I have flushed it out before, and will again. So, whoever you are, you have made a fatal mistake in not making your betrayal fatal to me. You have committed the error that brings down kings and liberators. And surely you're not that high.

On the seven-thirty flight to Paris I am the first to board, stiff and gummy from a nearly sleepless night. The take-off banks us back over a string of beaches still empty and pink under the low morning sun, and then over a yacht harbor where the masts of the larger boats threaten to snag our dipped wing. An optical illusion, probably. Alone on the cluttered foredeck of one small sloop, a woman stretching toward the sun twists through slow-motion Chinese exercises, oblivious of the voyeur flying over one of his own dreams, to cruise the world on a sailboat. But then, what does History care about sailboats?

Justina

ANOTHER OF THESE April mornings which incite every kind of passion. Today for some reason no imagined episodes of Kamal's mission are jolting me from bed. Today I let the sun work its magic on my body. When my imagination stirs at all it conjures someone's tongue between my legs. I know exactly how this kind of day spreads its restless pollens across the city. In Saint-Germain-des-Prés it will be a day of lavish infidelities. The display will be unbelievable: cocks semi-erect under skin-tight denim, bare breasts bouncing beneath transparent voile. And in the Quarter the students will be itching for a fight. If the morning offers them the least spark they will blow.

Later, so limp I can barely walk, I trickle down toward Mich and Germain to find something to stir me up again. Even half a dozen blocks away the vibrations of trouble in the air are unmistakable. By instinct I stop at the first newspaper kiosk to see what might have provoked it. The sober papers don't say much, except recounting a few more American outrages in Cambodia and more of Nixon's troubles. But *L'Humanité* has a headline which may be the fuse: another assassination, an Iraqi named Koubaissi gunned down in the street by several men with small-caliber pistols. That is the Israeli modus operandi, says the paper. And this Koubaissi was a professor in Beirut and thought to have association with the Palestinian movement.

This will be enough to set something off. Self-appointed Palestinian sympathizers will already have started a confrontation with the regularly stationed police. And by now it will be feeding on itself like a grassfire, the original cause of the protest unknown to all but the first few dozen. It is one of those days.

At the intersection of the great boulevards cars are blocked and trying to back away. Like tidal currents whipped by a wind, eddies of yelling, jeering people swirl across the pavement. On the peripheries kids climb lampposts to get a view of the vortex's center, while four streams of humanity drawn by some magic suction converge from the four directions. At least half a dozen different causes are legible on the posters. And even a few FREE PALESTINE placards are there at the hub of it all. But no one in Paris needs an excuse; riot is one of the rites, and rights, of spring.

Now the CRS are responding at last. Their permanent contingent, backed up along the spiked iron Cluny fence, have been too heavily outnumbered and have sent for reinforcements. They come lumbering up through the river of humanity, wrong way up Saint-Germain, in their gray-green vans, sirens howling, their helmeted brains behind those wire windows trying to gauge the size and mood of the crowd. Where the vans can no longer penetrate the swarm, they halt and disgorge their centurions in a blue file which forces a channel to the beleaguered outpost at the Cluny Castle fence. Now they join and array behind riot shields along the length of the fence. Every spring it is the same. The crowd jeers the arrival of the enemy but continues to mill, awaiting its unifying cause.

After May '68 the city tarred over the streets here to deny future rebellions our traditional weapon: the paving stone. This has driven the militant to import new weapons. The crowd now waits for these to arrive as it once waited for picks, shovels and crowbars. Finally the lull is broken. A strong surge pushes me back, almost off my feet. It is impossible to resist. Some instinct has caused a path to be opened through the midst of the crowd to allow someone to pass to the front lines. By climbing onto the bumper of a car abandoned in the swarm I can see the man for whom the path opened. He is a very tall and scrawny student disguised behind large sunglasses and a turned-up peacoat collar. He has something in his right hand which he holds low and to his thigh until he reaches a point about fifteen meters from the Cluny fence. By some spell he manages to keep the path open behind him.

The gangly student stops. The crowd hushes. His hands come into sight above the heads of the rioters gripping a large flare gun. A loud crack, and a ball of flame arcs just above the swarm and dips into the middle of the CRS line, which buckles and staggers. Yelling and signaling. One CRS is down on the pavement with three others around him trying to smother the flames under their lead-weighted capes. Another flare soars into their disordered ranks. A deafening cheer leaps from the crowd. The CRS men start to wade forward, pushing people back with their shields. But the gangly assailant is already invisible to them, retreating crouched along the miraculously maintained groove in the crowd which closes up behind him like the Red Sea. The police, finding their way blocked, unleash their truncheons. Of course this is anticipated by the battle-hardened front lines of the mob. Both sides have played this game before. Each has its provocation. The real battle can begin, neither side having to accept the blame.

The CRS line is immediately driven back against the iron fence by the pressure of the crowd against its shields. A third of the flics are disarmed of their capes and sticks by teams of experienced streetfighters who close on their chosen target in coordinated movements: one blocking the truncheon arm, two others trampling on the leaded cape until the poor flic is dragged under by his own garment. And between the fighting teams the disorganized congeal into passive barriers preventing the flic's mates from rescuing him.

Suddenly there is another ripple through the crowd. Rumor spreads from the center like a radio wave: One of the captains has been relieved of his pistol by a rioter. That is serious business. Guns scare everybody. But only for a moment.

The flics' next move turns everyone's attention back to the fray. The CRS line is retreating to its vans in two columns with the injured man between them. Another cheer bursts from the crowd. Success is measured in captured ground. The "people" have won their first skirmish of the day.

In the meantime another CRS fleet has been making its way up Saint-Germain from the west. An ambulance arrives for the injured flic. The fighting squads by now have melted back into the crowd to avoid identification, leaving less experienced and less confident people in the front lines. Against these the CRS reinforcements quickly regain their position by the Cluny fence. They start making arrests, grabbing the least mobile members of the crowd, including a bunch of foreigners who came to spectate and got carried away on the exotic winds of liberation. The arrests spark a new wave of retaliation by the crowd. Several of the prisoners are pried from the CRS. A chant of "C-R-S, ASS-ASS-IN" now rolls overhead. Carried on the rhythm of the chant, the rioters renew the attack. The fighting teams materialize from nowhere, their faces wrapped in scarves like cowboy bandits. The CRS lose almost all their prisoners in their retreat to the vans. The fighting teams press the pursuit, the crowd on their heels. One of the vans starts to rock side to side, each time closer to the tipping point. The flics trapped on the far side fight to keep it from rolling onto them. A few dare to circle around to drive off the wall of attackers heaving at their vehicle. But before they reach the front bumper another flare hisses out over the crowd and lands in their midst, driving them back for cover.

Now suddenly there is a change of mood. Nothing has provoked it but an instinct that warns both sides when the stakes are about to be pushed higher. The mood hangs on the equilibrium of that van about to topple onto the CRS caught between it and another van alongside. The chant dies. The truncheons freeze. And then, as inevitable as grief, two small cylinders sail over the van and two muffled explosions pop the silence. Then a cry of protest, then a screaming. The van rights. People just ahead of me are choking and stumbling as the gray cloud catches up with them. Two prongs of flics advance in gas masks from behind the front and rear of the beleaguered van. Several more gas grenades fly from their columns. I am being swept backwards. Our feeble chant of "C-R-S, ASS-ASS-IN" is stifled by the gas. The crowd, trampling itself in its haste, retreats up Saint-Germain and spills both ways onto Saint-Michel.

The flics now hold the tear-gas-choked intersection while the prevailing breeze does the rest of their work for them. Despite the exhortations by self-appointed generals in the crowd to stand and hold, the chemical has ended the mass phase of the demonstration. Soon the guerrilla phase will begin to the tinkle of breaking glass, the rattle of rocks on the pavement, the crackle of bonfires. Small gangs will roam around engaging the CRS with stones or an occasional Molotov, and the CRS will chase them out of the smoky streets one by one for the rest of the afternoon.

The festive mood is completely dispersed. Now there is only anger and disappointment, the tending of injuries and a rankling urge to revenge which keeps many milling about the periphery hoping for something to reunite the mass. But I at this moment find myself clamped in the middle of a mob rolling like a slow embolism up Saint-Germain, a claustrophobic panic gathering just behind my sternum. Why, in this quarter where I usually know thousands of faces, can I not recognize one now? Are these all outsiders, or are the faces just so twisted by anger and the scorching of the gas that they have become unrecognizable?

But, calm, Justina! This is hardly your first demonstration. Remember how simple patience and a relaxed wide stance, elbows akimbo, will float you in this crazy ocean until its natural waves cast you up on a quiet shore. It is not size but attitude which determines buoyancy in this maelstrom of bodies. You've seen huge athletes trying to resist with their bulk, helplessly swept under the feet of frail students. . . . But here is that shore already. Behind me the crowd surges once more and, poof, I am cast up amid the afternoon window shoppers of Saint-Germain-des-Prés, a beached shipwreck survivor, raw-fleshed and teary, staggering slightly as I straighten my clothes and poke my sweat-soaked hair back from my face.

The lines for the rest rooms at Le Drugstore are too long to tolerate. So, with no more attempt to restore my grooming, I plop myself down for coffee and ice cream, studiously ignoring the supercilious frowns of the serveuse as she takes my order. Ma petite, one simply does not sneer at mutilées de guerre.

Kamal

THESE LAST FEW HOURS have passed like a season. Just as the last few days have passed like a lifetime. A life's effort undone . . . My mind refuses to grip it all at once. Pieces slide in and out. Pop up and down. Like targets at a shooting gallery. . . . Naturally I had to phone as soon as I hit Paris: Kamal mustn't spare himself a minute in facing an impending disaster.

"I wish to speak to Dr. U. M. al-Ghazw, please."

"Who is calling?" A woman's voice. Hard, accented, but well educated.

"Huck Finn."

Silence on the other end. Then: "Dr. al-Ghazw is out of town."

"When will he be back?"

"It isn't known."

"I have to speak to him."

"He is out of town."

"Where can I reach him? It is urgent. Crucial."

"He is out of town."

"Cut the bullshit, okay? This is no fucking joke. I've got to talk to Boudia."

Silence.

"Listen, you stupid cunt—"

Click.

For the next hour, no answer at the phone number of Dr. U. M. al-Ghazw. Later I saw the reason on a news kiosk: another Israeli hit. A professor this time. Suspected PFLP connections, but denied by Iraqi consulate. Koubaissi is the name claimed. So Boudia and the others must all be diving under again. Like seals. Who knows when or where they will come up next. What am I supposed to do now?

Sleep on it, Kamal.

Sleep on it! Do you think I can sleep? Even after two hours of streetfighting up and down the Quarter I'm still ready to explode. And nothing used to calm me down like a good riot. After the cold shoulder chez Dr. U. M. al-Ghazw, I was more than ready to crack a few heads. But as Esteban used to say, "A guerrilla never wastes a good riot." Fate was throwing me a riot and daring me not to waste it. She lined up her police, each with a shiny little MAB 7.65 automatic snug at his hip, like forbidden berries on a bush, and she said, "Pluck." In front of me one of the smallest flics was being dragged to the ground by four toughs masked with bandannas, as the crowd behind crushed forward to wreak its vengeance. Did no one notice a tall hawk-faced blond squat and reach through the flailing limbs to unsnap the holster and ease the pistol from it?

No one noticed, Kamal. If someone had, the flics would have been after you as you edged back through the crowd with the pistol jammed down in your pocket. Or they would have trapped you in the WC in the basement of the cafe when you were stuffing the pistol into the sweaty wads of clothing in your duffel. Those were the moments for a pounding heart. But what's the excuse now?

The additional weight in my bag is distinctly noticeable.

But no one knows what the bag weighed before, Kamal. You're coming down with paranoia.

Not paranoia. Just lack of sleep. When was the last time I really slept? I can't remember. Perhaps I'm sleeping now.

A stillness smothers the afternoon. Cops, like rows of dark bats, hang in every shadow of every doorway in the Quarter. Barbed molecules of CS gas still attack your eyes and lips as you move along the littered sidewalks. There is a great milling about, a poised threat of unfinished business. But this is the endemic disease of the Quarter. Nobody ever finishes business, nobody ever delivers the coup de grâce.

Maybe it's the weather. Historians never figure in the weather. Do we know if on the morning of the 18th Brumaire a red sky showed above a press of gray cumulus on the horizon? Or if the day turned muggy like this one? No. Because Karl Marx never got out from behind his desk except to harangue a bunch of scruffy socialists in some dark hall.

What does it matter?

What does it matter, city boy? I, ibn Jibral of the Howeitat, scoff at you. A single tuft of cloud on the

157

horizon tells me that I need not lift a finger against the invaders camped below in my wadi. Allah will do it for me. In just a few hours man and horse will suddenly disappear under a wall of charging water, and the next morning I will ride down at my leisure and strip the carcasses that will be strewn for miles on the drying sands of the ravine. Carcasses of men with crucifixes who shrug at puffs of cloud on the horizon.

What the fuck are you going on about, Kamal? You know damn well it's not the weather that's got you on edge. It's that extra weight in your Adidas bag.

It's also the weather. Just a little breeze off the river right now might put a very different end to this day. It would clear the air of its poison. Chase everyone off to the parks. But instead, with the lingering of the gas lingers the sting of the rout. The streets still belong to the flics. The Quarter wants them back.

Leave it, Kamal, you've had enough for the day, scored far better than you had any right to expect. And you've gotten away clean. Don't press your luck. Go home to Patriarches, have a closer look at the morning's booty. All you would need to bring the last three days to their most logical and pathetic conclusion is to get arrested and searched by the CRS. It's all over down here anyway. So the Quarter has lost again, what do you care? There were a few small victories today and you have the prize of one of them.

All right, I'm going, I'm going. But it's not over down here by any means. Even in the last half hour the density of the crowd along Saint-Michel has been building. They're coming in from along the river. Different people this time. Next to me on the sidewalk facing Place Saint-Michel is a contingent from Renault, six of them, still in company overalls. They've clocked out specifically for this next battle.

It must be something serious if the word's gone all the way across the city to Renault. These six are a hard crew. Machine oil and metal shavings in their hair, hands the color of old lead. They don't even notice the remains of the tear gas. I should have left my bag and its treasure back at the cafe where I stashed it all morning. I wouldn't have to be so fucking fastidious now. The Renault toughs are staring at me like I'm some rinky-dink tourist.

"And who have we here?" The voice from behind me is too familiar.

"Hello, Hervé."

He looks like he's been in it all morning as well. His face is covered with a clear grease. He came prepared for the gas. As did the two men with him. They also look like Algerians, and are irritated that their buddy should stop to talk with an obvious bystander like me. All three are padded out with old sweaters and look formidably burly. All three have their skulls protected by stocking caps stuffed with rags and are wearing water-soaked scarves around their necks, ready to pull up over their noses in case of another round of gas. Hervé has ski goggles pushed up on his forehead, and leather gloves clipped to his belt. He is now eyeing my rumpled civilian outfit and my traveling bag.

"I thought you were off in foreign lands fighting the Infidel, Kamal."

"But here I am." How the hell did he know about that?

"The infidel must have put up a good battle, eh? Have you seen Justina? She will be as surprised as I am to see you back so soon."

Hervé's companions are getting restless. One of them tugs at his sweater and points out the flow of the crowd in Rue Saint-Séverin and Rue de la Harpe. Hervé nods.

"Well, Kamal, I advise you to get out of here while

you still can. It is going to become very unhealthy very soon."

"Sounds terribly dangerous, Hervé,"

"Tsk, tsk. All I'm saying is that you're not equipped for what is coming." He gestures to his sweaters and scarves.

"I'll manage."

"Of course you will. This is just child's play to a professional like you. I keep forgetting. My friends, we are honored with the company of the Palestinian James Bond"—why is the bastard pushing so hard?—"who has just come back from a secret mission overseas." Not secret enough, apparently. "Posing as a handsome American athlete." He prods my Adidas bag.

What are you trying to tell me, Hervé?

"We are all happy to see you back so soon and so safely from your exploits, Kamal. But we haven't time to stop and chat about them now. Some other time perhaps. But now take care."

"You too, Hervé. You too."

Take care against what? Were you expecting me to disappear forever?

Hervé and his buddies saunter off to merge with a clot of students pushing into the narrow Rue Saint-Séverin.

Yes, I know your type, Hervé. You were one of those instant Maccabees who sprung up overnight after the Six Day War, like mushrooms after a rain. You were one of the strutters with a spine borrowed from men thousands of miles away in a land you'd never seen, a freeze-dried Zionist reconstituted with the blood of Arabs spilled in the Sinai and in the Golan. Weren't you one of those, Hervé? Radical or no radical, in June '67 your true colors shone right through, didn't they? Or did you hide them diligently and find a more dangerous and devious way to express what lay under your red-painted exterior?

160

Now this is strange, all these people jamming into the narrow streets, pouring off the boulevards where all the action usually takes place. The flics haven't moved. They are still standing around in dispersed knots, perhaps in a stupor from their own gas.

Without volition I have been swept to the intersection of Séverin and Harpe. There is something happening just up the alley. A small squad, five or six flics, is pinned under the marquee of one of the little movie theaters facing a crowd of what must now have built to over a thousand people. The theater doors are locked behind them. The glass of the ticket booth is smashed, as is the glass covering the display of still photos of the best bare tits in the film. The flics are backed up against these. Taunts and jeers fly from the crowd's front lines.

Orders are crackling over the walkie-talkie for the flics to rejoin their main force on Saint-Germain. The orders provoke a gale of laughter from the crowd. The flics start pushing along the wall toward the boulevard. They have less than a hundred meters to go. Irresolute at first, the crowd allows them to edge perhaps twenty meters. Then somebody in the front lines starts chanting, "No pasaran, no pasaran," as if five scared flics are Franco's four columns. But the crowd takes up the chant and presses in to close off the squad's escape.

More consultations over the walkie-talkie. "Fight your way through," comes the word. More laughter. The squad tries to reverse its course and edge back toward the theater. Perhaps hoping to reach the intersection with Séverin and duck out the other way. But it is blocked that way too, pinned against a bare stone section of wall. Soon the vibrations of animal panic are beginning to incite the predator in the crowd. The flics against the wall feel their shields and sticks in the grip of a furious suction, an undertow stripping them and carrying away their equipment piece by piece. They all have heard what happened this morning and are clutching their holsters, where their last protection rests. They feel fingers beginning to clutch at their clothing.

A short close-eyed blond flic is the first to draw his pistol. The action freezes the front lines of the crowd. Encouraged by this the other flics draw their pistols, though the terror of what this may provoke shows clearly on the ashen faces behind the plexiglass masks. Less than a meter separates the front lines from the row of flics.

For a minute, or perhaps more, the confrontation remains as immobile as a painting. Events have never before gotten to this point. Neither side knows what to do. The flics will not put away their pistols: they have no other defense. And the front lines will not retreat. It is no longer possible. A few meters back nobody knows what is happening up here. Behind us we feel a terrible pressing forward. The gap between us and the flics is being squeezed. We press back, digging in our heels. But to no avail. The flics raise their pistols, one by reluctant one. They are each alone now. Each alone with a crowd of thousands. And the pushing continues from behind, a kind of malignant effort to ignite the explosion by compressing the fuel. I manage to slip one row back from the front line, now clutching my bag under my arm to keep it from being ripped away. The push comes directly from behind, in waves. At the next lull I manage to twist again and let another body slip by. One more between me and the guns. And now the source of the pushing is directly behind me. "They shall not pass, they shall not pass." It is Hervé. He gives me a sour smile, then resumes his chant. And his pushing.

BLAM! The flics' first shot into the air. Then another. The screaming starts. And the swarm is suddenly heaving in every direction.

But all I can see is Hervé, foaming and ugly, bent on finishing the job his friends failed to finish in Jerusalem: he is trying to push me onto the guns. Now I have twisted around to face him fully, while my free hand, finding what it has been seeking deep among the crumpled clothes in my bag, closes around the solid certain steel. Like the grip of an old friend.

It barely makes a sound. No more than a low thud lost in the screaming. Hervé is no longer thrusting forward. Spine sprung into an arc, hands fluttering upward, eyes and mouth dark holes crying mute horror at the alley's narrow sky, he hovers in mid-flight. But only for a second. Then he is sucked down beneath the stampede as it bursts sideways in terror, recoiling from the leveled pistols of the flics. They will waste no more shots into the air.

In a moment the crowd has decided on retreat. Hervé's body emerges from under it crumpled and limp as a drowned bird thrown up by a tide. While I am swept back on the tide, back toward the river, back toward the open air, back away from the guns of the panicking flics and a rolling cloud of gas behind which a relief party of CRS is advancing from Saint-Germain. The elbow of the street puts Hervé's corpse out of sight. But at the last glimpse he looked very dead, very dead. So dead that the flics weren't even bothering to check.

Justina

THE NEWS CAME in pieces. First rumors of gunfire. Then a whisper that a man had been killed. The demonstration dissolved very quickly after that. But it wasn't until early evening that the newspapers came out with the identification. Half an hour later everyone associated with *La Flamme* was at the office. Françoise and Pierre were already planning the next issue: 102 Years of Police Violence in Paris. Starting with the Commune and ending with Hervé. Nothing less to "respond" to Hervé's death. He was already a cause. Nobody but me could remember when he was born. It made me nauseous, but it brought *La Flamme* to life as it hadn't been for years. Once I supplied Françoise with Hervé's "personal data" I left. No one noticed. I swore I'd never return.

If I had not been so numbed by Hervé's death I might have been shocked to find Kamal sprawled out on the bed, fully dressed and emitting a painful wheeze with each breath, as if every tissue in his sinuses had been flayed with wire. Nothing would wake him. His clothes lay scattered across the floor, along with the camera and some other things. The Adidas bag lay on the bed next to him. As I picked it up to make a space for myself I noticed a hole near the zipper end. A bullet hole! He had been shot at too. I had nearly lost two men in one day. That broke the dam. I must have gone completely hysterical, because the next thing I was conscious of was Kamal holding me down on the bed and trying to comfort me at the same time.

"They nearly got you too!" I wailed.

"Got me?"

"The bullet hole, Kamal. Didn't you see the bullet hole in your bag? The dirty pigs nearly shot you too!"

"Oh that. I'm O.K. Close call, huh?"

"Close call! Kamal, they killed Hervé. Didn't you hear?"

"I heard."

"I'm sorry, Kamal. It was all just too much for me. I'll be calmer now. But, oh God, am I glad you're back."

That night was special. The shock and grief of death cracked away both of our brittle shells of self.

We lay together raw and silent, yet so eloquent through our sex, our palms, our lips. Later, in the absolute dark listening to the muffled midnight sounds of the city putting itself to sleep, I understood the poets for the first time. It is true that sex needs death to find itself. When we call on it to liberate us from the petty frustrations of everyday life we condemn it to the same petty scale.

At once the entire ancient spectrum of passion was revealed to me in a way I had never seen it before. You had to have felt the pain of blood sacrifice to feel such a lust it could make you move a nation to war over a woman. It took Hervé's blood to allow me and Kamal to experience something intense enough to be called love, something which the ancients would not scoff at as they must scoff at the rest of our pitiful simulations of it.

But this was a vision one could only see in the dark. Daylight crushed it, reduced it, trivialized it down to a necklace of words. The dirty yellow sun glared at me and made me wither with shame to have indulged in such neolithic desires. In the street, surrounded by the masses of ordinary mortals struggling to get where they were going on time—that was challenge enough—in order to pay the bills, I felt unutterably guilty that my single night of passion should have to be paid for with the life of a young man. What right did I have? Did I think I was Cleopatra?

At the same time I felt soaringly proud. How many of these other women clicking along the pavement looking so chic had ever known a night like mine? Damn few. For how many had the necessary blood sacrifice been made, by Fate or whomever?

Whomever? I shut off the even darker vision unleashed by this mental slip, but too late. It was lodged like a tiny pellet of radium in my unconscious. There would be no forgetting what I had just seen for that brief instant. Over the next few days it would ambush me. The first time, when I discovered Kamal had incinerated the Adidas bag because the bullet hole "bugged" him. And the second time, when the newspaper reported on an inside page that the laboratory could not match the fatal bullet with any of the five pistols carried by the flics in Rue de la Harpe, though it was of the same caliber. No criminal charges could therefore be brought against any of the CRS men; the five would be reprimanded as a group. Every faction of the Left was crying, "Fraud!" But I remembered the rumor that had swept the crowd of a pistol stolen from a CRS captain.

Kamal's reaction to the news article was normal. He shrugged his shoulders and said, "What do you expect?" But from that morning his habits changed radically. Where before he used to spend his day roaming the streets or hanging out in cafes, now he chose to stay put in Patriarches, reading or staring at the peeling paint over our bed. Only after dark could he be persuaded to leave, and then only for the dark of a movie theater or for a quick furtive walk along the nearby streets. He blamed his reluctance on the Koubaissi assassination, and the mission he had just been on.

Then, a few days later, when the Israelis sent their commandos into Beirut and killed three top Palestinian leaders and destroyed their offices, Kamal nodded and said, "You see, they're on a rampage." I only nodded ambiguously. We both knew the truth. We were a conspiracy. Our conspiracy fueled our passion. Every time we looked into each other's eyes we reaffirmed the culpability. I had no desire at all to shed it. Because to shed my share of the guilt meant at the same time to kill off the passion that Hervé's death bought us. Kamal was mine more than ever now. More mine than anyone had ever been. And the ecstasy that possession gave to my body would have been worth dying for. I didn't care. Any consequence was all right so long as I could make this last just another night. Yet we were living inside the most delicate equilibrium. Anything could tip it. So I said nothing. And Kamal said nothing. And I held my breath for the inevitable which would send it all crashing to the ground.

Kamal

THE LONGEST WEEK in my life. Waiting for the axe to fall. Staving off the horror with desperate fucking. Each time as if it's the last and they're going to come crashing in the door. What seemed like the perfect crime now seems the worst amateur botch. Justina suspects. And it excites her. That is better than the opposite: terrified withdrawal. I thought I might have to kill her too. But instead she acts as if she also had had her hand on the pistol. Both of us are getting giddy from the danger. Bonnie and Clyde. It's good for sex, I'll say that for it.

Now it's all up to the police. They know it wasn't one of their own men. They always have photographers everywhere during a demonstration like that. They will already be poring over the pictures to see who was near Hervé at the time of the confrontation. And there I will be. Sooner or later they will also recall that a CRS officer was disarmed a few hours earlier. They will look at the photos of that event. And there I will be too. A pretty tight case. This is France: I will have to prove myself innocent! Good night, Kamal. The only question is whether the police care enough about the death of a Trotskyist Algerian Jew to go to all this trouble, and then create a cause célèbre for the Left, which will never accept the story anyway. And then there is the question of whether they will turn over their evidence to the Israelis, who damn well will care who terminated their agent.

So why don't I leave Paris?

Where else is there to go? Beirut? Benghazi? To be marched around in the dirt waiting for my time to die on the barbed wire for the glory of the Revolution? And yet there is no place else to go without giving up on everything I have been living for. Get a job, but a yacht, sail around the world into utterly obscure banality? Rather die in the dust. Yet the only stop between here and the dust is Boudia. I must stay here and find him, no matter what the risk. I've got the little MAB 7.65 and a full clip minus one. I might as well stay until I have to shoot my way out. And if I'm guillotined, it will be as a cause célèbre, at least.

So Kamal becomes a vampire, entombed in Patriarches during the sun's hours and venturing out by dark in search of his life-blood. Starting with a young girl, of course. But she proves as elusive as Boudia himself. A long chilly walk out to Elaine's apartment near the Université Américain gets me nothing but the hollow echo of my knuckles on her door. There is a millimeter of undisturbed dust on the doorsill and a musty odor from under the door. Elaine likes fresh air. She has not been here for days. She's dived with the rest of the ducks.

This is confirmed several nights later by another millimeter of dust on her doorsill. I stalk back to Patriarches in an evil and vengeful mood. Justina is waiting up. My anger only seems to stir her own heat. Once again she draws me into it, obliterating the world for me. If this oblivion in sex ever fails me, what would be left but heroin?

The telephone of Dr. U. M. al-Ghazw continues to ring without an answer. Only one option remains.

The next night I hitchhike out to Villejuif and after some wandering recognize the street that Elaine directed the taxi to that night of the interview with Ghassan, Tony and Saleh. In a few minutes I have found the building and reassure myself that it is the same one by recalling the odd sweep of the lights from the highway across its facade.

This is the first time I have ventured into the street armed. I feel the weight of the incriminating pistol nestled in the small of my back; it is vaguely reassuring nonetheless. Before I left Patriarches I removed the plastic grips and wrapped the butt with electrical tape to reduce the weapon's thickness.

Justina watched this operation silently. It was the first time she'd seen the gun. When I was standing in front of the mirror to see if the bulge was visible under my jacket, she asked in a voice even small for her, "Is that . . . the same one?"

I nodded.

"You ought, oughtn't you, to get rid of it?"

I don't know why I hadn't. It should have been lying in the mud at the bottom of the Seine. But a revolutionary doesn't throw away his weapon. Only a criminal does that.

I climb slowly and silently up the dark stairwell. I hear voices inside the apartment and smell olive oil and garlic wafting onto the landing. A nice domestic scene. Must be Ghassan's family. At least it is a place to start.

A young teenage girl answers my knock. She seems disappointed.

"Can I speak to your father?"

She leaves the door open but does not invite me in. A minute later she returns followed by a portly Egyptian-featured man I have never seen before. "Can I please help you?"

"Yes. I need to speak with Ghassan."

"Ghassan? There is no Ghassan here."

"No Ghassan? How about Saleh or Tony?"

"I am truly sorry, but you must have the wrong address."

"No, I'm certain. I met them here just a few weeks ago."

"Here? Impossible."

"Can I look at your living room? Perhaps I have made a mistake."

"Yes, of course, come in. What is your name?"

"Kamal."

It is the same room.

"Perhaps you were away and rented the apartment?"

The girl interrupts. "We were not away. We haven't been away."

"Please, my dear," her father pushing her gently toward the kitchen, "I would like to speak to this man alone."

He guides me toward the door. "I am sorry. If there is any way I can help you . . . Kamal?" He stares very intently into my eyes, trying to tell me something, or warn me. But the message is too ambiguous.

"Kamal Jibral is my name. I'm sorry to have disturbed your dinner. I must have gotten the building confused."

"That is quite all right, Mr. Jibral. Think nothing of it."

I walk all the way back to Patriarches trying to decipher that encounter. Of course he knows who Ghassan and the others are. In function if not in person. The family must have been out visiting that night and lent the Organization the key. The father may know nothing more than that, and not want to know. But he was sympathetic to me. If he can pass on the word he will. There is nothing more to be done.

It is after one by the time I reach Patriarches. Jus-

tina, lying awake, turns her back to me. I climb into
bed and also lie awake waiting for her to explain.
But she isn't ready. A quiver just short of nausea
lodges in my gut.

Justina

I HAD BEEN living in silent horror of that "something" which would end it all, without any idea of
what form that "something" would come in. So when
I came home to find Kamal working on a pistol it did
not occur to me at first that there was any connection
with Hervé. I did not want it to occur to me. The killing was still just a story in my mind: a dirty forbidden adventure, but not a fact. One oily black pistol
and one question, answered with a nod, turned the
story into a murder, a vicious puncturing of tissue
and bone and a heart desperately pumping its blood
out of a new hole. I still could barely connect this to a
man I used to hold, who had so many times been inside me, pumped hard by the same heart. But now I
had to ask myself the question which the storybook
killing did not require to be asked. Why did Kamal
kill him?

I tried to push the question out of my mind at
work. There was no answer with any logic. I felt as if
I was slipping on ice. I thought about calling Raymond. But there would be no comfort from that quarter; this time the consequences were too enormous.

By early afternoon the stockroom of the bookstore
seemed like a prison. I slipped out the back into the
clatter and bustle of the streets. I thought about
going to stay at my Stalinist friends' home, but
found myself in front of Patriarches before I was able
to make up my mind. And immediately I noticed
something that made the question vanish. There
was a man across from our building watching. An

171

Arab-looking man, very lean, very tough. When he saw me he continued to watch as if I were some kind of bug. I smiled at him. No response. By the time I reached our apartment my heart was beating so fast I thought I would pass out. Kamal was lying on the bed, as usual.

"Kamal, there's a man out in the street watching."

"Oh? What does he look like?"

"Arab. Tough, mean-looking."

"Watching this building?"

"Absolutely."

Fortunately we had no window onto the street. Kamal thought a moment, sprang up, jammed on his shoes and yanked the pistol from above the water heater. I'd never noticed that he kept it there.

"I'm going to go out the back way and circle around. Don't worry."

He was at the door already, pulling on his jacket and tucking the gun into his pants behind his back. His eyes had a very nasty glitter.

"Kamal, don't . . . If you don't have to, I mean."

He seemed to ignore that.

"Kamal . . . Why? I mean, why Hervé?"

He paused with his hand on the dead bolt, without turning to me. "Why Hervé? Because I ran into some trouble in Israel, Justina. Somehow Hervé knew I was there. Someone here told the Israelis I was coming. Hervé was a spy. It had to be done."

He said it just like that. Without emotion. As if reading from a history book. And then he left. Left me with the full horror of the consequences of my little chats with Raymond.

Kamal

EVEN FROM THE POOR VANTAGE of the corner of Passage des Patriarches the figure is vaguely famil-

172

iar. Huddling behind the collar of a dark peacoat, hands plunged deeply into the pockets, he has stationed himself so there is no way to approach without being spotted. The weather does not call for a heavy coat; he must be armed. There is no one else in sight. I have to retreat around the corner to chamber a round. The clack of the slide closing seems to fill the street. But the man in the peacoat is still unaware. I tuck the pistol back in my pants, step out into full view, and whistle loud between my fingers. He spins toward me, jolted out of some trance. Now I can see why the profile was familiar. It is Saleh. I make a wide gesture to show that my hands are empty.

"Salut!"

He pauses, then does the same. "Salut, monvieux."

We approach each other rapidly and clasp hands like two old friends. To cover the muttered exchange.

"Where the fuck have you guys disappeared to?"

"There has been trouble, Kamal."

"Don't I know? Where's Boudia?"

"Do you have the film?"

"Yeah, I have the film."

"Will you give it to me please?"

"I will give it to Boudia, nobody else."

"I have been sent for it."

"That's too bad. Boudia's the only one I trust. Nothing personal, you understand."

"Do you have the film on you now?"

"Of course not."

"You will go get it, and then I will take you to Boudia."

I reach out and pat the steel lump under his arm. "Please, please, my dear Saleh. I'm not a fool. That film is my security. Take me to Boudia and I will take him to the film." I am not expecting much from this gambit. Saleh nods and shakes his head alternately.

"Come with me. This is a change of plan. I must make a telephone call."

We head down toward Contrescarpe.

"By the way, Saleh, how did you know where I live?"

"We had you followed."

"Naturally."

He makes his call from the cafe opposite the little square. I am wondering what to do with the pistol. There is no safe place to stash it.

Saleh returns very quickly. "Come."

We walk briskly down to Ecoles, then through the heart of the Quarter. Right past the spot Hervé met his fate. It is full of tourists gawking at the erotic movie posters outside the theater. This is the first time I've been back. I catch myself searching the pavement for bloodstains. Two minutes later we are down at the river, where Saleh suddenly stops. The traffic careens by. We wait. Suddenly a green Renault 16 jerks to a halt in front of us, the passenger door swings open, Saleh almost pushes me in, then climbs in back himself, and the car shoots back into the traffic, heading down onto the express lanes on the quai.

The driver is the bearded man of the back-lit encounter in the park.

"Comrade Boudia."

"Comrade Jibral." He grins. In the light of day his face is no surprise: a distinct touch of humor softening the intensity of the eyes. Otherwise slightly thick-featured, which imparts a kind of toughness and immunity. "And how was your journey to the homeland?"

"Interesting."

"I should imagine so. By the way, are you armed?"

"Yes."

"May I see?"

I can feel the muzzle of Saleh's weapon pointed at

my back through the seat. I pull out the MAB and lay it on my thigh.

"Very nice. A police weapon."

"Yes."

"Would you remove the magazine and clear the chamber. Loaded guns make me uncomfortable."

I comply, and make a gesture of offering him the gun.

"No, by all means keep it."

I stick the gun back in my belt and the clip in my jacket pocket.

"Is that better?"

"Much better, thank you. Saleh, will Invalides do for you?"

A grunt from the back. Boudia jerks the car to a stop. Saleh jumps out. The car springs ahead.

"Good acceleration. This doesn't look like a fast car."

"But it is. Except in this traffic. So . . . We continue where we left off. You parted having posed me a riddle, Kamal."

"I did?"

"Yes. You asked me if I had been in the Soviet Union. Do you recall now? It was an odd question. It puzzled me for a time, and then I figured it out."

"Well?"

"Mark Twain. Don't the Russians hold up Mark Twain as your greatest writer? I think that was your deduction."

"It was a guess. Most of the world has barely heard of Twain."

"However, my dear Huck Finn, I assure you I came to Mark Twain entirely on my own. Long before I ever met a Russian. I discovered him in prison as a matter of fact. Laughter is precious in prison. More important than food. So you will have to deduce in another way whether I have been in the Soviet Union. If that matters to you."

175

"Not a bit. I was interested in how you got to Twain."

"Are you not interested in why I was imprisoned?"

"Stealing a loaf of bread."

"Do I not appear just a little more flamboyant than Jean Valjean?"

"Conspiring with Napoleon."

"That is closer. But they have closed down the Château d'If, fortunately."

"Attempting to assassinate De Gaulle?"

"Allah forbid! It was my good friend De Gaulle who let me out of prison. Not because he liked me, you must realize, but as a goodwill gesture to Ben Bella."

"You are Algerian?"

"Mais oui."

"So what was your crime?"

"I just blew up an oil tank or two outside of Marseilles back during the Algerian war."

"Now that must have been a kick in the ass."

"Glorious. Absolutely glorious. Better than sex. I could barely tear myself away from those beautiful flames, and the roar . . . You have never experienced anything like it. It gets to be a habit. Perhaps you heard of a similar event at Trieste last August?"

"As a matter of fact I did read about it. That was you?"

"It was. The Italians are trying to have me extradited from France, but the French are not too anxious to cooperate. Here they are very careful to avoid provoking terroristic retaliations. The safest man in Paris is a member of PFLP or Fatah."

"Tell that to Koubaissi."

"Ah yes, I have to admit the Israelis are a problem. But not for you, I understand. Or so Saleh said. Why would you not trust him with the film?"

"I had no reason to believe you trusted him, either.

176

You did not tell me he would be picking it up. That's in lesson one."

"Admirable caution. Do you trust him now?"

"Anyone you trust behind your back with a loaded gun I also trust, Boudia."

"Call me Mohammed, please. So will you trust me with the precious film now?"

Call him Mohammed! Am I really here? Half an hour ago this man was no more than an elusive abstraction, a ghost of my hopes, whom I had willed myself to hunt down in spite of the doubt that he really existed. Now suddenly here he is, jesting and boasting and smelling faintly of stale sweat. How many scripts have I written for exactly this moment? The moment of having to build the case to exonerate my failure to carry out a mission. Every script is falling flat. None of them reckons with this kind of a Boudia: one who can laugh.

"Trust you with the film, Mohammed? As a matter of fact I would trust anybody with the film. Since there's nothing on it."

"No pictures on the film? Why?" His voice is neutral.

"I did not consider it safe to shoot the pictures under the circumstances."

"What circumstances?"

"I was arrested the morning after I arrived, in Jerusalem, by Miutim: a department dealing with Minorities."

"But I see they let you go."

"They had nothing on me. They got suspicious because I went directly from the airport to a slum called Katamon and spent an hour wandering around there. You're supposed to go to the Old City, you see. Anything else is suspicious behavior."

"Why did you go to this slum?"

"It was where my parents lived before 1948."

"I see. And so they let you go when you explained this to them."

"No. They clobbered me for being a wise guy. After a while they came back and said they'd made a terrible mistake and let me go."

"Why did you not proceed with your mission then?"

"You've got to be kidding, Boudia."

"Where did they take you when they arrested you?"

"To a police compound near the Old City."

"Yes, Moscobiya. And there they interrogated you. What did they ask?"

"Who I went to see in Katamon. Over and over. And then what terrorist organization did I belong to. I told them to go fuck themselves and started yelling 'Gestapo, Gestapo,' until the whole building was shouting along with me."

"And then they let you go?"

"First they tied me up and gagged me. Hit me in the neck a few times. Then left and came back in an hour to tell me it was all a ghastly mistake and could they do anything to make it up. Couldn't have made it more damning, could they?"

"Damning?"

"Come on, Boudia. If someone came to me with a story like that I'd be tempted to shoot him in the head and dump him in the river."

"You're a harsh man, comrade Jibral. And very quick to reach conclusions. I'm much slower, luckily for you."

He steers onto the Pont de Bir-Hakeim, now so sluggishly that the cars behind are starting to honk. Which is illegal.

"One of my favorite places in this city. The whimsey to prop a Métro on a Roman viaduct on top of a bridge. Formidable!"

Lectures on architecture now. What next? When

we reach the end of the arches he speeds up. He reminds me of Ferdinand the bull. I hope nobody throws him flowers in the middle of a firefight.

"But to return, you were in the process of concluding for me that your interlude with the Israelis was highly damning. While I myself was perfectly ready to accept your first interpretation: that the police found it odd that you should be wandering around a slum an hour after you arrived, picked you up, harassed you a bit, then discovered why you had gone there and let you go. Yes, it seems perfectly reasonable."

"Why should they have paid any attention to me in the first place? To be aware that I had gone to Katamon they had to have been suspicious of me in the first place." I wonder for a moment why I have said this, when I could have simply agreed with Boudia. But with a slight wrench in the gut I realize that I am not defending myself before Boudia but defending my case against Hervé before . . . Before whom?

"But, Kamal, my friend, put yourself in the position of the Israeli police. Would you not want to be notified instantly whenever a young angry-looking Arab carrying an American passport lands at your airport?"

"I suppose I would."

"How did you get from the airport to Jerusalem?"

"I rented a car at the airport. They said I was lucky they had one."

"If you were working at the car rental desk would you not be equally alert to this same angry young Arab, and be certain to find him a car so that his movements could be easily traced by your internal security services?"

"I suppose I would."

"And then when the car appeared in a troubled area not known for its tourist attractions, would you

179

not, as internal security officer, be curious to know why this angry young Arab was in such a hurry to get there?"

"I suppose so."

"There! A perfectly innocent explanation of what befell you. That is good enough for me, comrade Kamal. Quite good enough. In fact, if you had returned successful from this mission I would be much more troubled. I would be asking myself, How could this man have succeeded when he is such a prime candidate for Israeli suspicions? Why was he not intercepted? Why was he not followed? But as it is, my slow mind chews contentedly on the facts as you have presented them, and it concludes, All is well, all is well. Like an English lamplighter, you know? So relax, my dear Kamal, you have passed your test."

What must Boudia make of the bleakness these words of his have cast across your features, Kamal? When you should be rejoicing. It can only appear to be one of those inexplicable inversions of mood, like a post-coital tristesse. But if his supposedly contented cow of a mind knew the other facts, it would be churning. Oh yes. If it knew, it might advise him to take your own prescription for yourself, Kamal: to put a bullet in your head and dump you in the river.

"By the way, Kamal, did Saleh interrupt you from something important? We need time for a long talk."

"I assumed that is what we are doing now."

"It may take us several days."

"That's no problem."

"What about your girlfriend, the Cuban?"

"She's no problem either."

"Good. You are not tied down to her in any way."

"Not in any way. Where are we headed?"

"Somewhere to talk comfortably. Do you have any preference?"

"No."

"Tell me about your father."

"He's dead."

"And before that?"

"He was alive."

"That is more than could be said for some. How did he stay alive?"

"He worked for IntraBank's office in New York."

"A bitter choice. What did he do after the collapse?"

"He withered and died a little over a year later."

"Did he believe that Intra was brought down by a conspiracy of the Lebanese bourgeoisie?"

"Was there any question? He knew exactly who organized it."

"Did he talk about it?"

"Oh yes. My father wasn't the silent sufferer. He said that destroying Intra was the most self-destructive thing the Lebanese ever did, because in destroying the bank they wrecked the Palestinian bourgeoisie, which was the only force protecting them from the revolutionism of the rest of the Palestinians in Lebanon."

"He was correct. What did he do before IntraBank?"

"He worked for UNRWA. That is why we were brought to the States. It was arranged from Amman."

"And before 1948?"

"He worked as an administrator in the Mandatory."

"For the British."

"Yes."

"How did he feel about the British?"

"He loathed them and wished he were one."

Boudia turns to look at me with skeptical surprise.

"You are as hard on him as you are on yourself, Kamal. Life was very hard for that generation.

Harder than for us, because they had to submit to colonial values which—"

"I have read Fanon."

"But not lived it, my friend."

A long unfriendly silence as we roll onto the Périphérique.

"And Vietnam?" He springs the end of a long chain of thought.

"What about Vietnam?"

"Did you fight in Vietnam?"

"No."

"You were not called into the Army?"

"No."

"How was that? I thought toward the end they were calling up every young man."

"Perhaps they did call. I was in Montevideo."

"That was in 1970, I believe you said. What about before?"

"I was deferred as a student."

"Why did you not stay in the U.S. and join the underground?"

"What underground?"

"The group calling themselves Weathermen."

"Comrade Boudia, do you know where they took their name? From a line in a song, also an old adage, 'You don't need a weatherman to know which way the wind blows.' That was their political line."

"What do the Americans call that—built-in obsolescence? As I understand, their forecast was staggeringly inaccurate. Did you have any contact with the Black Panthers?"

"I'm not black."

"You are not Latin American, either."

"So I discovered."

"Is that why you left Montevideo?"

"More or less. The Committee wanted me out. I was wanted and my face was probably known to the police."

"You mentioned last time we met that you had killed."

"Yes. A Death Squad goon, who was also a flunky in the Ministerio del Interior. And before that, an infiltrator in our cell."

"Have you killed anyone else?"

"No." Did he hear your heart thump? Did he sense the pause that felt so enormous to you?

"What does it feel like to kill a man? I never have."

"If you ever need a powerful anesthetic, try killing. There's nothing like it."

"You don't like to talk about it."

"Very perceptive, comrade Boudia."

You wonder what you've missed, do you? A pervading sourness which wells up a few days, or a few weeks, after the act when you discover that the reality around you has not been altered one iota. Despite the ultimate moral commitment you have made by accepting to kill. Nor is there any entertainment in a man dying of a bullet hole. No bright orange and crimson flames, no thunderous roars. It doesn't even compare to chopping down a tree; there's no majesty in a body slumping to the ground. Stick to your oil tanks, Boudia. For pranks like that you can only be praised and giggled at. But gun down a man and, even if he was a torturer, you will suddenly discover that your comrades are loathing your presence and are searching for any implausible reason to banish you or drop a social hood over your unloved face.

"Where are we?"

"The town of Versailles."

"What's here?"

"Please, my dear Kamal. Don't remind me that Philistine and Palestinian were once the same word."

"Fuck off, Algerian scum."

"That brought you out of your shell! Now I know a useful secret, don't I?"

"It only works once."

He parks amidst a mass of tourists in front of the gate of the Versailles palace. I have been expecting to be taken to some safehouse in the woods, and here we are shuffling along graveled garden paths watched over by fake Greek gods and nymphs in their faggoty poses. I'm beginning to wonder if this Boudia isn't a bit of a loon. He has become the doddering art professor, his left hand thrust deep into his pants pocket, hiking up the jacket, and his right hand gesturing pedantically at the sculptures. He's even adopted a little academic stoop.

"It's a remarkable creation, no? Poseidon rising from the sea." He makes a magnificent sweep of his right hand over the circular pool before us. ". . . Notice how the fountain spray imparts a feeling of movement, as if the chariot has at this very moment burst from the waves, scattering the dolphins, infuriated, to all sides. Doesn't the water gloss make the horses look lathered? And see how the mist breaks up the light, imparting an almost supernatural luminescence to the event. . . . Or have you no taste for these pleasures, my friend?"

"I have a great hunger for them."

"Do you indulge it?"

"Not often."

"That is a mistake. Particularly with the uncertainties of our profession."

"Indulging those hungers too much can make you lose your taste for our profession altogether."

"Have you tried?"

"No. I dare not."

"How can you know if you haven't tried? It is just another empty theory to flagellate yourself with. This fountain, this sculpture of Poseidon, makes me wonder if our ancestors made a fatal mistake abandoning polytheistic religion. I have always felt that a family of vociferous squabblers is far less oppressive than a solemn patriarchy. Where there is one voice of authority only, you obey it in abjection or exile yourself into the terrifying vacuum of apostasy. Where there are many voices you have the freedom to play the diplomat with them. Like Ulysses. They were braver people then: they had enough faith in themselves to give themselves a choice. They didn't need commandments to whip themselves into line."

"They weren't living in the desert."

"Nor were the majority of people who swallowed the so-called desert deity. Monotheism wasn't born in the desert, it was born in the city. The Moslem's prophet was a merchant, the Christian's a carpenter, and the Hebrew's an adopted prince. City boys, all of them. Swallowed first by city people. In fact the bedouins themselves barely tolerated Islam for the longest time.

"No. The motivation for abandoning our lovely herd of deities is directly related to leaving the desert, the forest, the sea and finding ourselves in an increasingly anarchic world that made us as helpless as children. Leaving the world of Nature we left behind that simple relationship where the results of one's work could be seen and where the forces of Nature acted on one directly, without disguise. If the sea refused to yield up fish you complained to Poseidon. If it was generous, you thanked him. And if at the same time your wife was infertile, you could curse the god responsible for that, while thanking Poseidon. What do you do if there is only one God and he is giving with one hand and holding back with the other?

"But that, you see, is the condition of city life. We live in a vortex in which every force reaches us twisted and distorted, from a direction we can't see.

185

No fish in the market? Is it the sea, or the fishermen on strike, or the speculators, or the fish inspectors. And our own efforts, where do they go? All is confusion. So what is the natural response? Reimpose the Father. He must know what's happening even if you don't. Somebody better know."

"What I don't understand, Boudia, is where all this is leading. I mean, what are you trying to tell me?"

"Leading? I am leading nowhere. This is play: play of the mind. Just the same as play of the body."

"You should have told me this was recess. I'm not used to talk as play."

"Is anything play to you?"

"Sex, sports . . ."

"What would you do with your life if it were not for the injustice in the world?"

"If it were not for the injustice in the world I would be a completely different person."

"That is an evasion. Not only of my question but of yourself. I, for example, am an actor. I would be an actor in Paradise or in the Inferno. In this world I chose to act in the play of revolution because it is the stage that draws the most intensely involved audience. But it is too demanding a role to play all the time. The police and their spies are very critical of flaws in the performance. So I find relief in playing comedy on the smaller stage of the Théâtre de l'Ouest. You must know the story of Scaramouche."

"Of course."

"Ah, good. So it's not just sex and sports that are your pleasures. I was afraid you might be one of those madmen who lie on beds of nails and read *Materialism and Empirio-Criticism* before going to sleep. Do you know Rimbaud's *Season in Hell?*

"To whom shall I hire myself out?
What beast should I adore?

186

What holy image attack, what hearts break,
What lies uphold?
In what blood tread?

"Now tell me, Kamal, in all truth, how far are you
from this poet's state of mind?"

"Isn't that exactly what you're looking for, Boudia? Someone ready to tread up to the knees in
blood?"

"When we recruit young fellows to throw bombs
into royal carriages, yes, that is what we look for.
But to lead our struggle we need people who have
overcome this particular demon. We look for people
who elicit respect and love, not horror."

"Then I suppose you will just have to put me
aboard with your next planeload of JRA kamika-
zes."

"If that is how Kamal Jibral ends his days it will
have been his own choice, nothing we've imposed on
him. However, I haven't as poor hopes for you as you
pretend to have for yourself. Come, enough of Poseidon. Let us get a little further out of earshot and
closer to substance. Do you recall my little homily
about roots and trees? To find out what you may
bloom into, let us have a look at what you have
grown out of. Do you have any objection to returning
to the subject of Montevideo for a while?"

"No."

Boudia is leading us away from the pools toward a
grove of maples, along a path that the tourists seem
not to have discovered. White marble goddesses peek
at us from the deep shadows.

"Earlier you remarked with some bitterness that
something you called the 'Committee' wanted you
out. Were you implying that you were not trusted?"

"No. It was not lack of trust. By then I had more
than proven myself. But I had always been problem-
atic because of my peculiar identity."

"Then why were you accepted in the first place?"

"I performed a service of great value to them. I arranged a shipment of nearly a hundred weapons."

"How did you come to be in a position to do this?"

"I was asked by an old friend from elementary school, the son of a Uruguayan consul. He was up in the States trying to make contact with groups who could ship arms. He asked my advice, because he knew he could trust me absolutely. So I advised him not to contact groups, but to have his guns shipped by individuals who could operate on their own. He asked me if I would do it, so I said sure."

"With no hesitation?"

"No. There wasn't much risk for me."

"But an individual can't procure arms."

"In the U.S. one can. I drove out west with twenty thousand dollars in cash, went around to the gun shows and bought an AR-15 here, a Garand there—"

"Gun shows?"

"It's a great American tradition. Firearms hobbyists rent a hall every year in each city and sell or trade the toys they don't want anymore."

"No police permits, no registration?"

"The right to bear arms, comrade Boudia, is in the Constitution. There are a few cities where it can't be done. New York is one. But the rest of the country is wide open. I picked up over fifty M-16s from Vietnam veterans by simply following up personal introductions. Everything else I bought perfectly legally."

"That is truly incredible. One hears of this, but it is difficult to believe. And you can buy any weapon?"

"Only shotguns, rifles and pistols legally. But so much stuff is coming back from Vietnam in duffel bags that you can buy just about anything if you ask discreetly. The Cuban exiles are also a good source. They accumulated an incredible arsenal during the early '60s which they are selling off now that their bank accounts and hopes are drying up. Weapons

188

flow like rum from the Keys. It was from Florida that I arranged to have the guns shipped out. By yacht. Usually those people make runs down to Venezuela or Guayana. It took a little convincing to get them to go down as far as Punta del Este."

"This friend of yours, he is in the Tupamaros?"

"Was. He was assassinated by the Death Squad."

"But at the time you arrived in Montevideo, he enabled you to join."

"Yes. He vouched for me. Once the arms arrived."

"And you were trusted from that point as a full member?"

"Gradually. As I did more and more, I was trusted more and more."

"Did you smuggle any more weapons?"

"I haven't been back to the States since that first load. I had to fly down to arrange the unloading of the guns, because the skipper's condition was that he would not make a landfall with the weapons aboard. Nor would he turn them over to anyone but me. I rode in the launch out to the rendezvous."

"So for the two years and more that you were there, what did you do?"

"I started out as a courier, because I could cross borders very easily under my U.S. passport."

"You carried papers?"

"Occasionally. Often tape cassettes, with the voice recorded in such a way that it could not be heard on a normal machine. It was very clever. One of their engineers had worked it out. I could trot through customs with the music blaring from my portable recorder, like some jack-off tourist. The guards always liked to hear what I had, particularly coming into Argentina. After a few crossings they started calling me Rock 'n' Roll. 'Hey, Rock 'n' Roll, Qué tal?' Had they only known that between Jagger and Richards were detailed instructions for an attack on some prison or military outpost they might not have been so smiley."

"Those instructions would be coming from whom?"

"From some planning group. When the heat was on, action squads often holed up across the Plata, and popped across for the operation. Particularly heavily armed squads whose equipment was hard to conceal."

"These did not operate independently?"

"Oh no. Typically an operation would involve several squads. For example, one of the biggest operations was an attack on a provincial prison in which we succeeded in springing one hundred and ten comrades. That operation took a coordinated effort of two intelligence groups, half a dozen transportation groups, four attack groups, and I don't know how many escape groups to handle one hundred and ten plus all of the action people! There must have been two dozen escape groups involved."

"What is an escape group?"

"They consisted of field medical personnel and special people who were entrusted with locations of the safehouses for the escapees. Also the locations of sympathetic medical clinics and doctors who would take care of the seriously wounded. All these were known only by code name, except to the escape group specialist, who knew the actual location of his particular three or four."

"So these plans were very detailed."

"Detailed down to the minute, specifying rendezvous points, routes of approach and escape, deployment of forces during the attack. There was very little improvisation."

"Did the planners participate in the attacks?"

"Often not. Many of them were respectable citizens by day, whose professions gave them access to the targets: doctors, journalists, engineers."

"And these were the people you carried the tapes from."

"Not directly. Someone played the go-between."

"How did you carry maps and floor plans?"

"Before I came along they were using traditional secret inks and taking their chances. I invented a little trick which made the job a lot safer. I carried a camera with a roll half full of tourist snapshots. But the last frame to be exposed carried a deep underexposure of the documents to be transmitted. That frame was rewound so it was the one behind the lens of the camera as I went across the border. If I had ever been asked to surrender the film I would have simply snapped a brightly overexposed picture of the troublesome customs officer and handed over the camera with the evidence completely erased in the most innocent thirtieth of a second. When I did deliver the film, the technician at the receiving end knew to develop it for the very underexposed documents instead of the normally exposed tourist shots."

"Ah, Kamal. A stroke of genius. If we had only known you earlier. You see, some young friends of mine were arrested in the mountains a few months ago. They had a list of names they were unable to destroy in time. Now they are on trial and that list is in the hands of the DST. And probably in the hands of Mossad, which is worse."

"They were arrested for carrying a list?"

"For smuggling plastique. But it is the list which will do the harm. They should not have been carrying both. Your South Americans sound much better organized than we. Did you ever participate in any of these actions other than as a courier?"

"Not during the first year. But later on, yes. The first break was a kidnapping. They had grabbed an American oil executive, and the negotiations were at a standstill. They had put off deadlines a dozen times. I had to point out to them that they had lost the credibility of their threat with the company. It also turned out that the man had a heart ailment and was not expected to live very long anyway. They didn't want him to die on their hands, of course, so they asked me if I could act as a 'neutral' arbitrator.

"How did you represent yourself?"

"As a traveler who had stumbled on the situation and had a humanitarian interest in the outcome, but didn't want to become publicly involved for obvious reasons."

"The Americans accepted that?"

"Gratefully. It was all done over the phone. They thought they were dealing with a lily-white gringo. Their own racism kept them from suspecting my true allegiance."

"You didn't tell them your name."

"I was 'George' to both sides as far as the company was concerned."

"Did you meet with the hostage?"

"No. I didn't even know where he was kept, until afterward. This was regarded as another test of my loyalty."

"So you succeeded."

"Oh yes. I was able to convince the company that their man was getting enough medical care to keep him alive even if he had a heart attack, and so they could not hope to be let out of it that way. And then, with Esteban, I worked out a scenario by which they would be convinced that the 'duros,' the hardliners, were gradually getting the upper hand and would have their man shot, like Mitrione, if the company did not capitulate. They were talking to both Esteban and to me on different phone lines. Over the three days he became more and more hysterical while I became more and more hopeless, until they finally panicked and gave in."

"They paid the ransom."

"Yes. And got their man back in the best shape he'd been in for years. The wardens had put him on a healthy diet at the advice of the physician who diagnosed the heart condition, and made him exercise regularly to keep down his blood pressure. We received a card later from one of the company executives volunteering to be held hostage if we'd put him on the same regimen."

"What was the reaction to your success among your comrades?"

"Most were delighted. A few suspicious souls were made more suspicious by the fact that I had succeeded where they had failed."

"Were you involved in any more negotiations after that?"

"No. 'George' vanished from the face of the earth. I'm sure it was all taped. Even the gringo companies aren't dumb enough to fall for the same trick twice."

"So what were you assigned to after that?"

"Esteban and I started planning a huge operation to take place in June in Punta del Este. There was going to be a meeting of some committees of the Organization of American States. We had inside information that a good number of the Uruguayan honchos were going to be there, including possibly the secretary to the President, who, we had just found out from an informer, was giving direct orders to the Death Squad. So we were planning to grab the whole lot of them in a direct military operation."

"You say it as if it did not happen."

"We were on a reconnaissance to Punta when Esteban was assassinated. There was a spy inside the cell. He knew the entire plan and must have passed it on. We couldn't take any chances after Esteban was betrayed."

"Was this the spy you executed?"

"Yes."

"Did he confess?"

"No. But there were only three of us who knew where and when we were going to be in Punta on the reconnaissance: Esteban, me, and Alain Castellan. So it wasn't too difficult to figure out who was responsible."

"He must have known he would be exposed then. It was a sacrifice from the outset."

"I don't think so. I think he expected that they would kill us all, except him. But Esteban's body fell behind the door and blocked it just long enough. I had brought an AR which had been converted for full automatic fire, and when that started ripping through the door the goons changed their minds. If it had been police it would have been another story. But it was Death Squad, and they squealed off as soon as I started shooting back."

"Yes I know about those kinds. We had the French equivalent in Algeria: sober bureaucrats who put on hoods and threw bombs in crowded apartment buildings by night. Did you give this informer a trial?"

"Yes. We fled up to the forest above Punta. I took over command of the cell. We stopped for an hour and had a court-martial. He tried to pass the blame onto me. Nobody believed him. The vote was unanimous."

"But you shot him."

"No one else would. They were all in a panic without Esteban to make up their minds for them. He was too charismatic. They all fell apart when it turned out he was mortal."

"But not you?"

"Oh, I fell apart, but only inside. I'd never seen anybody killed before. It unleashed a steel man I always suspected was in here but never met before."

"That is very useful, to know that he is in there and can take over if he has to, Kamal. Very few people know that. The ones who do are special."

"Tell the Committee that."

"You are implying your relationship with the Tupamaros was changed after this incident."

"To put it mildly. The Committee disbanded our cell rather than have me as its commander. I realized then just how little I had been accepted on my own. I was tolerated only because of Esteban's prestige. He had one of those intellects that could obliterate any opposing argument, but so graciously and quietly that the defeat stung twice as badly, the victim having failed even to provoke irritation in Esteban's voice. I was the only person to whom he showed any deference at all, though I didn't understand why his manner to me was different than to any of his compatriots until Mariangela, his lover, explained it to me after he was killed.

"We were hiding together before we were dispersed to real safehouses. That was a very bleak time. The behavior of the Committee was disillusioning all of us. She said, 'Why do you suppose you can never be accepted among us, 'Nardo?' I went by that name always. 'You must have seen by now that to us the U.S. is the adult, Uruguay is the child-State which has whims but no will of its own. It is impossible to grow up in a child-State until the child-State grows up itself. That is what we see when we look to Cuba. One might say that Fidel is the only *man* in Latin America. The North Americans are also men in our eyes. Even Mitrione. Though no one but the women will admit it. So you, as a gringo, also somehow automatically stand above us. Even making you a messenger boy does not reduce you enough to make some of our own boys comfortable.'"

"Ah, women can be very hard."

"Sometimes they see what we don't want to see."

"So it was hopeless for you there?"

"Yes."

"Then who was this other man you executed?"

"He was one of the names on the informer Bardesio's list. The People's Tribunal issued a mandate to execute anyone on the list. I was getting very angry sitting in my cellar. Esteban had been a very important leader. Alain Castellan had been a mere worm of an agent. That was like exchanging a knight for a pawn. I decided if I were to do nothing else in Monte I would at least even it up a little."

"This was the man in the Ministry of the Interior?"

"Yes."

"You were not asked to do it by the Tribunal or the Committee?"

"That was not how executions were initiated. The Tribunal sentenced them to death after investigation. They issued a general mandate: 'All revolutionaries are urged to carry out these sentences whenever, wherever and however possible.' The names and addresses and functions were listed afterward."

"You operated alone?"

"Always for executions. That is one of Marighella's basic principles. There is never a need to compromise anyone else."

"How did you proceed?"

"I waited in an unlocked car near the house early in the morning. I assumed he would leave for the Ministry at a normal hour. He did. When he appeared, I got out, greeted him . . . I was already sighted in when he turned. I gave him a few seconds to think it over. And then I shot."

"With a pistol?"

"Yes."

"You carried it out in the open. Were there people around?"

"It was not a busy street, but we were not alone."

"You fired more than one shot?"

"No. One was all that was necessary. It was a .357."

"How close were you?"

"Fifteen, twenty feet. That's five or six meters."

"That was a very risky technique. You might have had to shoot more than once, and if there had been any detectives or disguised police around, it could have gone very badly for you. You could just as well have walked up and put the muzzle in his ear or to his chest. I am curious why you didn't.

"My way worked. He's dead. I'm alive. That's good enough for me."

"Believe me, Kamal, I am not trying to upbraid you on your technique. I know you have a reason for doing what you do the way you do it. But I suspect there was a reason beyond the mere execution of the man for the particular theatrical style. So what was it you were trying to achieve?"

"Since it has such significance to you, comrade Boudia, perhaps you should first tell me why I should dig around in my soul for the answer to that question."

"As I have said: to determine what kind of tree you may grow into from these roots."

"You won't stop until you get it down in black and white, species and genus—"

"Did not the grand Colonel Lawrence write about us: 'Semites have no halftones in their register of vision. They are at ease only in extremes.' Perhaps I am ill at ease."

But mock himself as he might, this Boudia was most alert to halftones and nuances. We talked. He questioned, led forward and backward, spiraled inward onto minutiae, outward onto political theory.

"You are not a Communist, Kamal, I conclude."

"You need a country to have an economic system."

"But one needs an analysis to guide one's actions."

"I'll leave that to those who have studied the distinctions."

"You sound like you belong with Fatah."

"I belong with whomever is the most active. Isn't that you, Boudia?"

"You will make a fine ambassador someday. We will make you ambassador to the United States. I think very soon you will start to miss it. If not already. Though I know you would never admit it."

We must have circled the gardens a few dozen times when he finally brought the interview to a close.

"Well, I think you've had enough, eh? For today at least. Let us go dine and have a relaxing evening. This is grueling work for both of us. I can see it in your face. It gets paler every hour."

"Just hunger, Mohammed."

"No need to deny the truth, Kamal. There are many disturbing memories inside you which would prefer to lie forgotten. It reassures me to know that you are not unmoved by killing, by having to kill. But enough of this. A good dinner. You are my guest."

He gently prodded my shoulder to turn me back toward the palace, but it was such a tentative gesture, almost shy, that I gleaned a hint of what underlay the actor's stage manners. I wondered why he kept returning to the execution. It was a voyeur's curiosity of something beyond his limits; that and something else. He was too certain of his right to probe around in my secrets. Did he have to know for some particular reason why and how I killed and what happened to me inside afterward? If so, it could only be because he had me in mind for some particular armed action. Suddenly the evening was looking much more gracious, the day's discomforts whisked into the elms by a cool sunset breeze.

I must have sped ahead without realizing, for Boudia's laugh rang from behind me. "Eh, I didn't see her. Which one are you chasing?"

We filed under the gold-crested gate with the last

of the tourists. The green Renault stood nearly alone in the parking lot. Boudia unlocked the passenger door, then circled to the driver's side. As always, I waited before climbing into a stranger's car until the driver had taken his seat. Another instinctive precaution. Boudia noticed, and also paused. Then resting his elbows on the roof, he stared at me narrowly. I could almost hear the workings behind the pale forehead. I waited, meeting his gaze without difficulty. We were at some crucial point in the calculations. The sum of what I had presented had been totaled and, as always, found to be a little short of what he saw and sensed before him.

Now he had to fall back on his intuition to fill the discrepancy. Before I left for Israel Boudia had said he didn't believe in intuition. Rather wished he didn't have to believe in it from time to time. I realized that if I had not paused before opening the car door this moment would simply have been put off to another day. But I had accidentally forced him to the decision of whether or not to trust me right there outside of the Versailles palace. By logic or instinct he knew that the precautions he had taken were very weak.

He must have known that it was I who accosted Saleh—he had undoubtedly been told over the phone—and therefore there could be no way of being sure that I had not dragged a tail with me all the way to where he picked us up by the river. The tail would have gotten a description of the Renault and the direction in which it was heading; it would have been trivial to put a car behind us anywhere along the route. And now the Renault had been sitting untended for several hours. Was this the reason, Boudia was now asking himself, the young man was hesitating to open the car door? Or was he hesitating because the owner hadn't made even a rudimentary inspection of the tailpipe, wheels or hood.

I decided to give Boudia the answer to his question. Sucking in a nerve-steadying breath of the cool evening air, I yanked open the door and slid into the passenger's seat. He immediately took his seat and started the engine without a blink. As we rolled out of the parking lot he was nodding his head, with a small smile lifting the corners of his mustache. He muttered, "Eh, I have a better idea."

Our drive took us along back roads through little towns just beyond the new suburbs. When we came to one called Petit-Clamart Boudia commented, "Did you know my friend De Gaulle was almost assassinated here? It missed by inches, just like all the other attempts. I have a theory that it was not for lack of marksmanship that he was never hit. Neither was Hitler, Nasser or Hussein. While your Kennedys, Martin Luther King and Patrice Lumumba fell like cut flowers. Why the difference? Because the former all inspired fear in addition to whatever else they inspired. The assassin's hand was trembling before he ever picked up the weapon. He feared the target was immortal, though that immortality existed only in the mind of the assassin. That is what makes the Israelis so dangerous: Jews have a very strong sense of mortality."

"So do Palestinians."

"And you are dangerous. But many Moslems don't have that sense. Myself for example.

"Know that the present life is but
a sport and a diversion, an adornment
and a cause for boasting among you.
And a rivalry in wealth and children.
It is a rain whose vegetation pleases
the unbelievers, then it withers
and thou seest it turning yellow
then it becomes broken orts.

200

"That, if you were wondering, is the reason I don't look for booby traps under my car. You don't know the Koran, do you? Ah, but here we are."

He turned into a lane beside a modern apartment building that looked like a Swiss cheese with rectangular holes. Each apartment appeared to have a balcony. Boudia scanned these and snapped his fingers.

"I thought we were going to a restaurant, Mohammed."

"Dinners are served other places as well." He hurried inside and raced up the stairs. On the top landing he paused with his knuckles a centimeter from the door and whispered, "Our guidance for this evening also comes from the Koran. 'Your women are a tillage for you, So come unto your tillage as you wish.' But don't quote me tonight, eh?" He rapped loudly. A light appeared at the inspection hole, then the door swished open.

"Mohammed, c'est vraiment bête, hein? Il y a six mois que . . ." She was very dark-skinned, heavy-featured but very lively around the eyes, full-figured and so short that Boudia had to stoop to kiss her in spite of her platforms. Then he pushed her back into the apartment with one palm against her breast and with the other dragged me in after him.

"But where is Nadia?"

"You don't love me anymore, Momo?"

"Ah Sophie, I could love no one else. But my friend Kamal here, I told him about Nadia. What a disappointment!"

"Sois sage, Momo. She will be back. She has gone to buy dinner. Now I see I will have to send her out again."

Embarrassed, I volunteered to go out and pick up some extra food. They both stared at me in disbelief.

"Mais il est vraiment drôle," Sophie concluded.

"No. He's not strange. But he's had the misfortune to be raised in the United States. That is all."

201

We left with the women at eight the next morning. Sophie's 2CV was parked adjacent to Boudia's Renault. He kissed her and ran around to help Nadia into the other side. This chivalry prompted more laughter. We followed them to the autoroute, where we parted company with much waving.

"Nadia's not bad, eh?"

"You've tried her out? . . . Mo-mo?"

"Oh yes, of course. Both of them. In all combinations. I prefer Sophie only because of her name. Sophi-a. It sounds so good drawn out, don't you think? Nadia's much prettier, but she hasn't got so much to hold on to."

"Come on, Boudia, you can tell me now. Who are they?"

"What do you mean, Who are they? They are two beautiful women. But perhaps you don't find them so." Boudia was grinning through his beard.

"I've seen prettier. My friend Momo, I wasn't born yesterday."

"That is a nice expression. I have never heard it before. But what are you referring to?"

"Mohammed, if you're not running those two I'll retire right now and become a postman."

"That is the trouble with you Americans: everything is business. Even if it is, sometimes you have to pretend it isn't."

"I've pretended for an entire night. Now, would you mind if I brought up a subject of some importance to me?"

"What would that be, my friend?"

"When do I start to work?"

"Soon."

"How soon? And doing what?"

"There is a big operation coming up. Very big. I have in mind that you might very well lead the operation in the field."

"Fine. What is the operation?"

"I can't reveal it to you just yet. Certain approvals have to be obtained first. But I can assure you it will call on some of your special talents. There will be a phase requiring very stern but patient negotiation."

"And?"

"And this negotiation will have to be backed up by a willingness to kill."

"Hostages?"

"Or anyone who might try to liberate them before the demands are met. A man who has already killed has a certain air which no virgin can simulate. The negotiators on the other side, and the psychologists they always bring in, can discern that. It gives us a great advantage."

"Will this be a public operation?"

"Do you mean, will your face be shown to the world? Very much so."

"Then I will have to go underground again afterward."

"Not necessarily. We can have your face changed."

"I've gotten sort of used to this face."

"Or you may be invited to Beirut or Aden to join the command. If this operation succeeds it will make our reputations forever. This will put Munich in the shadow. And without spilling blood, hopefully."

"How certain is this operation to take place?"

"There are major forces committed to seeing it happen. Whether or not we are the expediters, that is the question now."

"How major are these forces?"

"Major. There are none bigger."

"The Russians?"

Boudia shrugged.

"Is that hearsay or fact?"

"Fact. Firsthand knowledge."

"When is this operation to happen?

"By the end of the summer."

"And who is coordinating it?"

"I am."

"What am I to do between now and then?"

"Remember, Kamal, that this operation is not ours yet. Once it becomes ours it will be very important that the operatives do not draw any attention to themselves until the moment of action. So, in short, you will do nothing but live a very normal life. You are used to waiting. That is one of the abilities I have been looking for. But this is all premature. It may be another month before I can say, Yes, this is going to happen. And even then, who knows, you may decide you don't like the operation once you have heard the plan."

More waiting. But at least now not in a vacuum. I have been waiting for some kind of swearing-in ceremony, a committee sitting in judgment. Perhaps that is yet to come. But thinking about it, that was not how it happened in Montevideo either. In fact, it was very much like this: six weeks of milling around in a strange, hostile city, being run through a maze of blind rendezvous at non-existent or vacant addresses. Sitting for the fifth or seventh time like some jilted teenager on that same designated bench on the Rambla. By then my rage had gathered to such a dark anvil-headed cloud, rolling and thundering inside my skull with such a din, that I was quite ready to let the lightning strike anywhere, at comrade or enemy without caring for the difference.

It was a windy afternoon, the Plata blown into a frantic chop that had chased the small boats back to their moorings. It was not a day for strolling or waiting, but a young couple kept strolling by, chirping overloudly to each other in a poor charade of affection. Finally I bolted off the bench to confront them. At my abrupt motion they instantly separated in a well-rehearsed choreography and plunged their hands into the deep pockets of the overcoats they were both wearing to grasp weapons of some kind. This response was oddly reassuring. I realized I was not as isolated as I thought. I was being watched, but also being watched over.

I sat down again. They resumed their strolling embrace and hurried out of sight. The next day at the same time I returned to the bench as I had been instructed to do several weeks before. A young woman with the hungry air of a recent divorcée or widow was sitting there. She spoke English and struck up a conversation. An hour later we went back to her apartment by a circuitous route involving two bus rides. Esteban arrived an hour later.

Two nights after that, some forty miles off the coast, Esteban and I stood soaked and shivering on the bridge of a Chris-Craft that had been left unlocked for us to "steal" from its mooring in the bay. Both of us had become seasick from scouring the virtually invisible horizon for running lights. But through the superficial nausea I recognized the need that had carried me through all those desolate weeks of waiting. It was a hunger for this profound flush of companionship that was warming us on the spray-whipped bridge of the Chris-Craft: a dream made real at last. What more could I ask of life?

Except that it might happen like that again. With Mohammed Boudia there is a chance. Whatever this operation of his entails, there will be that moment of success and that same flush of companionship when my plane lands at whichever Arab capital has been chosen as the culmination. Yes, that will be ten times the satisfaction of the moment when we finally spotted the starboard light of my yacht through the haze, and signaled and received the pass-signal flashes back. Ten times that joy at least. . . .

"Comrade Boudia, I have a feeling that I will find your operation perfectly to my taste."

He glances over at me with a grin. "Comrade Jibral, I dare say you will. Inshallah."

Justina

HE DISAPPEARS all day. Then all night. He's dead. I lie awake with the image of him gliding down the stairs, eyes glittering, showing not a tremor of fear for what he was going to meet.

As he left I had braced myself for the sound of gunshots, the thud of a body falling, fleeing footsteps, certain that the man in the door was an assassin sent by Dieter. But when there were no shots, no sirens, no ambulance, and the neighbor tenants continued to trudge the steps as usual, I found myself nursing what could only be called disappointment.

What? Did you want more blood, little bitch? Does murder thrill you?

No, no. It is only that I am sickened and want out of all this. That taped-up pistol, his lethal stealth, those last words as he left . . . How can I blind myself to it any longer? I am living with a killer.

And knowing this blows away the entire pretense of my so-called political existence. Not just mine, but Hervé's, Raymond's, all the spring rioters'. Kamal takes our play-acted game to its real conclusion. We will all end up with his bullets in our hearts. And until then we can live writhing with the nausea and horror, too terrified to escape into sleep, longing to be let out of our wide-awake nightmare by a mysterious dark agent in the opposite doorway.

And then suddenly Kamal is back again, smiling and as giddy as a teenager in love. What right does he have? With Hervé's corpse hanging over him. Or perhaps it doesn't hang over him, only over me. He still thinks Hervé was a spy and that makes it all right to have murdered him.

"Out screwing your blonde again?"

He looks startled.

"I found some long straight blond hairs snagged on your jacket button, Kamal. Any explanation?"

"I didn't know you were one of those women, Justina."

"What the hell are you acting so smug about?"

"Smug? I just feel good. You ought to try it."

"Feel good? Why? Did you kill the hood out there in the doorway?"

"Ease off, Cubana."

"Or was he your boss? The one who ordered you to murder Hervé. Or did he just order you to go to Israel? And you ordered yourself to kill Hervé."

Kamal rises slowly, like that morning with Dieter, his face as hard and jagged as a piece of broken steel.

"Me you can probably kill with one hand, my love."

But he only glares for a moment, then turns his back. The motion is almost creaky. He stands with his hands against the window sashes. There is a twitch in his lower back I've never seen before. Oh, Kamal, these somber theatrics don't move me. I'm packing, can't you hear. This is no bluff. If you are going to kill me you'd better turn around soon and do it. How long does it take to stuff a suitcase? I won't even close the door behind me, so you can hear my footsteps all the way down to the street and know that this is no bluff, sweetie. You've dragged me over the brink into your own special species of madness.

"Raymond, this is really important."

"Did you have to telephone? Couldn't you have waited for the monthly?"

"Don't sound so irritated. I haven't the patience. I'm leaving France. If you want the information that is making me leave, be on our soccer field in one hour. After that, up yours."

"You are talking on a telephone, Justina."

"Yes, on a telephone, to Raymond Whoever of the noble DST, who spies on wimpy Trotskyites and thinks he's a hero. One hour, hero. And I'm sorry it is too early for the soccer game."

I am quivering with excitement and fury all the way to Boulogne. No one but strolling mothers and their babies here now. Very pastoral. Blissfully unaware of the grown-up brats killing each other with real guns for imagined wrongs.

"Finally, Raymond. You took your damned time."

His face is gray. There will be no wry preachings today. He's afraid of me, standing off at a distance hunched under his raincoat. "What has bitten you, Justina?"

"Do you want it straight? Or with the usual meanderings? No. Straight this time. My lover Kamal murdered my ex-lover Hervé. Nice twist, eh?"

"I suppose he simply told you this."

"Not only did he tell me, he still has the gun. It is the pistol that was stolen during the demonstration. You see, he thought Hervé was the spy who betrayed him to the Israelis. I don't care to be around when he learns the truth. I don't care to be around even if he doesn't. So go ahead, Raymond, he's all yours. It will be a great coup. The Police Judiciaire obviously haven't a clue. Arrest him and your career will be made."

"Aren't you a vindictive little one."

"You should be thanking me. Who's brought you a better morsel of espionage lately?"

"It's interesting."

"Interesting, he says."

"Interesting, that is all it is. Now go on home. Don't worry, there will be no arrests."

"Why not? Don't you believe me?"

"Justina, you know very well that our business is

208

the security of the State. The demise of an Algerian
Jew is not a threat to the security of the State. It is a
criminal matter only, and if the Police Judiciaire
cannot solve it, too bad. I am not going to waste the
American just because you have a lover's grudge
against him. Damn it, Justina, we are in a serious
business."

"I can't believe what you're telling me, Raymond."

"I've told you too much already. Now go home."

"Yes you've told me too much. More than any person with a shred of morality could bear to hear.
Adieu, Raymond. Fuck you and France both."

And borne on this incredible, almost orgasmic
flood of rage, I stride away with the seed of my next
move already bursting inside my brain. It has been
there for days. Yes, since I first suspected who was
responsible for Hervé's death: I glimpsed the seed as
it was planted. Then it hid from thought, awaiting
certainty. But meanwhile it has been sending roots
down to levels of primeval memory, drilling through
historical strata implanted by my ancient ancestors.
And now the sprout surfacing sucks up from the
deepest plunging root a memory of medieval Paris,
of a Jew sprawled in a muddy street of the ancient
city, soaking in his own blood, his head beaten in
with a heavy wooden cross. The Jew is Hervé's
ancestor. The massive cross is an ancestor of the little gold one I used to wear between my breasts, before . . .

Don't stop now. Don't wait for the flood to subside.
You have something to do which can only be done on
the high tide of fury. Reason will only betray you if
you hold back. Reason will find plausible excuses to
be prudent, to let things ride, to fall back into the
mire of your pathetic cowardly existence.

Yes, Justina—the Métro decelerates on its slick
wheels—this is your station: Wagram. Let the flood

bear you onto the platform, let it bear you up the stairs. Yes, now across the avenue, feel the fear starting up from your coccyx, keep moving on the flood, yes, toward the building number 143 under the blue-striped flag with its six-pointed star, past the guards looking at you so strangely keep moving, up the stairs, the heavy doors, to whom, to whom? They see something is wrong, here is a military man, Can I help you please, miss? Yes, in his ear, Justina, and then there will be no going back: the fear will be defeated forever.

"Yes, please, I have some very, very important information for"—don't break down now, Justina—"for your Mossad officer. Oh God! Quickly. So important. Life and death, an Arab terrorist, a man named Kamal Jibral, Oh please . . ."

part three

Kamal

MY NEIGHBORS SMILE at me on the stairs now. I have become respectable in the last month. I live alone, I have a schedule. The French are a tolerant people; they ask nothing more. The concierge assures me the old tenants have begun to speak well of me. She would not be surprised if I were invited to dinner by one of them before the year is out. It was the "foreign girl" who provoked that terrible fight, they were all certain. Things have been very peaceful since she left; doesn't that prove it? The American boy has settled down to his studies and his athletics—he is so fit and healthy-looking—and he holds down a regular job. Five evenings a week, anyone passing in the Rue Descartes can see him loading long steel skewers with luscious cubes of lamb and beef, fat white mushroom caps, bleeding tomato slices, verdant bell peppers. And he is so cute; he always winks at the people who stop to gawk and lick their lips, and gives the skewers a turn on the grill so the fat dribbles down and ignites in great leaping yellow flames.

But it is his dedication to athletics that truly shows his character. Not like these limp Parisian students with their pallid skin and curved backs. The American boy is like we used to be before the war. Do you know he rides the Métro out to the Bois de Vincennes every morning and runs at least ten kilometers, or rents a shell and whips it around the artificial lake there at least a dozen laps? Why don't our sons do that anymore? France is going to the dogs. There are too many foreigners like that dark girl, and they all stir up trouble. Just look how he has improved since she ran out on him. He may have been sad for a while, the poor boy, but it has been for the best, as anyone can see. Not that he lives the life of a monk, you understand; such would be quite unnatural for a healthy young man. That very well groomed young French woman who visits his room occasionally, perhaps you have noticed? Yes, she might be four or five years older than he, but that is no scandal. At one glance you can see that she is from a respectable family, and close to Paris, to judge from her pronunciation. She does not distract him from his serious pursuits. And she does not drag other foreigners up to visit, and even to stay overnight, the way the *other* one did. Mon Dieu, we used to worry that the police would come crashing in at any hour. But no longer. He is really a nice boy. And speaks French so well, for an American.

So I've done quite well for myself, haven't I, Mohammed? You would probably be contented to hear that Justina removed herself from the scene, very likely from Paris itself—no one has seen her for a month now—and so I am all but cut adrift of visible political circles. Just as you advised. And now I simply wait, hypnotized by the repetitions of the daily pattern: in bed by two, up by nine, to the park by eleven, back by three, showered, napped and changed and loping to my shish kebabs by five-thirty. And between these marks on the clock I study in my room. The books piling in and out keep up appearances of sobriety. It's a sober subject, too: French foreign policy since the war. After all, don't I need a credible reason for hanging out here? And something to talk about with my lovely blond divorcée a few times a week? Mireille believes in France religiously. That touches me. I'm getting tired of dialectical grumblers. Is this a bad sign, Mohammed?

"Ya, Kamal!" A strong hand grabs me by the shoulder and spins me around as I absent-mindedly jog toward Descartes to play chef. I find myself blinking as stupidly as a grazing cow at Saleh's tough visage. I did not even notice him. The contempt I see in his eyes is well deserved. "What is with you?"

"What is with me? The idiocy of urban life. That's all."

He doesn't recognize the allusion to Karl and thinks I'm insulting him in some mysterious American way. The sneer elongates into truculence. "Come with me now. He wants to see you."

This is what the astronaut must feel stepping out of his cozy capsule into space. Suddenly nothing under the feet, yet not falling.

"Now?"

"Yes. I will drive."

I hear all sorts of pathetic protests vying for my tongue: I can't, I'm expected at work. Tomorrow. I'm not ready. You can't just show up like Mercury with a summons from Jove.

But the old Kamal who has been waiting mutely for this very moment throttles the anxious cook, and replies, "Lead on, Saleh," as calm as a glacier. If only on the exterior.

A few times in life one arrives at a moment when the efforts of years focus like the sun through a lens on a single decisive point. Success or failure, advance or stagnation, peace or despair, all hang on the fateful moment. With the bright burst of ignition, all proceeds happily. But should any mischance move the focus even slightly off the mark, then all is wasted for a little smoke and nothing more. I can only pretend to confront this rendezvous coolly.

According to Saleh, Boudia and I are to meet by accident over the same album of Carlos Santana in a record shop on the ground floor of a gaudy shopping complex south of the city.

"Excuse me, I have been trying to find that particular Santana," I whine.

"What a shame, there is only one. . . . Why, what a surprise, it is you, my friend."

"Yes, I just happened to be feeling homesick. You know there is nothing like familiar music to bring one's country back."

"In that case, I will have to let you keep this copy. To me it is just another recording. But at least I can take the opportunity it has offered to invite you to an early dinner. There is a very mediocre restaurant upstairs, if you have the time."

"For you I will make the time. It will take only one phone call, to tell my employer that I am indisposed."

"This is quite something." Boudia gestures around him once we are in the main corridor of the complex. It rises three tiers above us, shops on every level on either side along balcony walkways running the entire quarter-mile length of the building. A spiky stainless steel sculpture jumps two and a half stories out of an impotent fountain in the middle of all this. A new Maserati-Citroen sits on a velvet platform in front of it, reciting its performance statistics over and over to nobody. Boudia's eyes are wide like a child's.

"Have you noticed the cathedralesque echo, the almost reverent silence? This is the Chartres of modern France. It is larger than Chartres, by the way, and the interior is higher. Also you must have noticed the double cruciform floor plan; in homage to

De Gaulle, no doubt. And of course along the nave in place of confessionals these wonderful shops where you can buy peace of mind and have something to show for it afterward. How can Catholicism compete? Look at the choice around us. It is a wonder they don't have to clear away corpses of the devout exhausted to death by the St. Vitus's dance of deciding where to spend their money. Driving off the Devil of Social Unrest, these poor middle classes can never rest. As soon as they've driven off the Devil for a while, they find themselves stalked by the Minotaur of Debt. Isn't it sad?"

Why is he going on like this? He is not blind. He must see me chafing. I have come to hear a decision which will shape my entire life. Yet he continues to prate away.

". . . But don't think you can point the finger at Capitalism, my friend. Oh no. They are building these cathedrals of Social Peace in Moscow, too. And how long before they start rising around Peking? And perhaps, but only if you and I are successful, there may be giant toy stores like this rising out of the Gaza desert, and all of the faces of the happy shoppers will look like yours and mine. Allah willing, they may even call one of those temples Centre Jibral. Or at least plant our graves side by side at the entrance to the parking lot. Eh, what do you think, Kamal? Is it so written?"

He extends me his hand as a broad smile spreads his beard.

"Muktub, Mohammed, you crazy mother. Muktub!"

So this is how one is sworn into the Revolution.

Boudia continues to prattle through a quick dinner. I hardly hear him, his voice seems to roll in from the distance, fade in and out, like a river heard through woods. Afterward he drives us in the green

217

Renault in a wide circle eastward around Paris. There are still stretches of farm land out here, and little stone villages through which the road suddenly narrows to two cart widths. And then just as suddenly we will whip past a meadow of raw dirt out of which four enormous white apartment buildings have sprouted, seemingly having drained the life out of the surrounding half kilometer to nourish their own cancerous growth. There is no coherence to the landscape when you are cutting across the radial grain as we are.

Here we wind through a sixteenth-century farming village, and are held up waiting for a three-wheeled produce truck to maneuver a right turn off the main road onto a side alley. Next the road sweeps past a new industrial park tenanted by Hewlett-Packard and Honeywell Bull. And now we have entered a lush suburban township of turn-of-the-century villas behind high gates and stone fences. The sorts of places Buñuel would take us to mock the dirty passions of the bourgeoisie.

And to my surprise it is before one of these villa gates that Boudia stops the Renault, jumps out and unlocks a giant padlock. The iron grill swings open remarkably smoothly. It looks like it has not been touched since the fall of the First Republic. Nor do the grounds inside. They have been left to go completely feral. The grasses and weeds are waist-high on both sides of the driveway. The fruit trees, which are in bloom, have grown so high and ragged that they form a canopy over the gravel path we are following. Their branches scrape the car's roof every so often. Occasional dirt paths penetrate the undergrowth. From these, several dogs lope out to investigate our arrival, silently, suspiciously, though they seem to recognize the smell of the car. The dogs look as wild as the trees. Shit and rotting fruit perfume the evening air. Under the trees it is difficult to see that it is still quite light out. The path seems to wind on for a mile. But of course this is only because we are inching along.

Finally the mansion of this decayed estate appears before us in a clearing: a blocky two-story stone farmhouse with a very steeply pitched pyramidal roof rising above four chimneys on the corners of the building. The walls are smothered by moss and climbing vines. All the upper-story windows are shuttered. The unshuttered lower-story windows are just out of reach from the ground. They have not been washed since the last century. There are lights on behind the windows to the right of the entrance.

The dogs who have followed us to this clearing now sniff at our heels as we pick our way up the paving-stone path to the front door, and then they squat behind us to make sure the way out is more challenging than the way in. One terrier who is too anxious to learn my scent catches his nose on the edge of my heel. His yelp flushes a hundred birds from nearby branches, which wheel and screech and alarm a thousand more throughout the jungle, before they all settle back to pecking the cherries and plums and whatever else is hidden in the foliage.

The front door is not locked. Our footsteps echo on the bare wood floor of the corridor. Arabic conversation drifts from the first lighted room. Two men, one quite small, in tennis clothes and sneakers, and the other bearded and in fatigues, like a reduced Fidel Castro, are standing face to face and gesturing vehemently at one another. Nearby a woman is sitting in a threadbare stuffed armchair. She is listening but not watching. Her eyes are on an old painting. Her eyes and skin are dark, but her hair is very blond. Her legs and waist seem very trim for her age, which must be close to fifty. She is dressed like a fashionable Parisienne. She could be the wife of the tennis player.

Our entrance interrupts the argument. The two men approach and shake hands with Boudia, greeting him in Arabic. Boudia appears to shift the subject to me, for suddenly the tennis player is looking me up and down.

The Fidel type extends a muscular hand and introduces himself in English. "I am Issa. You are Kamal Jibral? We were beginning to wonder if you really existed, or if Momo had just made you up."

A contest of grips. This Issa nods with appreciation when he finds his big mitt thwarted. Yes, I exist.

But the tennis player does not offer to shake my hand. Instead he addresses Issa and Boudia in English. "Let us get down to business. I am expected at ten at an official function. I don't care to arrive dressed like this."

Short obligated chuckles from Boudia and Issa. The woman continues to more or less ignore the proceedings.

TENNIS: "Where do we stand, Mohammed?"

BOUDIA: "To confess a problem, sir, I think we will have to content ourselves with the train option. According to Kotov, the Israelis picked up some of the planning documents of the original operation during the raid on Nahar el Bard. And with these Golda was able to pressure Kreisky into stationing a heavy guard around Schonau."

TENNIS: "How heavy?"

BOUDIA: "According to Kotov, up to a hundred men."

TENNIS: "Impossible. That's half the Vienna constabulary. Don't believe it. Kotov is trying to dissuade you from our plan so you will need him."

BOUDIA: "Our people in Austria confirm that the guard is very heavy. The Austrians are on the alert. You heard that they picked up a Fatah reconnaissance a few months ago."

TENNIS: "That was the Italians. The Austrians knew about it, but have been avoiding any confrontation. That is why we can consider this operation at all."

BOUDIA: "Yet they have mounted a guard around the transit facility. Even if it is a quarter of what Kotov said—say, twenty-five men. Plus whatever the Israelis have inside, now that they are expecting trouble. Issa, how many would you say we would need to mount a direct attack and still have the numbers left to hold the hostages inside?"

ISSA: "I would say even two to one in our favor would be very risky against an emplaced defense. And that is assuming we were using battle-trained men. I don't know where we could find even fifty."

TENNIS: "There are always Abu Ahmet's boys."

ISSA: "He wouldn't let go of ten of them, not to speak of fifty."

TENNIS: "He could be persuaded."

ISSA: "Not even by you. He is no longer the same man as a year ago. But that is irrelevant, because his fighters are trained for the mountains. They would be picked up or picked off in five minutes inside Europe. And how would you smuggle them in? As a boys' school? As a soccer team?"

TENNIS: "And there is no other option but the Eastern conduit?"

BOUDIA: "Not without a major gun battle."

The woman has finally taken an interest in the debate. She has been nodding imperceptibly at Boudia's arguments.

WOMAN: "And please keep in mind that another moral fiasco like Munich or Lod sets us back further than any success advances us. In Munich there were no Germans killed, at least."

ISSA: "Wrong. There were at least two. And here there might be some Austrians killed. That isn't the problem. The problem is failing to take the tar-

221

get, and as a result having nothing to bargain with. If all twenty-five Austrians were killed we would capture the target and then there would be no problem."

BOUDIA: "Twenty-five is our invented number. KGB says one hundred. We have no information to the contrary."

TENNIS: "It appears that twenty-five and fifty or a hundred is the same to us. We cannot mount a sufficient force against it without drawing on a national army, and that is not a diplomatic possibility. Kreisky will bow before terrorism, not invasion. So we must stick to terroristic means. But is there no way we could have our men board the train carrying the emigrés inside Austria?"

BOUDIA: "No. The Austrians and the Israelis both put aboard a security force as soon as the train stops inside Austria. So we would be left with a smaller version of the castle. We would need at least a dozen men, heavily armed."

TENNIS: "A dozen sounds like a reasonable number."

BOUDIA: "Too easy to pick up at the point they concentrate. And even if the Austrians declined the fight, the Israelis would probably open fire and force them into it. And there is one other problem. The emigrés come into Austria over two routes, one via Hohenau, one via Marchegg. We need the KGB to tell us which one, and on which particular train, and in which particular car and cabin the Jews are. So we are dependent on the Russians in any event."

TENNIS: "Using their information and using their conduit are two different matters, Mohammed. You will be running up quite a bill depending on both."

ISSA: "What about taking hostages somewhere else in Austria? Why do the hostages have to be Russian Jews? Kreisky will be more likely to give in if the lives in danger are Austrian."

TENNIS: "On the contrary. Kreisky's constituency, our reports indicate, will force him to take the hard line if the hostages are Austrian. It must appear as entirely an external affair so Kreisky can shrug his shoulders and say 'It is not our business.' Already the Austrian farmer has little sympathy with the Israelis and the Russians using Austria as a refugee camp. Don't forget, all we want to do is give him the excuse to say to Golda, 'Enough of this. Take your Jews somewhere else.' Fortunately for us, Kreisky is anxious to have the Austrians forget about the fact that he is a Jew himself."

WOMAN: "Then this is all the more reason to keep the operation as bloodless as possible. If you raise the specter of the Nazis in Austria, the people who will have to pay for it will be the Palestinian community. You people did not have to live with the consequences of Munich. But we did, and we do. It is not pleasant to be questioned every other week by the security police. It is not pleasant to be regarded as a bloodthirsty maniac by your neighbors and associates at work. The established community pays for these bloodbaths of yours. Try to remember that when you make your plans."

ISSA: "Do you expect us to stop the fight for the homeland just so that a few doctors won't lose patients?"

WOMAN: "I expect you to weigh what you may gain against what your brothers may lose."

ISSA: "Bourgeois doctors and lawyers are not my brothers if they put their own interests above the interests of the struggle."

WOMAN: "I am not speaking of lawyers. I am speaking of fathers who work in factories around Vienna and Munich and who depend on the goodwill of the police to keep their work permits. Do you have any idea how many Palestinian families were forced back onto the UNRWA rolls after Munich?"

ISSA: "I am perfectly aware. But this is not something we have to debate every time. It is our principle that the struggle takes precedence."

BOUDIA: "Particularly in this case we do not have to debate it. We have no choice but to put our men aboard the train inside Czechoslovakia. The Jews will be taken hostage before any sympathetic security men come aboard in Austria. As a consequence the operation will be bloodless. Kamal here will lead the operation in the field. You all know his experience and qualifications. I feel perfectly confident that he will keep the situation from getting out of hand. He has negotiated in far more brutal circumstances than this will be. And neither he nor Kreisky will repeat the mistakes of Munich."

TENNIS: "Mr. Jibral, we have been assured you have unusually steady nerves and implacable patience. Mr. Boudia has carried out some very difficult and important operations for us in the past. I respect his judgment implicitly. It will now be up to you to make certain that my faith in Mr. Boudia is justified. That is a great responsibility, not just toward your people, but to him and to me. I assume you recognize that."

KAMAL: "Yes sir. And a great responsibility to myself as well."

TENNIS: "You do realize, of course, that if things go wrong your responsibility may demand that you become a martyr for the struggle."

KAMAL: "That is always assumed."

TENNIS: "And under certain circumstances your responsibility may call on you to terminate the lives of innocent, or I should say unarmed, individuals."

KAMAL: "I am not unexperienced, sir."

TENNIS: "So I am informed. Very well, Mohammed. Go ahead with the Czechoslovakian boarding. I will have a passport issued for Mr. Jibral under another name, and arrange the Czech visa. You will send me some photographs of him, as usual. The other man will be meeting him inside Czechoslovakia as I understand it?"

BOUDIA: "Yes. And we can count on you to make the weapons available to him at your consulate in Prague?"

TENNIS: "As we discussed. There has been one new development in that area. The Czechs will only tolerate the operation if the weapons bear our marks. Of course, so they will have somebody to pass the blame onto if things go wrong. We will take that responsibility on, but you will have to give us a list of material we can get out of our own inventory."

ISSA: "Why don't we give them U.S. weapons, and claim it's a CIA provocation if it blows. After all, Momo, your man's an American."

BOUDIA: "There's something to that. I imagine the Czechs and the Russians both would be very happy with it."

KAMAL: "I would not be happy with it."

BOUDIA: "But you would cooperate if it had to be."
I would? They sell you quickly in this business. If they think I'm going to die with the world, and my family, believing I'm a CIA agent, they'd better rethink quickly.

TENNIS: "A quaint notion, gentlemen. But I'm afraid my Foreign Minister would rather have to apologize to Kreisky than to incur the cost of trying to implicate the CIA. We do have relations with the United States, please remember, even if they appear chilly on the surface."

ISSA: "It is reassuring to know just how many barrels of oil one *is* worth."

TENNIS: "Not many, Issa, not many. But it is getting late now, too late even to be explained by five long sets. So if you will excuse me, gentlemen. I wish you good luck, Mohammed. I will try to persuade the Russians not to levy too heavy a duty on your importation, but I can't promise much. I assume you are prepared to make good your debt."

BOUDIA: "As always."

TENNIS: "Very well. Bon soir. Madame, can I offer you a ride back to Paris?"

WOMAN: "Thank you, I have my car."

The tennis player struts out of the room like a rooster. From the window I see a Mercedes pull into the clearing to meet him. So this villa is not quite as deserted as it appears. The cars must be driven behind the building, or under the trees. It seemed inconceivable that a conference like this would be held in a house with no security. But the security is impressively discreet.

ISSA: "Well congratulations, Momo."

BOUDIA: "Congratulations, Kamal. What is the matter? You are looking very grim."

KAMAL: "I just need some air."

A heavy cloudburst just after dark has stirred up the jungle odors of the compound. Two gulps of this damp feral air clear my lungs of the smoky aftertaste of the conversation. The cacophony of rejoicing crickets and foliage rustling under its fresh load of moisture smothers the cadences of Boudia's and Issa's voices. The congratulations seem to have quickly turned to argument. But ten steps further into the foliage, and the fecund darkness swallows the last hints of civilization: no more voices, no more yellow glow of the lights in the mansion windows. I have an urge to strip and scrub myself clean against the glistening leaves, and then flee naked through the forest to a new, unsmirched land.

But isn't this just what you have been hungering for, Kamal? A chance to put your name and face in History. What is this urge to run away from it?

Perhaps this is not how I hoped to see my face in History: grimacing above a submachine gun pointed at the cowering chests of a shabby Russian Jewish family. Or perhaps sneering over their torn corpses still clutching their children, under the headline AUSTRIAN CHANCELLOR REFUSES TO BOW TO TERRORISM on the front page of the *New York Times* beside my mother's breakfast coffee.

But suppose I say, No, comrade Boudia, I don't like your operation, I don't like that weasel of a tennis player who is calling your shots and is not even a Palestinian in spirit, as perhaps you may be. And what do we hope to accomplish by this? Other than appear heirs to the Nazis, as the bleached blond lady fears.

Of course comrade Boudia will frown at his well-polished shoes for a silent minute as he gathers his disapproval. This is what I feared, Kamal . . . and yet hoped would not be. It seems the charges of your Uruguayan comrades were not far off the mark. An individualist, they said. Undisciplined. No politics. He is less interested in the consequences of his acts than how they appear in the newspaper. He raises himself to general without having been a private. He sets himself above the Committee, picking and rejecting orders as if acts of revolution were cans of soup on an American supermarket shelf.

Panting and low growls from the dark nearby. Then slow, heavy, uncertain footfalls approaching, following the dogs. A match flares at the edge of the clearing, then flickers out in a downward arc. The heavy steps start toward me, marked by a faint red beacon. The smell of acrid tobacco smoke instantly poisons this sweet feral atmosphere.

"Cigarette, Kamal?" It is Boudia.

I don't answer.

"Ah, that's right, you don't smoke. And you came out here to clear your lungs. Although that is usually a euphemism for cooling one's head, is it not? You did not like Issa's whimsey about making it appear a CIA provocation. You will have to get used to that. It is the way we joke here. Or did you take some other offense, Kamal?"

"Other offense? To what could I possibly take offense?"

"Good. Then you are favorable to this operation. I am very happy to hear that."

"Who is the guy in the tennies?"

"A very good friend of the movement. An important man. He does not like much to be known about him, I'm sorry. He wanted to see you. Otherwise you would never know of his existence."

"He made it sound as though we were working for him."

"That is just his manner. Aristocrat, you must have noticed. We do not work for him, but with him. You are seeing how differently we work from what you are used to. Here we have no ocean to swim in, so our survival depends on staying close to the summits of power. We need embassies, diplomatic mails, intelligence from national services. In return we must make ourselves useful to the men who make these things available to us. You must have realized that my little raid on the pipeline terminal at Trieste was not merely for theatrical effect. That pipeline is one of the major sources of oil for West Germany. We are not the only ones with an interest in reminding the Germans of that dependence. In this very complicated world one may scarcely hope to predict all the strange bedfellows one must fall in with in the course of a struggle like ours. So relax, Kamal, and accept that you will have to act on many decisions you cannot understand."

"Does that mean not to ask?"

"Ask, but you may receive no satisfactory answer."

"What is Issa's function?"

"He is not inside the organization."

"He is Palestinian?"

"Very much so."

"And the lady?"

"Also. She is the widow of one of our martyrs. She carries on his 'voice of reason,' as you heard. If she had her way, there would be no so-called terrorist activities. And she is not the only one in the organization who feels that way. We wage a constant battle against the bourgeois element."

"These people do not have names?"

"Not for you. Not until you have proven yourself. Your time will come, Kamal. Perhaps you will step into my shoes, perhaps higher, certainly higher if you survive. There is sixteen years difference between us. When I was your age my own national struggle was just gathering steam. I came to Marseilles to lead a cell. A year later: the first Boudia's Inferno."

"What was that?"

He rolls out several brief phrases in Arabic, like a short avalanche of smooth stones. Then remembering that I do not understand, he translates,

> "When heaven is split open
> When the stars are scattered
> When the seas swarm over
> When tombs are overthrown . . .

"Have you ever had a literary image stick so firmly in your mind that you knew, even when still a child, that someday you would have to live it out?"

"Yes. Mine is from *A Tale of Two Cities:* the man hanging under Evremond's carriage."

"I can see you using a dagger, Kamal. That is much more in your style than a pistol. A pistol is too much a weapon of expedience, too little of vengeance. But you can see why oil tanks have always appealed to me. With twenty kilos of plastique I can bring my vision to perfect realization. I have always wanted to film one. Perhaps the next. An event like that should be recorded. I did keep a photograph of the blaze in my prison cell."

"You were caught."

"Oh yes. When the DST sets its mind to catching terrorists there is very little hope of evading it. At that time they were very determined. Now, fortunately, they tolerate us. Prison itself is not so bad. Except for the lack of women. One has time to read and think. I wrote two plays, and when I was returned to Algeria after independence I was made director of the National Theater. I would still be, no doubt, were it not for the demise of Ben Bella. In 1965 I had to escape back to France, because Ahmed had liked me too well. The ironies of life, Kamal. You are just beginning. When you have been swept back and forth by history as I have you learn to take life with a sense of humor. It tears you in half if you don't."

"How did you get involved with the Palestinians, then?"

"I tried to get the left-wing exiles from Algeria organized for several years, published a paper called *La Charte,* hoping to build a movement against Boumédienne. But the fire was out, and I did not want to waste my life trying to kindle damp wood. So, when the Palestinian movement suddenly burst into flame after the '67 war, and was looking for revolutionaries with experience and sympathy and energy, I was ready to give myself to it. Does that answer your question?"

"I hear a sadness in your voice, Mohammed."

"It is true. Perhaps everyone loses his hope with age."

"You have no hope for our struggle?"

"Don't sound so offended. I believe it will succeed, sooner or later, Kamal. But the revolutionaries who make it succeed are always doomed to disappointment because the pragmatic result always falls far short of the idealistic dream which carries them through the agonies of the struggle. Yet knowing this full well, we proceed. I suppose because our natures will not let us do anything else."

"I don't have an idealistic vision, Mohammed."

"I know. That is why I think you may survive and succeed. You cannot be disappointed. You are like Stalin."

Boudia's cigarette flares in the dark. He draws a deep calming breath, and slowly exhales. "But if one cannot be disappointed, neither can one be satisfied. And that is the danger for you, Kamal. Life may stop having any value at all."

"And now what, comrade Boudia?"

He continues to drive without answering. By the headlights of the cars escaping the city a different Boudia is revealed: the man under the actor's sparkle, a creature with no light of his own. A moon. No wonder he is drawn to combustion.

"Now? Now we slip back into the drone of day-to-day life. I have a show to take on the road for three weeks. I will be back in Paris toward the end of June. By that time things will be arranged for your show, and we will begin rehearsals. Meanwhile enjoy yourself. You might begin to practice one particular skill that is certain to be called on: staying awake. You will have drugs, of course, but it is better not to rely

231

absolutely on them. You should be able to train yourself to stay awake for at least forty-eight hours without drugs. Try it once a week. Start with thirty hours and increase six hours a week. Don't try to do it all at once. And don't try more than once without sleeping seven normal nights in between. And aside from that, keep up your pretense of normal life. By the way, have you heard anything of your old girlfriend?"

"Not a word."

"Just as well, just as well. There's always Nadia and Sophie if you need comfort. Don't hesitate."

"I have a nice little affair going with a divorcée. Very light, very temporary. She thinks Pompidou is wonderful and that I should dress better."

"Perfect. And you have no problem with your job."

"None. They love me. They are getting American productivity at Arab wages. Who would complain?"

"And you have no financial difficulties?"

"I still have money. Don't worry, I'll tell you when I get low, Mohammed."

"After this operation you will never again have to worry about money. Now you have a sense of the magnitude of the interests behind it. In the meantime it is better if you continue to feel a little impoverished. For the realism of the performance. . . . But here we are, the Métro is still running. I would prefer not to drop you at your door."

"Of course. By the way, where is Elena these days?"

"She has been sent east. Her talents were being wasted here in Paris."

"And Tony?"

"It was deemed wise to separate them."

"Okay, Mohammed, I will not pester you with more questions until you get back. Break a leg!"

"What?"

"That's how you wish an actor good luck in American."

"May a thousand fleas infest your groin."

Oddly I am a little sad to see him drive off.

The pastel dawn over Paris approaches tenderly, even circumspectly, as if apologizing for its intrusion on the night. In Monte daylight ran up the eastern sky like a flag up a pole, wagging its colors. To remain in bed in the morning was an act of pure defiance. Not here. Here the travesty is in spying on the city's morning rituals. One is supposed to be asleep until it has put on its face.

Boudia was right: this has taken practice. On the first attempt I was hardly inclined to muse on the colors of the sunrise after twenty-odd hours. And when I tried to read, the words swam off the edges of the page. By thirty hours my ears felt stuffed with cotton, and whatever I put in my mouth tasted like cornstarch. The world was receding and leaving me behind. A forty-eight-hour stretch would certainly put me in the nut house. The experience left me in despair. Here the perfect commando was about to be rejected for the mission because he couldn't stay awake. What more pathetic failure could there be?

The second attempt was even worse. I dozed off for a few minutes before twenty-eight hours. I wanted to get down to the street for some exercise, but didn't dare. I'd be picked up for bizarre behavior in a minute, drugged and carted off to the Paris Bellevue. Could I count on Boudia to bail me out? Hah! I was about as useful to him as a cub scout. In Monte I knew people who could sit thirty hours at a card game, and still win. Those are the types he needed. Not Kamal, who started turning psychopath after twenty-four hours. Now I understood how the hostage massacres got started. After thirty hours even the lady pushing the vacuum cleaner upstairs was a mortal enemy. I made it to thirty-six on coffee and pushups, and vowed to resign from the mission as soon as Boudia got back.

That time the effects lasted. Two days afterward I missed by only a centimeter an attempt to add the hand of one of the waiters to the lamb cubes on a skewer. He had mixed up his orders three times. Everyone at the restaurant was sure I had been jilted by a lover. There was no other explanation for the radical deterioration of my personality. Mireille was convinced I had been fired from my job. Never again, I vowed.

But this time it is going easily. Twenty-five hours and I can still concentrate on reading without coffee or pushups. Boudia was right. This is a learned skill. The trick is to recall what it feels like to have had that night's sleep, and pretend.

It is a fine morning for a run, certainly too lovely a morning to waste reading indoors. Reaching the Métro is a small triumph. I've got this thing licked. My favorite biddy ticket-taker chirps a greeting from her guichet as I come bounding through. She has been like this since the technicians gave up trying to make the automatic turnstiles work. She sits on her stool and smirks at the passengers who try to stuff their yellow tickets into the inert stainless steel. On the platform two boys are passing a soccer ball between them, closer and closer to the edge, defying the rail pit with their confidence in their feet. Even my favorite pederast is exactly in his place on the bench, and turns his ogle from the kids to me as soon as I jog into sight. I've gotten used to his lipless lecherous smile; like a toad's, it spreads in a smooth curve halfway around his head. His posture is a bit toadlike as well, the head pushed forward and always looking up. Now for the first time I notice that his arms, resting on his knees, elbows outward, complete the toad stature. He is always waiting with a briefcase between his feet. I suspect he sometimes lets trains pass until I show up so he can board the same train and continue his ogling. Today I don't even bother to change seats when he sits down directly facing me. Suddenly I notice something sly in his eyes. He does not avert them in embarrassment as he usually does. But he says nothing and shuffles out at his habitual station. Just as the doors are closing I block them with my foot, and as they slide open for another try, I slip out onto the platform. My pédé is already teetering down the stairs from the elevated platform. Our train rattles away from the station. The little fellow pauses below at the first landing, steadying himself on the railing. Pauvre type, who can blame you for hungering after the young and healthy? With a faint wince of shame I decide to call off my spying. But some subliminal change, perhaps in his posture, keeps me watching as he starts down the next flight toward the street. I can't pinpoint it, yet there is a distinct quality of an actor leaving a set, still in character but suddenly safe behind the wings. The knees suddenly have a little more flexibility and strength. The head is a little more erect. That is all I can see from above and behind. Then he is out the gate, onto the street. Suddenly my heart is pounding. I would dash down and follow him, but I don't want to know. When did he first show up, four weeks ago, five? I can't remember. Maybe he's been riding this train for years. He's as natural a part of the scenery as the ticket-taker. He's good, perfect. He must have been a professional actor before he took up this line of work. But whose is he? And who picks up where he drops me? There is no familiar face on the platform here. Of course, whoever it is gets on a station or two before the pédé gets off. Whoever-it-is is still on the train, left behind by my sudden move. But whoever-it-is also knows that his

235

partner is blown. Tomorrow they'll send someone else.

Whoa, Kamal. Don't you recognize this? It's the paranoia of sleep deficiency in a more subtle dose. Tomorrow your little pederast will be right there leering at you. As sure as the sunrise.

But tomorrow turns out to have no sunrise. It hides behind a roof of leaden cloud. And my little pederast hides too, his absence silencing the scoffer. No, never ignore coincidences, Esteban used to say. Coincidences kill.

Yet three days later the sun and the pederast reappear, waking me from my paranoid daymare. I stop memorizing faces. Running gets easy again. Mireille assures me in her mothering voice that I seem to be recovering from my illness. Boudia will be back any day now, and I realize that it is not really the passengers on the Métro that are worrying me, but the passengers of a train which will carry me into Austria and into History.

Again I have nearly succeeded in not recognizing Saleh's cheerful countenance. But he has cornered me at the entrance to the Métro with a commentary on the French Open and who's going to win at Wimbledon. It doesn't seem a natural subject for a Palestinian poet. But he has his own twist. Even in that most bourgeois sport the decay of the imperialist West is becoming apparent, don't I see. Capitalism is helpless to produce anything that can hope to compete with Nastase. He doesn't realize he's talking to the Great Palestinian Hope. Saleh's angle on tennis recalls the little diplomat in his whites, and I wonder if I wouldn't have helped my people a lot more if I'd won the 400-meter hurdles at Munich. An antidote to Mark Spitz. But as Coach used to say, I don't want to hear no woulda's, coulda's or shoulda's. And my new coach is waiting. At least I can tell him I've made forty-two hours with ease.

A strange memory surfaces on the way down to the Faculté des Sciences where I am to meet Boudia. My mother and father had just landed in JFK, then called Idlewild, from their first trip abroad—the first trip in either of their lives that was not an escape or an emigration. It had been preceded by months of anguished wrangling. I was too young then to understand why. Now it is perfectly apparent. For my father, any travel meant never returning to the place he was leaving. He couldn't push that fear out of his head. As the departure date drew closer his work grew increasingly demanding. Then he got sick. But my mother remained adamant. She hadn't been home since the war started twenty years before. Nothing would stop her now, particularly my father's "crazy" worries. They fought like alley cats. For once she didn't protect him. And when the day came, she packed and pushed him into the taxi with the threat that she was quite ready to go alone.

I was about eleven or twelve, and experienced again that fatal shame for my father. I was glad when they disappeared into the tunnel to the plane, and not particularly glad when they were about to reappear from it three months later.

But my mother's face almost changed that. She emerged beautiful from that corridor which had swallowed her bitter and pinched. I was shocked to find her so appealing. And my father? I don't know how he looked. I couldn't meet his eyes.

For months afterward my mother sang in French, read in French, dragged my father to French movies. She brought her home home with her. Then the Algerian war started in earnest, and my father went on the attack. France became the essence of racist repression, reaction, effete decadence and moral corruption. He turned on their music, their films, their painting, their literature, with a violence which frequently crossed the border into hysteria but never

237

lost the cutting edge of logic. My mother crumpled under the onslaught, and lost the radiance she had brought back from the country of her childhood. It was the only battle against the "whites" my father ever won.

We are to stumble on each other in the library of the Faculté. It is uncomfortably hot and muggy already, a heavy turbulent cloud cover imparts an ash tone to faces and buildings alike. The complex is nearly deserted, which puzzles me until I recall that we are just a few days from July. It takes me nearly ten minutes to find someone who knows where the library is inside this labyrinth. When I find it, Boudia is either in the stacks or hasn't arrived yet. I sit down with a few back issues of *Scientific American* and begin reading the ads: warmup. The articles themselves would sprain my underexercised cortex. Boudia saunters into the library about twenty minutes later.

"My friend, you look so much like a student I almost didn't recognize you."

"Sorry, professor."

"That was never one of my ambitions, I'm afraid."

"How did your show go over?"

"I keep forgetting that the provinces are exactly what the Parisians always say they are: simulacrums of death. It is good to go out there every so often, to better appreciate life. . . . Allah forgive me. But since last night I have made up for the entire three weeks."

"Shit, man, you boast like a virgin."

"And you, you are as discreet as an Engish apothecary."

"We make a good comedy team. Let's get on with our routine."

"Patience, patience. Slowness comes from God, haste from the devil. How much do you know about chemistry?"

238

"The first symptoms are burning and itching."

"I am quite serious. I have to know about phosphate."

"I think, knowing you, you would be more interested in nitrate: cellulose or potassium."

"Not right now. Now I am interested in phosphate."

"Which phosphate? There must be fifty phosphates, at least."

"Algerian phosphate. I mean Spanish Saharan phosphate."

"Is that calcium phosphate?"

"How would I know? All I know is that it is Political Phosphate, and that there is going to be a war between Morocco and Algeria over it."

"Then why do you want to know the chemistry of it? To find out if it will explode?"

"Hush. Here we are: mining . . . calcium phosphate, raw material for fertilizer. There, what is the good of your college education, American, if you have to go look it up the same as I do? Fertilizer. Shedding blood over fertilizer. What a world!"

"Would you feel better if it were rocket fuel?"

"I would find that less of an irony than digging fertilizer out of the middle of the Saharan desert. That can't be the reason for a war. Boumédienne has something else in mind. But I will read about this phosphate, anyway. Amuse yourself for a while."

I return to my *Scientific American*s to attempt an article on quarks. I can concentrate only with difficulty: another of the casualties of living on adrenaline for three years: my intelligence has spoiled to cunning. For a physics major to be taxed by *Scientific American* . . .

But here's Boudia again, emerging from the stacks muttering, "No. Phosphate can't be the reason. Let's go. I am parked out on Fossés Saint-Bernard."

Boudia is really upset about this phosphate non-sense. He muses all the way to the street. Finally I can no longer resist asking him why.

"Oh, just an argument. With Issa." He steps into the street, unlocks his door, jumps in, reaches across to unlock . . .

Even from a few yards away it appears no more than a shudder punctuated by a mild pop and a tinkle of glass. In the next moment a split, twisted wreck sits silently smoking where the green Renault sat a moment ago. And in place of a friend, blood, se-vered limbs, shreds of skin and cloth. The roof of the car is punctured in a hundred places. Blood oozing through torn steel: red rivulets on green. A white thing on the hood is a hand. But I see no head. This can't be my friend. He is around here somewhere. I just blinked and lost sight of him. This is too quiet. No screeching departure of a soul. No ululating wails of grief from the heavens. Turn around, you simply misplaced him. Mohammed? There is a famil-iar face smiling weirdly at me. But it isn't Moham-med. Two mechanics in overalls are shouting. About what? Oh, they are warning about the spreading gasoline. Don't push me away. That was my friend. Who was he? He was . . .

That smile is familiar. It is still there. Lipless liz-ard smile. You!

The mechanics are dragging me back from the gas-oline as I recognize the face. It is the pederast, out of costume. He is still watching me. I lurch out of the grip of the mechanics. The ex-toad slips a hand under his jacket, warning. What a fucking moment not to be armed. The mechanics grab my arms again and pull me across the street, twisting me away from the wreck and the toad. When I manage to twist back for a glimpse, he is gone. They are pulling me down the street toward Saint-Germain. I have no strength to resist. They have me just above the elbows. Like in

Jerusalem. But they look French. They are just trying to keep me from getting killed too. Or arrested. The sirens are wailing behind me. The steel Kamal takes control at last, wakened by the sirens.

"Merci, mes amis."

They nod and let go. The steel Kamal is suppressing this exploding urge to turn and chase the toad. The steel Kamal keeps marching ahead, not looking back, though he feels the heat of the burning gas on his neck. He turns the corner onto Saint-Germain, treads the five blocks, evenly and steadily, to the Maubert Métro as the ambulances and police cars and fire trucks wail by. . . . You didn't want to die in silence, Mohammed. You wanted to go out to gunfire, flames and bellows of rage. Not have your life ended by some little gadget under your car seat. If you had to die you wanted to die like mad Rasputin, pumped full of lead and poison, bound hand and foot, yet finally killed not by men but by the Neva ice. Or like Ahab, bound onto the back of his whale. What a bitter fate, Mohammed, to have your end marked only by a pop, a grunt and a tinkle of glass. And to have your corpse sniffed at by curious bystanders while the assassin slips away with a leer. A bitter fate, a bitter fate to die on the side of a street like a dog who wandered out without looking.

Concentrate, Kamal! There are decisions that have to be made. What are you trying to accomplish zigzagging across Paris below the ground like some punch-drunk boxer trying to pretend he's still game? No one's chasing you. The toad is on his way to the airport to be whisked away by El Al. Don't you remember all those rumors the Arabs were muttering in the cafes after Hamchari bought it: how the El Al pilots have instructions to take off even against the tower's orders if it's a question of saving a Mossad agent. Someone at Magoo's said he heard their 707s have .50-caliber machine guns in the wings, hidden behind plastic which breaks away on the first shot, and special armor against grenades so the pilots can keep flying even if a hijacker drops one in the passenger compartment. When you know you are likely to be attacked it's insane not to take some precaution. Boudia didn't even glance at his hood or tailpipe. Fatalist. It was his own fault. He must have thought a bit of caution cramped his style. Admittedly it is hard to look dapper poking your nose under your car every time you get in. But why should it be my fault if he was too damn dapper to even take a glance?

Who said it was your fault, Kamal?

Well, can I deny that the toad followed me to Boudia?

But you did not deliberately lead him to Boudia. If there was any guilt it was inadvertent.

We have to judge by consequences, not by intent. Isn't that what I told Alain Castellan?

Alain Castellan made no attempt to avenge Esteban. That was an admission of intent, whether conscious or not.

And Kamal? Is he making any attempt to intercept the toad to avenge Boudia? Is he rushing to pick up his pistol and get to the airport before the toad gets on his armored jet?

Which airport? There are three outside Paris.

Two which count. Even a fifty-fifty chance is worth acting on. With a few minutes' research you can make the guess even better than that. Would you have accepted an excuse like that from Alain Castellan? Get off the Métro at Opéra, persuade the Valkyrie at the travel agency to let you have a look at her airlines schedule book.

But how will I get the pistol? It would be stupid to show up at Patriarches now. The police are probably there already.

How would the police know? It will take them hours just to figure out who died in the Renault. Even if someone on the scene remembers your face it will take days to identify the description as you. And if the Israelis wanted you dead, the toad would have shot you on the spot. But why would they want you dead? You have been very useful to them.

From now on I will make certain Kamal Jibral is quite the opposite of useful to the Israelis, if it costs my life.

Stop posturing and do something. Here's Opéra.

An exhausting effort of will to ride the escalator out of the sanctuary of the burrow into daylight.

But see, there are no police waiting with machine guns, no hitmen in trench coats with Beretta .22s poking out their pockets, no witnesses screaming and pointing, no one slipping into step behind you.

The next flight to Israel on El Al leaves in a little over an hour from Roissy. Plenty of time by taxi. First Patriarches.

Patriarches is as quiet as ever. Not a flic in sight, nor anyone else for that matter. The apartment is just as I left it. Everything in place: pistol, passport, stash of traveler's checks.

You see?

Why do I have this feeling I will never be coming back here again?

Because if you do intercept the toad, this is the first place his compatriots will come looking for you.

And if I don't?

One step at a time, Kamal.

The taxi reaches Roissy with fifteen minutes to spare. The driver wanted to know why I was going to the airport without luggage. To see off a woman. He sped up without being asked. The French still believe in romance. Or pretend to. What else do they have to believe in? La Gloire? Hardly a soul at the El

243

Al ticket counter. But the toad would not have to check in his baggage. Try the gate. What a ridiculous vanity, these plexiglass tubes crisscrossing in midair. All this to go up a floor and over a few yards. Actually it is very good from a security point of view, they've got you in a test tube. All they have to do is cork it at both ends and watch you smother. Why didn't I think about this? The El Al search lines, the armed guards. The toad will be whisked past all this, while I stand here with a pistol tucked into my belt which could send me to the guillotine. Remember Hervé.

What the hell did you think you were going to do, Kamal?

Improvise.

Improvise? Have you forgotten Esteban's First Law already? Organisar al triunfo, improvisar al verdugo. Organize our way to victory, improvise our way to the executioner.

And here you are attracting attention just standing by. These Israeli guards have a nose for trouble. Keep walking, Arab. Shit, here comes a plainclothes.

"Je peux vous aider, monsieur?"

"You speak English?"

"Yes, I do. May I help you?"

"I am supposed to meet someone on an arriving flight."

"This is a departing flight, as you can see."

"I can see. Where is arrival?"

"You are on the wrong level. You will have to go back down the moving ramp to the main floor. Are you not well?"

"Not well?"

"You are sweating and trembling. Perhaps you should see one of the nurses." He is trying to read my eyes, ben sharmoota. Or perhaps he recognizes my face from one of their photographs.

Why can't you remember, Kamal? You're blown.

No one has ever forgotten *your* face. Every Israeli agent in Paris, every airport security man in Europe, and God knows who else has memorized those mug shots they took in Jerusalem. You're blown sky high, Jibral. You're useless to anyone now, and dangerous to everyone. It's Monte all over again, only ten times worse, because this time you *are* guilty.

"Let me guide you to one of our nurses, sir."

Back off, motherfucker, before I blow you away in the toad's place. Why don't you say, come along with me, Mr. Jibral? Fuck this little game with the nurse. Let's have it out right here. An eye for an eye. I can nail three of you before you get me. That will make three kikes for two Arabs. Such a deal.

So what are you waiting for, Kamal? You wanted vengeance. Here's your opportunity.

It would be trading a knight for a pawn. Again.

Oh, is that the excuse? Or is it that you had a grander vision for yourself than a pathetic little shootout at an airport? That is hardly much of a place in History. Not even a footnote. What you wanted was to ride the lead tank of your own battalion, call it the Boudia Battalion, into Jerusalem. That is more like what you had envisioned for yourself.

And wouldn't that be the kind of vengeance Mohammed would really have hoped for? Not the death of a security guard or two.

Naturally.

Then control yourself, Kamal. One step backward, two steps forward. The man who seeks vengeance digs two graves.

"Thanks for the offer of the nurse, but I'll be all right." And I'll be back when the odds are better. Organisar al triunfo, improvisar al verdugo.

His eyes are on my back all the way down the tube. If it weren't for these fucking tubes I could have nailed him and gotten away. Another time, another place.

And now what, Kamal?

Back to Paris. By airport bus. Save the twenty bucks. This world is overwhelmingly immense. Look at all those people going by who haven't an inkling that a killing very nearly took place. But it wouldn't have been a very important killing, so why should they have an inkling. It is the De Gaulles and the Fidels and the Hitlers whose deaths count for something. And the Ben-Gurions and the Goldas. But they are all impossible to kill.

And now what, Kamal?

The future shrinks every time I think about it. One inescapable conclusion slaps me across the face: without an Esteban, without a Boudia, I am nothing but a daydreamer riding an imaginary tank at the head of an imaginary battalion into a city which I barely know.

But isn't the lesson clear enough now, Kamal? There must be no more Estebans, no more Boudias in your life. And no more Justinas. Whenever you let someone touch your heart you are one step away from disaster. You must hone the ability to sniff at the death of a comrade the way a cat sniffs at a dead mouse. Unmoved. Until you can do that you are still an amateur, an amateur whose discipline will blow apart at the first shock, an amateur who will whirl in futile circles when there is no one to tell him, Now put your left foot in front of the right.

Perhaps. But now what?

I must find my way back to the villa. There is still the Austrian operation. If I remain at large with that story in my head, the organization will send someone to blow it off for me. With Boudia dead, I had better check in immediately, or, given the circumstances, I will be the number-one suspect.

That is true. You are beginning to think clearly, at last.

One step at a time.

But if you proceed to the villa you'd better make damn sure that no one is following this time.

Of course.

Well, Kamal, you seem to be back in control. I think I can let you take care of yourself now.

Thanks.

Any time, my friend.

Where the hell is that walled-in compost heap of a villa? I thought I'd memorized the route so thoroughly. But all these precious suburbs look exactly alike, so groomed, so quiet, so discreet, so solidly set under their elms and maples that it is inconceivable their inhabitants shit, cry and have nervous breakdowns. Here everything is "comme il faut." Here things run their course. One knows what lies ahead, and behind, and to the sides.

Yes, but do you know what lies in your very midst, you snoring bourgeoises, behind this respectable wall too high to peer over, behind this solidly padlocked spiked iron gate? Let me climb over and tell you. Dark shadows, snuffling curs, smells like fetid death, rotten fruit and dogshit sliming under foot, a house with no warm lights in the windows like yours, and instead of lush Mozart from the stereo, the click of a submachine-gun bolt being drawn.

I duck behind a tree just before a spotlight blazes onto the clearing in front of the house. The dogs peer up at it.

"Ce n'est que les chiens." The voice is Issa's.

"Are you calling me a dog, Issa?"

"Qui est là? Who is there?"

"Momo's friend Kamal."

"Show yourself."

"Don't be lewd, Issa."

247

"This is not a time to jest. Step into the light."

"All right. Don't shoot."

I crunch noisily across the gravel. The front door opens, seemingly by itself. The hall is pitch-black. The door closes behind. It is operated by a mechanical arm. A light switches on at the end of the hall. Seconds later it goes off.

"Please come down to the foot of the stairs." Still Issa's voice.

I can feel the presence of several people above me in the dark. Also the presence of weapons: a very chilly, ringing aura always surrounds firearms.

"Come up the stairs. Are you armed?"

"Just the pistol I always carry."

The light comes on. I am on the first landing. Issa and a woman, both in bathrobes, are leaning over the railing of the second-story landing pointing AK-47s at me.

"We have had people out looking for you all day. Where have you been?"

"That is a long story. Do you know what happened?"

"The entire world knows."

Is this an accusaton, Issa? You see it really is me here peering up at you. Why the firing squad? I trust your trigger finger, Issa. But that storm trooper next to you, she looks like she's itching to kill something. Whatever you see in her from the neck down, it's a wonder that face doesn't shrivel you up like a worm under a blowtorch.

"Who is this person, Issa?" Her voice is a deep tobacco rasp of an accent as unidentifiable as her physiognomy. Either could have originated anywhere from the primeval forests of eastern Poland to the canyons of Yemen. Her face is not ugly, but fierce without charm: broad-browed, high-cheekboned, sun-tautened, thin-lipped, a trace of Mongol around the eyes. The robe completely hides her body, but her hands are thick and aim the AK with a familiar, certain grasp.

"Who is he? That is a more profound question than you could guess. Eh Kamal? Who are you?"

"Why ask? Obviously I'm a hired professional assassin who was engaged by the Zionists to bump off Boudia. And that's why I've come scampering here for safety."

"One day your joking is going to cost you dear, comrade Jibral. Come up here."

"At last."

"Where is your pistol?" He has pushed back my jacket with his free hand.

"In my belt behind my back."

The Fury pokes up the tail of my jacket with the muzzle of her AK, grabs my pistol and backs off turning it over contemptuously in her left hand. Don't sneer, sweetheart. It can kill you just as dead as a clipful from your AK. Issa leads us down the hall to a narrow windowless room. The Fury takes one step in, then on a signal from Issa, leaves, closing the door behind her. The room is bare except for a metal bed and a black-painted wooden chair with the rungs falling out. The door, I noticed before it was closed, can be locked from the hall by a sliding bolt. This is to be my cell. Perhaps it was stupid to come here. But suddenly I'm very tired, and glad to have someone else making the decisions. This must be how one winds up in prison: the effort of staying free suddenly seems too great for the freedom it buys. I throw myself on the bed.

"Wake me for breakfast, Issa."

He sits down on the rickety chair—another rung pops out—with the AK across his lap.

"Don't tell me you're going to start interrogating me now."

"What happened in Rue Fossés Saint-Bernard?"

"I thought the entire world knew. Somebody

planted a bomb in Boudia's Renault. He got in. . . . Boom."

"And you? Saleh phoned to say you were to meet him just before it happened. Did you meet him?"

"Yes."

"Then why were you not in the car when the bomb went off?"

"It sounds like you wish I had been."

"There would now be fewer questions for you to answer."

"Thanks all the same, but I'll take the questions."

"Why were you not in the car with him, then?"

"Because he hadn't unlocked the passenger-side door."

"Are you implying that he started up the engine before he opened up the passenger door? I have driven with Boudia. That was not his habit."

"I know it wasn't. He never started the engine. He unlocked his own door, sat down, reached across to unlock the passenger door, and that is when the bomb went off. It must have been on a delay triggered by opening the driver's door or sitting down on the driver's seat."

"Never heard of such a thing."

"And before Hamchari, had you heard of a bomb set off by a tone sent over a telephone? Whoever can pick the locks on a Paris apartment can pick the lock on a Renault in ten seconds."

"Where were you when the bomb went off?"

"A few yards from the hood."

"You were not injured, I see."

"The car contained the blast, except for some flying glass. It's not like the movies, Issa. If someone had been right next to his window they might have gotten pretty badly cut up, but that's all."

"But *you* were some meters distant."

"Boudia rushed ahead. You know how he walked. What's the point, Issa? I had a lucky break. If it had been an ignition bomb I'd be dead now and you'd be happy. So why don't you just come out and fucking say what you've got to say and let me go to sleep. If you want me to be an Israeli assassin, I'm an Israeli assassin. Okay?"

"I have not accused you of anything. I simply need to know certain facts."

"They will still be facts tomorrow. But I'll give you one fact to sleep on, Issa. The reason Boudia was at the Faculté des Sciences had to do with an argument he was having with you. Over Algerian or Spanish Saharan phosphates? He never got a chance to explain. If he had used the normal pickup he would not have had to park the car. So how about that, Issa? How would you like to die for looking up a chemical fertilizer in a textbook?"

"Death finds us where and when it will." He stands. The chair creaks its gratitude. Issa is not big but unusually solid; one of the few men I would be reluctant to tangle with. The AK swings like a toy gun at the end of his bulky arm. He is staring at me, not sure whether to press the interview any further. He knows he'll get nowhere. And perhaps he is afraid I will ask what the phosphate argument was about, and why it so upset Boudia. Ah, Issa, wouldn't you like to know just how Death did find our friend in the Rue des Fossés Saint-Bernard. It seems we both led him there.

"Who is taking over Boudia's operation in Austria, by the way?"

Issa replies with a sniff of contempt, turns and leaves the room. I expect to hear the bolt shot outside, but the heavy steps do not pause until they have reached the end of the hall. A door creaks, clicks shut. I pad silently to my own door. It opens. But for some reason I have no urge to slip away.

* * *

251

Ink-black night. A thump. Steps. Someone is coming into the room. Wake up, Kamal, wake up. The fog of sleep parts slowly, too slowly. A pillow is smothering my face, arms, torso. I cannot resist. My muscles buzz but lie limp. Oh, it is so much easier to give in to this, so much easier to give in. Like floating, like going to sleep, like dying, so much easier.

But wait. He will get Justina next. There, she is awake, backing up against the wall with horror and contempt while I let myself be smothered. No, this mustn't be. I must make the effort, wake my liquid muscles, now coil for the counterattack, giving no warning for he has been lulled by my passivity, one, two, three, kick.

Fuck! Silent room. Nobody here. And so thick with CO_2 I can barely breathe. What is this sourness in my gut? Have I been poisoned? Got to get the door open. Here it is.

The snick of a safety catch being switched fills the silent opaque hallway. Yes, he would like me to go sneaking out in the hall. Then he could make his questions moot. "Mistook him for an intruder. He should have spoken out." Sorry, Issa. You can't get rid of me that easily. You'll have to shoot me in bed.

Cool air replenishing the room. I feel quite awake, but the sourness still fills my abdomen. It has to do with Justina. I thought she left out of fear for the consequences of Hervé's death. Why have I never understood before why she couldn't believe he was a spy? She had to convince herself I killed him for jealousy. If she only knew where his betrayal has led.

Perhaps if I hadn't killed him, they would have forgotten about me. But once their informer was silenced they knew he was onto something big. They knew it then would be worth following me back to the man who ran me. Now, too late, it is so obvious how they did it. The first time Saleh took me to meet Boudia down at the river, whoever tailed us must

252

have seen us climb into Boudia's Renault. From that moment they had a description, or even a photo, of Boudia and the car. They also knew that Saleh was the messenger boy and that whenever he contacted me there was a good chance I would be meeting Boudia again.

Or if they missed the meeting by the river, the Israelis had another, even easier opportunity to glean the same information when Saleh drove me to meet Boudia at the shopping center south of the city.

When Saleh next came for me we led them straight to Fossés Saint-Bernard, just in time to let them watch Boudia drive up in the same Renault. This opportunity could not have been more perfect. They needed only a minute to pick the lock, slip the bomb under the driver's seat, and set the trip wire.

Too easy, we all made it too fucking easy for them: me, Saleh, Boudia himself. We were all too soft, too lazy, too self-indulgent, to observe strict security procedures. I mean, what's the fun in that? Here we are in Paris. La vie est gaie! The city is the grave of the guerrilla; how absolutely right you are, Fidel. First it sucks down his spirit, after that his body follows without a struggle. Look at me for your proof, Fidel. Just minutes ago I was ready to let my body smother under a pillow. Is this the same Kamal that landed in Paris just six and a half months ago? I can hardly recall that one. It seems to me he was full of fervor and hope. No, that must have been someone else. This Kamal can think of nothing better than to hide in a windowless cell.

Morning barely managed to reach my room. It was a halfhearted morning to begin with, thickly overcast, still as death. What light did pass the dusty ancient panes at the ends of the hallway was swallowed by the dark wood of the floor and doors, so by the time it reflected into my cell it was no more than a hint of day. I thought I had wakened at dawn. It turned out to be nearly noon. There was no one standing guard in the hall. No one anywhere, until I found the kitchen, where the Fury sat reading a magazine with a cup of coffee by her left hand and the AK lying across the table by her right hand. She did not look up as I walked in. I asked her if she minded if I helped myself to some coffee.

"Allez."

"Where's Issa?"

"En ville."

All right, I get the message. I took my cup and wandered through the dining room into a dark shelf-lined study. Examining someone's personal library is almost like peeking into his mind. But whose library was this? The books hadn't been touched for years, to judge by the dust on them. It was not a revolutionary's library: no Lenin, no Mao, just a single Collected Works of Marx and Engels. Mostly French historical and philosophical titles. A large section on the Napoleonic Wars, and a generous collection of English literature, including Churchill and, lo, *Seven Pillars of Wisdom*. My free hand pulled that down before the thought formed in my mind. Forbidden Lawrence; he was one of my father's anathemas. There was no copy of *Pillars* in my father's copious library. But a year or two before he died a tome with the title *T. E. Lawrence: An Arab View* appeared on the shelf and he pushed it at me one evening after I came home under the spell of Peter O'Toole's Lawrence. "There is no trick. The trick is not to mind."

I practiced snuffing out candles without wetting my fingers for weeks afterward. Finally my father asked over dinner if I'd read the book he'd lent me.

To avoid discussing it I replied, "I haven't had a chance."

"Read it. Why do you think I gave it to you?"

"I'll read it."

254

"No you won't, Kamal. I know you. You'd rather remain blind to the truth about this man you've taken as your hero. You'd rather not know that your Lawrence was a homosexual, a runt, a masochist, a sadist, a megalomaniac and an inveterate liar, a racist, a misogynist, an imperialist, a spy and a coward."

"It was just a movie, dad."

"No, not just a movie. Nothing is *just* anything. It's a piece of racist propaganda. Why should they need to use an Englishman with a stuffed nose to impersonate Faisal?"

"You went to see the movie?" I was dumbfounded.

"Yes," he snarled, not having anticipated giving his secret away that carelessly. "Yes, I went to see it. To know what deceptions you and your brothers have swallowed. The great warrior Lawrence, hah! If you study History you will find out he never went to Aqaba, and that his only battle experience before he was made colonel lasted three minutes, after which he accidentally shot his camel in the head and was knocked unconscious by the fall. They didn't put *that* into your movie, did they?"

That finished Lawrence for me. It was a bitter loss to inflict on a seventeen-year-old. I never gave Lawrence another glance until late in those five months incubating under Pollo Rojo when I'd sickened of all that revolutionist crap that had been passed to me down there for my self-criticism and consciousness-raising and I asked the owner to bring me something to do with the Middle East written in good old English. Of all things, he brought back a battered copy of *Pillars*. I pushed it away for two days, then devoured it. Few changes are as painful as unloading oneself of a parent's most passionate prejudices, and few so liberating. I reread *Pillars* so many times my dreams shifted from Monte to the Hejaz and the

Wadi Rumm. I rediscovered my hero: braggart, faggot, runt and all.

So this dusty edition of *Pillars* from the villa library fell into my hand like an illicit lover. "Some of the evil of my tale may have been inherent in our circumstances. For years we lived anyhow with one another in the naked desert, under the indifferent heaven. By day the hot sun fermented us; and we were dizzied by the beating wind. At night we were stained by dew, and shamed into pettiness by the innumerable silences of the stars. We were a self-centered army without parade or gesture, devoted to freedom, the second of man's creeds, a purpose so ravenous that it devoured all our strength, a hope so transcendent that our earlier ambitions faded in its glare."

The words made my skin electric. Here was the antidote to the sourness that was poisoning me: the desert, the sky. In the city it was impossible to keep the notion of freedom from shriveling into rhetoric, and without the *feeling* called freedom there was nothing to sustain the will to fight for freedom. Except ambition. Ambition for power, ambition for pleasure; these were what had grown in the spot in Boudia's heart vacated by the pure feeling for freedom. He must have known that the pure feeling would never return—the explosions of Trieste could not bring back the explosions of Marseilles. So there was really nothing to live for except the pleasure of power, and that pleasure would be spoiled by too vigilant, too serious an approach to life. So he opened the door to Death, who does not respect those who do not resist him and deals them squalid ends, au bord d'un fossé.

Boudia had very nearly dragged me into the ditch with him. But Death kept some respect for me yet. I was still sparked by a vestige of the pure feeling of what we were fighting for, and I had remained vigilant. That instinctive vigilance had saved me from sharing Boudia's end, and now I could fan my spark back into a flame. But the only place the air was pure enough to feed it was the Middle East. If I stayed here in Paris it would only smother again.

I read on in *Pillars* with fright and exultation. It was a different work than the one I had read a half dozen times beneath Pollo Rojo. It breathed this time, it spoke into my ear as if it had been written for no one else. I had to turn it face down on my knee to keep from being swept down the cataract. In the respite I glimpsed another dimension of the urban guerrilla's futility. He must have two faces. He claims the fighter is the real one and the daily bore is the pretense. But it is exactly the other way around, and his own Marxist theory makes that inescapable: existence determines consciousness. His existence in the city conditions in him the reflexes of the daily bore. Against the persistent conditioning he pits fuzzy fantasy images of revolutionism, and he hopes that when it is time to act he will have mind-trained himself from the daily bore into the fighter. But it is futile. One needs to live on the battleground to be a fighter.

"The Beduin of the desert, born and grown up in it, had embraced with all his soul this nakedness too harsh for volunteers, for the reason, felt but inarticulate, that there he found himself indubitably free. He lost material ties, comforts, all superfluities and other complications to achieve a personal liberty which haunted starvation and death. He saw no virtue in poverty herself: he enjoyed the little vices and luxuries—coffee, fresh water, women—which he could still preserve. In his life he had air and winds, sun and light, open spaces and a great emptiness. . . .

"The desert Arab found no joy like the joy of voluntarily holding back. He found luxury in abnegation, renunciation, self-restraint. He made nakedness of the mind as sensuous as nakedness of the body. He saved his own soul, perhaps, and without danger, but in a hard selfishness."

Ah, Boudia, you should have read this before it was too late for you.

Issa returned just before dusk. He found me reading in the library and gnawing on a piece of bread.

"You will be glad to know I have asked her to make dinner."

"Thank you, Issa. I wouldn't have dared. What's happening in the city?"

"There will be a protest march for Mohammed. The police have accepted the fact that it was an assassination and not an accident as they first claimed. They have lodged a protest with the Israelis."

"Are there going to be any retaliations in kind?"

"Undoubtedly. Are you volunteering?"

"As a matter of fact, no. I've been through that. There's no point."

He appraised that reply with a frown. He must have been expecting the opposite. He muttered, "Any retaliations will be done by people who did not know him, for whom he was a symbol, not a man. Vengeance is for the guilty at heart. I am reassured by the fact that you have no urge to it, Kamal."

How simple: Vengeance is for the guilty at heart. A searing truth. This must have been something he discovered by experience, as I had. Yet he had been able to distill it as I never had.

"Apparently the Israelis had been looking for Boudia since February or March. They found his name in a file they grabbed on one of their raids into Lebanon. One can't lead a double life as he did and expect to survive long. In fact, I don't think he expected to survive long. But Boudia was an actor. It was hard to know what lay under the clown. I knew him for years but could not really call him a friend. We never bared our hearts. Anyway, there is no place for that in our business.

"By the way, you will be glad to hear that I am taking over the Austrian operation. . . . No? You are not glad, I see in your face."

"Issa, this is something we have to discuss. The close brush with death has changed my feelings. I realized that Europe is doing to me what it did to Boudia: its worms are gnawing my will. I can't lead the double life much longer. I want to go east."

"I see."

"Who is Abu Ahmet? His name came up that night I was brought here by Boudia."

"Abu Ahmet? Why?"

"You said his men were used to fighting in the mountains."

"That is true. But that is not for you."

"Why not?"

"First, you do not speak Arabic. Second, you are too valuable. The casualty rate during his operations across the border is close to one hundred percent."

"It sounds as if he needs some better officers."

"No. That casualty rate is in the nature of the terrain and the goals of his raids."

"There must be others I could join."

"You would be of little use there."

"I will soon be of no use here."

"Give yourself a few days to recover from the shock. Then we will see if you are still so pessimistic. Meanwhile come to dinner. Anna is not as fierce as she looks."

Ground lamb, onions and yogurt sauce in home-baked pocket bread. And good old hummus, just like at the Uncle's house. The Fury did not look so furious at the stove. She even smiled at Issa. Then I noticed the wedding ring, and a little gold cross at her neck and one at his. Husband and wife! A real incongruity in revolutionary circles. I felt a surge of warmth for them both. Everything had been distorted into grotesque forms by fear and anger last night. Now the villa was seeming touchingly domestic.

"Anna, he is interested in Abu Ahmet. Tell him about Abu Ahmet."

She sniffed. It was the same gesture as Issa's. "They say, if he cuts himself with his razor he bleeds mercury."

"Heavy dude, huh?"

"Excuse me, I do not . . . Oh I see: heavy because of the mercury." She looked away, embarrassed by incomprehension.

"It's an American expression meaning . . . What does it mean? Tough, dangerous, hard. Or it means really important and powerful, depending on the context."

"Heavy dude? Yes, perhaps."

"Your image is much more graphic. Bleeds mercury. I like that."

"Anna heard that from her brother. He served with Abu Ahmet."

"And now?"

Issa shook his head.

"I'm sorry."

Anna quickly replied, "That is not uncommon. Every family from the camp has lost at least one brother."

"Which camp is that?"

"Tal al-Zatar. It is outside of Beirut."

"I have heard of it many times."

A silence fell. What can two people say to each other who have suffered the same calamity so differently? Another reason for me to go east. I wondered how her brother died. This Abu Ahmet was beginning to carve his own image in my thoughts. A man of metal; Issa and Anna thought they could chill me with such a description. How could they have known that after Esteban and after Boudia, I would follow no man but one impervious as metal to human emotions. Issa had seen the disappointment on my face when he announced that he would take over Boudia's Austrian operation. I didn't dare tell him that he was too human, too capable of being a friend, for Kamal Jibral to trust the outcome. The crimson blood of one more friend would drive Kamal Jibral mad. Now, a man who bled mercury on the other hand . . .

After dinner Issa challenged me to a game of chess in the study. Anna sat back in a stuffed chair, reading and watching, her AK, as ever, close to hand. From the opening it was clear that Issa was a king's-pawn kind of player. Even with white's opening advantage he played defensively. I sacrificed a knight to bring my bishops over to the attack on the king's side. In response he cleared his last rank on the queen's side and then castled. Just as I had expected. Yet I found I could not mount an attack on that side. My bishops were stuck on the wrong side of the board, one of them defended by my remaining knight. Only my queen was free to attack on the important side, yet I dared not bring her out, because in clearing out his last rank to castle Issa had also mounted a very formidable front against my weak side. I had to retreat my bishops to bring them to bear on the weak side. But he was now attacking by pushing his unneeded pawns. I had to sacrifice one of the bishops to save the remaining knight, and suddenly I was back in the starting configuration, minus a knight, a bishop and a couple of pawns, with no defense developed.

I was getting furious with my own stupidity. Issa had done nothing aggressive to cut me down this far. I had done it to myself. But now if I played conservatively he would simply grind me down, using his material and positional advantage. The only hope for me was to make a raid on his weak side with my queen and bishop and hope to pin his king behind the lines with a rook. But all it gained was an even exchange: rook for rook, one of his knights for my last bishop, and I had to back off my queen all the way to my own decimated ranks. It was hopeless. I stared at the board a few minutes and resigned.

"Very interesting," Issa commented. "Another one?"

"No thanks. I'm too tired to think clearly." But I was thinking very clearly: I couldn't beat him. If I tried to play his careful game he would grind me down with my own small mistakes and if I played again in my own raiding style he would be even more ready for it than last time. "I think I will just read a bit and go to sleep." I picked up Lawrence.

"Perhaps tomorrow evening?"

"I hate to plan that far in advance these days, Issa."

"I can appreciate that feeling."

I went upstairs feeling small and furious. Very interesting, eh? Yes, Kamal, it is very interesting. You play chess the way you live: in stabs. And when they are deflected, or blunted, you stab all the more wildly until there is nothing left to do but resign and go on to a different game. Poker, anyone? Kamal likes games in which he can bluff.

The next morning Issa was gone again. Did he always commute like an office worker, suit, tie and all? Anna, over coffee, said, no, this was very unusual, and very dangerous. It took hours to be sure no one was following him back here. The problem arose from the fearfulness of the people he had to meet. Everyone was seeing Israelis around every corner.

She sniffed. "For each one of us the Jews kill, our Arab 'brothers' kill a dozen. My brother was killed by a Lebanese Army patrol trying to stop them crossing the border to raid the kibbutz at Dan. I hate the Lebanese ten times as much as I hate the Israelis."

Then she stopped talking as abruptly as if a wire had been cut. She nodded or shook her head at a few more questions, and then I gave up. She didn't like me. The ones who were stuck in the camps never had much love for the ones who escaped, in particular for the ones who made their deals with elites of the countries of exile.

I buried myself in *Pillars* for the rest of the day. Issa returned after dark, muttering only "Bon soir," as he marched into the kitchen, shedding his tie and jacket. A vigorous conversation in Arabic echoed into the study. Issa sounded upset, Anna almost triumphant. Then Issa yelled in English, "Hey Kamal, dinner is ready."

I walked in and sat down. They both stared at me.

"Kamal, do you drink whiskey?" Issa had already poured himself a glass. "I have some bad news for you."

"Sure, I drink whiskey. What's the bad news?"

He poured. "Have you heard of the Direction de Surveillance du Territoire? It is the French equivalent of your FBI."

"I've heard of it."

"When the DST is looking for somebody of foreign nationality it often informs, unofficially, of course, the various embassies and consulates with which this person might have contact that it is interested in speaking to him. That is a way of communicating that the DST is not interested in making an arrest but rather in gathering some information. It seems, Kamal, that the DST has taken an interest in you. Or what you know, presumably, about Boudia's demise. It seems you were recognized at the scene of the assassination, and an hour or so later at the El

Al gate at De Gaulle airport. May I ask what you were doing at the airport?"

"It's very simple. I was going to avenge Boudia. That seemed like the best place to find Israelis. I calmed down a bit after I got there, and changed my mind."

"Were you armed?"

"Yes. I had that little MAB."

"It is a lucky thing you changed your mind."

"I was a little out of my mind when I had the idea."

"A bit like your chess playing, no?"

"A bit."

"Under the circumstances it is probably not a good idea for you to remain in France. The DST may mean you no harm, but they are very good at tricking information out of people, and following them. In your present distressed frame of mind it might be better if you were beyond their grasp, do you not agree?"

I nodded. My throat was too tight to talk.

"You were anxious to go to the Middle East. Under the present circumstances that might be the best place. At least until this storm blows over. Do you have any objections?"

"No." I could only get out a hoarse whisper.

"I am afraid that it will not be possible for you to reclaim your possessions at Passage des Patriarches. It is under surveillance. So you will have to travel with just what you have now. But you will be taken care of, don't worry about that."

"Where?"

"I cannot tell you that now. Until you are outside of French jurisdiction it is better for you to know as little as possible."

"When?"

"We leave here in about twenty minutes, if you do not object."

I shook my head. Suddenly my world had closed down to nothing. The T. E. Lawrence fantasy vanished. I was not ready to go east, not like this, as a virtual prisoner. And yet was there a choice? None that I could see. I nodded my acquiescence and finished dinner in silence. Then I went upstairs for my jacket—at least I had that—and my passport. I had nothing else here. Those few things at Patriarches, my camera, the prints Justina had bought—the wistful barmaid and Monet's windmills—I nearly cried to think I was having to leave those few sentimental things behind. Traded for what? The image was blank, and its blankness chilled, almost a resurrection of my father's terror as he faced the final void. Issa was waiting by the front door. I followed him around the house in the dark to a stable where the cars were parked. He drove a Volkswagen. A terrible pain was mounting behind my ribs. I couldn't get Justina off my mind. Issa drove very carefully to the gate, scattering the dogs, which were drawn by the headlights. Once outside the villa, I closed my eyes. It didn't matter anymore where I was going, or by what route I was being taken there. I was not coming back.

After about twenty minutes of driving Issa pulled off on a secluded road in sight of the lights of Orly. We waited. Soon a light-colored BMW cruised slowly by and pulled over to the side of the road a hundred yards ahead.

"You will be going with them. It has been arranged this way for other people before you." Issa tapped the steering wheel with his knuckles, and stared at his lap for a moment. "I don't know whether to tell you this or not. . . . Yes, it is something you ought to know. Apparently the DST has also informed your embassy, the U.S. embassy, that it is searching for you. I don't know how these things work in the United States. In other countries, of course, they have serious repercussions. I did not want to say anything in front of Anna, but there was another part of the rumor. A possible criminal charge having to do with an Algerian Jew? It will not matter now. But it is well that you know about it."

"Thank you. Is that all?"

"Yes. Just walk to that car. It belongs to the pilot of the plane."

I pulled myself out of the car. Then decided to take one small chance on Issa's sympathy. I walked back to his window and tapped. He lowered it.

"Issa, you know that pistol you took from me?"

"Yes?"

"Dump it in the river."

The BMW sped off as soon as I climbed in. The driver was dressed in a pilot's uniform. He drove a few minutes and stopped under a grove of trees. He reached into the back seat and pushed a pair of overalls at me. "Put these on over your clothes now, please. Quickly."

I had to get out of the car to do it. When I slid in again he explained, "You are an instrument technician. You are going to replace some bulbs which have burnt out in the instrument panel. You will find your tool kit behind the seat; when we park you will follow me directly to the plane. As you may have noticed on your overalls, you are Peter Dawkins of Lockheed Instruments. If you are challenged, it is your problem to be persuasive. I know nothing more than that you are the technician sent to fix my instrument panel. Understood, Mr. Dawkins?"

"Understood, captain."

But we were not challenged. We strode through the private corridors of the airport building and emerged onto the field under the dark shadow of a giant wing. Across an immense stretch of tarmac swept by the lights of jets taxiing away from the terminal stood a solitary 707, gleaming white, the

266

script on its tail too poorly illuminated to be legible from this distance. We paused behind the landing gear of the jet next to the terminal, the pilot pretending to point out something amiss on the strut's hydraulic system, until there was a lull in the ground traffic. Then we hurried out onto the darkened taxiway toward the solitary jet and reached it just before the probing lights of an incoming plane bore down on our path. Again we inspected landing gear until the bulk of the 747 passed between us and the terminal. Just as its lights fell beyond us we scampered up the boarding ladder into the empty plane.

It was the first time I'd ever been in a completely shut-down jet; the inertness was eerie. I followed the sound of the captain's steps to the cockpit. He instructed me to sit down in the navigator's chair, open my tool kit and not touch anything. I asked him if he could fly the plane alone if need be. He looked at me queerly, then replied, in his strange crisp accent, "Of course!"

I asked no more questions, but sat silently observing his checkout procedure and trying to memorize it. How preposterous had been my gambit to intercept the toad at Roissy. He had undoubtedly boarded his plane just as I had boarded this one. It had never occurred to me that such a thing could be done: too many years in South America, where the last thing we expected was the cooperation of an institution like an airline. This was certainly a different game in Europe. Issa had probably arranged my escape through the little consul in tennis clothes, and no doubt heard the DST rumors from him or someone equally highly placed. What could you do in a sophisticated continent like Europe without access to some of its sophisticated resources? Hide in a student quarter until someone ratted on you. Without the indigenous ocean to swim in, all you could do was fly. And for that, one needed powerful friends.

Were it not for Issa, I would be falling into the hands of the DST any day, or hour, now. And probably with the incriminating MAB still tucked behind my back. The city is the grave of the guerrilla! I could hear the lid of the coffin being pounded shut just behind me. Whenever this jet would tuck its wheels up would be none too soon for me.

We boarded the rest of the crew and passengers about an hour later. For the take-off I was strapped into a kind of jump seat behind the navigator. It wasn't until we were taxiing to the runway that I heard our destination mentioned in the request for clearance for take-off. We were flying to Kuwait via Damascus. I fell asleep as soon as we were in the air.

The captain waked me while we were still over water. We would soon be beginning our descent into Damascus. A few lights of coastal towns in northern Lebanon were visible ahead. I asked if I was to be put off the plane in Damascus, and the pilot again gave me that queer look. I assumed I was, or he would not have awakened me. Perhaps he was expecting me to keep playing the role of instrument technician.

I tried to conjure up some kind of image of Damascus. But to me it was only the end point of Lawrence's adventure, or a destination for caravans and crusades. It did not exist into the twentieth century. I only knew that it had been threatened by the army of Israel during '67 and supposedly had not been taken only because it was of no strategic importance. A little while later I recalled comments by the Uncles that their nephews had found Damascus a grim place to make a life: if it wasn't the Syrian landlords and shopkeepers cheating you, it was the bloody Deuxième listening in on your conversations or breaking down your door in the middle of the night. And what was I, also their nephew, supposed to be doing down there in Damascus? I wished I'd had their addresses. How reassuring it would have been to know that one of those lights making up that ragged glow in the midst of infinite blackness marked the house of family, no matter how remote. But there were no reassurances to be found in any aspect of the situation. Even the lights of the city did not resolve into the normal grid as we approached, but lay scattered helter-skelter like jewels spilled on black velvet. A few linear veins crisscrossed the scatter, but too few to impart any scale. We left the lights to our left as we descended and aligned with a bright swath of blue miles south of the city. As we taxied toward the lights of the terminal I thought I could make out military planes standing off in the shadows.

I was kept aboard until the passengers had emptied into the transit lounge. From the cockpit I saw a black car prowl onto the tarmac and stop under the nose of the plane. Now I was instructed to shed my Lockheed overalls. A few minutes later a man in fatigues opened the door to the cockpit and spoke in Arabic to the captain. I heard my name mentioned. The man in fatigues extended his hand, and the captain explained that I was to give him my passport and follow him. I thanked him coolly for the smooth flight and stepped out onto the boarding ladder, into a heat as thick and still as motor oil.

Now, minus even my passport, I was leaving behind the last connection to Paris. The dispossession was complete. I had no more control over my own life here: no identity, no function or rank, no money, no weapons, no friends, no language. The last dispossession was the most frightening of all. The man in fatigues gestured me into his car. Once that was accomplished he had nothing further to communicate. He focused all his attention on the dark road carrying us away from the airport. I was merely baggage; once picked up, I ceased to exist.

Clear of the lights of the airport I was able to determine from the Dipper that we were headed generally southwest. It could not be a long ride, as the Israeli-occupied zone lay not further than about thirty miles in this direction from Damascus. And even were we to turn abruptly south, the border with Jordan lay not further than fifty or sixty miles, as I recalled from the maps I'd studied in Paris. But we continued southwest, and soon the road began to gain elevation. The night was too dark to make out any of the features of the surrounding landscape. Our headlights illuminated only low scrub by the side of the road and occasionally picked out squat buildings in clusters set back twenty or thirty yards. We passed only one oncoming vehicle, a truck, during the entire journey.

Suddenly, without slowing, the driver swerved from the main road into a narrow canyon whose walls steepened as we climbed past two switchbacks into a ravine. The road ran level along the floor of this ravine, but the vegetation revealed by the lights thickened dramatically as we proceeded deeper. After about two miles the road began to climb again and brought us into a tiny settlement, a knot of poor huts squeezed into a slight widening of the gorge. Past the huts the road turned to dirt. The driver shifted into first gear and worked the car past a series of deep runnels which could have easily swallowed a wheel. The walls of the ravine closed in again on either side, and the steepness of the climb threatened to defeat even first gear at several places. I had noted the odometer when we passed through the settlement. Three kilometers later the grade eased, and though the ravine walls were steepening they now diverged to leave a level clearing perhaps a hundred meters wide on either side of the dirt track. After another half kilometer the ravine walls suddenly converged again and the road made an abrupt left turn. Here we were blocked by a pole gate lowered across the road. Coils of barbed wire prevented passage on either side of the track.

After we stopped, a guard approached the car and peered in the driver's window. He was no more than sixteen years old, with a little incipient wisp of a mustache. He saluted the driver, backed off and lifted the gate by climbing onto the counterweighted end. As soon as he had enough clearance, the driver shot ahead and negotiated the rock-strewn grade for at least another kilometer until we reached a cluster of tents and two bunkerlike structures. Here he stopped, killed the engine and doused the lights. The scene instantly reverted to vague shadows.

The driver leaned against the door and lit up a cigarette. I stepped out of the car to stretch my legs. The air was much cooler than at the airport. We must have gained several thousand feet. Overhead the stars punctuated only a narrow slot of the sky, indicating that the canyon walls rose nearly vertical on either side. There was no motion or light from any of the tents or bunkers. When I looked back into the car the driver had stretched himself across the front seat. He pointed to the back seat. Apparently no one was waiting up for us, and it seemed there must be a few hours left till dawn. I took the driver's suggestion and curled up in the back seat. I woke only as the first light of dawn was trickling into the canyon.

The end of my road. Our headlights had barely given a hint of the finality of the place last night. Now under a chilly gray dusting of illumination the ravine's dimension appears dramatically magnified. Though the floor where we are parked has not grown, the cliffs rising from this fifty-yard-wide slot open to the sky at least a thousand feet above us: a thousand feet of brush-covered rock and scree too steep to climb except by clinging to the vegetation.

Ahead the gorge continues to climb into the mountainside, narrowing and hooking left out of view. Behind the car the road slopes down toward the pole gate and wire barrier and beyond, perhaps half a mile from this encampment, the canyon widens and swings away to the right. Its far wall blocks a view of any terrain further down the mountain or in the valley below. There is no view except up. We are sitting in a vast open grave.

The road, in fact, does end right under our tires. We are parked in a roughly circular clearing, ringed by piles of boulders which have been bulldozed away to where the ground starts to rise. This hundred-foot-diameter field is the only part of the ravine floor which is not littered with boulders. On the right-hand edge of the clearing stand two bunkers constructed of cinder block and concrete. Both have heavy steel doors. A gray Land Cruiser is parked by the far bunker. The only other vehicle is a black VW minibus parked to our left. Up-canyon, past the ring of cleared boulders, a dozen pieces of tarpaulin-covered equipment stand guard; whether guns or rocket launchers is impossible to tell. And past these, among the naturally strewn boulders, are hidden small brown pup tents, so difficult to distinguish in this ambiguous light from the boulders themselves that some seem to appear and disappear each time I glance toward them. And now concentrating on a nearer group of tents, I think I can make out some activity between the rocks.

Impossible to sit still any longer. The driver continues to snore in the front seat as I ease open the back door and slide out into the cold mountain dawn. The dirt feels good under my feet. A faint smell of coffee hangs in the thin, clean air. My legs want to shake out the logginess of too long confinement. I have an urge to jog down to the fence and back, but it's a dangerous idea. Though none are visible, there must be guards among the rocks. One could hardly ask for a more easily secured redoubt; one well-armed man at each end could hold off an army. The smell of the coffee is becoming irresistible. It must be wafting down from the area of the tents. What the hell! Who could begrudge me a cup of coffee?

Two men are squatting in front of the first tent—two teenagers, rather—tending a small hissing stove. They glance up as I approach and say something in Arabic. I shrug and mime drinking a cup of coffee. "Ahwa?" They laugh at my poor attempt, but pour out a spare gulp of the viscous black fluid into a tin cup and hand it to me. It tastes like hot liquid rubber, but comforts all the same. The two kids watch me and talk low and quickly. Then one springs up from his squat and bounds away among the boulders. A few minutes later he returns with a man about my age, still tousled from sleep, but dignified in his walk and manner. He is dressed in rumpled fatigues, which seem out of character with his fine long features. He resembles the portraits of Faisal in *Pillars*, except in place of the sadness of Faisal's eyes, his eyes almost quiver in a struggle to contain some force exploding behind them. He scrutinizes me for a moment, as I do him, then rears his head back slightly and concludes in nearly perfect Oxfordian, "So you must be the American."

"I must be. And who must you be, pray?"

"I am Samir. Did Abu send you over here to be fed?"

"Abu? No." I point at my stomach, and he mutters to the teenagers in Arabic.

"They will feed you. Then I suggest you wait in front of the far bunker. Abu Ahmet will want to interview you."

"Abu Ahmet? The Abu Ahmet who bleeds mercury?"

"I've never seen him bleed. This one is the commander of our camp. He will give you instructions. . . . Yes, you see they are looking for you already."

Down in the clearing the driver and a very tall stooped man in uniform are scanning the canyon floor toward the pole gate. They must be thinking I have fled.

"You had better return."

"All right." I help myself to another half cup of coffee from the boiling pot, and a flat hard roll warming in a pan next to the coffee. Then cup in one hand and roll in the other I stroll back to the clearing.

The tall, stooped officer strides toward me. "Come, pliss!"

I follow as he leads to the first bunker. The steel door is now open to a shoulder-width passage. He has to duck to clear the opening. A single bare bulb lights the tunnel. Thin pipes run along its ceiling. It extends perhaps thirty feet into the slope, not more. The mutter of a gasoline generator echoes through the concrete. I can feel its thrumming in my feet.

About halfway into the tunnel the tall officer turns and peers down at me. The bulb is directly overhead and exaggerates his vulturelike appearance. He reaches for the tin coffee cup. "Search, pliss." He kneels and does a quick pat-down, as usual skipping my back. Then he knocks on the low metal door next to us. A syllable sounds from within. He swings open the door with a creak and nods me in. He remains outside in the tunnel.

This room is surprisingly spacious after the squeeze through the passageway. On either side the walls are lined with metal shelves sagging under boxes and books and stacks of papers. There is another door at the far end of the right-hand wall. Next to it on the far wall begins a row of posters of heroes of the struggle, just below these a vast topological map. And in front of this map, behind a steel table that extends nearly the full width of the room, sits the object of this visit. But he sits so still that at first he appears as inanimate as the rest of the fixtures of the room. Only two gray irises, like galvanized steel washers, move in a broad expanse of face, flicking methodically over my full length. The blankness of the expression stops me in my tracks as I try to read even the vaguest hint from its features. It is not an Arab face. Either every one of the world's races have contributed to it or none have. It could be the progenitor of a post-human race which will emerge as the equilibrium point of all the explosive racial chemistry of this age.

Just to provoke some response and break the spell I stick out my right hand and march up to the desk. His hands remain folded. Then the thin taut lips part and a few seconds of Arabic rattle from deep in the throat. The steel washer irises stay fixed on my face through the address. I have an urge to clamp my open offered hand into a fist and drive his nose back into his brain. But just as I feel the tendons tighten, I recognize words that are coming from his lips.

"So it is true you do not speak Arabic."

"Good morning." My hand falls back to my side.

"Either that or what I said was fact, and so you take no offense."

"What did you say?"

"That you are a spy, a profligate, a murderer and a homosexual."

"No offense." I feel my mouth trembling and twisting. "So it must all be true."

His hands have parted, and now I notice that under a newspaper by his right hand is a submachine gun of some kind; the wire stock protruding close to his elbow.

"Apparently you have been recommended highly by Mohammed Boudia. One should never ignore the recommendations of a dead man. While he was still alive I had no use for Boudia. So were he still alive his recommendation would mean less to me than a fistful of sand." He stares his blank stare.

"And now that he is dead?"

"You have no comprehension of what I am saying. We must begin at the beginning. What was Boudia?"

"What was he? I don't understand the question."

"I am asking you what the man Boudia was when he was alive. But I see I have to answer my own question. Boudis was a cosmopolite, a sophisticate, a moral degenerate, a drug addict, an opportunist, a careerist. He was also a foreigner, as are you."

"I am a Palestinian."

"No. Your father may have been a Palestinian once. But Palestine is here, not ten thousand kilometers over there." He jabs his forefinger westward. "Perhaps you see the truth now. You may have been of use to a man like Boudia; for that very reason you are no use here except as an example."

"Example?"

"Of what happens to a man when he loses the connection to his homeland. So while you are with us, it is my order that you remain in civilian clothes."

"This is all I have. I'll at least need a change of shirt."

"You are no longer in Paris. That is all any of us have: just what we are wearing. Realize as your clothes wear thin your bourgeois Western attitudes will wear thin as well. That is the best we can hope for, is it not?"

He raps twice on his desk. The Vulture steps heavily into the cell and coughs in the direction of the passageway.

"Comrade Ahmet, can I ask one last question? Why am I here?"

He slowly spreads his hands, turning his palms up

in mock supplication. "Did you not ask to be sent here?"

Samir

WHATEVER HE IS, his walk is unmistakably American. On the assumption there is no place they aren't welcome, that arrogant race lets its ungoverned swagger carry them where it will—ungoverned, that is, by conscience. They do not believe the concept of trespass applies to them. Haven't we posted our lands clearly enough? The British and the French have surely learned to tread with a more confined gait. However, not the Americans. Not yet.

But Abu knows how to clip a swagger. The American emerged from his quarter hour in the Chamber in a surly, silent rage. He barely grunted as I led him through the supply bunker issuing his bedding and mess gear. For some reason he is to have no military clothing or weapons except during marksmanship training. There is no explanation of why he is here; he can't even speak our language.

"We are tentmates now, you know. I'm to act as your interpreter."

"You don't sound too happy about it.

"It's nothing to do with happiness."

"What's it to do with?"

"Duty."

"Oh shit!" The American raises his eyes to his godless heaven, then peers at me quizzically. "Where did you learn to speak English so well?"

"So well? I speak as well as any Englishman."

"I take that to mean in England."

"In English schools, and Swiss schools, and the University of London, and the London School of Economics."

"Pretty plooty. Your parents left to England?"

"My parents live in Dubai, as have all my recorded ancestors."

"You were sent abroad for you education."

"Yes, it is not uncommon in our families."

"You're a princeling of some kind?"

"I am closely related to the royal family."

"What do ya know! A real prince. And what is a real prince doing up here?"

"Fighting for his people."

"His people? Dubai is a long way from here."

"All Arabs are one people."

"Listen, man. If I want to hear that shit I can turn on Radio Free Libya. Why don't you lighten up a little?"

Another form of the American trespass: they'll swagger into your mind if they don't like what is being thought there. Having no religion, they have no temples, and thus respect no sanctuary. Our traditional barriers of formality are to the American just fences to vault. He assumes the right to be inside. And persists.

"I have a hard time understanding why a prince would leave his palaces to come sit on a cold hard rock."

"One might ask the same thing of an American. Why do you leave your air conditioning?"

"I am a Palestinian."

"Aren't we all?"

This American has a violent streak in him. He is clenching up his fists. Is he insane? Doesn't he see I'm wearing a pistol?

"No, we aren't all, princeling. Not all of us were born in refugee camps outside of Amman."

"So you really are a Palestinian. Your persona is American, as American as . . . John Wayne. Ah, life is complicated, is it not?"

"You could simplify it a little by explaining why

278

you, who are neither Palestinian nor refugee, are here in a guerrilla camp."

"Oh, it is a sort of rite of passage among us. There have been others like me. One of the sons of the royal family of Kuwait, for example. He was wounded by an Israeli bomb a few years ago."

"How long have you been with Abu Ahmet?"

"We call him Abu, for short. About eleven months now."

"What do you think of him?"

"I will let you draw your own conclusions."

He does not seem dismayed by the prospect of sleeping on the hard ground in a tent that is just big enough to sit up in. I expected a complaint. But instead he unrolls his bedding and stretches out on it for a minute, concluding, "Not bad."

Then hopping out of the tent, he demands to know what is next on the "agenda."

"For you, nothing. For the rest of us, morning training exercises."

"Why not for me?"

"Abu's orders. Something about serving as a lesson to the rest of us in the decaying influences of life in the bourgeois West."

He has no reply for this. I leave him brooding on a rock to fall in with my squads down at the clearing. Hamid has already begun the drills. The in-place calisthenics will be brief today; it is the morning for our terrain run. We are all conserving our energy.

Toward the last of the exercises I catch sight of the American observing from the periphery of the clearing. He cuts a ludicrous figure, with his wild blond hair and corduroy student's jacket, blue jeans and silly leather sneakers. When the workout is terminated by Hamid's whistle the murmurs and snickers over the newcomer's appearance ripple through the files. Hamid's whistle dismisses us for a fifteen-minute rest.

The American ambles over to me. "And that was training?"

"There is more coming."

"They worked us harder than that in grade school. What's next, croquet?"

A sort of circle has formed around us. Hamid now shoulders through to investigate the distraction. He demands to know why this new person is not participating in exercises. I explain Abu's orders concerning the American. Hamid shakes his head. Everyone participates in exercises. If he is not participating send him away. He is a distraction.

I translate this for the American.

He replies, "Tell him I'll participate."

"The orders are—"

"Fuck orders." He strips off his jacket and then his shirt, revealing a surprisingly fit torso.

Hamid demands to know what is going on. I explain that the newcomer insists upon being included in the training exercises. Hamid sweeps his powerful arm in a dismissing gesture.

"I'm afraid it's no go. Orders are orders. And besides, you should be happy to skip the next trial. We are all trained to it, yet it nearly kills us every time. You see, we will now run up goat trails on the canyon wall for many, many kilometers."

"Tell Superman there that this worm-eaten specimen of bourgeois decay will come along for the ride."

I translate. A peal of laughter from the circle. Hamid frowns and again dismisses him with a wave of the arm. Now he turns and leaves the circle. Three blasts of his whistle bring everyone into formation again. Most have removed their shirts. At the next blast we begin to run in place. The American is standing alongside watching. Hamid now turns and leads out of the clearing. Behind him our six files merge into one and follow onto the narrow boot-beaten track which snakes between the rocks toward the high end of the canyon. Glancing back, I see the American still waiting in the clearing as the last of the boys file out. I am almost sorry he has thought better of making a fool of himself. Sooner or later he will not be able to resist it.

The first kilometer is not the steepest, but the worst. The trail twists and turns around the boulders. It is impossible to keep an even stride. We are all on each other's heels. And all gasping for breath until the sweat starts to flow freely, which is when the second wind also comes. Later on, the heat and the increasing steepness of the trail will be the principal tortures. Then the thirst . . .

A hand taps my shoulder. It is the American pulling alongside, striding lightly. "Chin up, chest out. Ta ta."

He shoots ahead with a smirk. The men ahead, hearing the rapidly closing steps, glance back and stumble aside to let him pass. In minutes he is on Hamid's heels at the head of the line. Now he taps Hamid on the shoulder. Hamid glances back and flares. The American gives a little wave and points ahead mockingly. Hamid's muscles tighten and he lunges ahead. His increased pace ripples back through the line. But the American remains in lockstep with him. Again he taps Hamid's shoulder and signals to pass. Hamid strains for more speed. He is now breathing very hard. He must know he cannot win this race. The American is still striding very lightly and easily. And the rest of us are suffering from the unaccustomed pace. I know Hamid. He will change the rules of the race very soon. Hopefully before the rest of us are worn down. Hamid is a powerful man, but it is doubtful even he can keep this up for long. He has to act soon.

And he does. He suddenly curls into a squat and flings himself at the American's knees. But the challenger simply hurdles the sweaty muscular trunk and shoots out ahead. Twenty of us have passed Hamid before he manages to regain his feet. He is dark red and trembling, but he waves us on. The lithe figure of the American is vanishing up the trail.

An hour later, reaching the crest, I find him reclining under a large bush taking in the scenery. "I assume this is the finish line. The boot prints seem to mill about suddenly."

Collapsing next to him, I wait until I have the breath to speak intelligibly. "Well, I must admit you've won that round. But you were lucky."

"Not lucky, princeling. It is a basic guerrilla principle: Never engage the enemy unless you are certain you can win. Che said it, or Mao. I can't remember."

"How could you be so certain you were going to win?"

"I chose the battleground."

Kamal

THE BOURGEOIS decadent strikes back. In itself it is a hollow victory, running down a clumsy weight lifter in combat boots. It's that monstrosity in the bunker I would like to run into the ground, but he will not meet me on my ground. So I will have to gnaw away at his. And this is not a bad start. Look at this panting princeling, how he suddenly is regarding me with dog's eyes. Or these others staggering onto the ridge, the younger ones goggle-eyed with admiration as they flop down in a wide circle, even willing to forgo a place in the shade to be near me. The older ones will not be brought around so easily. It will take more than a foot race. But it's not a bad beginning. So long as you don't let them see what it's cost. Word of this will get back to Abu, and he'll know he has a battle on his hands. Better be ready for the next round, Kamal.

The drill sergeant reaches the crest near the tail of the pack. The early duel must have burnt him out. He makes his way between the prone bodies to my bush. He is strong. He has almost regained his breath.

The princeling translates his words. "He says you should be the drill master. The men have never run so hard."

"Tell him he ran a good race until he tripped."

"He didn't trip. He was trying to tackle you."

"I know that, princeling. Just tell him what I said."

The translation brought a smile to the square red face. Be magnanimous in victory, Kamal. Always give a man's pride a way out of defeat. Some of my father's good advice. My first bit of diplomacy appears to have won me a friend. The drill sergeant retreats, still smiling, to find a spot in the shade and begins an animated discussion with the boys around him, gesturing regularly in my direction.

"So, princeling, where are we? Geographically speaking, that is."

"To be precise we are at a few meters below two thousand meters elevation. If we were to climb a little higher you would see the summit of Jebel ash-Shaykh, what the Israelis call Mount Hermon, due north about nine kilometers. The dark patch far out on the plain to the northeast is Damascus. It is about fifty kilometers as the crow flies. If you follow this ridge down due eastward and then look south, you see a small cluster of buildings and a road leading in and out?"

"Several miles down the canyon?"

"Yes. That is Beit Jinn. That is how you came into the camp, along that road. You can see past Beit Jinn, where the road flattens out there is a green

283

patch in the brown. That is Mazraat Beit Jinn. An old oasis."

"And across our own dear canyon here, to the south?"

"Do you see the line across the facing slope that drops down into our canyon?"

"Just above the drop-off? A few hundred feet lower than where we are now?"

"Yes. That is the Syrian boundary of the demilitarized zone. The Israeli fence lies just along the top of the ridge, a kilometer or two further south. In fact, the peaklet you see, which is only two hundred meters higher than our present elevation, is the very corner of the occupied zone. The boundary shoots south-southwest from that point to Majdal Chams and then south to Kuneitra. If we were two hundred meters higher you could see into the occupied territory."

"So the camp is within mortar range of the Israelis."

"Quite within mortar range. Fortunately the canyon walls are too steep for them to see into the canyon, so they are shooting blind. The first round always hits somewhere up on the slopes overhead. It gives us plenty of warning to take cover."

"That's nice."

"It is really very similar to being in a large trench. A trench is a safe place to be. It is the leaving of the trench that is dangerous."

"What about air strikes?"

"We haven't received any, so far. Just a few reconnaissance flights overhead. This corner of the border has been remarkably quiet for the six months we have been up here."

"Where were you before?"

"In a camp near Hamma, north of Damascus."

"Why were you moved?"

"The struggle is down here, not up there."

* * *

The canyon floor receives direct sunlight for only
five or six hours. By three the shadow of the steep
southern wall has moved halfway up the brush and
broken rock of the northern wall. Above the shadow
the rocks turn bright ocher against the darkening
blue sky. In the trench's depth now all colors have
become shades of somber slate gray. There has not
been much activity since the sun slid out of sight. It
is hard to resist staring up at the luminous rim of the
canyon, trying to absorb some warmth through your
eyes. With evening the chill pours down from the
west end of the ravine like a palpable fluid. As at
dawn, the hissing blue flames of the kerosene stoves
send their sweet vapors down-canyon. But now the
fuel smells are also laced with light veins of acrid
hashish. The boys cluster around their stoves for
warmth as well as for whiffs of the porridgey stuff
that is called dinner. The pipes pass back and forth.

"Hey Sami"—that is the princeling's nickname—
"how come a moral ramrod like Abu tolerates dope
smoking?"

"He is a realist. Without hashish what do sixty
healthy young men do for pleasure?"

"Even with hashish . . . There remain other
needs."

"In what way do we slake our passions—as the expression goes—is that what you are asking?"

"Trips down to the city perhaps?"

"*That* is not permitted."

"But the other is . . . permitted?"

"Yes, but not talked about. Nor joked about."

"Where are all the budding young Leila Khaleds
one hears about? In the States they always put a
girls' camp nearby."

"Then you are doomed to disappointment, Kamal.
By this and other differences. Perhaps you would
find the Israeli Army more to your taste."

"Don't say that too loud."

"No, I'm serious. That is a real problem. What do these kids come back to after battle? Veils, or the moral equivalent. Compared to the Israeli soldier of the same age. There is a joke about why the Six Day War lasted only six days."

"We could steal a truck and bring up a load of girls from Damascus."

"Our commander might take that as a challenge to his authority. If Sophia Loren were standing nude in the middle of the drill ground taking reservations, not one of Abu's boys would come forward."

"Nature is nature, Sami boy. Authority goes only so far."

"But here nature is overcome by will. It is what Abu calls the 'tempering.' I see you do not believe me, Kamal. Let me only make this point. If seeking women is part of man's nature, certainly avoiding Death is an even more deeply rooted instinct. And yet, through 'tempering' Abu is successful in excising the latter as well as the former. Perhaps you noticed some of the boys wearing on their sleeves black patches in the shape of hand grenades?"

"Yes, I did. About a dozen of them, in fact."

"Those call themselves the 'Grenades.' They volunteer for so-called one-way missions."

"There is such a thing? I thought suicide squads were an invention of Israeli propaganda."

"That particular term should never be used up here. Their act is not considered suicide."

"But when they go on a mission they know they will not survive it?"

"Yes."

"It is not simply a pessimistic euphemism?"

"No. Why do you have such trouble believing it?"

"If we were in the Middle Ages instead of the Middle East—"

"Are you really so Western that you are not at all moved by the charisma of sacrifice?"

"Only by the charisma of success."

"Then you will find life very disturbing here. Those boys with the grenade patches are considered the elite. I hope you are not offended by the deference the others pay them."

"But the 'others' don't volunteer for one-way missions, all their reverence notwithstanding."

"You misunderstand. That privilege is not offered them. The opportunity to become a hero is very precious. It is given only to the deserving."

"In other words, if you carry out a mission and die, you are a hero. If you carry out the same mission and survive, then you are not a hero. Is that the idea?"

"The voice of Anglo-Saxon utilitarianism. Do you see that those two are not the same mission? The sacrifice is part of the achievement."

"I'll tell you what I do see, Sami. I see that you are not wearing one of those patches."

He shrugs and flashes a momentary smile. "I am a product of Anglo-Saxon education, too. I was being pedagogic with you."

"The fervor in your voice was a bit too intense for mere pedagogy, Sami."

"Yes? Beware then, Kamal, the power of an idea in an empty place like this. It worms beneath the most cynicism-hardened skins after a while."

An empty place like this. He has put his finger on it. Even the tide of night air flowing through the canyon cannot explain this chill. Nor even my slight fever from overstraining this morning. It is the chill of a place that no one wants. Even the crows and field mice are a bit diffident in full daylight. They have no use for this ravine at night.

Sami squats loosely in front of our stove stirring the gruel. This was really once a prince? His squat belongs to a street Arab: comfortable, unselfconscious, and as undignified as taking a shit. He must have learned it up here. Just as he must have learned to tolerate sleeping on the ground and swallowing gruel up here. All this must be part of Abu Ahmet's process of "tempering." If it can undo Leysin and the London School of Economics it must, as Sami suggests, have an uncanny power. But the commander has realized that it will not work on me. That is why he has set me apart. I am to serve as the living proof of the corruptness and weakness of the "untempered" state. He will have me act the camp clown whose ineptitude, confusion and cowardice shame the rest of his subjects into even more devout application. But his scheme is already jumping the track. No one is laughing at his clown. And what would he make of his princeling officer squatting at the clown's feet stewing the clown's dinner?

But what does the princeling officer make of it himself? He could have asked me to prepare our dinner and mitigated my triumph on the ridge by having me squatting at his feet. But he never suggested it. Could it be that he was so awed by the victory of an obviously trained trackman over a herd of kids in combat boots? Or does he have another purpose in keeping my budding legend intact? If there is one area in which this aristocrat is not to be underestimated, it is in the realm of subtlety.

A nasty dream tears up my sleep sometime before dawn. But the dream itself evades my memory now that I am awake, so I'm left with the sourness and no way to purge it. Bits and pieces come back to me in the dark: the room at Patriarches, Justina's face. Yes, now it comes back. She is peering in the window of Patriarches, hovering thirty feet above the inner yard. And her sudden and impossible appearance there made my heart pound with fear. Yes, it is still pounding. As if she were about to pull back the flap

288

of the tent and stare at me: that accusing, haunted leer.

Or perhaps it is just the fever that has gotten worse. Or the cold of the ground leaking through the bottom of the tent and attacking my cramping calves. Inside the tent the blackness is absolute. I could be blind for all I know. Or dead. Except for Sami's wheezing snore.

So the rest of the night passes in concentric circles of distraction and discomfort moving farther and farther from sleep until the faintest dusting of gray touches the fabric of the tent. At first it pulsates in time to my heartbeat. Gradually it steadies until the seams where the fabric is folded form distinct dark lines, and now the clinking of pots, low muttering, nearby the hard hiss of urination and then its faint odor. And now Sami is sitting up in his blankets, yawning blasts of vapor, tugging off the ragged white undershirt which serves him for pajama top, peeking under the blanket to make sure his pecker is still there and then giving it a few grateful tugs. Day number two has begun.

There is no alienation like lacking a language. If anything drives me mad it will be this. I must lean on Sami for every detail. Take him away and I would be missing a limb. Except for the "ben sharmootas" which the kids use like commas, my ear cannot grab a single word out of their rapid chatter. Even the few words I know are indecipherable in this dialect. I might as well be deaf.

But not only their tongues put them beyond my reach. Their gestures, their shrugs, their grimaces flow as easily and quickly as their words. To them I must seem like an emotional hippo among gazelles. Sami, when he returns to his inherited language, completely sheds that rigid British shell. His intensity with the others reminds me of my father's mercurial temperament, so outlandish in the Anglo-Saxon world, so perfectly accepted here where nobody backs away with a squint from outbursts of joy or rage. Here they meet your eye, and if you look away they will step around in front of your gaze and demand with their eyes why you are trying to avoid them. Is this why my father complained that all the "whites" were avoiding him? Was he still too Arab, even after twenty years? If so why did he pass so little of it on to me? Now I see why these people insist on calling me "amriki." They feel no kinship at all.

What I do elicit from them, however, may be more potent than kindred spirit. I suspect their awe is not easily granted to strangers, and may be withdrawn at the first stumble. They are always watching me. Even fifty yards away I often feel a pair of eyes studying the way I walk, the way I stretch or pushup or run in place. Even the way I fold my blankets. I glimpse a challenge their scrutiny throws my way. They say, Show us you are a hero and we will emulate you in every detail we can see. But show us you are anything less, and our scrutiny will give us the material for endless mockery.

So day two continues, fortunately occupied by routine matters like digging new foxholes, moving stones to expose dirt to fill sandbags. Mindless, sweaty work offering no opportunity for heroic displays. Thank Allah. Around noon a barrage of gunfire echoes down the canyon. Sami explains that the camp is divided into three firing practice groups. Each group goes up to the firing ground twice a week. Each man is issued one clip, thirty rounds, per week for practice. There is a moderate shortage of ammunition. The bulk of it must be saved in case the canyon is attacked. Officers are issued pistols in addition to their Klashnikovs, but the Tokarev ammunition is in such short supply that they never practice with them. Special weapons such as the

RPG anti-tank launchers are dry-fired until a mission is in preparation. Then the active squads are given one or two live rounds to try out so they won't be caught by surprise by the sound and blast. This was not always the policy. But on one of the first missions out of the canyon the RPG man planted himself in front of one of the riflemen in his firing group and burned him to death with the blast of the rocket. He hadn't realized that anything came out of the back of the launch tube; he'd never seen one actually fired before he went on the mission. After that the survivors were so horrified they couldn't carry on with the mission. They returned to camp carrying the charred body of their comrade. Abu sent the three down to Hamma for their failure to carry on in spite of the loss. Being "sent down" was the worst of all disgraces.

"I would have expected harsher punishment to be meted out by a man like Abu."

"Ah, Kamal, you still do not understand. You can be whipped without losing face. You can even be shot without losing face. But there is no way you can be 'sent down' without humiliation. Up here there is no harsher punishment than humiliation."

"Thank you, Sami. I think I do begin to understand."

Samir

ON THE WAY to the firing range the American asks to borrow my Tokarev pistol. A little target practice, he explains. There is no reason to deny him this. Now I see he had a bigger purpose than perforating a piece of cardboard. He has just performed another of his carnival tricks. The firing group has left the line and is gathering around the sprawled carcass of a large crow. Kamal stands about ten meters away with the Tokarev dangling carelessly by his thigh. The boys stare from him to the bird. No one actually saw him shoot it. We heard the shot and saw the bird flutter to the ground. He could as well have picked up a dead bird, fired a shot in the air, and then thrown the bird out on the range. I don't put it past him. But the boys are convinced he shot it on the wing. You can see it in their faces.

Kuma, the tallest, steps up cautiously. "Bu Q'asidi," he murmurs with an expectant look.

"What's he saying?" the American asks.

"Don't you recognize it, Yank? He's saying Butch Cassidy. They think you shot the crow on the wing."

"I did."

Dark, gangling Kuma peers down at the American, eyes shining with admiration. "Po Nooman."

"Hey Yank, he thinks you look like Paul Newman. Personally I think it's an undeserved compliment. Must be the blond hair."

"Doesn't he know Newman's a Jew?"

"Yahud?" Kuma points at the American in wonder and horror. I explain that Kamal was referring to the actor. Kuma is relieved and begins chanting "Bu Q'asidi." Immediately the other boys take up the chant. "Bu Q'asidi, Bu Q'asidi!" The American has acquired a nom de guerre.

"You know, Yank, it's bad luck to shoot crows."

"Is that what they taught you at the London School of Economics, Sami?"

The American and I remain at Little Nefud after the others have spent their fifteen rounds and returned to camp. I thought I would drill him in the field-stripping of the AK and explain its quirks. But apparently he knows the rifle inside out.

"Do you know how many of these came from Vietnam? You could buy them for about two hundred dollars when I left the States."

"That crow, that was a lucky shot, wasn't it?"

"Call it an educated guess. I've been shooting since I was nineteen. It's not as hard as it looks, once you learn to aim with your body instead of aiming with your eye and hand separately. It's just like throwing a ball."

"Well, I was never very good at cricket, and I'm not very good with this pistol either."

"Who cares? A pistol is about as useful as a lawn mower up here. I assume this place is called Little Nefud because of the sand."

"Yes, our little desert. It is the largest piece of level terrain we ever set foot on since we came up here. It becomes a pond after winter, but this year it didn't last much after April. That is when we had to start trucking water up to fill our cistern. And when the daily baths stopped."

"Yes, I was wondering about that."

"One two-minute shower a week, my bourgeois friend. You will adjust."

"I hope I'm not here long enough to adjust to that."

"Really? Do you expect to be leaving soon?"

"I thought you knew, Sami. I'm just being parked here out of harm's way while things cool off in Europe. The man I was working for got himself blown up by the Israelis."

"You mean Mohammed Boudia?"

"Yes. You didn't know that?"

"Not a syllable of it. We were just told that an American was being brought."

"Well, there's no harm in you knowing, since the French Direction de Surveillance du Territoire seems to know. It was to avoid having to chat with them that I came here. But Boudia's operations have been taken over by others, and they will call me back when it is time to act."

"I see why Abu took such a disliking to you. He is quite dour on the 'cocktail' revolutionary set. I'm surprised he even let you come here. He must owe someone a favor. If I were you, I would not disseminate the news that you are only a wayfarer here. No one else knows. And it would undo the reputation you have gone to such trouble to establish. By the way, what is the next act in your magic show?"

"How about an eclipse? Would they go for that?"

"Sorry, Kamal. Wrong side of the Nile."

"Sami, do you know the story of the Pied Piper?"

"Of course."

"What am I going to do with all these kids?"

"You must have had an idea when you started piping."

He shrugs as he shoves a fresh clip into the AK. I am finding his shrug suspect, and the Pied Piper allusion a taunt. Who is this man? And why, when he appears so blond and bland, does his aura feel as shadowy and doubtful as a wizened dervish in a Baghdad souk? He is sighting the rifle at the targets and now toward the rocks at the far end of the sand bed. I wonder if Abu isn't right about the types who are drawn into the terrorist cells located in the European capitals. This one has anarchist written on his forehead. And just now a vague outline of Abu's probable intention emerges. He is going to turn his anarchist into an object lesson for the rest of us. The American looses a short burst from the AK. I'm about to reprimand him for firing off the range when my eye, following his line of aim, discerns a flurry of black feathers dancing above a rock over a hundred meters away.

"Do you have something against crows, Yank?"

"They'll do for the moment."

Kamal

PIECES OF THE COMPLICATED CLOCKWORK which calls itself Samir have been revealing themselves: each day a new gear, lever or bearing. The dark of night turns our tent into a confessional. A big chunk of the mainspring sprung out last night. Today Sami won't look me in the eye. He has the air of someone pressing his bowels back into his abdomen. Sami talks a great deal about his uncle, who is the Minister of Defense as well as other matters in his country, and takes a great personal interest in Sami's career.

"Is he your father's brother or your mother's." I realized last night he had never made that clear.

"My mother's brother. Though I'm sure they both would prefer it were not so."

"If there is no love lost between them, why is Uncle so paternal to you?"

A quivering cough. "Some think there is too much love between them: enough to make them prefer to be other than brother and sister."

"Do you believe that?"

"I wish I could disbelieve it."

"Does this love have something to do with why you are here and not back at the palace?"

"Well, you see, my uncle has always preferred me to my cousins. But bearing his name, they stand above me on the cliff of power, and when they climb into their inheritance they will be in a lethal position to avenge their father's displaced affections. This is knowledge I have grown up with. Proximity to a seat of power makes for precociousness, let me tell you. My mother and my uncle decided very early on that I would be best off abroad. Like Hamlet, I was sent away into England."

"And where was your father in all this? Ghosting around the ramparts?"

"He ghosts, yes, but in his racing yachts. He ignores me, as the English put it so well, studiously. And that was not difficult since I was usually a continent away. My uncle was always the one who came to visit, and the one who moved me from England to Switzerland when I complained too bitterly about the racism at the English schools."

"Why did he put you in an English school in the first place?"

"He believed that we Arabs were living in a world invented by Englishmen and only by becoming English to a certain extent could we hope to understand and thereby master it."

"And yet you never had much of a hope of going back to Dubai."

"Not until I was old enough to understand my situation. I still remember sitting staring at the Alps. We were drinking tea. He had come for one of his visits to take me skiing. I was fourteen only. That was the last day I was a child. I remember listening to him trying to explain. His voice was so full of pain, that was all I heard. Not the words. I couldn't absorb the words. I remember feeling that the only warm thing in the whole frozen universe was that cup of tea between my hands."

I wanted to ask how he had then come to end up in this cul-de-sac with Abu Ahmet, but I realized I would have to wait. I heard him roll over in the dark and grunt as if he were tensing his muscles against the sobs in his chest. I knew that feeling. I was happy for him when he won the struggle.

But now that this much of his confession is out, the rest will come sooner or later. And the pieces that I have picked up before now fit into place. He has made references to feudal delusions concerning the Palestinian movement. I had assumed he meant Hussein, but now I think he meant something closer to home. He once asked me if I ever intended to return to the U.S. I replied, "Of course, my family is there. Don't you intend to return to Dubai?" He gave a little snort. "Oh yes, I intend to return." Now I understand why I heard it as a threat. Sami's vision of his future is not spun around al-Quds, Jerusalem. For him that word does not have the magic it does for everyone else up here; it is not painted on our tent as it is on almost every other tent in camp. For him, the Return is to Dubai. And this is a way station, though I can't see the route yet.

But now, finally I see why Sami was so cooperative in establishing and preserving my legend. This was precisely what Abu had in mind. He simply provoked me into defying his accusations: the oldest coaching trick in the book. And now having set myself up as a hero to these kids, their idolatry will keep me toeing Abu's own line. Jibral, you're a stupid fucking rube! You ought to walk around with a ring in your nose. Pull here.

So, Abu's gotten exactly what he wants. No wonder he hasn't responded to my "provocations." Well, roll with the punches, rube. This guy is a heavyweight. Despite what you told Sami, you know nobody's going to call you back to Europe. So sit tight and try to figure out the moves here. Your survival depends on it.

Justina again. In my dreams almost every night now. Finally she came in from hovering outside the window and we screwed just the way we did those days after Hervé: in the heat of the sun streaming in the window, she sitting on me, arched back with her breasts pulled taut against her ribs, sweat glistening, the cords in her thighs quivering, pumping . . . The smell of jism and a warm stickiness on my stomach.

Shit, it's been years since I had one of these. So this is Army life. They're not putting enough saltpeter in the gruel. I have to get out of this insane trench. Am I never going to touch a woman again? And what happens if I don't? Do I start at the younger boys?

That is what started this. I must have been hearing that moaning again. Yes. They're at it again, the little punks. I ought to go out there and kick down their tent. If they get any louder they'll wake up the Israelis.

Aw, shut up, Kamal, and go back to sleep. Maybe you can coax up Mireille with her swan's neck swirled in blond tendrils and her pink nipples and the pale curls on her mons. Remember what it was like with her? She never got on top. It made her feel "trop au lointain." I gave up all that for this dust and dirt and rock? I can't believe it!

You didn't give it up, have you forgotten? It was taken away from you. Step by step: Hervé, the Jerusalem thugs, the toad, Boudia. Then Issa and the tennis player. Then the pilot and the man in the black car. Now Abu. And, though somehow in the process I've forgotten the purpose of it all, I plod on anyway. As if I have become part of an organism and need no reasons of my own any longer. But wasn't that exactly what I was seeking in the first place?

Yes, but you didn't realize what you would have to give up for it, did you?

No. Yet others survive this arid existence. How? Must be by giving in to it. I wish I had a copy of *Pillars*. He explains it somewhere in there, I'm sure. But the closest copy of *Pillars* is probably in Jerusalem. Or Haifa. Up here there are not only no books, but no newspapers, no radios. The outside world has fallen completely away. By comparison the hole in the ground under Pollo Rojo was downright cosmopolitan. Why, remember, you even got laid down there a few times!

That's true. Starvation must make you recall every hamburger you've ever eaten.

A piercing blast from an airhorn strips us out of sleep. No Mireille, no Justina left behind this time. Only a jangly havoc for which I'm just as happy to substitute dawn shivers, a gulp of last night's icy coffee and a stiff jog down to muster in the clearing. We are all at attention in front of the commander's bunker, the spotlight over its steel door shining directly in our eyes.

Major Daoud, the Vulture, stands before us, but Sami whispers, "I'm quite certain the Great Man will make an appearance any minute."

And sure enough, he emerges from the dark of the tunnel dressed in officer's khakis and a dazzling white kaffiyeh illuminated from behind by the spotlight. He walks with military poise to a spot just forward of the Vulture, halts and raises his hand. Despite the depth of the shadow on his face, the command of his gaze is absolute. He begins to speak in quiet, rich syllables which reach into our ranks and caress each one of us. No one dares breathe. Suddenly he stops and gestures toward himself. From our lines all the men with grenade patches are drawn forward, moving solemnly into a new rank before the commander. Now another phrase and another signal of his hand draws six more men from our lines. These more nervously assemble between the Grenades and Abu Ahmet.

At the next phrase from him, Sami taps my hands and whispers without moving his lips, "Be ready."

For what?

Six of the men from the line of Grenades march forward to the bunker wall, where they pick up and shoulder rifles which have been racked there. Among the six are Kuma, the tall kid who dubbed me Q'asidi, and the leader of the Grenades, a short muscular eighteen-year-old named Fawaz. They now split up and approach various people: Fawaz to the

Vulture, another whose name I don't know to Sami, one to Hamid, one to Naef, one on the other side of the lines to somebody I can't see, and Kuma, cautiously, to me. Then on a command from Abu, they all unshoulder the AKs and offer them to the men they have approached. I mimic Sami's nod of acceptance and grasp Kuma's rifle. On the next command the six Grenades rejoin their group. Abu salutes them, then turns and marches back into his bunker. The steel door creaks closed behind him. The spotlight is extinguished. There is a rustling and an exhaling, some stamping of feet. Then the line of Grenades snaps a left-face and marches out of the clearing down-canyon by the road. The six non-Grenades who have formed up follow them. Now Sami pokes me. "Our turn."

We form up behind the Vulture, the six of us with rifles.

"What is this, Sami? A firing squad?"

The Vulture turns and glares at me.

"Milles pardons, mon vieux." Sami informed me some time ago that the Major speaks French. Or at least understands it.

Now we six officers, or five and whatever I am, march down the road following the other two groups.

About five hundred meters from the clearing we turn from the road into the boulder field which lies between the guard fence and the camp. The sky is beginning to brighten now. A luminous edge of gold trims the crest above us. Down among the boulders the Grenades and the group of six are stretching and jumping, but their mood is still solemn. No one speaks. The only sounds are boot tramps, the hollow whistle of the dawn wind high on the canyon walls, and now the clink of sheet metal as the Vulture hands out a dozen banana clips to each of us from a rucksack.

"This is three hundred and sixty rounds! Are we having a massacre?"

"If you don't take a more serious attitude, Yank, we very well may. Have you ever shot at a man who wasn't painted on a piece of paper?"

"I've been known to. I hope you're not expecting me to shoot at these kids."

"Not at them. But very close to them. This is the famous trial by fire. It is a great honor to be chosen as one of the gunners."

"Who chose me?"

"The Grenades did. Or perhaps you were recommended. But you must realize that every so often there are mishaps, even fatal ones. That is why they have the right to choose by whose hand they may die. And why you have the right to refuse to be a gunner."

"But one doesn't refuse, does one?"

Sami glances up at me from under his brows. No, one doesn't refuse a man who's willing to put his life in your hands.

The course is painted in white arrows on the rocks and covers an arc of about four hundred meters sweeping from the road where we are standing uphill to just short of the clearing. Each of the gunners has a fixed firing position along the path. Sami's covers a large boulder with a notch in its top just deep enough to wriggle through. Sami will fire just above the notch from the side. I am covering a three-meter stretch of sand between two boulders. I will strafe into the sand at the feet of each commando as he makes the dash between the boulders. The least error at either Sami's station or mine could result in a maiming. It is a harsh test. All of the Grenade group submit to it each time any of them are psyching up for a mission. It must inject a special kind of fearlessness into those who are leaving, and a

301

powerful empathy into the ones who are staying behind. And into those of us manning the rifles, an awesome responsibility.

A burst of fire from the start of the course. Another. Now a long pause. A string of isolated shots. A silence after the echoes disperse up the canyon. Suddenly Sami looses a burst. I sight in at the foot of the boulder and listen for footsteps. Nothing. Then a scrape. A body springs out from behind the rock. I pause a beat, then spray a few rounds about a yard behind his heels. He lurches to a stop midway between the rocks. It is Fawaz, and he is curling his lip at me, and now proceeds to stroll toward the second rock. Insolent little twit. If he wants it closer he'll get it closer. I let a single round fly within an inch of his ear. His eyes go round and he flings himself at the rock, falls short. I put another round just over his hands, and on the next lurch he makes it to cover. A few minutes pass before we hear Hamid's burst. Then Fawaz appears on the grade up to the clearing. He is waving. Another burst at the start of the course. From now on one will be started every three minutes.

An hour and a half later the last one comes through. The six new recruits have been interspersed with the old Grenades. They have gotten the same treatment as the regulars and have all passed their induction. There is a general celebration going on up at the clearing from where the rest of the camp has watched. We six gunners are the last to join it. The sun is pouring into the canyon now. Soon our shirts are coming off. The rest of the day will be a holiday. Hamid appears from the supply bunker with three soccer balls in his arms. The new Grenades are elected captains and begin choosing teams. Little Fuad is the next to last chosen, I the last. This is evidently serious business, this soccer tournament, and nobody wants an unknown quantity no matter how fast he runs.

Twenty-four hours later I realize how subtly our transitions of mood have been orchestrated. Yesterday's ritual was merely a study for the major performance launched with today's death watch. Yes, I see how the prelude conditioned us. First Abu's dramatic dawn address imbued the impending ordeal with a mystical importance. The live-fire drill, which every army puts its men through, here is elevated to an initiation rite. So the very real tension of slithering under or being chased by hissing live rounds is exalted above the sordid question of survival into the realm of worthiness in the eyes of the Revolution, Abu, the Martyrs Who Have Gone Before, the People—if I can trust Sami's translation. And all of this then dissipated in the frenzy of the soccer matches and general hilarity of the afternoon. It still seems impossible that during the games everyone, except me, knew just how imminent the real performance was. Not even the four for whom today's death watch is being held gave a hint. Kuma and the other three raced after those soccer balls as though the outcomes of their matches were the most important thing on earth. And tonight they are preparing to leave it.

But perhaps that is not the expectation in their heart of hearts. Yesterday's ritual enactment anticipated a joyful, victorious resolution. The triumphant Return. Only there will be no return. I've seen the maps of that terrain. Once they drop out of the heights onto Neve Ativ there is no climbing back up. They will be as easy to pick off as ants on a wall. Assuming they get that far. I wonder if they know this, or if they are dreaming of a comic book escape.

No, they do realize they are not coming back, after all. Why else this orgy of photos? Fawaz has been

snapping pictures of them all afternoon: single portraits, group portraits, shots in combat poses among
the rocks. Click by click their four souls are being
sucked through the lens and trapped in Mr. East-
man's emulsions. All that will remain to be disinte-
grated on the border minefield or under the machine
guns of the Neve Ativ watchtower will be four empty
sacks of flesh which the souls have already abandoned on the way to immortality as posters on the
walls of Damascus and Beirut. They do realize and
they do not protest. They have learned that the dead
are better loved than the living, so why not make
haste toward that revered state?

I can understand them, all right. But what is one
to make of the man who sends them? Does Abu picture himself in a shaggy cloak kneeling on the Rock
with Kuma's throat beneath his dagger? Does he
think of himself as Ibrahim? Certainly he doesn't
think of what he's doing as a crime. Is there even a
word to designate the sacrifice of sons? It is not a
crime in any culture. It is called History.

So the reason I do not sleep tonight is that I am listening for footsteps outside the tent, the careful
tread of eight feet, too polite to wake the rest of us,
diminishing into the dark with a special finality.
Only, I can hear nothing except the wheezy ebb and
flow of Sami's snores. I'd like to throttle him, but I
already envy even this temporary oblivion of his too
much.

In the morning all that remains are two neatly
rolled tents and four stacks of bedding.

Samir

THE AMERICAN REACTS STRANGELY to the departure of
the four commandos. The camp, as always when
some of us have gone under the wire, is silent and re-

signed. Most activity is suspended. We go about our chores without complaining or joking, saying only what needs to be said. Only if there is news will any voice be raised: that of Fawaz who squats by the door of Abu's bunker waiting for any reports that Major Daoud may pick up on the shortwave receiver. Kamal is also silent. But it is the silence of a landmine. He is smoldering behind his eyelids. His body quivers like a drawn bow. But nothing comes out. And who would want to get close enough to find out the cause? So he sits on his rock and glares.

Then early in the afternoon he finds me standing in my knickers cranking the handle of our improvised clothes washing machine: a salvaged twenty-liter grout tin suspended by an axle between two wooden posts, spun end over end full of clothes, water and soap. He is beginning to look very ragged now in his civilian uniform. There are holes in the elbows of his shirt and knees of his jeans from practicing prone attacks. The sun has faded both completely colorless. And the soles of his precious sneakers are separating from the leather tops. His person has fared not much better. The bones of his cheeks are even more prominent than when he arrived, his hair has gone wild as weeds. His entire presence has become rather weedy, in fact. It is a pity he could not be stuffed into a twenty-liter drum with a bit of soap and water. But at very least the clothes.

"Hey, Kamal, throw your things in here and take a turn at the handle."

"They won't stand another washing."

"Well, if they disintegrate Abu will be forced to issue you fatigues. He can't have you running around naked, can he?"

"He seems to be able to have anything he damn pleases."

"Now, now."

305

"Who is he, Sami? How did he get here and what is he after?"

"Ask him."

"Sure."

"Suppose I confided the dark secret that Abu Ahmet is not even five years old. That is to say, the person who occupied our commander's body five years ago was not only not named Abu Ahmet, he was not even a revolutionary. Quite the other thing, in fact: a professor of history at the American University in Beirut. He was one of those 'good' Palestinians who made his way by being hard-working, amenable, even compliant, apolitical: what you Americans call an Uncle Tom.

"He had had all the advantages. He was sent to universities in France and Germany and England, returned to Beirut with a fine reputation and immediately received an appointment at the university. He was the living proof of the possibility of real assimilation into Lebanese society. Apparently he used to speak at various bourgeois gatherings about the 'illusion of the Palestinian problem.' "

"How do you know all this, Sami?"

"My uncle took an interest in the Professor."

"Your uncle? Why?"

"That should be obvious. You've seen the charisma of the man."

"But he was only a professor. Of what interest could he have been to a minister of state of a foreign country?"

"You *are* innocent. Do you realize that since we started exporting oil in 1969 we have been importing population at such a rate that now we have more foreigners than nationals? Most of those are Palestinians. So the Palestinian movement is of great importance to us. And therefore so are its leaders."

"But you said Abu was not a leader then. If anything, the opposite."

"That was before June, '67. We had no Palestinians and no interest in him then. But apparently the Professor underwent a chemical change as a result of the June war. When my uncle first became aware of him—it was toward the end of 1970—the Professor had quite metamorphosed. He was in prison. He had attempted to cross the border with four former students and enough plastique to blow up Mount Sinai, but they were cornered by a Lebanese Army patrol just short of the fence. Three of the students were killed in the firefight. He surrendered rather than sacrificing the fourth and himself for nothing."

"Surrendered! That must still rankle inside him."

"With Abu one never knows what goes on inside. His trial caused a sensation. Lebanese society was rather hurt by this ugly behavior on the part of someone on whom such favors had been lavished. But luckily for the Professor none of the Army patrol had been killed, so he was sentenced only to thirty years for having led an armed insurrection. The student who survived was only given a five-year sentence."

"It was a quick thirty years. Was he paroled?"

"No, that isn't the way things are done in Lebanon. The Professor's trial caught my uncle's attention. Then, a few months after our Professor went to prison he managed to smuggle out a manuscript entitled *What I Must Do*. The Syrian Deuxième intercepted it. My uncle persuaded them to hand it over to him. He was passing through Damascus on the way to visit me in London, so I got to read it. I remember being quite impressed by the power of the polemics, as was my uncle. Let me try to quote an example. It was in a passage in which he justified his attempt to cross the border and blow up something. He wrote, 'Crossing the wire has but one objective, not to kill our enemies but the meaning of a single word. That word has become our most insidious enemy. Its synonyms burn under our skins like acid: down-trodden, defeated, abject, squalid. Only by fighting back, even without hope, can we change the meaning of this word to make it sound from our lips with dignity. It is worth even death to be able to say the word once with pride. I am a *Palestinian.*'

"Good stuff, Kamal, don't you think?"

"I'm not too big on polemics. Did he make you memorize that?"

"Oh no. But Abu uses the good parts of his little book in all his speeches. They stick in your mind after a while."

"So how long did they keep him in prison, and why did they let him out?"

"They didn't let him out. He was rescued during a routine medical checkup. Did you notice how gray Abu's skin is?"

"Yes, as a matter of fact. Someone once told me he has mercury for blood."

"He has a heart condition. A serious heart condition."

"Who organized the rescue?"

"A group which called itself 'Al-Niquam'—Revenge. It took credit a few days after the break in a telegram sent to the Beirut newspapers. It said, 'We cannot defeat the Jews while there are traitors at our backs,' among other things. And it was signed 'Major Abu Ahmet.' Al-Niquam based itself in Syria. No one had ever heard of it before that telegram."

"So who was behind it?"

"The Syrians, perhaps. How would I know?"

"Then I don't understand your uncle's interest."

"Why not? Abu Ahmet was a dynamic new leader on the scene, still free of hampering alliances or loyalties, looking for help in establishing his place in the Revolution. I imagine my uncle was not the only minister of state interested in Abu at that time."

"Now it becomes clear. You're here looking after your uncle's interests."

"And after my own, of course."

Kamal

NIGHT SWALLOWS THE CANYON and, somewhere south of us, Kuma and his three companions. They will be coming out of hiding soon and making their advance down the bluff, knocking out the tower with a grenade, storming the residences for hostages, making their demands for the release of twenty-five imprisoned guerrillas . . . And it will end as it always does, if they haven't gotten lost yet or been flushed out of their hideout by a passing patrol. I was going to ask Sami what he thinks of this futility, but now that he has clarified his relation with Abu the answer is obvious: He regrets it but accepts the "necessity." The necessity, of course, is keeping Abu viable as a leader. A leader must have followers, and he must lead them against the enemy. Therefore . . .

Perhaps the logic sounds inverted, but that is only because the interests are inverted. There is no good reason for Sami's venerable uncle to want a Palestinian state to come into existence. Then the labor force on which they depend would have a place to come home to if their lives became too unpleasant in Dubai. So if the uncle is anxious to have a hand in the Palestinian Movement, it must be with the purpose of frustrating rather than advancing us. Could Abu be blind to that intention? Or does he share it? A horrifying possibility raises its head.

Again sleep is impossible. In reinterpreting everything I have seen here in terms of this bleak new hypothesis, I am finding nothing to put it to rest. If any single tactic could drain the Revolution dry, it is the "one-way mission." It drains us in dribs and drabs, so no one notices the stab wound in our back. No one wants to notice; all the heroes would be instantly transformed into dupes.

Sami snores. Somewhere south of us Kuma and the other three are bleeding to death. Abu studies in his bunker and makes plans for our future. The Vulture hunkers over his shortwave radio waiting for the announcement that our four boys have become martyrs. The rest of the Grenades lie awake hoping that this time it will end differently, they will make it back somehow, or at worst be taken alive after all their ammunition is used up. There has been a lot of hash smoked tonight. The dreams, if anyone does sleep, besides Sami, will be insane. In the morning all the faces will be gaunter than today. And still no one will suspect why their hopes have ebbed even closer to empty. No one except me, that is.

The dawn silence is different this morning. Instead of lying on the canyon floor like a thick fluid it buzzes like a swarm of insects just out of earshot. I find myself being drawn from the tent to hear it better in the open air. Hear the swarming silence? I've been inside the tent too long with Sami snoring in my ear. When I can't sleep, the tent becomes a torture chamber.

But I am not the only one to have been yanked from my tent by this undefinable commotion. It is still too dark down here to determine which ones, but at least twenty other men are pulling on their clothes in front of their tents with an ear or an eye cocked toward the steel-gray strip of sky. Now it is distinctly audible, a confused distant pulsing roar. And then it goes abruptly mute. I see a few men shrug nearby and bend to their stoves. Suddenly the noise resumes, but now building in intensity by the second. It sounds from the north. Everyone is watching that lip of the canyon when the thunder bursts from the south.

We spin to see a wave of helicopter silhouettes sweep over that crest. Incandescent rays of tracer bullets streak from their flanks. A bass muttering is added to the pulsing roar of the engines. But most of the fire is falling just below us, in the clearing, against the bunker. They have come a few minutes too early. The darkness at the foot of the canyon must make the tents indistinguishable from the boulders. Everyone is diving for cover behind boulders, into foxholes. There is no firing back. No one wants to draw the helicopters' misdirected fire.

After a few seconds of that muttering, the rain of tracers falling onto the clearing ceases. There are flames under the minibus. It is a wonder neither of the vehicles has exploded. Behind the boulder to my left I can see someone plugging an RPG round into a launcher and now inching the ugly lozenge-headed rocket over the rock. The helicopters are climbing vertically above the canyon. A jet streaks high overhead, high enough to be in the full light of the sun. How long will it take the fucking Syrians to respond to this invasion? The man with the RPG is sighting on one of the helicopters. He hasn't a chance of hitting it now that they are climbing and circling. I chuck him in the ribs with a small stone. He pulls his head back from the sights and glares at me, clenching a fist at my signal to hold his fire. But he obeys, though I have no official authority over him.

The helicopters now spread out. Below the leading one four parachutes suddenly mushroom and float languidly above the canyon. Another jet swoops into sight, turns and dives at the canyon from the lower end. We are all frozen by the sight for a moment, then scurry around to the other sides of our boulders, completely forgetting about the helicopters and the parachutists overhead. The jet closes without a

311

sound, drops into the canyon near the wire fence, then rears onto its tail and with a sudden burst and a howl slings itself out of the canyon. Its gift to us comes bounding end over end in long wild arcs; glinting metal, spraying sparks, a dreadful hollow clank at each bound, into the clearing, over the bunkers, it caroms into the north wall, hops in a high lob and falls a few hundred yards up-canyon. Its trajectory is now marked with a fierce orange blaze, on the rocks, on the bunker, up the wall of the canyon.

The jet has vanished. The helicopters are backing toward the border. The four parachutists are already below the lips of the trench. There is yelling, now firing. One of the parachutes collapses and plummets. The AKs have their range. The other three bodies are jerking under the impact as they float toward us. One is nearly cut loose from his chute, and hangs limp by a single shoulder. The firing doesn't stop until all four intruders have hit the canyon floor. The choppers have disappeared instead of coming in to provide covering fire.

There is something very weird about this operation. I signal the boy with the RPG to keep covering the rim of the canyon in case the chopper pilots change their mind. Then I follow the advance toward the intruders. The firing has stopped, but no one is taking any chances. We dive from boulder to boulder until we can see the vast orange blooms. To our side the napalm continues to suck and roar. I have to shield my cheek from the heat of the flames. Ahead, some of the boys are creeping near to the parachutes. Suddenly three of them stand up and run forward, throwing their rifles aside. Now a dozen follow. They begin plucking at the tangle of lines. Some are shrieking. When I get closer they look up at me with tear-stained faces. Amid the rocks, tangled in their own parachute shrouds, lie the torn corpses of our four Grenades.

The rumor is now a fact, made so by a thousand repetitions in the last few hours, "Yes, they were dead before they were dropped. Hamid said there was dried blood on the ropes which bound their hands. The Israelis killed them. Not us."

But it doesn't matter. Each of us chooses his own horror. We all knew that Kuma and his squad were prepared to die, but we were not prepared to see their shattered bodies. A martyr must die an abstract death. He mustn't lie in state for all to see his limbs or his face shot off. They are supposed to be remembered as in their parting photographs, eyes shining from a mixture of pride and fear, not glistening from a mixture of brain and blood.

Abu stands before the door of his bunker looking gravely down on the four stretchers, and on the straight files of men lined up behind them. His left eye and the left corner of his mouth twitch every few seconds, imparting a momentary leer. This was not part of the plan, was it, Abu? You smell the rage of your troops and you don't know what to do with it.

He begins a speech. There is no electricity this time. I sense a great restlessness around me. Sami can read it better than I can; he looks scared. Suddenly we all hear footsteps to our left and turn. Fawaz is striding into the clearing with his camera hanging from his neck. Ignoring Abu's speech, he walks to the stretchers and begins to photograph the corpses. Abu stops speaking and watches for a moment. He turns to the Vulture, who is standing behind him, as always. The Vulture steps forward and barks a command at Fawaz. Fawaz ignores him. The Vulture reaches for his pistol, but Abu taps him on the arm and he desists. They wait motionless until Fawaz has finished the roll of film and strides back to his tent. Then Abu resumes the speech. It does not last long. As soon as he has finished he returns to the bunker. The funeral procession continues to Little Nefud without him.

Later, in the tent, I ask Sami what Abu said in the speech.

"Same old thing. He promised that the four comrades would be avenged."

"I didn't hear any cheers."

"He forsook his usual declamatory style. The speech was purely a formality."

"In other words he really is going to do nothing to avenge this outrage, and doesn't want to get the boys too worked up."

"Quite possibly."

"You don't seem too upset about that possibility, comrade Samir. Why? Is it your uncle's policy that we sit on our asses and avoid seriously attacking the Israelis, even if this is the price?"

"If you are under the impression that my uncle controls Abu just because he donates a certain amount of aid, then you have grossly misread Abu's character. You have a child's grip on international politics, my friend."

"Well, guru, perhaps you can explain to this child why the royal family of Dubai should be so interested in the success of the Palestinian Revolution . . . rather than its failure."

"We are interested in its existence. We are not so vain as to think we can determine its success or failure. If it does succeed, we would like to have some influence on its course, since it is so likely to have an influence on ours. Your mind, my friend, always seems to run toward the most pernicious interpretations. If we were interested in the failure of the Revolution, Abu would certainly be able to discern that, and I would be the first victim. Do you think I would play such a dangerous game? Or is it that you think

Abu himself is working for the failure of the Revolution? It has to be one or the other, doesn't it?"

"One or the other."

"Your mind leads you down very dangerous paths. Be careful you don't plunge over the precipice on either side."

The moment of the attack hovers, hovers with an extraordinary clarity in the dark interior of the tent. Every detail, every nuance shimmers, magnified like the hairs of a petal under a drop of dew. It has the same refracted beauty. Splashes of crimson and yellow flame against the speckled gray rocks. Incandescent tracer streaks spilling from the just bluing sky, more like rays of thought than matter falling in their weightless parabolas. And our own tracers winging toward the translucent jellyfish canopies, lit up by the spikes of flame on the rocks. A painter's dream! And more: something for every one of the senses. Sweet chemical fumes of napalm garnished with acrid cordite. The flame's contented licking, punctuations of AK bursts, the retreating popping roar of the Hueys, our high-pitched shouts . . . If war is hell, hell must be intoxicatingly lovely.

This was my first taste, and I'm already addicted. It was very strange, but aside from the moment when we spun around to see the choppers pouring over the ridge, I felt no fear. Only an intense animal alertness and an exultation. Is this what one feels on a raid, when the firing begins and one has no more thoughts of the future? If so, I can see why one might be quite ready to die for it. With no future there is no anxiety. Without anxiety nothing clouds the senses. They absorb the fullest experience of the moment without a blink. What is traditionally a hell becomes a revelation.

Extraordinary! I see Abu's method with clear eyes at last. Here he strips us of all connection with the future: women, wealth, even knowledge. The aridity of existence gradually dries out our imaginations, which finally suck to pulp even the most trivial memories. Then desire dies. We are quarantined from all outside vectors of infection of desire—no books, no movies, no news, not even the tinny distraction of radios, are permitted to penetrate our cloister. If Abu has visions of a party or a program he keeps them a secret in his bunker. Such hopes are not for us either. Only one hope is permitted to survive: the longing for action. This our parched senses keep dangling before us like the mirage of an oasis. It is the only image our fantasies are given the colors and shapes to paint.

So we are ready for an attack like this incursion of the Israeli helicopters. We are ready for a futile rush down the bluff into Neve Ativ, AKs at the hip blazing into the windows of the settlement. Yes, we are ready to shoot and be shot back at. So ready, we long for it. But what we are not prepared for are the consequences. The empty eye sockets, the shot-off faces, the limbs dangling from a tendon, the crotches without genitals; those are supposed to remain outside the canyon walls. We are not supposed to infect our imaginations with such tangible images of death. Death is Martyr Kuma's smiling photo on a demonstration placard, not the gleam of his white brains showing through tufts of his jet black hair. Something went wrong with the plan today. From now on the image of four young men trudging out of the canyon bristling with AKs and grenades will always evoke the image of their four mangled corpses lying twisted in their own shroud lines. Like gnawed prey at a periphery of the web of some great spider which sits implacable, silent, machinelike, poised at the hub, listening through the perfect filaments for the desperate vibrations of his next victim.

Why didn't I think of this before? I have already

encountered the spider who sits at the hub of it all: my interrogator in Jerusalem! The sharp aristocratic features, the long slow-moving limbs, the brushed-back silver hair, all come into perfect focus. As does suddenly his purpose in letting me go free in Jerusalem. And then again in Fossés Saint-Bernard, where he could have had his toad end it all. He knew each time I would trail his fatal filament to greater prey than Kamal Jibral. God knows if I haven't trailed his filament to this canyon.

Well, I served my purpose, didn't I, monseigneur? And now you have no doubt forgotten me. That is too bad for you. It was my sworn oath to return. Now the time has come. I told Issa I would not care to avenge Boudia. But now I have myself to avenge, and the four boys who looked up to me. And I have one other purpose which your death, dear Count, could well serve: I intend to prove to everyone in this canyon it is possible to strike the enemy at the center of his web and return alive. So even for you, clever Israeli, the vicissitudes of History can fold back on themselves in unexpected ways. I will give you a few seconds to appreciate the irony, dear Count, just as I gave that pig from the Ministerio del Interior the moment to appreciate his fate. I want to see the flash of horror and regret twist your fine composed features before I splatter the Jerusalem limestone with your clever brains. A bientôt, mon ami. Je suis plus proche que tu peux imaginer.

Samir

AFTER A MORNING of desultory drills, from which the American was conspicuously absent, I return to find him sitting stark naked in front of our tent mending his leather sneakers with a heavy needle and pack thread. Around him, draped on smooth rocks, are all his clothes, freshly washed, drying stiff under the sun. He has also done something to his hair. It no longer has the look of a garden gone to seed.

"What is all this? Have you finally resolved to go to Damascus to find a girl, as you've been threatening?"

"Nothing to do with girls. Just respect for Death."

There is no point to talking with this man; every word is an obfuscation. Though this should not surprise me, since he sees conspiracies everywhere around him. If only they would call him back to Europe.

Crawling into the tent to escape the sun, I am confronted by an empty holster lying on my bedding. Checking further, I see that my English rucksack is also missing. And my compass. The American puts on a childish grin when I dangle the empty holster in front of his nose.

"Don't you know, Yank, that in this part of the world thievery is not exalted, as it is in your country, but despised. We cannot insult a man more profoundly than to call him a thief."

"To each according to his need. Is that not the principle we are fighting for, comrade Samir?"

"Well, my friend, if you need a compass to find your way to the latrines at night and a pistol to protect your privacy, so be it. But why my good Ben Nevis pack? That still troubles me."

"Maybe I'm going mountain climbing." He shrugs and resumes forcing the needle through the leather. This could be a scene in an asylum: the stark naked shoemaker. But now I see that he has also carefully repaired the rents in the knees of his pants and the elbows of his shirt. His corduroy jacket is also spread on a rock. It has been serving as his pillow until now.

"I must say, Yank, this all has the air of an imminent desertion."

"If that's the excuse you need to go squealing to Abu, go on. I can't stop you."

"Your Anglo-Saxon schoolyard code of honor binds no one up here. We say that two men cannot meet but Allah is the third among them. But if you are planning to desert, by all means make haste. I look forward eagerly to having my tent to myself again. Be sure to let Fawaz take your picture before you leave so we can start a gallery of deserters."

"Fawaz can take my picture when I get back from Jerusalem."

Jerusalem now! If this fellow could only see a reflection of the preposterous figure he cuts, sitting naked cobbling his sneakers and blithely babbling about what he is going to do when he *returns* from Jerusalem. If he would look up from his needle and thread, perhaps the incredulity on my face would shake him. But no, he is lost in his own fantastic world where neither I nor Abu nor the Israeli border patrols cast shadows. I don't believe Abu realizes what we are hosting here, so all schoolboy honor codes aside, I will have to apprise him of the mental disintegration of our guest.

Relations between Abu and myself are diplomatic. There is no love lost, but there is a realistic acceptance that we share the same lifeboat, and survival would be even more doubtful for both if either began to indulge his emotions. So we keep our conferences to a minimum. Our last was on the arrival of the American, so it is only fitting that our next should be concerned with his threatened departure.

Abu greets me in his office with a handshake and a forced smile. We avoid each other's narrowed glance so as not to expose the charade. We chat around the subject for a while, talking news, in particular Sadat and the Soviet Union and rumors of preparations for another war with Israel, which Abu dismisses as pure posturing. Then the subject drifts closer to the Struggle. He mentions with a smirk a radio report he picked up on his shortwave receiver on the twenty-first of July and has been following for over a week now, concerning a rather puzzling hijacking of a Japan Airlines jet out of Amsterdam. The plane had attempted to land in Syria, Iraq and Bahrain but had been refused. Finally—and this is his reason for mentioning it to me, says Abu—the 747 was allowed to land in Dubai so a wounded steward and a dead hijacker could be taken off the plane.

"Your family once again has displayed its independence and humane sensibilities." Irony twists the corners of his mouth.

"Thank you, professor." Let no one forget where he comes from. "Do you happen to know from which of the lunatic fringes this plot has unraveled?"

"A group calling itself Sons of the Occupied Territory. No one has heard of them, at least in this part of the globe. There are two Japanese and at least one dead German, a woman, among them, so perhaps it is a different occupier they are confronting. They issued no demands, except for the release of the JRA man Okamoto, pro forma. And then they flew off to Benghazi, released the passengers and blew up the jet."

"And now?"

"Muammar threatens to try them according to the precepts of his Green Book. If this comes to pass it will be a fitting last act to this little melodrama without a point. Perhaps it will discourage future theatrical careers from being built on the name of our struggle. But speaking of theatrical careers, how fares Boudia's protégé?"

"It is about him that I have come to speak."

"Then speak." Abu begins to trace invisible boxes on the desk with the end of his forefinger, tapping the center of each completed square. As I talk I find my words falling between the rhythm of his tracing: tick, tick, tick, tick, *tap*. He glances up only infrequently. When I pause he says nothing and his silence forces me to continue speaking, to reiterate, to speculate, even to invent to fill the void. Finally I have to force myself to stop. I have gone far past Kamal's boast of going to Jerusalem and the theft of my pistol. I could not keep from mentioning his suspicions concerning Abu's own loyalty and intentions vis-à-vis the Movement. It must sound as if I am trying to build a case against the American. After a minute of meditation Abu traces a large box around all the others and decisively raps the center of it.

"It is fortunate that this provocateur cannot yet broadcast his slanders in Arabic. One cannot count on that indefinitely."

"What about Jerusalem? What do you make of that?"

"I suppose one ought to find out what he hopes to accomplish there. If it is productive I see no reason not to let him go. Of course, I cannot encourage him, since I have promised to keep him out of harm's way until they call him back to Europe. I have no idea what they intend to use him for: another vapid theatrical, no doubt. But I owe them favors, so I cannot appear to be abducting their personnel. However, if the American chooses to go under the wire on his own initiative . . ."

"You will not try to stop him."

"He will only be an increasing irritation if he remains here."

"Suppose he is picked up by the Syrians or Lebanese as he tries to cross the border. Could that not be a severe embarrassment?"

"Old Nizar can get him across the border. Let the Israelis worry about him after that."

"So you accept to appear to the camp to be approving of this folly, commander? If you bring in a guide for him, his exit will hardly have the air of a desertion."

"We don't want a deserter. We want a martyr."

"Suppose he survives and returns as he is boasting. His popularity at that point could be troublesome."

"If he survives and returns, in addition to succeeding in his mission it will have been an honor to have helped him, no? I shouldn't fret on it. Or do I sense that you would rather thwart the American for personal reasons, comrade Samir?"

"I can hardly be accused of attempting to thwart him."

"That is quite true. I apologize for the insinuation."

But apologizing does not retract it, as Abu knows perfectly well. It is a trick that may work inside the civilized walls of a university, but out here Abu will find his too finely aimed sniping either falling short or ricocheting back at him from unexpected obstacles. I sometimes wonder if the professor has adapted at all to his new venue, or if he hides in this crude simulation of an academician's office because the brutishness of our life among the rocks horrifies him. For him this camp is, he hopes, just an intermediate step toward greater offices, so there is no reason to romanticize it, or even get used to it. Abu is no Che, no Fidel. He had already passed briefly through that stage by the time he emerged from prison. His intellect had allowed him to leap over the futile idealisms slower men exhaust by bitter experience.

Uncle saw this immediately when he finally met Abu. He described him to me in a snowbound chalet in Gstaad, before a licking fire which had no doubt warmed discussions that toppled more than one Middle Eastern regime. "The man is no firebrand, I discovered to my surprise. His flame has gone out some time ago. But what remains is a clear vision of what the flame could have ignited, and could still ignite were the spark still in him. Now his ambition is to be the hand that wields the torch. It is the oldest story: When passion dies it leaves a hunger for the one thing in which there is no nourishment at all, that is power. But it also leaves the brain cool. All we have to do is look to Europe to see how much states benefit from being run by well-chilled brains. In Europe, they are common. In our part of the world, they are precious jewels."

I must remind myself from time to time that the gray man who sits before me is a precious jewel.

Kamal

SAMI, just as I expected, ran straight to Abu. A while later he returned with an even longer face than usual.

Early in the afternoon the Vulture strode up and announced that I was wanted "to assist at the commander." I pulled on my fresh repaired clothes and took a few light bounds to test the new seams of my sneakers, then allowed the Vulture to lead me into the bowels of darkness to "assist at" Abu. This was my first personal meeting with him since the morning I arrived.

He seemed almost a different person. He rose from his desk as I entered and extended his hand. "Welcome, comrade Jibral. Please have a seat. Major Daoud will bring us some fresh coffee."

As the Vulture folded himself out the door I studied Abu's face to see how he could have flattened it into the metallic mask of our first meeting. Now his eyes, if not smiling, were animated. Two fleshy creases bracketed his mouth, giving him almost a sensual and a peculiarly French air. And his hands, frozen during our first meeting, were now restless.

The right forefinger swirled circles on the table in front of him. But he watched me and not his fingers as he spoke.

"I received very favorable reports of your comportment during the helicopter raid. Is it true that you ordered Naef to hold his fire?"

"I couldn't see who it was. I told someone with an RPG not to fire at the choppers. You were pretty safe in here with concrete and rock over your head. But there would have been quite a mess if we had drawn the fire of their flexies up among the tents."

"That was a commendable judgment." New affability to complement his new face?

"A second matter concerns your comportment in general since you arrived here. I must apologize for my own not so commendable judgment of you during our first meeting. I should not have let your association with Boudia color my perception. Now I can say that your influence here has, on the whole, been worthy of praise. I do not underestimate the importance of physical leadership. Because of my health I cannot provide a good example in that domain, so I have great respect for those who can. Perhaps your handicap of language has been almost beneficial because it has forced you to communicate through the medium of physical achievement. The boys hold you very high in their estimation . . ."

I nodded, wondering where all this flattery was leading.

". . . and I would encourage you to carry on setting this kind of example . . ."

But?

". . . however, I understand you are entertaining thoughts of leaving us. To Jerusalem, if the rumors are correct."

"Rumors often are."

"Must I remind you that this is an army, not a uni-

324

versity, comrade Jibral? One does not pursue an independent course of study."

"I am not one of your soldiers."

"But you are under my orders."

"Only while I am in your camp."

"I can keep you here by force."

"That would be a rather unpopular gesture just now."

For some reason that drew a smile. Not a mean one. He rocked his head from side to side a few times as if weighing to himself: on the one hand this, on the other hand that. What this and that were I had no idea.

After a minute he asked in a lowered voice, "And what draws you so powerfully to Jerusalem?"

At this moment the Vulture returned with a blue enamel coffeepot and cups on a copper tray. He slid it onto Abu's table and left again without a word. Abu poured two cups and raised his own, but paused and repeated, "Jerusalem?"

"Vengeance."

He took his sip. "Ah yes? Whom would you avenge?"

"The list grows longer every day."

"And what revenge do you feel would balance this growing list?"

"Not balance, but begin to tip the scales in the other direction."

"That is no answer. You have something specific in mind."

"I don't know his name, but he is one of the top men in a group called Miutim in Jerusalem."

"Yes, Miutim. It means 'minorities' in Hebrew. How did you happen to pick on this man in particular?"

"I was one of his victims."

"Oh yes? Then you have already been inside so-called Israel."

"Yes. Boudia sent me."

"This I hadn't heard! On what business?"

"A mission. To photograph the Hermon region. But I was picked up before I had a chance to get there. In Jerusalem."

"And you were interrogated?"

"Yes. But I admitted nothing. Told them nothing."

"In Moscobiya? The old Russian compound?"

"Yes."

"Were you beaten?"

"Well, roughed up."

"And then they let you go?"

"Yes."

"And for this you want mortal revenge?"

"Not just for this. For Boudia. For Kuma and the others. You promised us revenge for their deaths. I am ready."

"How would you carry out this reprisal?"

"I will cross the border, ride to Jerusalem by bus, wait for the man to leave work, follow him until I find a good place to carry out the execution . . ."

"With what weapon?"

"Pistol."

"Ah yes, the pistol. I have heard of your remarkable skills with a pistol. Against crows. It is another matter to execute a human."

"I know. I have done it before. . . . In Uruguay."

"I was not aware. They mentioned you had been in South America for some time. Nothing of this nature, however."

"I assassinated a condemned Death Squad commander."

"This part of your legend unfortunately did not precede you. Had I known I was dealing with an expert . . . You plan to return to us?"

"They will be expecting the assassin to escape by the normal routes, probably into the West Bank, and

326

then Jordan. Who would be expecting an escape route through the middle of the country to its furthest border? Once back in the mountains I will navigate by compass at night."

"Are you aware of the danger of interception by the Syrian or Lebanese patrols? The very American identity which will help you move freely inside Israel will assure you the firing squad as a spy in Syria. And probably prison in Lebanon."

"That is one of the risks."

"I cannot afford that risk, even if you are willing to. But without a guide to take you across the border you are certain to blow yourself up in a minefield even if you are not intercepted."

"Then I will take a guide."

"I was not aware you knew any guides, comrade Jibral."

"But you do. And since you are so anxious for me not to be arrested you will make the necessary arrangements for me to safely cross the border."

"I see you have thought it out quite thoroughly, for me as well as for yourself. When does your plan call for you to be starting out?"

"As soon as certain information is gathered and the guide can be made available."

"What information?"

"The name, address and daily schedule of the target. I assume you have people in Jerusalem who can obtain those easily enough."

"Of course we do. But whether I will expose them for such a project remains to be seen."

"The exposure should be minimal. This man is a visible figure. I've been through these kinds of preliminaries in South America. There is virtually no risk to the spotter."

"Naturally I am grateful to benefit from the advice of your experience. However, Jerusalem is not Montevideo. Our spotters must operate in the midst

327

of a hostile population, so the risk to them is not 'negligible.' The question must always be asked, Is the information worth the price?"

"What kind of price? If it's money, I've got money. I'll reimburse you for any expenses incurred."

"That was not the price I was speaking of. I was speaking of obligation."

"Obligation? You mean you trade favors? There must be a few revolutionaries in this Movement who would help out of principle."

"Possibly. But you would have to ask them yourself, and I doubt that they would find your project compelling. However—"

"I don't understand this Revolution."

"Revolutions are only understood after the fact. Meanwhile we must content ourselves with guiding the disorder. And if that requires 'trading favors' —as you call it—with associations of petty criminals who have just discovered their 'oppression,' we must just pinch our noses and proceed. You will not claim your comrades in Montevideo were above recruiting certain criminal elements; they did not learn the skills of bank robbery in the university.

"However, we are straying from the important topic, which is your plan. Aside from the intelligence you requested, is there any other support it would require?"

"Support? No. But I would need some Israeli currency, and of course my passport."

"Ah yes, your passport." He reached for a lower drawer and after some rummaging produced the familiar gray-green booklet. The sight of it made me feel as if I were being restored to a more wholesome earlier version of myself: fixed shoes, patched clean clothes, now my passport!

But as I held my hand out for it he covered the precious document with his own hand. "I'm afraid I cannot accommodate you in this. You see, I have made a commitment to keep you safely here in the camp. I have to be able to say to my associates in Europe that you left on your own initiative. Should you encounter some trouble in enemy territory, or be arrested by the Syrians or Lebanese, your possession of this passport would prove my complicity in your mission. I'm sorry, but you will have to find a way to do without it. You can appreciate my position."

"You can appreciate mine."

"You Americans have an expression: Possession is nine-tenths of the law."

"Some of your followers would be shocked to hear you justify yourself with such a nakedly capitalistic proverb."

"I make it a practice to speak to my followers each in their own idiom." He slid my passport from the desk and returned it to the drawer with a slow, deliberate sweep. "By the way, I meant to ask how Boudia responded to the failure of your mission."

"It was a test of loyalty. He did not expect me to succeed in the first place."

"I find his logic and methods doubtful. But I suppose if he had the opportunity to re-evaluate them himself now, he would also find them so." We stared at each other a moment over this comment.

How true it was that Boudia would have regretted sending me to Israel.

"But, of course," Abu continued, "if any of us had the opportunity to re-evaluate, which of us would not find our own logic and methods doubtful? Still we carry on. . . . This man of Miutim who so provokes your wrath; since he hasn't a name or a position, at least a physical description might help identify him."

I described the Count and his office in the barrack in great detail.

Abu took notes as I spoke, then responded, "He has unquestionably made a lasting impression in

329

your gallery of rogues. I must say this has been an informative conversation, comrade Jibral. I would like to chat further, but there are other matters which prey on my attention."

"You haven't said whether you approve of my mission."

"I was under the impression that my approval was completely irrelevant to you. As you so shrewdly observed earlier, I cannot force you to remain here."

"But I do need a certain degree of cooperation from you."

"Is that a request, comrade Jibral?"

"It is a statement of fact."

"I agree. That is a fact. Good afternoon."

But now two weeks have passed without a word: Abu is trying a new tactic. He is waiting me out, to see if I am desperate enough to pack up one night and cross the border, without a guide, without intelligence, without currency, without a passport. Wouldn't he love to get rid of me that way.

Meanwhile the rumor of my mission is on the air like a breeze: "Q'asidi is going to Jerusalem to avenge the Four." The boys wait and watch every gesture I make. Suddenly they are no longer interested in their beloved AKs, which are left leaning like derelicts against the rocks. The few pistols which they have wheedled from Hamid are passed from hand to hand, reverently dry-fired at paper cutouts from stances perfectly copied from my own practice sessions up at Little Nefud. They allow themselves two live rounds each per day, and spend minutes adjusting their aim before squeezing the trigger those two times. Watching them I am amazed how young they really are.

Their idolatry has been given no outlet, I realize. Abu is too chilly and remote a figure. Hamid is a bumbler, a good-natured camp counselor. Sami is strange and weak. Naef is completely colorless. I forget from time to time which one he is since he looks no older than most of the other boys. And Major Daoud is completely Abu's man. So that leaves them no one to admire except the toughest and smartest of themselves, that is Fawaz. And now Q'asidi, the exotic athlete who has fought revolutions all over the world, the master of martial arts and marksmanship who can kill with his bare hands or any weapon, and who can navigate in the dark without a guide. This is the latest fascination. I always hear two or three of them scraping over the rocks behind me until they finally fall too far behind to distinguish my shadow against the slopes, give up and stumble back to camp. But they are always waiting up to reassure themselves that the commando specialist has completed his nocturnal course on the mountain by 0230 hours and has not fallen into the hands of the Syrians or fallen off a cliff from misreading his map and compass.

"It go good?" they ask with the phrase they learned from Fawaz.

"I'm back in one piece, it go good." I've gone as far as the Lebanese border on the ridge and watched from the cover of those peculiar lava extrusions while a patrol from the Syrian lookout tried to locate the cause of a clattering avalanche of stones I accidentally dislodged. I wish I could tell them that, too. The frustrations of my muteness in their language still gnaw at me.

Finally an event to break the monotony: Hamid has driven down from the canyon in the Land Cruiser. This puts everyone in a state of expectancy. The last time he left, it signaled that the raid of Kuma and the other three would commence, because he returned with the old guide Nizar. And while the speculations are flying around the camp as to the portent of Hamid's present errand, my own guess is quietly confirmed by a note passed to me by the Vulture: an invitation to Abu's bunker at 1645 hours. My patience has forced his hand at last. When Hamid returns a few hours later with the white-maned Druze sitting stiffly in the passenger's seat it is no surprise to me. Before the guide has taken the few steps to the maw of the bunker the boys are already voicing the same conclusion. I overhear the words " 'l quds" and "Q'asidi." Q'asidi is going to Jerusalem. The ball is on your side of the net, Abu.

I squeeze through the tunnel to Abu's office at exactly 1645 hours. He is standing near the door and greets me warmly, the fleshy parentheses at the corners of his mouth creased deeply by smiling as he introduces the guide.

"Nizar stutters in at least six languages, including French and English, so you should have no problem communicating. I have already explained what you want of him. He assures me that there will be no problem if you can walk quickly. Can you walk quickly?"

"Quickly enough for him."

The old man stands to the side with his hands folded into the armpits of his gray djellaba. He has the hood drawn up around his neck like a winter collar, and watches us from the deep shadows of his brows, aloof, skeptical and contemptuous. The Druzes are not notoriously sympathetic to the Palestinian cause. Inside Israel they voted to volunteer their youths for conscription into the IDF. So one might wonder what brings this gnarled, hoary specimen into our service.

On Abu's desk is spread a military map of the Hermon region.

"Nizar suggests that our normal infiltration route across the ridge into Lebanon and then into enemy territory at Jebel Haourata may not be the best for this mission. He thinks there may be informers at Cheb'aa keeping a watch on the route and radioing the Israelis."

"What does he suggest then?"

Abu points to a town inside Israeli-held territory near the foot of the easternmost flank of the Hermon ridge. "Majdal Chams. It is a Druze town, completely sympathetic to the occupiers. Nizar has relatives there. Because you are an American he would be willing to go into Majdal Chams and persuade his relatives to let you hide in their house for a few hours until morning. It is a very colorful little hamlet, a tourist attraction, so it would be perfectly natural for an American tourist to be visiting. There is a bus which takes workers down to Qiryat Shemona at six-thirty in the morning. You could hitch on that bus and take one of the regular buses from Qiryat Shemona to Jerusalem."

"What's the catch?"

"Catch? I don't understand what that means."

"The drawback, the problem, the trick. It sounds too good."

"Of course there are several problems. First, your hosts will have to be paid for their hospitality. Second, they will have to be given a plausible explanation of your presence. The only one that may convince them is that you are an American agent returning from a mission inside Syria. Hopefully it would take them more than a few hours to realize the preposterousness of such a tale. They are, after all, peasants and tend to take things as they are presented. But there is always the risk of betrayal. You must weigh that. And third, there is the problem of crossing the zone."

"I begin to like the sound of Jebel Haourata."

Abu exchanges a few words with the old man.

"To translate loosely, you will have to enjoy its euphony by yourself. He will not take you there."

"Well, that decides it. How much will his relatives' hospitality cost?"

"I imagine about one hundred dollars would make them susceptible to your cover story. And you should be prepared to pay Nizar as well."

"What about the return trip?"

More conversation between them. The old man speaks in adamant tones.

"He says on no account must you return to Majdal Chams."

"Then I must find my own way back?"

"Nizar suggests Jebel Haourata. But as you can see on the map, the terrain is quite steep there. He says you must arrive there no later than two in the morning if you hope to cross the border into Syria while it is still dark."

"What about the minefields and the fence?"

"I was under the impression you have all the necessary skills of a commando, which include crossing minefields, cutting fences and avoiding patrols. I assumed those are the talents you have been refreshing during your midnight rambles."

He must know I've never crossed a minefield or cut a fence. Where would I have learned? In Montevideo? Perhaps he is trying to humiliate me. Or more likely, he doesn't expect I'll have the opportunity to try out those skills at the border because no one gets back that far. The hell with Jebel Haourata. From the road to the border that way is an eight-mile hike gaining over three thousand feet of elevation. And after that another six miles and another few thousand feet of climbing to reach the Syrian border. No thanks, Abu. If I go in via Majdal Chams I'll come out exactly the same way, step for step, through the same holes in the fences, through the same gaps in the minefields. Let Nizar worry about his relatives' reputations with the Jews.

I give him a wan smile.

"Well, commander, one prefers not to have to rely on infrequently practiced skills, but what must be done must be done."

"I appreciate your philosophical attitude. If this is decided then we can proceed to other aspects of the mission."

He mutters a few gracious phrases at the old man, who, without uncrossing his arms, steps from the cell with haughty slowness. Behind him the Vulture clanks shut the steel door. Abu lowers himself into his chair as if tired out by the effort of standing. His face has gone grayish and blank in the last few minutes. He now folds the map precisely along its former creases and returns it to a lower drawer in his desk. Then he slides a thin brown folder from the stack of papers by his left elbow, opens it and flips through some sheets of paper inside. Now I recall that the first time I sat before him there was a submachine gun lying under some newspaper by his right hand. Today it is nowhere in sight. Does this mean he finally trusts me not to assassinate him?

He pushes a roughly torn sheet of newspaper with a photo portrait under my nose.

"I'm sorry, commander, but this isn't the man. I told you he was silver-haired and elegant. This one is a Latin dumpling."

"Quite. The man who interrogated you is named Weizman. But he is, if anything, a liberal and we do not want him dead."

"Some liberal."

"For a policeman he is not a bad man. There are far worse in Miutim. The man you see before you is named Ehud Migdal, and is someone we would very much like to see put out of the way."

"That's all very well, but I don't give a damn about this Ehud Migdal of yours. It's Weizman I'm going after."

"In Montevideo, perhaps, it was the common practice for individual comrades to assassinate whomever they held grudges against. Here that is not the practice. Still, I would be interested to know what this Weizman has done that so inflames you. He is not known as a particularly brutal man. You yourself admitted that you were only 'roughed up.' "

"Do you want to know what inflames me against him? All right. This kind and liberal Weizman was instrumental in the assassination of Boudia."

He stares at me a moment. Then asks quietly, "How did you come by this knowledge?"

"Logic.

"Let me hear this logic."

"It's a long story."

"Do you expect me to wave it aside? That is a serious allegation. Did you think I would send you off to assassinate Weizman without even hearing the evidence against him?"

"There is evidence."

"I am waiting to hear it."

Where does it begin? All so long ago, and far . . . It begins with the betrayal by Hervé. "There was an Algerian, an Algerian Jew, I met in Paris not long after I arrived. I had been beating my head against a wall trying to make contact with the underground. This Algerian, Hervé, implied he had connections with the Palestinian clandestine movement."

"A Jew?"

"That is not unheard of, political principles taking precedence over ancestral associations."

"Not unheard of, no. Nor ever to be trusted. How did you meet him?"

"He worked on a small Trotskyite newspaper in the Latin Quarter. I knew someone who also worked on it. I met Hervé in the office."

"Who was the other person?"

"A girl. A Cuban."

"And you became friendly with this Algerian?"

336

"Not friendly. We talked several times. He was writing a piece on Kissinger and wanted to pick my brain on the subject, but we never became friendly."

"Because he was Jewish."

"No. I had many Jewish friends when I was growing up. But between me and Hervé there was a certain point of hostility over the fact that he had once been involved with this Cuban girl."

"So you were involved with her as well."

"To a degree."

"Go on."

"I suppose I must have implied to Hervé that I was looking for the Palestinian underground."

"That was not discreet."

"No, but at the time I was going crazy with frustration and was ready to follow any lead."

"Did he provide the 'lead' you were searching for?"

"No. Instead he warned me not to try to make contact."

"Why?"

"He claimed that everyone was deadly suspicious because of the wave of assassinations that had hit Paris, and my attempts to make contact would just turn the suspicion on me."

"Quite reasonable advice."

"It seemed so at the time."

"So when you did make contact with Boudia's group it was not through this Hervé."

"Boudia's group made contact with me. They said they had been aware of me almost from the time I landed in Paris."

"But not through the Algerian?"

"No. They must have heard of me through the grapevine. You know what emigré circles are like. Word gets around very quickly. I used to hang out in bars where Arabs often came in. I made no secret of the fact that I was Palestinian."

"So what does the Algerian, Hervé, have to do with your story?"

"At that point, nothing. Only later, when I returned from Jerusalem, did my suspicions turn to him."

"Suspicions? For what?"

"My mission had been blown by advance information to the Israelis. Someone had betrayed me. I never suspected Hervé until I ran into him by chance at a demonstration the day I returned to Paris. He was with some buddies, and started goading me about being the Palestinian James Bond, and how had my mission to the homeland gone off, and so on. There was only one conclusion to be drawn."

"Did you communicate your suspicion to Boudia?"

"I couldn't for some time. I was kept in the cold for weeks."

"But you did finally meet with Boudia. Did you express your suspicions then?"

"Yes. But he dismissed them."

"Why?"

"He was not of a suspicious frame of mind. I told you, he did not expect me to succeed. The mission was only a kind of test."

"But you yourself did not dismiss those suspicions."

"No. I still hold them."

"Did you communicate them to anyone else? After all, the alleged informer was still at large."

"No, he wasn't. He had been killed . . . by the police, in that same demonstration."

Abu jerks his head back at this, and then tries to stare through me. "Killed?"

"Shot."

"By the police?"

"CRS."

"Was this known publicly?"

"It was reported in the leftist newspapers."

"Killed. How convenient. But, then, I fail to see how this Algerian fellow could have had anything to do with Boudia's death, which took place quite some time later."

"A couple of months later. So what? The connection is not complicated. Hervé informed the Israelis that I would enter the country on a mission. Weizman was alerted, intercepted me, took my picture, sent that to their men in Paris, where I was followed until I inadvertently led them to Boudia."

"Not complicated? To me it seems rather extraordinary. First, do you suppose the Israelis can afford to have every suspicious Arab in Europe followed for months on the hope that they will be led to a terrorist leader?"

"Of course not. But if they know that one of those Arabs in particular is connected to a Mohammed Boudia . . ."

"How would they have known that you in particular—? Did you tell your Algerian friend that you were working for Boudia?"

"Of course not. I never even saw him, let me recall, from a month before I ever heard of Boudia to the day I returned from Israel."

"Then how could he have known that you were going to Israel at all, this Algerian?"

"But he knew. The day I got back, he knew."

"Someone else must have told him. Perhaps the Cuban girl."

"She wouldn't have told him."

"Are you so sure?"

"She didn't know where I was going until the morning I left."

"But perhaps she told him while you were away. In order to let him know she was . . . available?"

"I was in Katamon the afternoon of the day I left Paris. Weizman was already having me followed.

Even if she let it slip sometime that day it would have been too late."

"But that proves that the informer could not have been your Algerian friend, doesn't it?"

"It could look that way." Why haven't I figured this out before, myself?

"Well?" Abu purrs over joined fingertips.

My brain whirls. The great crystal of logic I have been holding in my chest of certainties shatters, obscuring all the others with a cloud of acrid dust. And through the midst of it all two images coagulate: Boudia's blood oozing from torn green-painted steel, and Hervé's crumpled body emerging from under the feet of the retreating crowd.

But someone told the toad to follow me until I led him to Boudia. That is not obscured by the dust. If not Hervé, and not Weizman, then who? Then who?

"Is there a problem, comrade Jibral? I am still interested to hear how Weizman was instrumental in the assassination of Boudia."

"I thought I'd reasoned it out. I was wrong."

"Of course you were wrong. Miutim has nothing to do with assassinations abroad. They have their hands quite full with civil disorder in Jerusalem. They simply mistook you for an Arab looking to cause some mischief in Katamon. Ironic, eh? On the other hand, Ehud Migdal . . ."

Abu's words seem to drift in from a great distance, so faint they are lost under the pounding litany which fills my skull: If not Hervé, and not Weizman, then who? If not Hervé, and not Weizman, then who?

Aie, Kamal! How could you have done that? How could you have persuaded yourself to kill Hervé on such flimsy—no, faulty—logic? But it wasn't logic at all, was it? It was the heat and the tear gas, the rage in the air, and the frustration and fatigue and bitter sense of failure you brought back from Jerusalem. It was Hervé's stupid goading, and his pushing from

340

behind when the flics were so close to shooting. It was the weight of that little pistol in your Adidas bag. And it was jealousy, too, wasn't it?

All of which makes you no better than a barroom murderer, Kamal. Everyone has frustrations. But you call your outbursts revolutionary acts. Hah! Go on, tell Abu the whole truth of the affair. What's the point in letting him babble on about this Ehud Migdal, whoever he is.

"I'm sorry, commander, but I don't have any interest in your Migdal."

"But this is the only mission I am offering you."

"I decline it."

He nods sharply. "Decline it? Very well. I will send Nizar home to Beit Jinn. However, you might consider that the entire camp is very well aware of the significance of Nizar's presence tonight. You will have to provide your own excuses for having declined to carry out the mission for which you have been making such ostentatious preparations. I must say I am not surprised. Now you have confirmed the suspicion about you that has been in my mind from the day you arrived here." He snaps closed the folder before him. "As an actor, Boudia should have been able to discern posturings of bravado put up to mask the true but quite contrary nature—"

"I'll take your mission."

"So abrupt a change of heart?

"It is not a change of heart. Only a change of target. Should it make any difference to me who the victim is? If you say Weizman does not deserve to be killed, fine. If you say my comrades will be satisfied with the blood of this Migdal, then . . ."

His fleshy creases bracket a sneerish grin. "In that case . . ." He flips open the folder again. "Let me say that you have talents that cry out to be proven in action. A man who sits too long without testing himself becomes a coward in spite of himself."

"Don't try to goad me. I have no doubts about my courage."

"But you do have doubts about your purpose. Those are far more difficult to live with. A coward driven by a clear and powerful purpose can be a very effective revolutionary." (Are you speaking of yourself, Abu?) ". . . But the man of action who swings like a weathervane with every breeze toward a new battleground, he is more dangerous to his comrades than to the enemy."

"Why don't you save the speech until I get back? Just tell me where I can find your Ehud Migdal."

"Very well. I will write down the address. It is a fifth-floor flat in a new suburb of Jerusalem they call Ramat Eshkol."

"Did the person who substituted Migdal for Weizman at least obtain the other intelligence I requested?"

"You asked for a schedule of the target's routine movements. I have that here. I could translate it all for you, but I believe all you need to know is when you can find him at home."

"I would prefer to have some options."

"Very well. But let me advise you on the matter of your escape. Israel is very small country and extremely alert and practiced in the business of intercepting terrorists. Very few reach their targets. Far fewer return. While you may have an unusual freedom to travel inside Israel because of your American nationality, once you are identified as a terrorist your description will be radioed all over the country in minutes. You will have no hope of escaping. Therefore if you do hope to escape you will have to act in the dark. And escape in the dark. That rather implies that you will have to find him at home."

"That is not absolute. But I agree, it is probably best."

"And there is one other factor that you may want

342

to consider, in case things don't go as well as you hope. The Israelis, oddly, have no death penalty for terrorism, at least for the time being. So the choice to die, if your escape should fail, is your own."

"The choice seems pretty obvious to me."

"It is not so for everyone. We do not make heroes of those who allow themselves to be taken alive if they can still fight. But no one can order a man to be a martyr."

"It is hardly the act of a martyr, eh, to kill a man you've never heard of."

"How you view it is your own business. However, don't think you can change your mind once you are across the border and divert your attention to the good Mr. Weizman. If I hear over the radio that he has been killed you will not survive the return trip. Be assured of that."

"An unnecessary threat, commander. Weizman, Migdal, anyone else you care to put on the list— they're all Schlomo ben Yahud to me."

"I will call Nizar back. We can continue with the rest of the 'arrangements.'"

Samir

IT IS NEARLY dark when the American emerges from the bunker. His walk is a little uncertain, not his normal stride, as if he has been drugged. When he comes closer I can see that he is ashen. But when he notices my scrutiny, he fakes a grin and a chipper voice. "Okay Sami boy, let's get the Last Supper cooked up."

"You are leaving tonight, then."

"Abu's in a hurry all of a sudden. I'll be back by sunrise the day after tomorrow. So have breakfast ready, what do you say."

"You're bloody cocky."

Hamid now joins us by the stove. He has brought two yellow T-shirts with the Coca-Cola logo in Hebrew letters emblazoned in red across the chest. And cradled on these are two of the Russian-style cast-iron hand grenades and three extra magazines for the Tokarev. Kamal accepts this contribution with a nod and places the pile reverently inside the tent. Hamid warms his hands over the stove, though it is not even cool yet, perhaps to have an excuse to hang around Kamal. But he has nothing to say and soon shuffles off in his embarrassment.

"Do you expect to buy off a border guard with a pair of T-shirts, Yank?"

"No. I expect to wear them. 'Verisimilitude' Abu calls it."

"Practicing his long words on you, is he?"

He doesn't answer. At first I attribute his silence to irritation at my jocularity. But then I see that he is watching an argument some distance away among several of the Grenades. Out of the blustering knot of them Fawaz strides toward us, his camera swinging on his neck. As he reaches our tent he points to the lens and then to Kamal and grunts, "Photo."

"They think you're going on a one-way mission, Yank. So he wants to immortalize you."

"No pictures, Fawaz." The American waves his hand to dismiss him.

"No photo?" The boy is puzzled.

"You understand a little English, Fawaz. No photos now. When I come back from Jerusalem, photos, all you like. Understand?"

"You come back?" He pokes his head forward in disbelief.

"Two days."

"In Palestine two days?"

"In Palestine one day. Just one day."

"Hey Yank, you're supposed to say 'in'shallah'

when making a statement of that audacity. It is a sacrilege not to ask Allah's cooperation."

Fawaz narrows his eyes and retreats one step. Then he wheels and stalks away angrily. He thinks he is being fooled. Don't worry, Fawaz, there's only one person being fooled, and he's doing it to himself.

But even as he is folding his weapons into the rough woolen blanket and pushing the lumpy wad into my purloined rucksack I secretly wait for the ruse to be sprung. The T-shirts follow the blanket. Then his corduroy jacket, neatly folded. And the map and compass on top. He tugs the drawstring tight and buckles the flap down over the puckered mouth of the sack. Can it be that he is truly leaving us? Something is missing. I've seen dozens march out of camps on missions; none were this casual. He acts as if he were going mountain climbing. Nervous but not solemn. Fawaz and I are not the only ones disoriented by his manner. Everyone is watching now. Kamal knows this and is playing to it just the way he did up at the target range. To him this is not a mission but another and grander scene in the spectacle he has been staging for us since he arrived. He fully expects to return to a standing ovation.

"You know, Yank, you remind me of a cartoon I once saw. It depicted a bearded, wild-eyed anarchist in a cellar with his comrades. He is holding open his coat to reveal a belt formed of sticks of dynamite, and he is saying, 'All right, I walk into the Palace and light the fuse. Where do I meet you guys afterward?' "

He stands up with that peculiar uncoiling motion, at the same time liquidly slinging the rucksack over his right shoulder. Style to the end. He steps up to me and suddenly pats, almost slaps, my cheek so hard my teeth click. Once, twice, three times.

"Don't forget, Sami boy, breakfast at dawn."

And swaggers off toward the bunker as if he has

just struck a mortal blow to the enemy. If there was any cranny of my soul which grieved the American's departure, it has united firmly with the rest of my being to wish the Israelis good hunting.

Kamal

THIS OLD DRUZE must be silently cursing me in every one of his six languages. On leaving the camp, he steered us up-canyon, to the northwest. Majdal Chams lies due south. The obvious way to approach it, the route requiring least climbing and the shortest exposure inside enemy territory, is to drop out of the canyon toward Beit Jinn and then skirt due south along the bluffs which form the eastern boundary of the occupied zone.

When I mentioned this he spat and replied, "What you know? Here go nort' to go sout'. Go sout', end up nort'. Nort' in Dimashq."

"Damascus?"

"Yes, nort' in Dimashq, in front of firey squad. You want, goodbye, go sout'. One kilometer say hello to patrol Surian. Nizar goes which way he goes, else goes home. O.K.?"

"O.K., old man, you're the boss."

"And not so old."

"No? You walk like the grave's already got your feet."

"Not must Nizar teach you humility. Must Allah."

So he persists in his enervating shuffle, past the switchback in the trail which would lead us up the north wall of the canyon and to the regular route over the Hermon ridge into Lebanon. Instead he picks a path through the talus and brush on the steeper south wall of the canyon. At times we have to climb on all fours, and whenever I dislodge a stone he turns on me with a sharp hiss.

It is difficult to tell how much distance we have covered when the terrain is as rough as this. After an hour of hard scrambling we can peer back and see faint lights flickering in the camp, halfway down the canyon, a thousand feet below us. If those stoves and lanterns were blacked out it would be impossible to spot any habitation there, even under this intense moonlight. But above us, where the slopes begin to relent, the moon exposes the terrain like a prison searchlight. Somewhere to the west, not more than two miles away, the Syrian observation post has a line of sight on the slope we have to cross to reach the fence. Here we are hidden by the twists of the terrain, but the abrupt exposure ahead of us gives me a chill.

There is no color colder than the moon's silvery blue. It highlights every boulder and every bush between here and the crest. The fence cuts a dark cicatrice across the moon-mottled incline. Beyond it the ground sweeps up to form two shining hummocks. Though their baldness is a trick of illumination and distance, they are the deadliest stretch of terrain imaginable. We will stand out like telephone poles on a glacier. Just beyond their summits is enemy territory.

The old man signals me to lie flat and he himself merges with the terrain by squatting under the gray folds of his cloak. After a minute I can no longer distinguish him from the rocks. Then suddenly he glides back to my side and points down toward the shadows from which we have just climbed.

"Why?"

"Patrol." He says the word like "petrol."

"I don't see any patrol."

He points to his ear.

"I don't hear anything except the wind."

347

"That why Nizar guide."

He glides another fifty yards lower, where the shadow swallows him like a pool of bunker oil. When I find him he has already unshouldered his little pack and is tugging out another gray cloak. "Put on."

"Gladly."

"We wait."

"How long?"

"Until safe."

Subject dismissed. We huddle in the shadows for another half hour without a word. I am trying to remember names of constellations when Nizar shakes me and points toward the fence. Two tiny silhouette figures are stepping carefully along a section of fence that rises toward our right. No sound of them touches my ear. They pass like phantoms across the eerie blue landscape.

Nizar whispers, "They look for cuts."

"Cuts in the fence? They are a little early."

"Yes, but only because we wait."

"You're a pro, old man."

"Not so old."

It takes the two figures fifteen minutes to climb the rise, which takes them out of sight. They are either very thorough or very weary; it is impossible to tell at this distance.

"How long before it is safe to continue?"

"Half hour. One hour. Must move fast later. Rest now."

He draws his hood over his face and leans back against a rock. He trusts his ears better than his eyes. I will trust them too, for the strain of peering into the dark is making things swim. The dark and damp warmth of my breath inside the hood soothes. Except for the cold spots on my knees it is just like being in the tent.

* * *

"You! Wake now."

But I am only drowsing. The hour has passed very slowly. I feel stiff and chilled. Nizar starts ahead. On my first step I kick loose a stone.

He spins. "Stupid."

I hike the cloak up to my knees and hurry after him. Soon we are within a few yards of the fence where it climbs the steepest section of the slope. He signals me into the shadow of some nearby rocks and slithers forward on all fours like a great loose-skinned gray lizard. A few minutes later I hear the metallic pinging of wire being cut. Now he is back, beckoning me to follow. Halfway there I loose a clatter of pebbles.

"You!" he snaps. "Look you, like this. No animal walk on his knees." He demonstrates his technique: a low straddling pushup supported on palms, fingers and toes. He advances one limb at a time, making certain to land on something solid before giving it weight. He accelerates this into a rapid glide and reaches the fence in a few seconds.

When I reach him he is grimacing with contempt. Or perhaps from the effort of cutting the intertwined coils of barbed wire with a bayonet-and-scabbard chopper. He has made all the cuts where the coils touch the ground instead of where the wire comes closest to hand, and to do this he had to reach into the tangle up to the elbows of both arms. Now holding the loops gingerly he spreads a foot-wide passage for me to push my pack through and then wriggle after on my side. As I turn to hold the wire for him, I find he is already halfway through himself, holding the loops apart and slithering in the same motion. A second later he is on his knees, binding the cut ends back together with some short pieces of fine copper wire. These joints he buries in the dirt and covers with small pebbles. It was worth the trouble making the cuts at the bottoms of the loops for this. The restored fence looks undisturbed. But it would take only a quick tug to break the fine binding wire and open up the loops again. I make a point to memorize the features of the terrain and the distance from the nearest post while he puts the final touches on his surgery.

"Now, must hurry."

He is on his feet, running in a low crouch toward the lowest point on the saddle to the right of the two hummocks. We are moving almost due west, by no means the shortest direction to the crest. But I have no urge to question him about it. He is an artist in this medium. And he is also twenty yards ahead.

"Look you." He points northward when I catch up. The Syrian observation post stands out very clearly, squat and pale except for the dark sockets of its gun ports. It is no more than a mile from us, but here we are showing them our shadowed side, and the slope is more strewn with boulders and brush than it appeared from lower down. In our gray cloaks we must be invisible even in a pair of binoculars. If they have infrared scopes, however . . .

Nizar interrupts the thought with a whisper. "From here, very, very dangerous. Many old mine from war. Now you follow close. Not worry now, worry later. Nizar goes here many time. Only must you follow close, very close."

He rises to his feet and throws back his hood. From here on I will imitate every gesture. Suddenly the mountain is full of sounds that the hood has muffled: tiny percussions, low whistles of wind passing among the rocks on the crest, a faint roar of a distant jet. Far below on the plain a string of lights in close formation are crawling south along what must be the main highway from Damascus, whose glow sits on the edge of the moonlit plain. Luminous markers of civilization. Ahead, beyond the shallow notch in the ridge, the world drops away in darkness. Enemy territory.

We are no longer running. Nizar advances five or ten steps at a time, stops, looks left and right, sometimes squats to peer along the surface of the ground, perhaps trying to spot the dark lines of trip wires against the illuminated slopes. I mimic every step. After a while each reflection of the moon on the ground looks like a trip wire or trigger plate. At each step he is walking a little faster, and every time I miss one of his footplants by a few inches I feel the thread hook my shoe and tense for the blast of the Claymore to shred away my legs.

If we catch it out here between the fences, in no man's land, which side comes to retrieve our upper halves? Or do they continue to grimace at each other across this desolate kilometer while the crows shred what's left? Perhaps some bored sentry back at that Syrian post is now watching us through his infrared telescope, eagerly waiting for the bright flash and the distant pop.

Here we have stopped again. The old man is looking back over the path by which we have come and scratching his head. What's the matter now? Did we take the wrong turn at the fence?

"Strange thing. Very strange. They take away mine, all mine gone. Bad news. Going to be 'nother war."

"Another war?"

He nods with the solemn certainty of a peasant predicting a drought. Whatever the reason they've taken away the mines is fine with me. The prospect of having to find my own way back over this last half mile on my hands and knees feeling for trip wires could make me change my mind about this mission. No, not quite. But twenty-four hours from now, without sleep, I will be in no mood to be painstaking. Mines or no mines, I will take a deep breath, tell myself the hell with it, and make a dash for the fence. So this is hardly bad news, old man. And if there's going to be another war, all the better. Maybe I'll be spared the trouble of making the return trip entirely.

Still shaking his head at the puzzle of the missing mines, the old man resumes his crouched advance uphill. We are now just short of the crest of the saddle. He drops into his lizard crawl for the last twenty yards, bidding me to wait until he gives me the signal to follow. I use the pause to fish out Sami's compass and take a bearing. As I suspected, we have been climbing due west since we cut the fence. The shortest route across the zone would have been south-southwest, but that would have taken us straight over the further hummock of the pair. The route the old man has chosen, though twice as long, takes the best advantage of the cover provided by the folds of the ridge. Perhaps before this area was cut up by the Six Day War, he herded sheep or goats up here, and now the only people who will buy his knowledge of this patch of mountain are infiltrators like me. Perhaps he did not get to choose the side he serves, but had it thrust upon him because the Israelis stopped their advance at the ridge line instead of a few kilometers further in Beit Jinn. Everyone from this part of the world is a victim of History. And everyone who comes here from other parts of the world, too.

This Ehud Migdal, his parents probably fled here from somewhere in Europe. Maybe they wanted to go to America and found the door closed. Or maybe they wanted to make the desert bloom and dance the hora and sing soulful folk songs. And then their son Ehud, who was probably thinking he was only making the land safe for his children—he looks old enough to have children—by some mischance caught the attention of an Abu Ahmet who needed a victim and happened to have at hand a young man willing and skilled to satisfy that need. But if Abu merely needed a victim, Weizman would have sufficed. There is something more to this Ehud Migdal affair. I should have asked. He was purposely being vague. Instinct tells me it's a personal grudge.

"Psst! You. Come now."

He has slid back to my side and now drags me to the actual crest. My first view of enemy territory! The saddle falls away gently for a few hundred yards then plunges into a deep twisting canyon. From near the summit of the mound to our left the Israeli fence slashes down the slope, its new wire gleaming in the moonlight, leveling only across a short shelf before sidling down the far wall of this narrow canyon below us. There the shadows swallow it. But it must rise again out of the canyon because the crest of the far wall is also the Lebanese border. We will infiltrate into the very northernmost corner of the land occupied by Israel.

There is no point on the border farther from Jerusalem, and yet, as we slither across to the descending slope, Jerusalem suddenly seems closer than anything behind us. Even the camp, no more than four thousand yards away as the crow flies, is History. Like Damascus, like Paris, like Montevideo. All these have been mere steps toward the ultimate goal which lies in the dark below me: Jerusalem. The great meander which I began just over three years ago now seems a single lunge.

The old man has squatted again. As I kneel beside him he jabs his forefinger emphatically to another hummock on the crest of the buttress where it turns south. It takes me a moment to recognize the structure: a squat geometric platform set into the crown of the hill.

"Israeli lookout?"

He nods.

"What is that below it?" I am wondering about a line of what appear to be giant stakes in the hillside.

"She-a."

"What-a?"

He holds two fingers parallel and snakes them down his thigh while making a whoshing sound.

"Skiing!" The stakes are ski-lift towers.

"Um, ski-a."

"Cheeky sons of bitches. They really send their kids up there to wiggle their asses at the Syrians?"

"Yanayir."

"January?"

"Um. Talg . . . la neige, partout ici."

"Snow everywhere here."

"Yes, snow. Most year."

"Good, let's get out of here before it starts snowing, old man."

"Not so old." He hops up and sets off down the slope in his crouched run. He doesn't seem particularly worried about the Israeli post. But with the moon now to our right, and the lookout to our left, we are showing them, too, our shadowed side. This must have been another reason for the long diagonal across no man's land. Nizar, you really are an artist.

We reach the fence just where it drops down the steep pitch to the shelf. We are now below the lookout post's line of sight. Nizar is already chopping away at the fence. This one is more difficult than the Syrian side. It is fabricated with chainlink mesh and barbed wire—more like a prison fence than a military barrier. There will be no way to hide the damage. He has hacked away a couple of feet of the overhanging barbed wire and is now trimming the lethal top edge of the chainlink. He looks nervous for the first time, and keeps glancing in both directions along the fence for patrols. The cutting is making too much noise. As each wire breaks, the snap of the bayonet against the hollow scabbard echoes along the fence mesh. It's making me nervous, too.

"Forget about making it perfect. I'll just fold up my cape and stick it on top of the spikes."

For the first time he defers to a suggestion of mine. Every kid raised in New York can climb chainlink as easily as a staircase. The thick fabric of the cloak, doubled twice, bates the spike ends enough to give a good handhold. In a few seconds I'm over, to the nods of the old man who follows almost as spryly.

"Good, good," he mutters as I pluck the cloak from the fence and put it on again. "But must hurry."

He leads to the right along the patrol path which follows the fence. Abruptly the shelf narrows and the slope again plunges into the canyon. Here we leave the fence to climb along a lava outcropping which quickly steepens until we have to find footholds and handholds for each step as we descend.

"On rock, no mines," Nizar excuses himself.

"On rock, break neck. Who needs a mine?"

But soon the rock merges with a dirt slope and we skid down another fifty feet to a goat trail. Below us the ravine wall steepens and plunges away into shadows. A false step off this six-inch-wide notch in the slope could be the beginning of a fatal fall. But Nizar sighs theatrically as if to indicate all our difficulties are behind us and launches ahead at nearly a run. It is not his pace but the precision of his footwork which keeps me on the verge of falling behind. The trail follows the contour, giving up altitude only as we turn more directly southward several kilometers from the fence. The ridge to our right, across the ravine, along the crest of which runs the Lebanese border, has dropped noticeably now. All around us the terrain is relenting. Suddenly, just ahead of me, Nizar has squatted on the trail. But before I reach him he is on his feet and hurrying down a steep embankment. In a moment I see the reason for his caution. Our path crosses a dirt road carved into the hillside. This must lead to the observation post or the ski lift. It is well packed. Nizar stoops to examine some tire tracks and waves me on to where the trail picks up at the foot of the shoulder. Below, the road curls down into the blackness of the valley, a bright tan ribbon abruptly swallowed. We are losing the moon, but perhaps it is just as well; there is a vague presence of humanity here, perhaps the smells of animals or domestic vegetation replacing the dry, sharp chill of the high mountains.

Nizar descends from the road as silently as a bat. "Hey, old man, far to go?"

He hisses me to be silent and hurries ahead. In a few minutes we encounter the first low stone fence. Now a hut. A donkey tethered to a stunted tree watching us pass with his incomprehensible animal complacence. I can't resist scratching him between the ears. Nizar hisses again. Soon more huts emerge from the darkness on either side of the trail, which has now widened into a cart path. On our right an ankle-high stone footing appears to mark the boundary of some property. On our left the first cluster of trees, perhaps olives. Just past these Nizar steers us off the path, across a small cleared field, then along a stone wall higher than my head. He stops abruptly at an aperture in the wall and directs me to enter. Inside is a stone-paved courtyard before a single-story house. Nizar knocks lightly, almost inaudibly, on the rough wood door. After a minute the bolt is drawn with a scrape, the door creaks open, Nizar drags me inside by the sleeve. Our host appears to be a teenage boy. A brief conversation ensues. The only word I recognize is "amriki." Me, the American. Then, without having let go of my sleeve, Nizar leads me down a hall to a small room.

"Rest now." He pushes me onto a high bed. I strike a match to read my watch: 3:05. The old man slumps into a high-back chair but continues peering at me from the depths of his hood, while the watch burns down to my fingers. He looks angry.

"What for you come here?" Not whispered, but barely audible in the way only a deep voice can be. The flame stings my thumb and I wave it out, using the distraction as an excuse not to answer.

"What for you come here? To kill yahud? So, you kill one, maybe two. Then they kill you. Muktub. Filistin, yes, they crazy with sorrow. Want to die. But American, what for to die? All foreignyer that come here, they die. Have Deutsch girl, have Italien, have Jap men—all dead. No American. You first one. Why not you go home to America? I tell Ahmet patrol shoots you. You hero all the same. Except live hero. All others dead hero. Ahmet, too, soon dead hero. Five years, all dead. No one remember them. But same five year, you rich in America, five son, beautiful wife with yellow hairs, Mercedey Benzi. Nizar come visit. You thank him."

"I thank you now, Nizar. But it is not written that way. My father had five sons, a beautiful wife with yellow hairs—you see mine?—and even had a Mercedes-Benz for a while. And he died a very unhappy man, anyway."

"What know you, too smart fellow? Nizar already not a young man before the fences come here. All this land of Nizar and father of Nizar and father of father of Nizar. We come and go across mountain free like streams of water in Maayu. Fences not stop water."

In his own mind perhaps this is an answer to my riddle, but to me it is just a peasant's guff. If I answer it he will then argue on through the rest of the night. So I shrug and pretend to be pondering his wisdom. The night has been long enough already. My stomach feels as though I've been eating limestone. My eyes are scratchy. Whenever I think of what lies ahead my gut withers in a surge of acid.

The rucksack is lying next to me on the sagging mattress. My hand, almost of its own volition, creeps in among the layers of the blanket to feel the reassuring solidity of the pistol grip, the slick, cold machined surfaces of the frame, the sharply knurled spur, the trigger's smooth pivot. I've always loved the feel of a pistol. Ever since I and my brothers sneaked the first secret grasp of the Luger my father used to keep locked, he thought, in the upper right-hand drawer of his maple desk. "Every Palestinian must learn to use a gun," he pontificated to my mother, who used to quail at the illegal weapon. And in my heart I vociferously rallied to his support.

This Tokarev is a strange weapon. Its excessive Cyrillic engravings on the grip and the flanks of the slide feel uncomfortable under my fingers. It is not a pretty weapon. Not like the classic and functional lines of a P-38 or a Browning HP. And then this Tokarev is burdened with an almost rifle-sized cartridge. For what? A 9mm never let anyone down. And why they left off the damned safety when they copied the rest of the design straight from the Colt . . . With this machine you have to leave the hammer at half cock. But stop complaining. It will do the job as well as any other gun. A good workman never blames . . . and all that.

Yes, there's the trick. Think of yourself as a workman on this mission. No, a craftsman. The craftsman doesn't judge the purpose of the blueprints in front of him. He takes pride in executing the design perfectly. And then basks in the warming accolades of those who commissioned the work. You've never killed to specification before. Hervé, Castellan, the pig from the Ministerio del Interior: all of them were victims of passion. Who hasn't, inside his brain, killed a thousand times for a slight? So when the grievance is great is it any surprise that the impulse sometimes jumps the microscopic synapse from thought to action? And in revolution the grievances are always great.

But I have no grievance against this Ehud Migdal. He exists only on a few scraps of paper: a blurry newspaper photo, an address, a schedule. Specifications. From which I am to craft an extinction to order. Abu's order. What made me change my mind back there in the bunker and accept this mission? Certainly not his taunts at my courage.

Abu was a million miles away when I changed my mind. Who was there just then? Boudia, Hervé, also my father, and a picture of myself in front of the Grenades—Fawaz, grim and judging, at the center of the line. I saw Abu shrug as if to say, "Weizman, Migdal: same thing to us," and admitted to myself that Weizman would have been another mistake— wincing under the sting of the truth from the back of my head to my groin—another mistake like Hervé . . .

I jump up as if hit by lightning. What the hell are you doing to yourself, Jibral? Talking yourself a way out, from the sound of it. Softening yourself up with regret. Somebody tipped off the Israelis, and you don't know that it wasn't Hervé.

"Hey, old man."

No answer. No motion. He is sitting erect with the hood far over his eyes. So he can't see this first trickle of light from the tiny window high above the bed. Another match. The hands of my watch are crawling toward five. I must have dozed off for some time. My mind raced through it as if I'd been wide awake. Tension does that to me.

"Hey old man . . . Nizar."

Still no motion, but after a few seconds the voice sounds from the cavern of his hood. "What you want?"

"Coffee."

"Cafe cost money."

"I'll pay, damnit. I'll pay ten bucks for a pot of coffee."

He nods, stands, leaves the room for a few minutes, and comes back empty-handed.

"Well?"

No reply. He has resumed his trance.

After another twenty minutes there is a tentative tap at the door. An elderly woman enters, almost backwards, her head bowed, though she manages a furtive glance from the very corner of her eye to see who I am. She's brought a tray with a silver pot and two tiny white cups which she sets down on the vacant chair and quickly backs out of the room. It is good thick coffee. Nizar makes no move toward the remaining cup, and before long I have drunk down the entire potful. The room is now visible, more a cell than a room with its bare walls and one scant aperture to the sky. There are no signs that it is lived in, though it has been kept scrupulously clean. Perhaps Druzes share fastidiousness with the rest of Islam. This cubicle is a little too bare for my taste.

"Nizar, is there no bus before six-thirty?"

"In such a hurry to die? No, no bus before."

"Keep your opinions to yourself, old man. You're paid to play guide, not social worker."

"Pay? Yes, now you pay. One thousand pounds Israeli for Nizar. Four hundred pounds for room. Forty pounds for cafe."

"Thousand pounds? No way. That's two hundred and fifty bucks. Abu said one hundred."

"Ahmet not guide."

"Ahmet also didn't give me that many pounds. Here's four hundred pounds for you. And, say, two hundred for the room. And the forty I idiotically promised you for the coffee. Take it in bad conscience."

360

He refuses to reach for the currency.

"No pay, no leave." The old native shakedown. They used to pull that one on us all the time outside of Monte. You would have thought we were making the revolution for ourselves the way those peasants tried to extort us. No pay, no guide; no pay, no hide; no pay . . . sometimes even worse. When we protested and explained the principles of socialism they shrugged and replied that they would be the victims no matter who was running the country from the city. So just a few more pesos in the pocket to prove they weren't being taken for fools once again.

"No pay, no leave, huh? Okay. Let's wait here until the sayeret patrol comes knocking on the door. Would your relatives prefer that to two hundred pounds?" I hold it out to him again.

"You are not good man, amriki. You will have bad luck."

"If that's a threat, old man, you will regret it. Bitterly. But I'll take it metaphorically."

He glares at me, probably understanding only the warning tone in my voice, and knowing from that he will not succeed at his dickering. Finally he grabs the wad of bills I've been holding out to him. Then he pulls his hood down and waits.

At six-twenty I stick my arm in front of the hood to show him my watch. No response.

At six-thirty, again.

And again at six-forty-five.

I am about to repeat the demonstration again at five to seven when the faint bellow of a heavy vehicle straining up a hill scratches at the window. Nizar is on his feet at once. We leave the house the way we entered: along the wall, across the small cleared field, into the grove of olive trees. The ridge behind us looks impressively huge. It is a pity we couldn't have made the crossing by day. The slope above us is speckled with wild flowers. And the town below, as

Abu described, a picturesque muddle of very Arab dwellings tucked against the hillside. There is more greenery here than I expected, though through the notch by which the road climbs to the town there is a view of a vast barren plain. Nizar points down the rocky slope toward the road. Dozens of men are converging on the point where the road enters the town. Most are wearing work clothes. A few are wearing black cloaks and white kaffiyehs. A rumble of diesel reaches us. I am about to rush toward it when Nizar grabs the grey djellaba he gave me last night. I pull it off and hand it to him, but he pushes it back at me. "You need again."

"That's true. Thank you." No charge for this? Apparently he has been smitten with a pang of generosity.

I stuff the cloak into the top of my rucksack as the bus roars again. We have time only to nod at each other. The bus is already starting up as I reach the road. I wave it down and the driver stops to let me board. He is a dark, bald man. He mutters angrily in Hebrew.

I shrug back. "Sorry."

"Amairicaan?"

"Yup." Might as well start the act on the right note.

"Where go-eeng?"

"Qiryat Shemona? Then maybe Tel Aviv. I don't know yet."

He slaps the door shut and accelerates down the hill, nearly knocking me over. The passengers all glare angrily as I stagger down the aisle to the first free seat. But the bus driver only shakes his head. What can you do with a crazy American hippie who doesn't even know where he's going. Then he turns up his radio.

The bus slides down the grade from Majdal Chams. Its next stop is an even smaller hamlet at the foot of the bluffs. The other passengers are ignoring me by now. Even the leathery fellow who sits next to me, who tried to exchange a few words, has given up and turned to chatter with someone across the aisle. The driver, though, keeps glancing in the mirror. I must be a novelty on this route.

The road, clinging to the foot of the steep grassy slopes at the base of the Hermon, crosses over a large fenced pipeline. This must be the infamous TAP line. Industrial arrogance manifest, to stretch a metal tube from the Persian Gulf to the Mediterranean, across four countries and a few emirates, protected by nothing but a pair of chainlink fences, and expect it to rest unmolested. Well, those days are over. I read that some of our comrades knocked out the terminal in Lebanon last April after the Israeli raids. Then the company said it was going to be shut down anyway. Not enough capacity for the gluttons on the receiving end.

Now, abruptly, we turn away from the bluffs, roll past some small farming settlements, cleared fields, still slowly descending. Another stop. Several more men board. The bus lurches ahead and stops again in ten minutes. There is no one waiting by the road, and no one leaves the bus. After a few minutes the driver turns around and shouts in Arabic. The passengers respond with laughter. The driver slaps the door closed and grinds into first gear. We are on the plain now, far enough to see the highest ridge of the mountain behind us. It seems inconceivable that just a few hours ago the old man and I were hiking way up there. Ahead lies a mass of new construction, bulldozed fields, rows of heavy equipment. There are other tattered yellow buses like this one disgorging men who look like the men next to me. They seem to be building an entire city at once. Huge square faceless highrises grow out of the dirt, out of place, as if some wag substituted architect's plans that were drawn up for Houston. We pull up in front of a cafe across from a bulldozed excavation. Construction dirt gives everything a brownish hue.

The bus empties, except for me and the driver, who finally shambles back up the aisle. "End of route here. Sorry. But you can go to the regulair buses station not far on this road. From there bus to Haifa or where you say you are going. I don't remember."

"All right. Thanks for the ride."

"No trouble."

The bus station is in a more complete part of the city, and crowded with an odd assortment of people. At least a dozen of them are speaking a strange language, which on closer listening turns out to be Russian. Emigrés. Brought here by the same human pipeline that Boudia's, and now Issa's, operation is going to breach. This world is as interknotted as a fishnet. But not nearly as neat. My father, Boudia, Esteban, Abu, Issa, these voluble Russians, the pig from the Ministerio del Interior, Hervé, Weizman, Alain Castellan, and now this fellow Migdal: all joined by one thread, Kamal Jibral.

A very different group of passengers is boarding the bus to Jerusalem. Young women in short skirts with suntanned legs. Four men in military uniform. Unarmed. Several older men in white shirts, already sweat-stained around the armpits from the morning heat. No one gives me a second glance. Odd that those Arabs should have found me so curious while these Jews barely notice me at all. The bus is already resounding with conversation and laughter. The soldiers are flirting with some of the girls.

Israel and sex: I wonder why that association is so deeply planted in my brain? It's been there forever, it seems. Skillful propaganda must have put it there. Or was it what's-her-name? Beth, Zionist Beth, who sat in the next row all the way through high school

364

with her single thick braid and delicate ankles. She was the first girl who didn't wear a bra. And she had a generous pair, too. Every summer she went off to the "kibbutz" and in the fall returned with the glow of a woman, even when she was fifteen, while the rest of us were going pimply with frustration. Oh yes, I remember the guilty longing for the "Jewess." Instead I gave her my hard eyes. She thought I hated her guts. It's summer now. I wouldn't be surprised to see her climb aboard at the next stop.

These spotty settlements along the road could be kibbutzim. I always pictured them lusher than this, though, from her impassioned descriptions. Israel, the Garden of Eden, reclaimed from the desert by muscular Sabras and sexy American teenage girls.

Ah well. Probably the '60s found her a cause closer to home. Perhaps a Resistance draft counselor, then a community organizer in some Brooklyn slum, now a women's self-helper. It's not a bad guess, though I must admit I'd prefer to imagine her as a helicopter pilot stationed somewhere on the Golan Heights. . . . Beth, a bright-eyed, fine-fingered predator pouncing out of the sky on her old classmate. Shit, I can still give myself a hard-on thinking about her.

This is not a beautiful country. It reminds me of Nevada, dusty and ungenerous. It is hard to think of the desolation out of which this appeared as a Promised Land of milk and honey. If you spilled milk on the ground down here it would fry to a chalky spot in a few seconds. How bitterly disappointed our young commandos must be when they descend from the mountain and for the first time see what they have been taught to long for all their lives. Confusion, doubt. Did we follow the map right? This can't be it. Let's go home.

Soldier with an Uzi boards. He, too, barely glances at me, but then sits down next to me planting the submachine gun across his lap as if it were a brief-case. The muzzle is pointing at my knees. But there is no magazine in the grip.

"Where do you come from?" he asks immediately in English.

"You mean right now or in general?"

"Your home."

The way he asks almost sounds like an interrogation, but I realize it is just Israeli "directness." At least I had better react as if it is.

"New York. More or less."

"Vacation?"

"Traveling around."

"First time to Israel?"

"No. I was here very briefly once before."

"You are going to Jerusalem."

"That's where this bus goes, isn't it?"

"Yes. You have been there already?"

"Yes."

"Well, then you know how beautiful it is."

"Even more beautiful than Houston."

He shrugs. "I don't know Houston."

"Take my word for it."

He shrugs again, then starts chatting with the four other soldiers who are sitting halfway across the bus. And in a few minutes excuses himself to sit closer to them. I am glad to see his Uzi depart, loaded or not.

It is extraordinary how good my cover is. Better even than the Jackal's. I could do anything here. Hit Golda herself. Why am I wasting it on this obscure Migdal? But the principle is that there are no innocent people on either side. Otherwise you could drive yourself crazy trying to sort out the equations of revenge and counterrevenge. They never balance right. You remember what it was like in trigonometric functions: all those sines and $\cos^2 x$'s proliferating all over the page like viruses. You wanted to take that hefty text and smash Dobbin's face in with it. But then he would show you your mistake and it would all combine into one terse formula as smoothly and perfectly as a Chinese puzzle. So, similarly this may all make perfect sense to Abu. He shrugged his shoulders at your fury against Weizman as Dobbins calmly shrugged at your wayward solutions to his problem sets. No, not $\cos 2x$ here, but $1 - \sin^2 x$. No, not Weizman but Migdal.

Another stop in a good-sized town. More men in uniform board. Is there no one in this country but soldiers? All of these have spindled berets tucked into their epaulets. A minute later half a dozen girl soldiers rush aboard, all with knee-length khaki skirts and gnomish black ankle booties. One of the men squeezes back against the flow and takes the seat next to me. He is very burly. His thighs look ready to rip his trousers as he sits down and tucks his legs into the tight space. He is wearing a different set of insignia from the others. In a very casual manner he mutters something to me. I run through my ritual of incomprehension. He persists. He is speaking Arabic.

The knot tightens in my stomach. I interrupt. "Sorry. I don't speak Hebrew."

He studies me for a moment, feature by feature. "Excuse me, I thought you were Arab."

"Me? You've got to be kidding."

"You are American, of course. But you are not Jewish."

"And why am I not Jewish?" In my best New York mock Yiddish accent.

"I'm sorry." He offers his hand. "We are all on edge since Lod and Munich. It creates a bad air."

More stiff banter. He's been all over the States. Yoni his name is. Bernie is mine. He even studied at Columbia for a few months, before the June war called him back. He got stuck in London, and the war was over by the time he landed in Tel Aviv. So we were in Columbia at the same time. Almost neighbors. He shakes his head at Watergate. Even America has its troubles. Do I understand this Nixon? Does Nixon understand himself? It's a terrible thing, the Americans giving up in the war in Vietnam. Perhaps it was a mistake in the first place, yes, but think how this will hurt the power of your country in the world. Winning may be cruel, we have discovered, but not a fraction so cruel as losing. Yes, Yoni, I agree wholeheartedly. I am no bleeding-heart liberal.

"You know"—his tone is suddenly half intimate, half embarrassed—"you should consider emigrating here to Israel. We need people with tough minds. And education. The States has more educated people than they need. Here, if you have a degree, you do not drive a taxi or make sandals. Nothing is wasted. Perhaps there is material hardship, yes, but knowing that what you do is making your people secure . . ."

Of all ironies, this one really scorches. You inviting me to live in Palestine! Did Abu plant you here to provoke me?

". . . Having been in the States, I can appreciate how hard it would be to give up that sense of space and security. Before '67 one could understand the reluctance. But now with our natural geographic boundaries we can offer the security of a normal country. Of course there is still the danger from Fatah terrorists. But that is not just here. Also in Europe. Though what they expect to accomplish when the combined armies of Egypt and Syria and Jordan were powerless, I can't imagine. Still, their leaders must convince their people that they continue to fight, so they continue to come and to die."

I can't suppress a glance at his watch, one of those bulky diver's models.

He notices. "Twenty minutes to twelve. Not long now. An hour and a half if there are no accidents on the road. We lose ten times as many people to crazy driving as to terrorists. There is the real danger of life in Israel. The psychologists say this madness with cars is a symptom of the external pressures. I don't believe them. I think it is just in our natures."

The hills of Jerusalem are a welcome sight, if for no more than to mark the end of this trying bus ride. Every passenger but me is pushing forward in the aisle before the bus has found its place in the chaotic jam of vehicles and passengers. I am again the last one off the bus. I wander around for a few minutes to let my fellow passengers disperse into the city. My ears are still ringing from the hours of unwanted conversation. I must collect my thoughts. Every step now must be reasoned out, weighed, and then executed with perfect attention. Any mistake, any oversight could turn this into a one-way mission. I have half a dozen hours to kill until dark. And two objectives: first, not to get picked up; second, to reconnoiter the field of action. So I must stay well away from Moscobiya, and away from any area like Katamon where I will look out of place. I can while away some hours in the Old City as a tourist, or at the university, or a museum. But business comes first. I stick my head into a bus which is waiting to board passengers. The driver is fixing something under his dashboard.

"Does this bus stop near Ramat Eshkol?"

"You know someone who lives in Ramat Eshkol?" Shit, man, can't anyone give a straight answer.

"My cousin Schlomo. This bus?" Control yourself, Kamal. Lose your temper now and you blow the entire mission.

"Who told you this bus? It is the fourth bus over there."

The "fourth bus over there" has dropped most of its passengers by the time it grinds past Ramat Eshkol. The driver is glancing at me from time to time. It is better if I debark somewhere else and not leave a connection in his mind between me and this place. Besides, I can see what I need to see. The buildings are widely spaced. There is no danger of getting trapped in an alley as there is in the heart of a city. In the dark I could even avoid a helicopter by darting from building to building. This is almost ideal. Only a forest could be better. It would take a small army to seal it off and search it. If the landscaping were done, it would not be unattractive. At least they've kept to the yellow limestone of the rest of the city; it won't look like Houston. The architecture is not thoughtless, actually. Nice carved details over the entranceways and along the walks. The apartments inside are probably not too skimpy either. And not too many in one building. In fact, it wouldn't be a bad place to live. We won't have to tear this down when we get it back.

The bus churns on. About a mile past the development it turns onto a kind of highway. This is where I'll pick up a ride after I'm done. I can cover the distance in a few minutes.

At the next stop I get off and begin walking. After half an hour I board another bus. It is nearly three o'clock. Now I can play tourist for the rest of the afternoon. But the question of where has been decided by the bus. This must be the university, to judge by the girls taking seats. I grab my rucksack and leap out just before the door snaps closed. Suddenly it hits me how long it's been since I've had a woman. The dust of the camp has plugged my pores. I feel old and desiccated. The proximity of nubile flesh makes me tremble. Are these girls, with their smooth calves and shining hair, all beautiful? Or has deprivation twisted my eyeballs.

I drift into a cafeteria and sit, hoping someone will start up a conversation. But no one does. I remain alone at my table. It is not crowded at this time. No one will be forced to sit down next to me. Anyway it's summer, and most of the students are off traveling. Traveling, flirting, screwing, laughing, sunning on the beaches. All the things Kamal no longer does. And why not? Nothing is stopping him. He could simply dump this rucksack in a locker and present himself at the U.S. embassy as a befuddled hippie who's been robbed of everything while sleeping under a tree: Oh won't you please issue me a new passport so I can go home. And then he can get the last bit of money out of his account in Lausanne and go cavort on the Côte d'Azur until the summer's gone. And then . . .

Pathetic, Jibral. My horniness is turning to a sour rage. Every time a girl walks by the window my fingers start curling for her tits, her ass, the warm juice of her cunt. You better get out of here and walk it off. But this can't be walked off. The city is too full of women. No wonder the boys don't come back from their missions. Suddenly they are hit in the face by everything they've been jailed from to satisfy Abu's twisted theories. It is he who is the torturer. Not old Weizman.

Shut up, Jibral. Get yourself in control. You've had your days as a student. And your good times. Not so long ago, either. Remember Mireille. Only a couple of months. No one forced the choice upon you. You could have been living a life out of *Playboy*. Instead you chose to make yourself the instrument of History. So plug up the whimper before it drains away your will. Harden your mind. The city is the grave of the guerrilla.

Five-twenty.

Tick-tock. Still forcing myself to sit, but now there is steel wool under my skin. I'm getting ready to put the Tokarev to my own head. How the hell did I ever sit through those months under Pollo Rojo? How the hell have I sat through the last three years? If I calculate honestly, not one percent of that time have I been in motion. And in real action? Only a fraction of that one percent. I should be much better at waiting than I seem to be. Perhaps I'm wearing out. They used to say in Monte that nobody was good for clandestine life for more than two years. I was already overdue when I left for Paris. And after Migdal tonight, how long will I have to wait again before I can be used for something else? No, there is a reason my brain and my cock and my skin are having hallucinations. They can't take any more waiting, any more abstention, any more fear. The machine is about to break down. It's giving you warning, Jibral.

All right, I hear. Migdal will be the last act. He will be my mark of blood on Jerusalem. Whether the equations balance or not in History's reckoning, I will call Kamal Jibral's accounts closed; for Boudia, for Kuma, for my father. Only promise to get me through tonight and not let me down until I cross the border at dawn tomorrow. And then it's quits, I promise. We'll pack up for the Côte d'Azur and bake in the sun and figure out what to do with the rest of our life. That's a promise, if you can just hold out until tomorrow at dawn. End of tour. Kamal Jibral's going home.

Six-forty-eight.

I am getting a little shaky again. It must be from thinking about sex on the beach at Ile du Levant. Suppose I picked up a girl tonight after the job. Spent the night in her bed. That would also be the safest place. God, I need the sleep. And then tomorrow travel north at my leisure . . .

372

Forget it, Jibral. Don't start playing tricks on yourself. That's what the plan is for. Discipline. Now, get something to eat and put your mind back on the problem of Ehud Migdal.

Seven-thirty. If you walk all the way from here to Ramat Eshkol it will be nicely dark when you get there. It will also help your digestion, calm your nerves, and give you the opportunity to get your weapons ready in the shadows of some construction site. You've been a very good boy, sitting here so patiently. Now you can start getting yourself limbered up for the final heat.

Eight-twelve. Just a few minutes' walk from here to the target. It's suddenly very quiet. The sound of the pistol snapping closed on a fresh round—you always have to check with an auto—echoes around the open foundation. I hope there are no kids hiding out in the shadows. It's dinnertime, I guess. They're all inside. Don't forget to replace the top round in the magazine, too. Might as well have your full nine. Though if I have to do that much shooting I will be in a pretty bad situation. But for discipline's sake. Also put one of the grenades in your left-hand jacket pocket. And straighten the pin, just in case you need it to cover your retreat. The other one can stay in the pack, but just under the flap in easy reach.

And now one last decision: whether to muffle the pistol inside the pack or use it in the open. If you muffle it there will be the same problem of the bullet hole as after Hervé. What is it about a bullet hole that attracts the eye so powerfully, so completely out of proportion to its size? Remember how Justina spotted the one in your Adidas bag almost the moment she walked into the room. Almost as if she already suspected just who it was who shot Hervé. Almost as if she already knew I had been betrayed to the Israelis and would be returning looking for revenge. Almost as if . . . as if she had been the one who betrayed me and was sighing with guilty relief that my vengeance had fallen on the wrong head. Justina? It's impossible. Yet who else but she ever knew I had been sent on a mission to Israel? Justina? Impossible. There is some other logical explanation. But now isn't the time to be worrying about it.

Eight-sixteen. Get moving, Jibral.

Here's the address. Ironic that is should be labeled in Arabic numerals. Perhaps the ancient Hebrews didn't know how to count. I hope you're counting now, Ehud Migdal. You've only minutes left. Nice of them to provide such a fast staircase: wide steps, good traction, with one landing between floors so there's no danger in jumping the flight. True, this would be easier if it were on the ground floor. Better check the photo and the apartment number just to prevent any unfortunate confusion. What kind of man is this Migdal? Hard to tell anything from the photo. Anyway it doesn't matter. Just be sure it's him. For some reason I can't get this idea about Justina off my mind.

Later, Kamal. Worry about it later!

Fifth floor. This stingy lighting in the halls and stairwell is a blessing. If there were some way of putting out the lights altogether . . . Here's the apartment. Lucky. It's the closest one to the stairs. No peephole. A glow from under the door. Sounds of clinking dinnerware. A man's voice. Or a radio. Still no one on the stairs. Dinner, it's the best time. You're doing well, Jibral. Now think. Rucksack on the floor, next to the door. No, not between you and the stairs. On the right side, so you won't trip over it if you have to bolt. Think! Pistol at half cock in your belt, well covered by your jacket. Now straighten your collar. Have to look a little respectable for the empty-handed introduction. Eight-twenty-two. Deep breath, shake out your arms.

One.

Two.

Three.

Knock. Knock. Hollow door. My hands are shaking. Not good. It must have been Justina, the snake . . . Steps inside. Unlocking sounds. Door cracks open. Damn, it's on a chain! Face of a girl, pretty, dark-eyed, round. About fifteen.

"Hullo. Speak English? I've come to see your father."

"Oh. Are you from the university? My father is eating dinner."

Beyond her head I can see the table. At least five people at it. A man is looking toward the door. Heavy-set. Dark. It is him. The girl turns, disappears behind the door, but leaves it open on the chain. Her voice, in Hebrew, questioning. The man stands. I step closer to the door. To jam my foot in, in case. He is much bigger than I expected. Or looks that way through the crack. He comes closer. He is almost a head taller than I am. And broad. He looks agitated.

He frowns at me from the crack and does not unchain the door. "Yes? Can I help you?" Educated English accent.

"Professor Guzman sent me to see you."

"Professor Guzman? I don't know any—"

"Bernard Guzman, from Columbia University." Stupid Kamal. Why use that name?

"No. I've never been in the States." He's going to close the door in a second.

"Professor Guzman was here last summer and—"

He turns toward the table and asks a question in Hebrew.

A female voice queries back, "Guzman?"

Now Kamal! While he's turned away. Get out the pistol. Every second is making it more iffy. Get the hammer back to full cock. At the click of the hammer there is a sudden shuffle and he has ducked away from the opening of the door. I thrust my pistol arm through just as he tries to slam it shut. The impact nearly breaks my grip on the pistol. Shouting inside the room. Do they have weapons? Oh shit, Kamal. Now what?

Grenade! Get out the grenade. That's why it's in your pocket. Now he's got a grip on the gun and is twisting it by the barrel. Never mind the gun! The grenade, yank the pin out with your teeth. Son of a fucking bitch, he's nearly got the gun. Cock the grenade, idiot. Start counting and hang on. One one thousand, two one thousand, now push it through the crack. Thunk! Three one thou—He's let go of the pistol. Get your arm out, out! Who's screaming? Dive, Jibral!

The floor and walls of the hall shudder with the explosion. There is a sudden silence. All I can hear is the ringing inside my ear tubes. The door has been lacerated by shrapnel. I lie next to the wall for a second collecting my wits.

Idiot! Are you going to lie here until the tenants start pouring out of their apartments to see what's happened?

I grab the pack and leap out to the top landing ready to start shooting. But the stairwell is still deserted. It is amazing how slow people are to react. Cautiously sidle down to the next floor. Still no one. Incredible, but don't argue with Luck's generosity. Hurry it, take them three at a time. Whoa, Kamal. First floor. No chances. Fire a few rounds into the hallway. If there's anyone waiting in ambush that will make them duck their heads while you go for the entrance.

But there is no one in the hall. Perhaps they couldn't hear the blast down here. Though just as I slip out into the dark I hear voices from the upper floors of the stairwell. Too late, my friends. Kamal

Jibral is already swallowed into the lovely cool anonymous sanctuary of night.

My legs want to sprint. Not from fear. From relief. It takes all my will to rein them in. At just a quick walk I am putting Ramat Eshkol far enough behind. No need to risk attracting attention. Eight-thirty-one. Nine minutes since I knocked on the door. Still no sirens. It could not have gone more perfectly. Except for a sore forearm. I wanted to use the pistol. But he was so quick when he heard the snick of the hammer being drawn back. Fucking Russians. If they'd just left the safety in the design . . . No one survived in that room. The F-1 grenade is lethal to a radius of sixty yards. So the little girl too. Oh God! Fucking Russians. Maybe he threw himself on the grenade to save his family. But all the screams stopped with the blast. Oh God, Kamal, how could you do that? Remember Katamon? ". . . The Jews advanced room by room behind hand grenades. Kamal, hope you never have to witness the effect of a hand grenade on a human body." Do you want to go back to Ramat Eshkol and look?

Sirens now, howling in the distance behind me. When I was here in Jerusalem the last time I listened to those wails drifting over the city and wondered what new grief they were heralding. Now I know. In another five minutes they will be carrying the corpses down on stretchers. And the investigators will be pressing their questions on the survivors, if there are any. She will say an American knocked at the door. And give a description, which will go out on the radio: a blond American. Who will believe it? They will be looking for Arabs escaping back to East Jerusalem. I am going the opposite direction. But still, it would be better to hitchhike. The bus drivers often keep their radios blaring. So might the driver of a private car, but if worst comes to worst I can always hijack the private driver.

Somehow I've missed the road I found this afternoon. It doesn't matter. There's a highway ahead. I can see the headlights. Another fifteen minutes' walk down the hill. Better get myself cleaned up, put away the gun, mop off the sweat, pull on one of Hamid's Hebrew Coca-Cola T-shirts, comb down my hair. I must look pretty much the hippie tourist this way. The T-shirt is a good touch. Must have been Abu's idea. How many shots did I fire back there? Two, three. Six left in this clip, and the grenade. That's enough. All just under the flap of the rucksack. Forethought is everything until I am back across the border. The job is only half done.

This is a main highway. Heavy trucks, buses still coming and going. What I want is a private car, though. Not so many of those passing now. A police Land Rover churns by, not even slowing to take a look at me. After the first gulp of adrenaline I find it reassuring. No description of me has gone out over their radio. The grenade must have gotten everyone. Everyone.

Wake up, Kamal. Look, someone's stopping for you. Don't make him back up. A Fiat 128. Yellow. Passenger door opening. Poke your head in, ask where he's going . . . A soldier! Everywhere you turn, a goddamn soldier. Never mind, he's just a man like any other.

"Hi! Speak English?"

He shrugs. I can barely see his face in the dark. Small dark line of a mustache. He is slightly built. Young.

"Are you going north? Toward . . . Haifa?" I point.

He gestures me to enter the car. I set the pack between my feet, in easy reach. There is no radio in the dash. Nor any weapons I can see. "American, you?"

"Yup." It suddenly hits me that I am not lying. Strange sensation.

"Go Haifa?"

"I don't know. Anywhere it's not so hot. To tell the truth I travel at night to save the price of a hotel room. In Europe I had a Eurailpass. Sometimes I would take the train at night just to have a place to sleep without paying for it. Also I like to keep moving. Keeps me cool, you know what I mean?"

"Sorry. Many words fast. Not good speak English."

"That's all right. I was just running on."

In fact it's a blessing. I don't have the energy to keep up a line of banter. What I really need is sleep. But I don't dare.

"Nice car."

"Nice, yes. Thank you."

"How far are you going?"

He peers closely at his odometer.

"Nine thousand and six hundred and thirty-four."

"I meant tonight. To . . . where . . . are . . . you . . . driving . . . tonight?"

"Ah! Rosh Pinna. You know?"

"I don't."

"Near to Safad."

Safad! That's almost to the border. I couldn't have asked for a better ride.

"Good."

"O.K.?"

"O.K. Listen, I appreciate this. I'll pay for half the gas."

"Gas?"

"Sure. Since I won't have to pay for a bus or hotel, that will help you out."

"Gas?"

"Gas, yes. Petrol."

"Ah, petrol. Petrol very . . . cost high."

"Yes, I know. How about ten pounds for petrol?" I hold a bill out to him.

"No, no." He waves it away.

"Are you sure?"

"No, no money."

"Thanks."

"O.K."

That exhausts the urge to converse for both of us.
We hum northward. I watch the digits roll up on the
odometer: each kilometer without a roadblock feels
like a gift. But after an hour or so I start feeling another anxiety creeping in. This mission has gone altogether too smoothly. It has just occurred to me that
had I succeeded in using the pistol on Migdal, his
daughter would still be alive to give the police my description. So this easy escape is only a gift of his
quick reflexes having forced me to use the grenade.
Nothing to attribute to my skills, just pure luck. And
I don't trust luck. Luck giveth, Luck taketh away.

Don't let down your guard.

Ten-seventeen. The peace of the night feels as thin
as a stage curtain. Behind it the Furies are stoking
up their vengeful tempers. It can't be that the Israelis will not respond to this massacre. Perhaps
they're already pulling apart East Jerusalem to find
the assassin. I can almost hear their rifle butts
smash through old brittle doors. And hear the cries
of protest and fury, and the grunts as the fists land.
But even if the Jews are following the wrong scent,
Lady Luck will not be satisfied. She knows where I
am. And the longer she continues to show me her
open hand, the more inevitable becomes the moment
she will clench it into a fist and strike back.

But when?

Examine it one step at a time. In the next hour or
two this fellow will leave you on the road some fifty
miles short of your destination. It will be around
midnight. There will be no buses at that hour. Little
traffic of any sort. And who would pick up a hitch-
hiker at that hour? So you will end up spending the
night by the side of the road and catching a ride first
thing in the morning, perhaps as far as the crusader

ruins at Baniyas, where you will have to play tourist all day. Risky. Suppose the little girl was only knocked unconscious by the concussion. Or suppose you are picked up tonight for vagrancy, or whatever they call it here. No. Either you must continue on tonight or check into a hotel and get some sleep. It's been twenty-four hours since you started across the border, over forty since you had your last real sleep. Not even the heroic Kamal Jibral can stay awake another twenty-four or more.

But how am I going to check into a hotel without a passport?

You can bluff. Say you left it in Jerusalem or Tel Aviv.

But suppose one of them has recovered enough to give a description back there. The hotel clerk always listens to his radio to pass the hours. I've come too far to let myself get nailed by a bored hotel clerk.

So therefore you must continue on tonight. If you could reach Majdal Chams by two-thirty you would just have time to make the hike back over the ridge.

I'm exhausted now.

You can force yourself that far. Don't underestimate the enemy to give yourself an excuse to let down now. Assume the worst. Assume the little girl regained consciousness. You must get to Majdal Chams tonight, in the next few hours. Isn't there a way? Hasn't it been just behind your eyes since you climbed into the Fiat? How long would it take to drive from Safad to Majdal Chams? An hour, at most. Why be squeamish now? If you'd been squeamish back at Ramat Eshkol you'd never have gotten this far. Is that not true?

The soldier is getting sleepy. I wonder if he is on his way home, or back to base. For all I know he could have been one of the gunners in the helicopters that attacked the camp. Remember how interknotted this world is. He could have been one of the patrol that intercepted Kuma. No, there is no reason to be squeamish about a soldier. It's me or him, in a way. I undertook this mission to prove that with sufficient will it is not necessary to go only one way. The means of finishing the work is a bullet away. I set out to avenge. I will avenge in full measure.

The soldier's head wobbles. I prod him in the ribs. He shudders, as if waking from a bad dream, and then glances at me sheepishly.

Eleven-thirty-one.

"You are tired."

He nods.

"Do you want me to drive?"

"No, no. I am O.K."

"You sure?"

"O.K. I am O.K."

Fifteen minutes later his head is wobbling again. We are passing through a deserted area. But the moon is strong. That would be a problem. His head drops forward. I grab the wheel and jerk the little car back and forth. He shudders awake to find me steering the car down the highway, and lifts his foot off the gas.

"Maybe I'd better drive."

"No." He is adamant.

"At least stop for a minute. Breathe some fresh air. Anyway, I want to stop and stretch my legs."

He brings the car to a halt on the gravel shoulder. I open the door and swing my legs out. It could be a highway in Nevada. He also opens his door and climbs out. My hands are quivering again. The soldier hops about to wake himself up, then jogs in circles in front of the car.

I stand up and stretch. "Beautiful night."

He stares up at the stars. I give a quick glance at the terrain by the side of the road. There is a steep embankment covered with low wild grass. Not good. But it is now or never.

"Hey, I just remembered. I have some chocolate. Like some?"

"Chocolate?" He looks down from the stars. He can't be more than twenty. How does he afford a new car? Rich parents? "Yes, I like chocolate. O.K."

"O.K." I reach for my rucksack and sling it up onto the hood. My heart sounds like a bass drum.

"Let's see, it's in here somewhere." I am pushing the Tokarev into the folds of the blanket, drawing back the hammer slowly, slowly. The soldier crunches up unsteadily. "Here it is, I've found it."

The report is louder than I expected, through blanket, rucksack and all. But the soldier slumps silently at my feet, his hand still held out. The pistol has jammed in the blanket, but I am shaking so badly I can barely hold it tight enough to free it. The soldier is wheezing. I didn't hit him in the heart. I don't have to kill him.

Yes you do, Kamal.

Why? I just need his car.

And a few hours with no patrol out looking for you. He is making noise. He could be found as soon as you drove off. You've got to put him to sleep. Why so squeamish all of a sudden?

He's a kid.

So was Kuma. So was the girl.

In a minute.

Not in a minute. Discipline. Now. Chamber another round, pull the blanket out of the pack and push it down on his face.

I can't do this.

Oh, yes you can. Remember Castellan. Now put the muzzle against the blanket, hard. Now squeeze.

The jolt of his body nearly knocks me over. This trembling is unbearable. And this nausea . . .

Get him off the road. Now!

I stick the pistol in my belt. As I bend to start dragging him the barrel pokes me in the groin.

Fucking idiot, Jibral. The hammer's still cocked! It has no safety, remember. This would be a fine way to end the mission. Blowing your own balls off. How they'll jeer when they find you.

Slowly, slowly I straighten up and slip my thumb in between the hammer and the pin. Then yank it out from my pants. I have an urge to throw it as far away as I can. But instead lower the hammer and push it back into the pack. Somehow this close brush with catastrophe has calmed me. Now the soldier's body is just a corpse. I resume dragging him from the shoulder of the road down to the foot of the embankment. It is steep enough to keep him out of the line of the headlights. He won't be noticed until morning. This will do well enough. If I cover him with the blanket he'll look like he's sleeping.

But don't forget to take his papers, just in case he is found tonight. That way it will take them hours to link the body to the missing Fiat.

I'm amazed at how steady my hands are suddenly, searching through the dead man's pockets. By the time I climb back in the car I am strangely relaxed and not at all sleepy. It feels good to drive. I have to buy myself a good car as soon as I get home. Maybe drive to California again. It will be good to be home.

Barren heights, sullen gray under the moonlight, stand guard to my right. To my left scattered lights of small settlements, and further on perhaps of a small city. Qiryat Shemona? I must be very close to the Hermon. Yes, there are the bluffs ahead. And what are those lights just by the side of the road? Checkpoint? We didn't stop at any checkpoint this morning. Or maybe I was sloppy and didn't notice. I was staring back at the mountains about here. The bus must have been waved through while I was gawking at the scenery. Is this where Luck finally takes back her gifts? You see, all it takes is a few careless seconds.

What have they got a checkpoint here for, anyway, inside the country? This hasn't been the border since '67. What are they checking? Maybe it's time to ditch the Fiat and proceed on foot. News of the attack in Jerusalem must have reached here by this time. Even if they have no physical description of the assassin they will be on alert. But if I start hiking here I'll never make it to the border by dawn. Not the Syrian border, at least. I could take my chances at the Lebanese fence. That's just a few miles away.

Forget it. It will be hard enough to cross by a route that you know. Impossible at a strange location. And then there would be a dozen miles of Lebanon to cross. In your state?

So I've got to take my chances at the checkpoint, it seems. It would be too suspicious to stop or turn around now, anyway. I will bluff my way through. I borrowed the car from my cousin, let's see . . . Damn, of course his papers are filled out in Hebrew. Well, if worse comes to worst there's the remaining hand grenade. That's the right weapon against a checkpoint. Some instinct made me bring them. Trust instinct. Straighten the pin. Stick it in my grenade pocket. If I keep the driver's window open I will be able to toss it out over the roof of the car. Then burn out this buggy in a race for the border. I can try to crash through on the other side of Majdal . . .

First things first. Here you are. Just act natural.

. . . The other side of Majdal, just a few hundred yards to the fence, and pray they've cleared the mines there too.

Slow up gradually as if you're in no hurry. A little bit sleepy. The soldier is holding up his hand. He's got an Uzi. Keep both hands on the wheel. Finesse before force. He's bending over at the waist to look at something. The license number? They can't have found the body already. Left hand to your pocket, slowly, while he's not looking at you. Remember to count before you throw. If he gets even a second to unlimber that Uzi . . .

What's this? He's waving me ahead. Shuffling back into his shelter. That's all? I'm free to go?

I accelerate very moderately from the lighted patch of road, perhaps two hundred yards before taking my hand from the grenade. No vehicles pull onto the road behind me. I reach the intersection at the foot of the cliffs and turn right, cross over the pipeline, still not another vehicle in sight. Why did he just wave me through? Am I driving into some kind of ambush? No. I could have turned either way at the intersection. He suspected nothing. As far as he could see, I was just another Israeli heading to the mountains for a vacation. And it is infiltration they worry about, not exfiltration. If I'd been going the other way it would have been a different story.

The slope begins to tax the little Fiat. But now there is no hurry. It is only one o'clock. In another twenty or thirty minutes I will leave the car parked just below that grove of trees in Majdal. I could drive up the dirt road toward the ski lift, but that might attract attention. No, Majdal is far enough. There is still moonlight. The hike will not be too difficult. It only took a few hours this morning. This morning? Was it just this morning? This has been the longest day of my life.

Infiltration, exfiltration: those try to lend a tinny dignity to what are no more than frightened scrambles. When I used to fantasize about guerrilla warfare I was never alone, never desperate, never disgusted with my mission and myself, never imagined the taste of these gases roiling up from my bowels, making me gag. The odor is of food rotting between the teeth, only it can't be spit out and even this vast grass-scented night can't dilute it. I wish I really did have some chocolate. God, it was just like shooting a little kid. The way he held out his hand. I shouldn't have done that. I'll never get the image out of my head.

This trail is much longer than I remember.

Or is it just that I am twenty-four hours more tired, trudging uphill instead of down, and having to pick my own way along this precipice instead of scuttling along after the old man who knew every pebble by genetic inheritance.

Or have I lost my way? No, the compass needle and my course are parallel. North will get me to the border. That's all I care about now: the border. And keeping my feet on the goat trail. Having come this far, it would be too bitter an irony to stub my toe and go cartwheeling into the gorge.

Three-eleven. It can't be that much farther now. The most dangerous hour of the mission is just ahead. Clear your mind of your stinging blisters and burning lungs. Those discomforts are not so bad. Think of being torn up by a hand grenade. Or cut down by an Uzi. Or dismembered by a Claymore. You should have brought a wire cutter. How are you going to get over the fence if they've fixed the barbed wire on top? Why didn't you ponder the problem of the fence on the way in? You could have bought a cutter in Jerusalem. But you weren't thinking of the problems of the way out. Not in detail. Admit it, Jibral. Unconsciously you slipped into a one-way state of mind.

Three-fifty. The moon is about to fall into Lebanon. Just when I will be needing it most. Somewhere along here I have to climb up to that rock outcropping. On rock, no mine. On rock, break neck. Who needs a mine?

I climb a hundred feet above the trail, but there is

387

no outcropping, so I carefully pick my way down again. I can smell deer or sheep turds. There was no smell like that where we climbed from the rock. I explore up the slope another two hundred yards along the trail. Still no outcropping. But the sweet dusty smell of lava is in the air now. It can't be far. I will try again after another hundred yards.

Jibral's luck! I knew I smelled rock. It feels so familiar under my hands, as if I'd grown up scampering around on these very potholes and nubbins. It is certainly easier ascending than descending. May Allah have made my enemies blind to the cuts in their fence. But suppose they have discovered the damage. Might they not just leave it as we left it and booby trap it instead, hoping for just what I am about to do? A black thread tied to the mesh, a Claymore staked to spray its shrapnel at the gap.

You have a nightmare for a mind, Jibral.

If I can think this way, so can they. They're not saints.

Four-twenty. Damn, that late already. There will be skylight in less than an hour. Much less than an hour. You can't stand here clinging to the rock. Think, Kamal. If there is a booby trap you have to trigger it from a safe distance.

If only there were still a moon, I could see.

But there isn't. You have to assume the worst again. There's a mine. You can't get any closer than this to trigger it. Even here . . .

If I cling to the rock I should be out of the line of it. Should be?

How am I going to set it off, anyway? And even if I did, the blast would bring a patrol here in ten minutes.

Ten minutes is a long time. It only takes a few seconds to vault the fence.

If it's cut. And what if it has been repaired?

Blow it up with your damn hand grenade!

Good thinking. Good thinking, Kamal, old boy. My hand grenade. My wonderful hand grenade will take care of all my problems in one easy toss. Blow any booby traps and tear a hole in the fence. It can't be this easy.

Why not? Do you want an excuse to give yourself up? Cling here much longer and you won't need one. Certainly they send a patrol along the fence at first light to see if there have been any infiltrations.

Four-twenty six. This isn't as easy as it seems. What happens if I miss my toss? Lots of noise. No hole in fence.

Live by the grenade, die by the grenade.

Just like that?

Just like that. Irony. For a two-buck wire cutter. You know: Organisar al triunfo, improvisar al verdugo.

Fuck it! I've lived long enough. If I survive this the rest of my life will be a gift. I'll switch to biochemistry and find the cure for cancer. Come here, little grenade, fly true.

It hits the fence with a clink and falls to the dirt. I press close to the rock. Oh God, not a dud! I should have counted. What the hell is going on up . . .

The blast fills the canyon. And a second one. Something slaps against my cheek and the side of my chest near my armpit. Two blasts? An echo? Or a booby trap? The roar rolls down the canyon and fades. It doesn't matter now what the second blast was. I start to scramble toward the fence. My mouth fills with blood, nearly choking me on the first breath. My tongue pokes through a hole in my cheek. A wave of dizziness nearly topples me from the rock. My teeth crunch on something hard.

Control, Kamal, control. It's just blood. Spit it out. Ignore it. Dizziness in your mind. Control your mind. Get through the fence. You've only got minutes. Minutes.

I spit out a mouthful of saliva and blood and hurl myself toward the fence. The air is still filled with dust from the blast. But from a few feet away I can see that the bottom edge of the mesh has been twisted up away from the ground, six, eight inches. Barely enough. I try to pull it up farther with my hands. It is too stiff. The dirt beneath the fence, however, has been loosened by the explosion. Just a few swipes clear away enough of a gap to let me wriggle through on my back. I am gagging on a throatful of blood before I manage to rip the cloak free of the snags. I lurch to my feet. Still no patrol? Of course not. It's only been a few minutes since I threw the grenade.

On all fours I claw up the steep embankment just beyond the fence. The bleeding is not so bad now. Whatever these wounds are they won't kill me. I won't let them kill me. I am on the easy slope now. The saddle shows up ahead as a dark shadow against the faint glow in the northeastern sky. Behind me, somewhere, is that Israeli observation post. It is invisible without the moon. Why haven't they got their searchlights on? They must have heard the blasts. Maybe they're using infrared, sighting in on me right now.

I try to push myself to a run. It is barely half a mile to the crest of the saddle. But my knees are rubbery and my head feels like a brick at the end of a stalk. So I stagger. There seems to be no hurry.

No hurry? What's that pulsing sound off to the right?

Right? I turn. The sound swings as I turn. I turn again. Again the sound eludes me to the right. I put my hand to my left ear. No difference. I've gone deaf in the left ear. So where is that sound coming from? I can't tell. And my hand is thick with blood.

Helicopter! That's what the sound is. No hurry?

Again I try to push myself to a run. Half a mile,

Kamal, even less. Less than an 880. You used to be able to do that in under two minutes. Why is this 880 taking you so long? Don't stop to look at the watch. Just keep pumping your thighs. You see, it's getting closer.

But so is the chopper.

But if you can't see it, it can't see you. You're a lot smaller than it is.

That's true.

I use this logic to stop and catch a breath and spit out more gunk. I look back toward the fence. I've covered more than half of the slope. The sky is taking on the first hint of color. Suddenly a light flashes on below, near where the canyon's blackness begins. That's the helicopter's searchlight. They're following the fence. It won't take them more than a minute or two to find where I blew it up. And then?

Suddenly I am surfing uphill on a throb of adrenaline. The crest is very close now. It is an illusory sanctuary, of course. The chopper can cover the same distance in twenty seconds. But reaching it means that the way home is all down hill.

One last look back. What are they doing, those stupid sons of whores? Giving up so soon? No, they're searching down the canyon. They've found the bent section of fence and think there has been an infiltration.

But naturally! Why would they expect anything else? No one ever returns from missions that enter from this border. They are looking for another four kids to mow down. Not this time, suckers. Just keep hovering along that trail until you find a yellow Fiat 128. And then do your homework. Then you'll know which way to fly.

Aw, shut up, Jibral. Stop congratulating yourself. It isn't over yet. Now if the old man was right about the mines being cleared, and the Syrians don't spot you and strafe you, and the cuts in the other fence which Nizar so carefully hid have not been discovered and repaired, and you don't bleed to death or collapse of exhaustion in the next hour, only then will it be over.

Sami better fucking well have breakfast ready.

Samir

A FARAWAY WARBLING CRY, then its strangely undiminished echoes, fluttered to the floor of the canyon with the first touch of morning light. Like the cries of animals searching for each other in a vast wilderness. I was already lying awake when they sounded. Who could sleep? A queasy feeling rose into my stomach. Well, at least now we knew. He had made it back.

Was I supposed to rejoice? My body stiffened at the recollection of his humiliating cuffs across my face. I should have struck back then. Instead of feebly invoking the Israelis to do it for me. Ah, Samir, that is so much like you. For most things in this life one only gets one good chance. I lay listening and realized I could not pretend to sleep through this event when the rest of the camp was turning out for it. Scurrying thuds of boots and clumsy rattles of pots and cups perfectly orchestrated the collective state of mind. No, I could no more sleep through this commotion any more than I could sleep through the rattling thoughts that filled the dark hours of my night.

Yet none of my attempts to probe this state of mind even hinted why Abu's solemn announcement in front of the bunker last night, that the American had succeeded in his mission—Abu had just heard a report on his shortwave radio—immediately loosed so many devils. Even while Abu still stood under the glaring spotlight I reminded myself that there was little chance that the American would survive the trip back.

Later last night I stood by and observed the Grenades, under the direction of Fawaz, deploy watches onto all the vantage points above the canyon which gave a view of either the zone or Lebanese fences. No one knew where he would attempt to make his crossing back into Syria. And Hamid on his own initiative hurried up the trail to the Syrian observation post to arrange, as was normally done for departures, with a certain sympathetic officer that their vigil be not too rigorous for the next number of hours. Vain hope. I shrugged and retired for the night. Yet there I lay, my imagination churning for a plausible speculation of how Q'asidi would go about making his escape from Jerusalem. And failing time after time, as the hours passed, the escape continued to seem impossible.

Now those distant warbles were telling me otherwise. I dressed and stuck my head out of the tent. Another drawn-out warble floated down, louder this time. Its tone was unmistakable: a chilling, exultant, piercing cry of victory.

I waited impatiently for my coffeepot to struggle to a boil, warming my hands by the heat around it, and glancing every few seconds toward the trail down from Nefud. It was still too dark to see very far up the canyon. Another city drifted down from the grayness. Suddenly, as I squatted, I became aware of a presence behind me. I turned to discover Abu standing, feet spread, hands behind his back, yet failing to disguise a great tension. He was wearing the white kaffiyeh which traditionally signaled that the occasion of his leaving the bunker was official. Already half an hour had passed since the first warble. The interval seemed quite long. Was it a false alarm? Just as the lid of the pot started to chatter a squad of four Grenades came jogging down the trail shouting and raising their AKs to the sky in triumph. A minute later the main contingent came into view, a taller gray-cloaked figure in their midst.

From the dispersed tents everyone converged on the trail. I felt the same tug, and before I knew it was waiting beside the foot trail with the rest. The tumult gradually smothered as the phalanx drew nearer and the American's physical state became apparent. For though he walked erect his head and cloak were drenched in blood. A flap of skin was hanging loose from his left cheek, and his left ear appeared deformed. The hair on that side of his head was matted and black with blood.

But still he walked with a swagger, even if a slower than normal swagger, as the escort peeled away and left him face to face with Abu, who had taken up a stance on the beaten foot trail. The magnitude this bestowed on the event caused everyone to draw a breath. The American, with my rucksack over his right shoulder, stepped up to the commander and extended his bloody hand. Abu's pause in responding to this gesture sent a ripple of tension through the spectators. Abu felt it, and as if under the collective will, raised his own hand and gripped the American's firmly. And then with both hands. After a moment he raised his own bloodied palms to the crowd. This brought a cheer. He turned back to the American and embraced him tightly. Abu's forehead barely reached the American's chin.

The embrace seemed even more false than the spectacle of the bloodied palms. But around me the cheers of the others announced they were satisfied: Abu was doing proper homage to the new hero. Who, in response, patted the little commander on the back, almost condescendingly, as a grown son comforts a suddenly dependent father.

After a very long minute they broke the embrace. Q'asidi then strode toward me. My stomach clenched.

394

Was he going to humiliate me by asking if breakfast was ready? I remembered that the coffeepot was boiling over back at the tent. But he said nothing about breakfast, only slung the rucksack off his shoulder and tossed it to me with a nod. I then realized he could neither speak nor eat. I had been afraid to look into his eyes until that moment, expecting a devastating sneer to be written there. But now I glanced up. I was ready to see an expression of great pain, but there was neither pain nor sneering. Nor even triumph. Rather a saturating sadness that belied his stride as an act for the benefit of the boys. Why sadness at a moment of complete supremacy? I wondered. His eyes seemed to lament: now I have put this all behind me and nothing looms ahead.

But, say, my friend, your mission to Jerusalem hasn't won the Revolution. I was ready to fling the taunt. Then a less bitter part of my brain stopped it with the recognition that Jerusalem was only a talisman for him, and that the struggle which it ended was his struggle with Abu. If one erased the grand bloodstained gestures to the assembled crowd, what had just taken place before us? Abu had bowed to Kamal. It was all there to be seen in Kamal's gesture of solace. Inside that diplomatic embrace something profound had passed between them.

Kamal walked off quickly toward our tent after tossing me the pack, but Hamid rushed up to him with a medical kit and tried to make him stand still so he could examine the wounds. He finally prevailed just outside the tent. The examination took only a few seconds. Then Hamid tugged him toward the clearing. The American complied with this too, mechanically, as if acknowledging his injuries had instantly drained him of his will. Hamid pushed him into the passenger's seat of the Land Cruiser and immediately started the engine. Seconds later they were lost in a cloud of dust, and leaving behind them in the camp a somber silence. Abu stood by without a word. I glanced at his face. He had removed the kaffiyeh, which had been bloodied in the embrace, and was now absentmindedly rubbing at the dried blood on his palms with it. He looked grayer than usual. There was a new roundness to his shoulders, even under the squaring effect of the military shirt. Whatever had held him erect was broken: perhaps some fine theory with which he had justified, until now, his command from the secure depths of his bunker. Suddenly his own expedient surrender back in Lebanon, and the now dozens of deaths of those whom he'd sent off from this camp must have crushed down on him. All I could read in his eyes was despair and defeat. And almost as if he felt the pressure of my thoughts from a meter away he turned to me, lowering his glance after a moment, and uttered hoarsely in English, "I did not expect this."

Then he walked, a sick man's walk, back to the bunker. I don't think anyone else noticed. They were all watching the dust of Hamid's Land Cruiser carrying the hero down to Damascus.

part four

Kamal

A VAST SLOPE of arthritic lava extrusions, an army of
encrusted guardsmen petrified in the act, thwarts
the way. But none reaches out an arm, or a weapon,
and soon they are all behind. Above, the crest widens
into a broad, brilliant dome of polished granite. Under its brow three vast rectangular apertures pierce
the rock. Their impenetrable depths command the
entire mountainside. The solitary figure struggling
up from the rubble below halts, confused by the incongruous transition in the terrain. He momentarily
fears that this charred skin of lava beneath his feet
will avalanche from the polished bone skull of the
mountain and, grinding him in its midst, plunge into
the canyon below. But a more immediate threat
draws his attention to the vacant sockets in the rock.
Instinctively he drops behind a boulder to escape
their gaze.

Too late. The challenge of whoever, or whatever,
hides in their shadows rolls down upon him. He wonders on what medium it is conveyed, since he hears
no voice, can identify no language or even a single
word. Yet the voiceless inquisitor unambiguously
demands to know his identity and his business. Now
the boulder which has been hiding him suddenly
vanishes, betraying him to the holes in the moun-

tain. He is naked, and though he thinks he is acting perfectly nonchalant, is burning with furious shame. But still he balks at answering the challenge. Why? Because he believes the sockets in the rock will not accept any of his answers.

"I am a brother, an Arab."

"You? An Arab?"

"Yes. My father was Arab."

"If you tell us that your father was a giraffe our eyes will not therefore see a giraffe. Our ears do not hear an Arab."

"Then look! Is this not the face of an Arab?"

Dry, hacking cachinnations from the rock. A moment later a dozen tracer bullets spit forth from the blackness and spray languidly over his head.

"Why are you shooting at me?" Panic rising. "I told you, I am a brother."

"Shooting at you? You accuse your brothers of shooting at you? What deluded mind calls bats bullets? Have you never seen bats flying from the mouth of a cave?"

"Bats fly at night."

"And now will you insist that this globe in our sky is the sun? We call it the moon."

He looks up and sees they are perfectly right. A nearly full moon hangs just above the polished dome of rock, still brick red from rising. He wonders how he could have been so confused. Another swarm of molten-eyed night-seeing bats streak by his head in low dangerous arcs before sailing on into the valley. Why are these bats flying so close? Perhaps it is a game they are playing. They terrify you, and then they let you pass. You heard them laughing. Laugh along with them. Show them that you are playing a game and are not offended.

He laughs a forced laugh at the dark apertures. They frown at the too obvious ingratiation. Then he hears low mutters in some language he's never heard but understands all the same.

"He goes too far with his inversions. We must teach this charlatan that laughing is not the same as crying."

At this, one of the bats dives from the formation and hurtles into his undefended face with a final, mortal shriek. Its carcas disintegrates as it tears through the soft flesh of his cheek, leaving a muck of blood, bones and tissue tangled among his teeth and dribbling from his paralyzed lips. The impact has knocked him to the ground. The remains of that bat are sucked into his lungs, deeper each time he tries to draw a breath. Is this how it ends? he wonders. Shameful, shameful. The muzzles flash deep inside the caves, and incandescent strands of death hiss through the obsidian night only inches above his good cheek. Now here is an honorable and quick end. You need only sit up and intersect your death.

With a sob he musters the last dregs of will and raises his head from the soft dirt. But no death comes. The luminous arcs lift away and fade into the morning sunlight. He watches them recede, almost disappointed. Then the warm, mucking blood choking him surges up his craw. He vomits . . .

And wakes.

Damn and hell. Wounds bleeding down my throat again.

"Water. I need water. I'm choking."

But on his chair in the hall the orderly snores on like Rip Van Winkle.

The bats are new tonight. You used to dream of bats long, long ago. Remember? But these aren't dreams, says the doctor.

"You have memories locked in your wounds which spring out like genies when the wound is suffering. These will vanish as the wounds heal."

Khalidi, I'd like to see your medical degree.

"Hey orderly asshole, damn you. Wake up and get me some water." What's the Arabic? "Mayya, ben sharmoota suryan."

That's done it. I hear him clicking down the hall. Go fetch a nurse who understands English or French, all right? Hey, fucker, you're not going to walk away and just leave me here choking.

Calm down, hero. Just spit it out into your cup. What kind of hero wakes quivering and in sweats from a mere dream? You were steady as a rock through the real thing. Mostly.

This delayed weakness must be a Jibral trait. My mother has said that my father was dry-eyed the dawn of their flight from Katamon. Even cold-blooded; she recalled being almost offended by his matter-of-factness. And yet for the following two decades the memory of that morning swam in a lake of his tears. We have too vivid imaginations, we Jibrals. It humiliates us. Even the damn mosquitoes in this hospital room have more dignity. They wait until my hand is almost upon them before they abandon their meal. And then they return to finish what they began, without a qualm, seconds after the threat is lifted. You'd make good revolutionaries. Nevertheless, brave mosquito, have a caution of imbibing too much Jibral blood. It carries a disease which will magnify your fears and paralyze you with trepidation. Your sleep will be haunted by nightmares of giant fists descending. You won't be much good as a mosquito then, will you? Even to feed on helpless patients in an antiquated Damascus hospital will be too terrifying. You will thirst to death: the first known mosquito fatality from a man-borne disease.

The doctor, Khalidi, is a sadist. His eyes glitter when he limps in to tear the dressings off my face. Still, I'd put up with a few more of his little brutalities if he'd make his visits more frequent. His rounds bring the only breath of life into this anteroom of Death. I wait for another body to be wheeled in to the second bed, which, sitting there empty, bothers me like some reflection in a mirror from which I have been erased. Did I lose that much blood? I've asked for an English-speaking orderly or nurse and been told there are none. Requested English books. Same response. So I must endure this Bergman-ish hell with nothing to do but count the inch-square white porcelain tiles which cover the floor and walls, and try to decode the blurry vague shapes on the frosted glass window which must remain shut to keep out the larger insects.

Meanwhile I wait for footsteps and hope each one is Khalidi about to barge in, plump his round body down on the stool by my bed, insult me a few times, rip the bandages off my scabs and poke his blunt fingers into my pussy wounds. He is also Palestinian. He speaks English. He hates Syrians. But he is an entrenched bourgeois.

"Well"—he claps his hands together cheerfully— "now that you've collected your souvenirs of our Revolution you'd better take them home before they heal up and disappear."

"Home?" I can only croak in the mornings until all the battered muscles in my face and throat limber. "Jerusalem is my home, Khalidi."

"Oh, please!" He throws up his hands. "If that is what is going to keep coming out of your mouth, I'll sew it up too. You are not in Ahmet's camp now. We can hold an adult conversation. I am surprised that you too are not sick by now of that incessant whine. Every kid who comes in here with a military wound —and every wound is, needless to say—raves on and on about 'home.' Where is that? I ask. Haifa, he replies. What does your house look like? I ask. It was a great mansion with twelve servants and an orange

403

grove. When did you see it last? In 1948. How old are you? Sixteen. That is old enough to know how to subtract.

"And you, monsieur le révolutionnaire, where were you born? Not Jerusalem, I'll wager."

"I was conceived in Jerusalem."

"Conceived! Ha! That is the thinnest title-deed yet. Here am I, born in Jerusalem, raised to the end of childhood in Jerusalem, having direct ancestors who lived in Jerusalem for a thousand years . . . yes, a thousand years. Yet you do not hear me whining about 'home.' Jerusalem is no longer my home. One has to have the humility to bow one's head before History. I have children. Their home is Damascus. A few years ago it was Beirut. Should I torture them with some notion of belonging in a city they have only seen on maps?"

"You do not mind being without a country?"

"Of course I mind. I also mind that this leg suffers from phlebitis. In fact I mind the latter a great deal more. But neither one is a reason to throw away life, mine or my son's."

"Some suffer more than you, doctor."

"If suffering were a land claim, what could we hold up to the Jews' claim. Eh? But history has always refused to recognize suffering as a claim to anything. Except pity."

"You have it very neatly worked out. Your world view is an excuse not to fight, it seems to me."

"I have had to rebuild too many young bodies dismembered for the sake of *your* world view. You were only lightly touched. Too lightly. I can show you some of the more serious achievements of your world view, just down the hall."

"Ugh, there is nothing more unbearable than the moral superiority of a doctor."

"Fine! I'll be happy to take it to the next room and let you heal yourself."

404

"But what would you do without someone to listen to your pontifications?"

"I can pontificate equally well in Arabic, my friend."

"Low blow, Khalidi."

"You brought it on yourself."

The battle continues the next afternoon. He tears off my plasters with glee. When I make no sounds he comments, "That did not hurt? Good. I do not have to be so careful next time. You know, sometimes when I see the results of the facial wounds these children come in with I want to cry. Often it takes me four or five operations to make a face less than horrifying to look at. So when I am presented with a case like yours I almost rejoice. Just a simple matter of cleaning out a few stone fragments, a few bits of metal, sewing up the more serious tears . . . I was describing your case to a colleague yesterday, puzzling over the stone fragments, and he suggested that your injury was very smiliar to injuries of racing bicyclists he had treated. I said, No, this fellow claims to be a revolutionist. He shook his head and asked, Is there such a great difference in the motivation? It is an interesting observation, eh? By the way, how did you do this to yourself?"

"I fell off my bicycle."

"Ah, my dear patient, I apologize. I mistook you for just another of the plague of revolutionists who buzz around this city. But as you are an athlete, that is another matter. I am certain my son would appreciate your autograph."

Khalidi pushes his prescription pad at me, then a pen. I scribble, To my cherished friend, Beni Oui-Oui. And push it back to him.

"Eh? No sense of humor: the unmistakable mark of a revolutionist. Too bad. My son will be disappointed." He crumples the sheet of paper. "Well, for a man so dedicated to pain and suffering, codeine is clearly an unwanted luxury. So we will discontinue administering it. I will drop by tomorrow to witness your exaltation. Farewell."

The next morning he bounds in waving an enormous hypodermic syringe. "Aha! The nurses tell me you refuse to eat."

"I can't eat, Khalidi. My fucking mouth hurts too much."

"Medically speaking, this is a problem, but philosophically it is a tremendous advance. You see! Withdrawing the drug was not a bad thing at all. It has cleared your intellect and your spirit both. In one night you have taken a leap from the eighth century to the twentieth: from Abbas as-Saffah to Gandhi."

"From who to Gandhi?"

"Who indeed? Abu al-Abbas as-Saffah. The Bloodshedder. The first Abbassid Caliph. You don't know your own history. He was the great uncle of Harun al-Rashid. You *have* heard of Harun? Now, if I were a politically ambitious man, which I am not, I would advocate the philosophies and tactics of Gandhi and Martin Luther King.

"It is my vision that we would gather a million exiles at the Allenby Bridge and begin a peaceful and unarmed march back to our homeland under the eyes of every television camera in the world. How would the Israelis stop that? With violence? And thus condemn themselves to global ostracism? Certainly not. The memory of their own refugee ships is not lost. Now it is we who possess the same weapon, against which, philosophically and culturally, they have no defense. A weak people with a just claim has to use its weakness as its power. But we, like doomed dinosaurs, bellow and bluff, and keep sending in people like you who provide the Jews' most violent and repressive elements with all the justification they need. Meanwhile, what do you accomplish, but make the words 'Palestinian' and 'terrorist' synonymous in the ears of the world. It will take decades to undo the damage you have done, before any of us can board airplanes without being eyed as criminals."

"But how many Palestinians can even afford to board an airplane? Or have passports, so they are not sent back from wherever they try to land?"

"And I have heard that platitude, as well. A million times. We Palestinians are the most mobile and educated of all Arab peoples. Travel through Syria, travel through Iraq. Then come back here and dare to repeat your nonsense. The result of your violence is only to guarantee that those of us who are still living in hovels, who are bombed and thrown out of one country and the next, will continue to live in hovels, be bombed and thrown out of each life they try to build. That is a fine accomplishment. Have you ever been to one of our refugee camps? No? Then come right now. You are not too sick to sit in a car."

"Don't you have anything more important to do than take me sight-seeing, Khalidi?"

"This isn't sight-seeing. This, hopefully, is saving your useless life and others, not so useless, that will be lost if you are not turned from your present course."

"Forget it. I'm staying here."

"Are you afraid to see the reality of your people?"

Khalidi summons the orderly and rattles off instructions. Then to me: "I will be back in an hour, more or less. The man will bring you clothes and shoes. And a razor. After all, the Vanguard of the Struggle must not represent himself to the People as a derelict. Eh?"

An hour passes before the orderly returns with worn fatigues and a pair of boots. The boots don't fit. He takes them away and does not return for another hour. But Khalidi has not made an appearance in the meantime, so I sit on the bed and wait.

Are you afraid to see the reality of your people? Of all his probes and taunts, this is the one that cuts. I *am* afraid to see the reality of my people, because I am afraid to discover that they are *not* mine. But if up to this point I have not known who they are, for whom have I been fighting? For whom did I go to Jerusalem? For whom did I kill Migdal and his family? And the soldier? Not for myself. And certainly not for Abu. For the boys in the camp? While they might celebrate the mission, to them it is the fact that I returned which holds some tangible meaning. The deed itself means no more to them than a victory of a favorite soccer team. After all, who was Migdal? Only Abu knows.

Then was there no motive for the undertaking but vanity? Did Khalidi's colleague touch the truth? Might you just as well have won a bicycle race?

I should have stuck to my hurdles. Why can't I tell Khalidi I have decided to quit and go home? He would approve heartily. Why do I feel shame to confess I have done all I can, that I have no spirit and no stomach for it anymore? Khalidi would applaud. Why do I keep pretending to him that I will carry on to the bitter end?

Damn, I don't want to go to the refugee camp. I don't want to see those people. I am done. They have no meaning to me. I have finished what I set out to do. I don't owe anyone . . .

Khalidi barges into the room, breathless. "All right, I have done four hours' work in two. I am sorry to be late. Get up, we're going."

My head pounds as I stand, but by the time we have reached the stairs at the end of the long bare corridor the pain has subsided. This is the first I have seen of the city since Hamid brought me down. Khalidi's car is parked just in front of the hospital steps: a dusty but not old Citroen. His service to humanity does not go unrewarded, apparently.

In a fit of jerks and lurches he races us through a gray, flaking suburb, indiscriminately challenging every bus, bicycle and cat for the right of way. When he finally slows down I assume it is because we have reached our destination.

"Khalidi, you're twice the terrorist I'll ever be."

"Eh? What do you mean?"

"Never mind."

He has stopped before a gate in a tall wire fence patrolled by two AK-armed civilians in sports jackets. They both appear to recognize him, and with only a glance at me wave us past with their rifles. I tighten my grip on the door handle. Khalidi's attitude has suddenly metamorphosed from reckless contempt to solicitous reverence. Here he is deferring to everything from a puddle in the dirt path to an old woman leaning against a wall who might at best be contemplating crossing the path sometime later in the afternoon. We proceed at a crawl down a rutted alley between two crooked, crumbling cinderblock walls. In places it becomes so narrow that pedestrians have to retreat into doorways to let us pass. Where these walls end, the doctor makes an abrupt right turn and heads down an alley somewhat wider than the last one. When we are nearly halfway to the next intersection a blue Japanese pickup truck enters from the far end. Khalidi immediately stops and backs up all the way to let it pass. The truck is carrying a dozen boys in fatigues, a few of whom recognize Khalidi and wave.

"You are pretty popular around here, doctor."

"I give them their inoculations, bandage their scrapes, soon I'll be treating their gonorrhea. They have to stay on my good side so I won't tell their mothers."

"They were in fatigues."

"They are going for training. Ashbal. In a few years they will be old enough to throw their lives away for Abu Ahmet, or whomever. Did you never wonder how your young compatriots up there acquired their bellicosity at such a tender age?"

"I assumed it was the effect of a hostile environment."

"The Syrians just on the other side of that fence live just as poorly. And yet make notoriously unwilling soldiers."

"They have the luxury of nationality."

"The placebo of nationality."

He stops the car in front of a clearing on the far side of which is a low whitewashed building. Children's voices in the air.

"The school?"

"Precisely. Come, we will go inside and be educated."

We knock at the first room. Fifty children sit up at attention. They appear to range from eight to eleven years old: younger by a few years than the boys on the pickup truck. The teacher—a lean pockmarked man of thirty, a most unprofessional type—greets Khalidi with an embrace. They converse quickly in Arabic, then turn to me.

The teacher extends his hand. "I am honored to meet you. I must tell the students who you are." He addresses the class.

I turn to Khalidi and whisper, "Who am I?"

He puts his finger to his lips. The teacher's speech continues for several minutes. Then four proud little fellows, whom he has pointed to, march up to shake my hand. No girls, though more than half the class is girls. One of the littlest boys returns to his seat staring at his right hand. What the hell did he tell these poor kids?

"Let's get out of here, Khalidi. I can't take this."

410

"But you are going to tell them the story of your proud revolutionary exploits."

"The hell I am."

"Why, this is your first chance for real immortality. Written on the tabula rasa of the next generation."

"Tell them I'm too injured to talk, and let's get out of here."

"I will tell them that you can't talk. But then we must stay and listen to their lesson. Otherwise the teacher will be insulted."

He makes a little speech before the class. Promptly, one of the boys abandons his seat and pushes alongside his neighbor.

The teacher nods to me sourly. "We are very sorry you are injured. Please sit and join our lesson."

Now that the kids have been enlisted in this game I cannot very well walk out on it. So I sit. Khalidi kneels next to me. The teacher lifts a large colored map of Israel from a side wall and hangs it over the arithmetic problems he was writing on the blackboard as we entered. He turns back to the class and asks a question. The children reply in unison in phonetic English, "This is Palestine. This is our home."

A little girl is summoned up and handed the pointer. She points and begins to recite: "I am from the city of Haifa. My family was driven out by the Zionists in . . . one thousand nine hundred and forty-eight. My mother and father lived in Haifa. They grew oranges and sheep. They grew milk and butter . . . made milk and butter. Now they are hungry. I will return to Haifa. No one will be hungry."

Another kid is called up to recite for Jaffa. This is making me very upset. I have the sense of watching children of settlers on the moon reciting about features of the earth none have ever seen except through a telescope. They are not upset. To them it is just recitation. Something they have to do. Like

411

arithmetic. The ache will come later. As they learn to feel that the place they are standing on is not a real place at all. Reality ceased in 1948. Reality lies to the southwest past those hazy mountains. You are ghosts, living ghost lives. While the Jews live real lives on your land. That is what they will learn, because that is what I learned. Whenever I think of turning my back on that border I feel like I'm giving up my right to live. It wasn't poverty or refugee camps that taught me to feel this way. It was the litany of my father's woes drilled into my brain for so many years that I never knew they were his and not mine.

"Excuse me." I stand up and walk out to the clearing, interrupting I don't know what.

A few minutes later Khalidi hurries out. "I told them you are more ill than you appear." He peers at me as if looking for the true reason for my bolting. I expected anger from him. Instead there is almost a smile of satisfaction.

"Let's go back to the hospital, Khalidi. Certainly there is something useful you could be doing there."

"I am doing something useful here. Come, let's have a drink. That's the only medicine you need now."

He leads us through a series of shoulder-width passages. Each one stinks of a different odor: stale urine, then rotting coffee, then dogshit. My sense of odor seems overly sensitive.

"Why don't they clean up this place? They have to live in it. It smells like a sewer."

"This is the sewer. This runnel carved by the rain in the dirt is the only sewage system here. They do the best they can under the circumstances. It could be worse."

"Why don't they get everyone out digging and laying pipe?"

412

"What pipe? And to where would they run it?"

"Why don't the Russians or Libyans supply some? For them it would be a drop in the bucket."

"They are generous with their AK-47s but not with sewage pipe, for good reason. It is not in their interest that we live too comfortably here. Discontent breeds faster in filth. And more virulent. But come along. As your doctor I prescribe a strong drink against the bitterness and disgust I see in your face."

The alleys lead to a wider street, not paved, but at least free of sewage runnels. Mostly older people walking to and fro, who scatter reluctantly before a water truck. When it passes we cross to a short arcade which shades a crudely poured concrete sidewalk. Above the arches the facade has been skillfully painted in a traditional pattern-work of blue and gold. It is the first decoration we've seen since the gate. Behind the arches is the entrance to a cafe. Inside at least a dozen men my own age are crowded around a fusbol machine near the side wall. The rattling of the game, the shouting dominate the entire space. Our entrance is scarcely noticed. Khalidi heads straight for the bar. I recoil. My hearing too has become oversensitive. Khalidi notices my wince and leads us back outside, under the arcade, where there are several tiny circular tables. A waiter arrives after a few minutes. He knows Khalidi. They talk for a few minutes. He returns inside. We sit for a while without saying anything. My mind has gone numb. Four or five of the young men from the fusbol machine drift by our table looking me over. Then drift back. One shoots a question at Khalidi.

"He wants to know if you are really brother Kamal."

"Who's brother Kamal? Tell him I'm Bugs Bunny."

Khalidi says something and they all laugh. A few

413

more jog out to see what's happening. Suddenly they all want to shake my hand.

"What do they think I've done?"

"They think you are one of Abu Ahmet's heroic commandos who has gone into enemy territory, carried out some daring secret mission and returned."

"If you'd known I was going to get such a royal reception here, doctor, you would have kept me strapped to the operating table, right?"

"If you are deriving any satisfaction from this, you have a shallower soul than I imagined. Tell me, brother Kamal; what you did in Jerusalem, does it deserve this?"

"Okay. Just lay off, Khalidi. You must have told them it was me out here. I didn't."

"Of course, they are respecting something real. Your courage. One must assume you possess a certain raw courage to cross the border the way you did. Most of them can't even get that far. So they stand around the machine all day and envy you and the few others who step out of the mire for a glorious moment. And they are very generous with their flattery. You could get drunk on it in one gulp. Declare yourself commander, like Abu Ahmet. Round up a herd of children to follow you by promising to put AK-47s in their hands. Send them across the border to make them heroes . . . But I needn't describe the process to you."

"That's right. Unless you're doing it to hear yourself preach."

"I'm sorry. I was letting myself get carried away. It is a sore subject for me. Drink up your arak. And have another. It will make things look more rosy."

We sit without talking for half an hour or more. I have finally arrived at an answer to the question that plagued me as I waited for Khalidi back there in the hospital: Was there no motive for the undertaking but vanity? Yes, there was vanity, but there was some need more important which would not have been satisfied by winning a bicycle race or setting a hurdling record. My father didn't give a damn about bicycle races. Or hurdles.

Khalidi taps my arm. "The arak, it is beginning to have an effect? Anyway, it is having an effect on me." He grins mischievously. I prefer him as the overgrown kid. As the preacher he risks driving his flock to apostasy with the weight of his sermons. "I was thinking, knowing what I know about your commander Ahmet, that it must be some time since you've laid eyes on a woman."

"You think correctly."

"Then, let us drain our glasses quickly. There is a woman who lives not far from here I would like you to meet. But perhaps you are not feeling fit enough and would prefer to return to the hospital."

"For you, Khalidi, I will wring my poor heart for its last few drops of courage. Lead on."

"Bravely spoken, comrade." He is on his feet with a leap. "Hurry."

"Such incontinence, Khalidi. For shame."

I struggle to follow him through a maze of alleys, quickly losing hope of remembering all the turns. "Hey, doctor, how much does this girl charge?"

"She's not that kind."

"You mean she gives it away for love of the Revolution."

"She gives all away for love of the Revolution. But quiet. We are almost there." He has slowed to a dignified walk, now straightens his jacket and restores his professional face. The alley we are entering is less narrow than the ones which brought us here. It is near the periphery of the camp. In many places erosion of the dirt under the walls has caused the bottom rows of cinder blocks to break away, leaving a gap to the interior. In several places these are

415

patched by flattened tin cans or cardboard, in others simply left open. Along this row not a single wall is still vertical. On the left side they hang out over the alley as if greeting us with a stiff bow. Between the top of this wall and the corrugated metal roof another row of gaps grins; from some of these laundry has been hung to dry.

Khalidi stops at the entrance to one of these huts and calls through the burlap which serves as a door. I am trying to picture the girl who lives here. The squalor arouses my compassion, and compassion arouses my sex. A poor, lovely girl, stripped of her inheritance but not her pride. There is some motion inside. The burlap curtain flies aside to reveal a figure as wide as the door itself.

Khalidi raises his hand and greets her in Arabic. The massive woman steps forward to scrutinize me with black, furious eyes. She spits out a few harsh syllables that sound like cracking concrete.

I mutter to Khalidi, "Her daughter isn't built like her, is she?"

"Um Yousef has no daughters. Only four sons, all of whom she has given to the Revolution. As I mentioned."

"Cheap trick, Khalidi."

"Um Yousef, give your blessing to this young fighter for freedom who has come all the way from America to join our struggle and who has been wounded, as you can see."

The woman speaks without enthusiasm.

"She blesses you and asks to know if you are the son of a Palestinian. Answer in English. She understands."

"Why didn't she ask the question in English, then?"

At this she sneers a reply in Arabic. Khalidi translates, "Because it is the language of the enemies and though she cannot control what falls on her ears she will no more willingly lend her tongue to the enemy's words than her hand to the enemy's weapons."

"Tell her that one of the principles of guerilla warfare is to turn the enemy's weapons against him."

"Um Yousef says, if you were the enemy she would gladly assault you with words of your own language. But since you are a comrade of her sons she will speak to you in the language of comfort and support."

"Tell her that I grieve I cannot reply in the same language."

At this the anger-hardened features of Um Yousef melt and a maternal fondness washes the glint of suspicion from her pupils. She steps down from her doorway with her arms extended and presses me powerfully to her massive soft body. "Ben, ben . . ." There are tears when she lets me loose.

"She says you remind her of her oldest son, Yousef, except for your beautiful blond hair."

Um Yousef now holds back the burlap flap to invite us into her dwelling. When she lets the curtain fall closed behind us there is no light but what slips in through the gaps under the eaves. It takes a full minute before my eyes adjust to the darkness.

Khalidi translates her next words. "She wonders if your eyes were damaged, since you have such difficulty seeing."

"There's nothing wrong with my eyes."

"She is asking that because her second son was blinded by a bomb. His sight has been partially restored by a cornea transplant operation which I arranged for him in Hamburg."

"Where is he now?"

"Still in Germany, under treatment."

Um Yousef interrupts.

"She says he will be the only one of us to see his homeland. And do you want some tea?"

"Tell her not to be so pessimistic, and yes I'd like some tea. Where are her other sons?"

"The oldest was killed in Amman during Black September. The one who was blinded also received his injury there. She then fled with her remaining two sons. Last year her third son was killed in an ambush during a raid near Nablus."

"And the fourth? You said there were four."

"Yes, the fourth. He is a compatriot of yours up there in the mountains with Abu Ahmet."

"He is? I must know him." Kuma? God, I hope not Kuma. But she would certainly know by now if her son was one of the four. Though who knows how long such news takes to reach here. If it is one of them, what will I say? Shall I use the Pentagon euphemism? Your last son, Um Yousef, was killed by friendly fire. But he was a hero all the same. All mothers' dead sons are heroes, Um Yousef.

"Her youngest son is called Fawaz."

"Of course. I know Fawaz. He looks just like her."

She has gotten up to rummage in a pile of jetsam on a wood crate near the doorway. After a minute she hands me a dusty Polaroid print of Fawaz with an RPG on his shoulder. He is grimacing to look fierce.

"Sure enough. Quite a coincidence, huh, Khalidi?"

Um Yousef's tea is sweet and minty. She has poured it with lavish ceremony, making certain we have noticed that the pot is handsomely tooled silver. It is the beauty spot of her life. The only item which shines in the gloom. An heirloom, perhaps? A symbol of the life she once had, whose last reminder she refused to pawn? Do you want us to see that you still savor a memory of some earlier grace?

"Um Yousef asks if you have brothers."

"Four."

"And she asks, where are they fighting?"

"They are fighting traffic in America."

"She asks, Why are they in America? Why are they not fighting by the side of their brother?"

"One might just as well ask why I am not a successful lawyer, professor or engineer by their sides."

"Um Yousef asks if their mother is not ashamed of them."

"Ashamed? No, she is proud of their success."

"Um Yousef says that if she had sons who would not fight she would spit on them. She says that a son who will not fight for his mother's home does not deserve a mother. She would disown him and spit on him in public."

She tosses her head. The glint has come back into her eye.

Khalidi, made nervous by the sudden change of mood, tries to calm her, addressing both of us. "Um Yousef, not all mothers have known the hardship you have known so close to the battles. You have been through every storm at its center. In 1948 you were driven from Lydda; in 1967 you had to leave Hebron. In 1970 you suffered the fury of Hussein's bedouins, lost one son, saw another blinded. Again you had to flee. Then you lost another son."

Um Yousef has slumped into her chair and merely nods at Khalidi's enumeration of her griefs. The hard folds of her face have collapsed in sadness.

But Khalidi continues. "You have only one son who has not been destroyed in the struggle."

Suddenly she straightens and shouts, pointing at me. "And why his mother keep all her five, when me has only one?"

"Um Yousef, have compassion. Kamal's mother is in a distant and foreign land with no one to protect her but her sons. She has no husband."

"And me? Who to protect me? A drunkard man who works at the oil fields of Iraq?"

"We wish all your sons were alive and well to protect you, Um Yousef. That they are not is no rea-

son to hate the mother of Kamal. You have given
enough, Um Yousef. No one asks you for your last
son, too. He can be returned to you to protect you and
comfort you and perhaps one day to reap some good
from the spilled blood of his brothers. If you order
him to return he will not disobey, Um Yousef. Abu
Ahmet will not stand in the way. Kamal knows Commander Ahmet and knows this to be true. He will deliver the message himself, by hand. Kamal is a hero
of the struggle. If he makes the request, no one can
look upon it as a cowardly request."

Um Yousef shakes her head without looking up.
This is an old drama between her and Khalidi. I am
simply a new tactic on his side. She is by no means
unmoved by his stratagem. Her next words are
barely audible, so choked is her throat.

"Um Yousef asks, Is it true you know her son?"

"It is true."

"She asks, Is he a good fighter?" Khalidi nods mi-
nutely as he translates.

"Yes, he is a very good fighter. But his grief for his
brothers weighs heavily." I glance at Khalidi to take
over the plea. I am afraid that what I say may have
the wrong effect.

"He is young yet, Um Yousef. He needs time to
mourn. The struggle will go on for many years. Let
him have a chance to fight in the final battle. You
owe it to his brothers that one of them should see the
victory."

She is silent for some time. Then replies gravely,
without looking at us.

Khalidi's voice trembles during the translation.
"It is written that none of Um Yousef's sons will see
the victory. One will be alive, but he will not see it
because he is blind. She says she will not make a
woman of the last son just so that she may have some
comfort from him. It would be a betrayal of his brothers. Other mothers have given all their sons. She

asks, May Allah give her the strength not to succumb in a weak moment so that it may not be said of her that she gave less than the other mothers."

She says nothing else. She refuses to lift her eyes from the floor. After a long enough wait, Khalidi stands.

"Brother Kamal is suffering from his wounds. We must leave now."

She does not respond.

When we have reached the Citroen Khalidi finally comments. "That shocked you."

"I never expected to hear that from a mother. From a father, yes, but not from a mother."

"Unfortunately her attitude is not uncommon. It is a death sentence on her own children. The only hope lies with the boy himself. You are a hero. He will respect your counsel."

"He will cease to respect it the moment I ask him to quit. You know that."

"There must be some more subtle approach you could use."

"And were I to persuade him, then you will say, What about the others? Right, Khalidi?"

"You said it, not I. Your moral sense is not yet totally drowned in the liquor of violence, I am reassured to see."

"And there's another thing. I'm not sure I want to go back up there at all."

"Aha!"

"All I said, Khalidi, was that I'm not sure."

"Yes." He unlocks the car.

The afternoon has taken its toll. Even propped in the soft plush seat of the Citroen I have to fight to keep the world from whirling. Now, when I wish he would step on it and get me to my bed, he is cruising along sedately. Absentmindedly. And his route leads, if anywhere, directly away from the hospital.

We soon leave the dusty district, picking up a highway which accompanies a canal or aqueduct along the periphery of the city. It takes us through a zone of modern apartment blocks. Just past these we slip off the highway. Now, closer to these buildings, it is apparent that they are shabbier than appears from the highway. They cannot be more than a few years old. Monuments of some dictator's illusion of progress. The residents whose paint crumbles from the ceiling into the soup aren't fooled. But to the passersby on the highway: Damascus the thriving modern city. Maybe it was always this way. T. E. was disillusioned here in Damascus, too.

Khalidi steers us to a smaller apartment building further from the highway. It is better, or more recently, constructed. Beyond lies a bulldozed field, and beyond that the yellow plain. The mountains themselves are almost obscured by haze, reduced to an ambiguous outline just below the sun that could be either rock or cloud. The heat is beginning to slacken its grip. A slight breeze from the west blows in the car window, whisking away my torpor. We sit in the parking lot watching a dozen boys battling a soccer ball back and forth across the dirt with incredible ferocity. I feel weak and jealous. If God offered me any gift right now I would ask without a moment's hesitation for Him to take back fifteen years and let me join the game.

A goal is scored. One of the boys on the scoring side, jogging back to defend his own goal, notices us and waves.

"My son." Khalidi shakes his head. "He wants to be another Pelé. I wonder where he gets it from. Look at me—hardly an athlete."

"Would you like him to be another Pelé?"

"What father wouldn't want that for his son?"

"Mine."

* * *

Khalidi's apartment is on the top floor. The clatter of our footsteps echoes off the painted concrete walls of the stairwell, emphasizing the slowness of my ascent. By the top landing I am dizzy, sweating and nauseous. And this is a flight less than Ramat Eshkol. A woman is standing by an open door. She gestures for me to enter. Khalidi says something. To her? To me? My hearing is muffled. The woman takes my arm and leads me down a hall to a bedroom. As I lie down the nausea subsides, but the bed continues to spin in looping figure eights even after I have closed my eyes. It is not an unpleasant sensation actually. Almost tranquilizing . . .

I wake with a cold damp cloth on my forehead. The room is completely dark. Clinking of dishes and laughter filters through the door: domestic sounds now so unfamiliar to me they sound staged. The last time I lay in the dark listening to those sounds was, yes, in the cellar of Pollo Rojo. How I longed to join them. But I had the discipline then to thwart trivial longings. No more. I am worn out.

I pull myself up from the bed, still clutching the wet cloth to my forehead, let myself quietly into the hall. The sounds from the dining room continue. The door to the bathroom stands open immediately across the hall. I stumble in, lock the door, and turn on the faucet. Running water, hot and cold; it's been a long time for that too. I start to lower my face into the bowl to rinse it under the tap when a face in the mirror stops me cold. A sunken-eyed, bony, haunted, prematurely-aged specter watches me suspiciously from the dark shadows of its brows. I've seen him before. I've known that face since I was a child. The very same leather-covered skull from which all expressions but distrust have emigrated. But whose face is it? Not mine.

The sharp blade of memory rips up from my sternum, my throat, into the base of my brain. Yes, I know you. Your tormented visage stared at me from the pages of my father's magazine. You are the wretched fedayee he wept for.

Suddenly tears appear in the reflection's sunken eyes. Sobs rack his bony shoulders. Why are you crying? Aren't you the hero your father praised? Haven't you made the mark he wanted to leave? Haven't you avenged the martyrs of Katamon who died by the Haganah hand grenades under the vaults of Saint Simeon?

I feel ashamed.

Ashamed? You are a hero.

But I am ashamed to walk down the hall and join these people at their dinner table. I am no hero to them.

Then return to your camp where you are a hero.

But it is not at the camp that I want to be. It is here, at dinner, with these people. But I don't dare . . .

You don't dare? The hero doesn't dare?

I don't dare because of this feeling. This feeling that my hand will reach into my pocket and throw a hand grenade into their dining room too.

You have no hand grenade.

But they will see the feeling. When they look at my face they will know.

They will know nothing.

They will know. Look in the mirror. It is right there for anyone to see. Carved in my face. The same thing that Justina saw after Hervé. What can any normal person do but recoil in horror and try to obliterate this presence from their life? I cannot face these people. I can face no one.

You can face Abu. You can face the boys up in the camp. Up there in that canyon they understand. There they are all like Fawaz. They know . . .

"Kamal?" Khalidi's voice at the door. "Are you all right?"

"I'm okay."

"Then come join us at dinner."

"I will. I'm washing up."

One more effort of will. It carries me down the hall to the dining area. At my appearance there is a sudden silence. I feel their eyes on my wounds. On their father's stitches.

After a moment of indecision Khalidi pops up and offers me his seat at the head of the table. "You are feeling stronger? Have something to eat. Some soup. You've had nothing all day but arak. It's hardly a surprise you are feeling weak. Ah, it's all my fault. I should have thought about food earlier."

A young woman changes the plate in front of me and places a bowl of soup on it.

Khalidi bumbles on. "Oh, excuse me. I have also forgotten to make introductions. Kamal is my patient. He is from America. My wife, my son whom you saw outside, my daughter, our old good friend Haroun, my children's governess Aicha. That's everyone." The old good friend attempts to test me with his gaze, playing the patriarch over his sharp gray beard. What is he looking for? To see if I avert my eyes to hide from his judgment. Khalidi, you haven't told them who I am, have you? Why did your wife and daughter and governess all glance down after their introductions?

Demureness, Kamal. Remember where you are. They know nothing. Not even distinguished Haroun. He did what patriarchs always do to young men here: They face you down. He's too old to know that this is a new era. Khalidi would not force it upon him by confiding that the anomalous guest is a terrorist, an assassin. He would not disturb his wife's lovely dinner. He would not risk creating an idol for his son. Nor for his daughter. The secret's safe with the doctor.

Secrets are never safe.

Relax, Kamal. Ignore Haroun. Let them make you feel welcome.

It is a comfortable apartment, though the furnishings are poorer than I expected for a Citroen-driving physician. The only decoration is a single small tapestry on the wall over the foot of the table. All the rest—chairs, tables, serving board, a bookshelf—is cheap, functional and disposable. As if they do not expect to be here long, and attachments to furnishings can be less well afforded than the furnishings themselves. This is sad, but it is a lesson learned subliminally. They probably don't even recognize how they advertise their transience. Khalidi's wife does not seem the kind of woman who would choose to live this way. She is slim and fit, her hair is short and coiffed. But for the darkness of her skin she would fit in perfectly in a bourgeois suburb of Paris. What they call a handsome woman.

The daughter, not quite ready for puberty, inherits her mother's high cheekbones and, for the moment at least, her father's chubbiness. My presence makes her shy. She diverts all her attention to her younger brother, bossing and teasing him. Neither Khalidi nor his wife nor the governess makes a gesture to quash their bickering. I don't mind. It restores the domesticity my entrance disrupted.

In minutes everything is back to normal. Khalidi sits back. The governess continues to serve dinner. She is quite pretty: big dark Persian eyes. Khalidi himself does not quite ignore her presence. His glance grazes her hips as she returns to the kitchen for the last serving dish. Once she sits down she is part of the family. Haroun is immune, a man retired to a world of words. Conversation has switched into English so naturally I scarcely notice. After a few polite questions about my health, never touching on the origin of my wounds, the talk turns to politics, which is what I assumed I interrupted.

"There is no question, though"—Haroun emphasizing an unresolved point—"that this time the mobilization is real. Assad's threats may be empty, I grant you that, but the Soviets are stuffing them with steel. And it is the steel, not Assad's 'liquidation of consequences of aggression' speeches, that the Israelis will respond to. I drove up from Derra two days ago. I have never seen so many tanks in my life. Not even in '67."

"More important," Khalidi's wife retorts, "where are they pointed, these tanks? Why not south, into Jordan? There is nothing Assad could dream of that would please him more than chasing Hussein to Switzerland."

"Nothing many of us could dream of. . . . But the Americans will never let it happen."

"Haroun, you forget," Khalidi interjects quietly, "Hussein was quite capable of chasing Syrian tanks back to Syria in September of '70."

"I am surprised to hear that you still believe that propaganda. The withdrawal was imposed by the Soviets."

"Please, please, let us not start on this again, both of you. That is past. This is something new."

"No, my dear. Nothing is new. Nothing is ever new in this part of the world. The Russians send tanks because hospitals and irrigation do not keep a dictator in power. Quite the reverse. Feed a people, make them healthy and educated, and suddenly they want democracy too. They don't want a Deuxième beating down the door in the middle of the night. They don't want torture—"

"But this has nothing to do with whether there is going to be another war."

"There will be no war, because if there is another

war the Israelis will march all the way here to Damascus and then there will be no more Assad."

"Such a pessimist, my friend. Such a pessimist. Yet the tanks I saw in Derra are an objective reality. They will not be so easily marched through. If there is no war being planned why did Sadat condescend to come to Damascus in June? What is the 'common policy' they announced in July? What is this 'tripartite agreement' of the front-line states that is being talked of? What, less than a war with Israel, would make Assad accept to talk with Hussein, even if through foreign ministers?"

"Empty talk, empty tanks, Haroun. Neither one is very formidable. And why are you all so anxious for another war? If Syria wins back the Golan Heights, if Egypt wins back the Sinai, what will that do for us? But if they lose again . . ."

"If Hussein wins back the West Bank . . ." his wife suggests.

"Hah! Not if the Prophet himself offered to lead the troops. As far as Hussein is concerned that border might as well be defended by American marines. He would not dare lift a finger."

Haroun nods. "With that I'm afraid I have to agree."

There is a brief silence. Perhaps left for me to fill, if I choose. After all, as an American and a guerrilla from the front lines, I should have something to say on the subject. But I don't. I know less about what is happening here in the Middle East than when I was back in Paris. A nasty irony. They would be better off talking to old Nizar.

"They have cleared the mines from the footpaths across the demilitarized zone." Suddenly everyone is staring at me. Why did I say that? They think I'm crazy. "They do that if they are planning to cross in a hurry. An invasion."

Haroun blinks. "They? Who?"

Who? Who removed the mines? Christ, I don't know who removed the mines. I don't even know who put them there. Why did I say that? They were talking about politics. Well, the mines were gone from the Syrian side of the slope.

"The Syrians removed them."

Haroun scrutinizes me. "How do you know this?"

Now Khalidi skewers me with a warning glance.

"How do I know? I talked to a Druze guide who crosses the zone regularly. He takes that as a sign there is going to be a war."

Haroun nods to Khalidi. "You see."

"Well"—Khalidi relaxes—"if the Druzes know, the Israelis know. And if the removed mines mean there is going to be an invasion and the Israelis are expecting it, then we should be thinking about where we are going to flee after their 'pre-emptive strikes' on Damascus."

"Ah, Khalidi, my friend, you must stick to doctoring and not torment yourself, or your family, with political and military divinations."

Haroun gathers himself to harangue his host. Khalidi's wife shrugs with exasperation at both of them. My idiotic contribution is already forgotten. I am lucky to have slipped out of it so easily. Glancing around the table, I catch the governess observing me. She instantly averts her eyes, but not before a moment of contact passes a message of lust between us. The argument recedes to a background drone. She is really a pretty girl. Sensuous, almost pouty, lips. And this charade of demureness, what an art! She knows I'm ready to leap over the table and carry her off.

Ah, Khalidi, you knew this was going to happen, you sly devil. You had this day all planned. Every scene of it. And of course it is too late, and you are too tired to drive back to the hospital tonight. And there is that spare bedroom. I can already see you lying awake gloating at the creakings from the next room.

Go on, Kamal. Why not give him this satisfaction? He is no Abu. You don't have to spite yourself to thwart him. He already knows you're ready to quit. Think about the living in the warmth of this family. Think of how Aicha will make love. Think of her soft breasts. Think of how she will tease you with her eyes. Think of the knowing looks you will exchange with her across the table. Think of learning the language from her tongue, her tongue . . .

Look at Khalidi, he is already beaming at us, pretending to listen to his friend's harangue. And the kids are silent. They can feel that something is happening to their beautiful companion. They interrogate their mother with their eyes. She replies silently, Hush, this is something you must not interfere with. This is something you must watch. Someday it will also happen to you, my children.

A bell rings. Khalidi's daughter jumps up before Aicha is stirred from her languorous trance. Rings again. Insistent. Doorbell! My gut tightens.

No, thank God, no, it is only the telephone.

But in the instant of fear my whole body has been set trembling. Aicha notices. Voice of the daughter on the phone. Now Khalidi and Haroun turn to listen. She calls. Khalidi jumps up, hurries into the kitchen. His voice sounds anxious. The daughter returns and slips into her seat without making a sound.

Khalidi walks back into the dining room. Ashen.

"That was the hospital. There has been an attack, a helicopter attack on Ahmet's camp. They are bringing in the casualties. They are afraid . . . No, the rumors are always extreme."

I know what he is saying.

"Khalidi, no survivors?"

"The reports are never reliable. Never." He turns

away while he tugs on his jacket. "I will call from the hospital. When I know more. I doubt I will be back tonight."

"I'm coming with you."

"No, stay here. You are in no condition to help."

"Khalidi, those are my comrades."

He glares. "You might have thought of that before you went to Jerusalem."

Silence. They are all staring at me. Even Aicha. Why, Khalidi, why did you say that? Why? Don't look away now. You have undone everything we both wanted. What has changed? Why are you putting this on my head? I only did what I had to do. That is what war is all about. Why do you put it on my head? Why, Khalidi?

"I'm coming with you."

He nods without looking at me. He won't say it, but he is thinking, Yes, come with me. I'd rather have you with the dead and mangled than with my family.

Three Syrian Army trucks lined up in front of the hospital steps, the bed of the one in front lit up by the glare of the lights of the one behind it, the bed of the last one in the glare of the Citroen's beams. Soldiers are pulling stretchers from the tailgates, passing them to others on the pavement, on the steps. It is too dark to recognize the twisted figures lying on them where they wait to be carried up the steps into the yellow glow of the main corridor. Khalidi rushes among them, bending for a moment over one boy who, in his agony, has writhed off his stretcher onto the steps. Khalidi yells to someone nearby. It is Hamid. He picks up the boy in his arms like a child—he is a child—and follows Khalidi at a run into the hospital. Another truck rumbles up. Two jets hiss by overhead trailing their fading roar toward the mountains. Soldiers leap from the truck before it has

431

stopped. They rush to pick up stretchers pointed out by a medic wearing a stethoscope. The dead remain on the pavement. Many of them. I don't want to count.

All this for Ehud Migdal? There is no logic to connect it. But who needs logic, Jibral? The smells of blood and vomit in the damp night air, the soft moaning from the stretchers being tipped from the tailgates of the trucks, the clatter of boots on the steps, the sirens in the distance—don't these convince you? And if not these, then the sudden freezing of Aicha's glance and the stiffening of her body. Convincing enough.

Hamid reappears and stares at me a moment, as if he does not recognize me and wonders why I'm standing here. Then suddenly he rushes forward. I poise to sidestep the onslaught. But he spreads his arms to embrace me. "Ya Q'asidi!" There are warm tears in his eyes.

"Ya Hamid." You, at least, don't blame me.

He clings to me for a long time. So long that my mind backs away and wonders why my grief is not as overwhelming as his. Finally he lets go, shaking his head in sorrow and disbelief. He nods toward the Land Cruiser, which is still idling at the head of the line of trucks. Another pair of jets roar past. When I look down Hamid is standing with one foot on the running board, ready to climb in and drive off. Back up to the camp. But he is waiting for something. Waiting for me. Waiting to see if I will return to the canyon with him.

My life seems to hang on which way I step right now. Into the hospital to help Khalidi? Or to the Land Cruiser and the camp to carry on with whoever may be left alive? Each future unfolds with perfect clarity. Up the steps lies a fevered night of bandages and cries and sheets pulled up over mangled faces. Khalidi's silent reproach, funerals, weeks of drunken milling around Damascus while the consulate processes my request for a replacement passport and money arrives from Lausanne, the flights home, the hostile stares at customs and immigration, the phone call to my mother to prepare her for the shock, my brothers' snide questions, hoofing around the city for a job . . .

And all the while chewing on my secret and waiting for the toad to step out in front of me with his Beretta drawn to finish what he must now realize he should have finished back in Fossés Saint-Bernard. Yes, by now they will have put it all together: the torn fence, the Fiat, the dead soldier by the road, Ramat Eshkol. Nizar's relatives will have volunteered my description, the photograph taken by Weizman will have been matched. And if they haven't completed the case yet it is only a matter of time.

And in the other direction, to the Land Cruiser?

Nothing but corpses among the rocks and a few dazed survivors, weeks of digging deeper shelters, desultory drills, initiations, speeches to fan the smoldering embers of revenge into another raid. Then waiting for the next reprisal from the sky: Spooky's steel rain, Muttering Death.

Not much of a choice.

What did you expect, Jibral?

What did I expect? I had a vision once, remember, of riding into Jerusalem on the lead tank of the liberating column.

Why are you laughing? Look at Hamid. He is also wondering why you are laughing.

Vicissitudes of History, Hamid. You know what I'm laughing about.

He knows nothing. He only finds it revolting that you are laughing in the midst of such a tragedy.

"I'm sorry, Hamid." How did I get over here? "Aasif, Hamid, aasif."

433

He's a good man, Hamid is. You see, he forgives you. But he thinks you are coming back to the camp with him. ―

Hamid, my friend, will you understand by this shrug that there is nothing for me to do up there? Please understand.

"Q'asidi. Samir O.K."

Sami's O.K.? I'm glad, but that doesn't mean much.

"Fawaz O.K."

"Fawaz? He wasn't hit? Fawaz is O.K.?"

Hamid nods energetically. "Yes, O.K. He . . ." Shaking his fist in frustration. "He . . . montagne."

"He was on the mountain, not in camp!"

Hamid shrugs, not understanding.

"Never mind. Let's go."

Well, you've made someone happy, at least. You can always climb into this buggy and drive back down. How did he know that Fawaz could drag you up here?

Humane instinct. If I could confide why the news that Fawaz is alive means so much to me right now. Every hope I have rests on it. Goddamn, Hamid, you better not have invented that.

From half a mile away we can see the glow of the lights on the canyon walls. Below the clearing we are stopped for a minute at a perimeter set up by regular Syrian Army soldiers. Behind them are three half-tracks whose headlights illuminate the clearing in front of the bunkers. Soldiers are standing beside the rocket launcher tubes mounted on the half-tracks, as if expecting another attack. The clearing itself is strewn with rubble. The front of Abu's bunker has either collapsed or been covered by an avalanche of the talus above it. Soldiers are working to excavate it, carrying away the rubble with their hands, stone by stone. The acrid smell of high explosive still hangs in the air. A very tall officer is leaning over the hood of a jeep writing, while another soldier holds a flashlight on the paper. A third, much slighter, man stands beside them, rubbing his hands over his face. Hamid stops the Land Cruiser next to them. The slight man turns to look up at us over his fingers. It is Sami.

"How many are left?"

Sami backs up as I jump from the car.

"How many, Sami?"

"Oh, it's you, Kamal." He sounds very weary. His face is black with smoke and sweat. His eyes seem to swim.

"Hey, Sami." I touch his shoulder to steady him. "How many are left?"

"You're left."

The Syrian officer now pushes between us. He is a head taller than me and peers down a nose like De Gaulle's. "Who are you?" he demands.

"I am one of Abu Ahmet's volunteers."

"Of what nationality?"

"Palestinian."

"That is not a nationality. Do you speak Arabic?"

"No."

"You are English?"

"I lived in America."

"May I see your passport?"

"It is in that buried bunker."

"What are you doing here in Syria?"

"Fighting for my people."

He curls his lip and gestures around him. "Is this fighting for your people?"

Sami bursts out, "What could we do? We couldn't do anything. We never heard them coming. First the jets and the damn bombs, and then if you survived that you looked up and there were the helicopters and the bullets coming down like rain. Just like rain.

If you happened to jump under a rock you stayed dry, otherwise—"

"Listen to him, captain! It was a full scale military invasion into your country. Aren't you going to retaliate?"

"Into our country? They undoubtedly launched that attack from part of our country which they took in '67. If we are not yet ready to retaliate for that, do you expect us to jump up and die for this little melee. It is your affair, not ours. They warn us before they do one of these."

"Then why the hell don't you warn us?"

"Warn you, retaliate for you, carry your dead bodies down to our hospitals . . . Perhaps I should give you my home as well?" He turns abruptly and goes back to his writing.

Sami is walking in circles.

I grab him by the shoulders. "Is it true Fawaz is still alive?"

He shrugs.

I shake him. "Listen, Sami. Go round up all the survivors and bring them here. We have to get everyone back under discipline or they'll get hysterical and wander off. You understand?"

He nods crookedly, with a strange smile. His eyes are black with resentment.

"Sami, everyone here in ten minutes. Particularly Fawaz."

"Yes . . . sir." He turns with a defiant roll of his shoulders and strolls from the clearing.

Now behind me there is a loud metallic creak and a bellow of diesel. They have driven one of the half-tracks up in front of Abu's bunker and hitched a steel cable from a drum under its bumper through a head-sized puncture in the bunker door. The hole must have been made by an armor-piercing rocket from a helicopter dead on. The cable tightens. The door creaks again. Now with a roar the half-track starts to grind backwards. The door groans, buckles and snaps open. Smoke pours out of the tunnel. I find myself rushing over the rubble to enter along with the Syrian medic. It is possible Abu is still alive. I can imagine him sitting at his desk, patiently working by flashlight on a stack of papers, nodding coolly as we pry open the secondary hatch to his bombproof cell. Then he will rise slowly, walk fastidiously along the blackened tunnel and emerge into the clearing silhouetted in the headlights' glow and make a speech to Sami and Fawaz and a few other tattered survivors: a speech about vengeance and pride. . . . And I will kill him. I will pick up the hook at the end of the cable and smash in his head.

"Aie!" The medic stops and points the flashlight at the floor in front of him. A headless, shoulderless corpse with a submachine gun tangled by the strap around its knees.

"Major Daoud."

The door to Abu's cell is shut and undamaged.

Calm, Kamal! He is alive.

Calm? What have I got to lose now?

Fawaz. Remember you came for Fawaz.

The medic flashes the light at my face to see why I have stopped.

"He's in here." The door swings open with a low scrape. The air inside is warm but fresh. There is no sound, no lights. I reach for the medic's flashlight. He doesn't know where to point it. He lets go reluctantly. In a second I have the desk lit up in its beam. The chair is empty. There is no smell of blood. It is like a professor's office during vacation: papers undisturbed on the desk. We search the floor. Nothing.

This is impossible. I slump down in Abu's chair. The medic grabs his flashlight from my hand and continues searching. Impossible. The Israelis couldn't have grabbed him. The main tunnel port was bolted. He could have only left before the attack. Fled. Deserted!

The medic returns and shines the light in my face. "No person here."

"You tried the little room in back?"

"Yes."

"Give me your flashlight for a minute."

He hands it over. I slide open the lower right-hand drawer. My passport is lying on top where he tossed it the evening we first discussed Jerusalem. My passport and the signed traveler's checks folded inside. I can drive down to Damascus, buy a ticket and fly home. Tomorrow.

"Hey, what you doing?" the medic protests.

"Look, it's me. See the photo?"

"O.K. Come out from here. Finished."

"That's right. Finished."

Sami is waiting outside with five or six of the boys, milling. The medic hurries over to the tall Syrian officer. I slip my passport under a rock in case he takes it into his head to demand it.

"Where's Abu, Sami?"

"Beirut, officially. In fact, Zurich, in a heart clinic."

"When did this happen?"

"A few days after you got back from Jerusalem."

"Heart clinic, hell. He's a fucking traitor."

"No. Just a sick man."

"Who did the sick man leave in command?"

"The Vulture."

"Not anymore. Where's Fawaz? I don't see him."

"Still up on lookout, above Nefud. He and two others. They refuse to come down. They're sure there's going to be another attack."

"Go up there and bring them down. So long as the Syrians are here there will be no attacks. Tell them I said that, and that I want them down here."

438

"*You* want them? Who put you in command?"

"There are only you and me left, princeling. That means if I'm not in command then it must be you who's in command."

He glowers.

"Well, Sami?"

He shuffles off. The boys continue to mill around the clearing. Better put them to work doing something, wear them out, get them some food, put them to bed. You're commander now, remember?

Until tomorrow.

Tomorrow's a long way off.

Six exhausted kids and a leader who can't even speak their language lugging stones away from the door of the supply bunker: a fine force we must appear to those Syrians. Fighting for our people. It makes me want to hide my head. If I could only go numb with the exertion. I'm supposed to be sick. I'm supposed to be lying in bed. In Aicha's arms. Where's all this strength coming from?

Rage! I felt it surge up as soon as we got inside that bunker. And there's the greatest humiliation of all: our brave commander running out on us. Like my father disappearing into his illness, leaving us with the rubble and the dead.

First light. The cough of the half-track diesels starting wakes me. Light snores ooze from the bullet-perforated sleeping bag next to me. It's been hit in ten places. Spooky's work. I should wake Sami, but I feel sorry for him. I feel sorry for every one of us. The Syrians are piling into their trucks.

The tall captain strides up to where I am sitting. "So you are in command now?"

"Some command."

"Of course these survivors will have to be incorporated in some other Palestinian unit. It may take a

439

week to arrange. You have enough supplies to last until then."

"See you next week, captain."

"No, you will not see me. Good day."

The captain's jeep leads the lumbering procession slowly down the road. One of the boys taps me on the shoulder. He has a cup of coffee for me. I take it and thank him, but he lingers nearby, kicking pebbles. What does he want? He wants me to tell him everything will be all right. I stand up and pat him on the shoulder. That will have to do.

Hamid is digging near the door of the bunker, which gapes black and empty like a deserted mine shaft. You're a prince of bad luck, poor Vulture. So snug and safe in there. Just like Abu. Only Abu was smart enough to realize he was no longer safe. He'll outlive the rest of us. Oh yes, my passport. The captain forgot to ask for it. I'd better retrieve it before Hamid shovels it into the Vulture's grave.

Fawaz appears at the entrance to the supply bunker carrying two large boxes of rations. He is the only one who has any will left. His gaze cuts through the others, now huddling around the stoves, as if there were no one there. He shoots me the same kind of glance and stalks back into the supply bunker. Why don't I order someone to help him? he is asking himself. Has Q'asidi gone as limp as the rest? I kick Sami in his sleeping bag. "Hey princeling, get up and help Fawaz."

He struggles out of his bag. I can see he is about to sneer or complain. I harden my face. He pulls on his boots and hops to the bunker just as Fawaz reappears with two more boxes. Fawaz's glance toward me carries something different this time: a secret but conditional complicity. With a hoarse shout he dispatches three of the boys to help Hamid carry the beheaded corpse from the tunnel.

Sami appears carrying two jerrycans of water. The

cistern pump has been damaged. Water has to be drawn by bucket.

"Sami, you saw the list last night. Did the little kid Fuad catch it?"

"Don't remember."

Fawaz, on his way back for another load, mutters without breaking stride, "Fuad, him kaput."

Him kaput. You can say it just like that? Fuad was a child with gleaming eyes and a piping voice. Kaput? You feel nothing? Nothing at all, Fawaz?

Fuad, him kaput: three little words fall as heavily as an avalanche of rocks, crushing the hope that carried me back here from Damascus. Khalidi, I cannot save Fawaz for you. If this horror does not touch him, nothing can. The hardness goes all the way to his core. This terrifies me. I don't know how to confront it. How do I order him, persuade him, wheedle him to come down from the mountain? I will wither up under his silent contempt.

Look. Now he is bringing out the RPGs. We all know what is coming. The others are transfixed. He is breaking through their numbness. And when that shell cracks, the pain and terror and humiliation of last night will come pouring in. And then they will look into Fawaz's eyes and discover how to cauterize pain with rage. They will start fingering their AKs, imagining the hail of bullets and the shredded bodies of the people on the other side of the ridge, and while their minds are full of these visions the pain and the humiliation will vanish. Until they sleep. Until they sleep. And when they wake with the horror renewed, they will grab their rifles to bury it again. Fawaz will show them the way.

And I? What can I show them? Can I keep them numb enough with drills to hold them here in this canyon? I can't send them off in dribbles the way Abu did. There is only a dribble left. In two days or three Fawaz will have them ready to follow him over

441

the ridge. All of them. Except Sami. And what will I do? Sit in the bunker and wait for their bodies to be dropped at my door?

Or will I slip my passport and traveler's checks into my pocket, sidle over to the Land Cruiser, and scuttle down to the Damascus airport? Deserting them like Abu.

No, Khalidi, Fawaz will not come down from the mountain. That was a humane but vain hope. And since he will not come down, none of the others will. If I were to kill him, yes, I might save the others, but I cannot kill anymore. Not even once more. I can only sit and wait, and when Fawaz comes before me with his obsidian stare to demand that I show them the way across the zone, I will take the bullets out of my gun, but I will show them the way.